Praise for Iris Johansen's Eve Duncan Novels

MIND GAME

"Enthralling . . . and completely satisfying."
—*Kirkus Reviews*

"A rapid-fire plot . . . a stunning climax."
—*Publishers Weekly*

"The right amount of complexity spiced with danger, thrills, and engrossing characters!"
—*RT Book Reviews* (Top Pick)

NIGHT AND DAY

"A winning combination of thriller elements and love story."
—*Booklist*

"Full of mysticism and mystery, this fast-paced novel is sure to appeal to all fans of romantic suspense."
—*Publishers Weekly*

HIDE AWAY

"This first-rate novel of romantic suspense will please Johansen's fans and newcomers alike."
—*Publishers Weekly* (starred review)

SHADOW PLAY

"Johansen delivers a no-holds-barred mystery that maintains suspense throughout and boasts a cast of multifaceted characters."
—*Publishers Weekly*

"Thrilling, emotional, and downright riveting certainly sum up this incredible tale!"
—*RT Book Reviews*

ALSO BY IRIS JOHANSEN

DARK TRIBUTE

IRIS JOHANSEN

St. Martin's Paperbacks

This is a work of fiction. All of the characters, organizations, and events portrayed in this novel are either products of the author's imagination or are used fictitiously.

Published in the United States by St. Martin's Paperbacks, an imprint of St. Martin's Publishing Group.

DARK TRIBUTE

For information, address St. Martin's Publishing Group, 120 Broadway, New York, NY 10271.

www.stmartins.com

Library of Congress Catalog Card Number: 2018045705

ISBN: 978-1-250-07595-6

Our books may be purchased in bulk for promotional, educational, or business use. Please contact your local bookseller or the Macmillan Corporate and Premium Sales Department at 1-800-221-7945, ext. 5442, or by email at MacmillanSpecialMarkets@macmillan.com.

Printed in the United States of America

St. Martin's Press hardcover edition / March 2019
St. Martin's Paperbacks edition / September 2019

10 9 8 7 6 5 4 3 2 1

PROLOGUE

The white lace gown Cara Delaney was wearing tonight was all wrong, John Svardak thought. But it should be fine once it was soaked with blood.

He slowly crushed the program in his hand as he gazed down from his box seat at the young violinist onstage. Cara Delaney had the audience in the palm of her hand. Or perhaps that wasn't quite the term those tone-deaf critics would use to refer to her. Since they were calling her the most brilliant violinist to come along since Yehudi Menuhin, they'd probably say that it was that magic bow that was holding those fools in the audience captive.

Why couldn't they see that she was *nothing*? he thought angrily. They had no idea what true artistry was about. She stood there with her long dark hair and olive skin dressed in that white lace gown that made her look like a young Juliet and let the music pour out of her to touch everyone in the audience. She was all passion and reaching out and becoming one with the entire world. It was disgusting. There should be control, the musician should stand above and superior when dispensing the perfection of their gifts as Anna had done. Cara Delaney looked as if she wasn't aware there was anything but the music itself. She was truly unworthy of all that adulation.

And he had clearly been right to mark her for destruction.

But her music was disturbing him and he had to close it out. It was too *wrong*. It made him feel things that he must not feel, things Anna had told him were stupid and only there because he didn't concentrate properly. It would be a betrayal.

Ignore Cara Delaney. He had come to see her because he'd had to be certain that she was all they'd said she was. He must not call attention to himself by getting up and leaving the concert, but there would be no betrayal if he spent this time planning for the destruction to come. He pulled out his notebook and flipped it open to the Delaney page. It had been a foregone conclusion that she would be the chosen one, and he'd already done the research.

But the research had been based on her travel plans to return straight to New York from Charlotte. She would have been easy enough to take on the way to the airport or after she'd arrived at her apartment in New York. But she'd made an unexpected change of plans yesterday, and now he'd have to adjust accordingly.

She was taking a flight to Atlanta, and that could be a problem. She had family there, and he'd found family was always trouble. They cared too much, and twice before, he'd nearly missed the kill because of family interference. It must not happen this time. He looked down at the report he'd pulled up on Cara Delaney's background. She'd probably go to the lake cottage where she'd spent much of her time since Eve Duncan and Joe Quinn had taken over her guardianship when she was only eleven. That shouldn't be difficult to overcome. Eve Duncan was one of the foremost forensic sculptors in the world, but she enjoyed the isolation of the lake cottage.

And so would Svardak: isolation was always helpful to his purpose. An artist like Duncan should not offer any challenge at all.

Joe Quinn, her husband, might be another matter. An ex-SEAL, ex-FBI, now a detective with the ATLPD, he might have to be dealt with in a special way.

Perhaps use the couple's young son?

But he mustn't be in a hurry to make any decisions. He'd already made the preparations, and only the final moves were left to complete. It would come to him. It always came to him.

Anna would tell him the best way to rid the world of Cara Delaney.

Excitement was beginning to tingle through him. This was the challenge for which he'd been waiting. This was the test to prove that those other clumsy artists he'd taken as tribute before that young woman on that stage had merely been a rehearsal. Listening to her tonight had confirmed what he'd known was true. She was everything that Anna would hate. That meant she was perfect for the kill.

And obviously destined to be his final triumph.

CHAPTER

1

"Cara's coming!"

Michael pressed the disconnect on his cell as he ran into the living room and plopped down on the couch beside Eve. "Her final concert is in Charlotte, North Carolina, tonight. She'll be here in Atlanta to-morrow night, but she won't be able to come home until day after tomorrow. She has to be at some fancy party in Buckhead for a benefit. She says it has something to do with a fund-raiser for St. Jude Hospital." He leaned back and stretched his legs out before him. "But she says we've got her for the next week . . . if we want her." He smiled mischievously. "I told her we'd talk it over and get back to her. What do you say, Mom?"

"I want to know what *she* said." Eve ruffled his chestnut-colored hair. "Did she put you in your place, young man? You nag her constantly to get her agent to stage her violin concerts as close to Atlanta as she can manage so that she can come home. And then you give her grief when she does?"

"Well, someone has to give her grief." Michael gave her a sly glance as he nestled his head on her shoulder. "Just teasing. Teasing is fun, right?"

"If you say so. It depends on whom you ask." But she knew that Michael was all joy and humor and very special in every way. She had known that from the moment he was born ten years ago and was even more aware of it now. "But Cara hasn't been around much for the last year. She might have forgotten what a brat you can be."

"She thinks I'm perfect," he said solemnly. "Most of the time." His amber-colored eyes were suddenly twinkling. "You're the only one who thinks I'm a brat."

"Because lately you've started trying to manipulate me." She looked him in the eye. "Haven't you, Michael?"

He hesitated. "Manipulate?" he repeated.

"A big word for a very devious act," she said. She'd been bracing herself for the past few days, and she might as well get the confrontation over. No matter that his actions were motivated purely by affection, it was her job as his mother to monitor and guide those actions. "And stop pretending you have no idea what it means. You probably have a bigger vocabulary than I do these days. Answer me."

"I wasn't pretending. That would be a lie. I never lie to you. I just had to think what to say."

"The truth. You've been trying to manipulate me?"

He didn't speak for a moment. "Yes. How did you know?"

"Oh, you've been very clever. Sometimes even subtle. Asking for help with your homework. You *never* need help with your homework. Persuading your dad and me to go on walks every evening. Bringing in Cara's CDs for me to listen to with you after supper." She paused. "Anything and everything to keep me from working on that reconstruction. Why, Michael?"

He was silent. Then he sighed and gave up. "You've been working too hard this month. You just got over the flu." His gaze went to the skull of the young boy on the dais of her worktable across the room. "It won't hurt you to take your time doing that reconstruction. Dennis wouldn't mind. He's probably a good guy."

He wasn't joking. From the first time he'd become aware of those skulls that appeared on her worktable when he was a toddler, he'd always treated them with gentleness and respect. He'd even given a few of them names just as Eve always did in order to better connect with them as human beings, not just as victims. "That's my decision, Michael. You're my son, not my guardian." She smiled. "And you're only ten years old. Put a few more years under your belt before you decide you're in charge of this family."

"Years don't really matter," he said absently. "You just have to make up your mind what's important and do it. Of course, people seem to object to letting you do what's right until you reach a certain age. But most of the time you don't, Mom."

"But what you think is right isn't always that," she said gently. "There's such a thing as free will."

"Yes." He was frowning. "But you were working too hard. I didn't want you sick again. You're never sick. It scared me."

"Did it?" She pulled him closer. Of course it had scared him. That bout of flu had come out of nowhere and attacked her like a nuclear bomb. She had come very close to pneumonia. It had taken her almost a month to get over it, and she'd been aware how upset he'd been. The bond between them was even closer than between most mothers and sons. Sometimes it seemed as if they could read each other's thoughts. "Then talk to me about it. Don't try to manipulate me."

"It seemed the easiest way." He was still frowning. "I've been finding it works with other people."

And Michael was so clever, so innovative, that it would be simple for him to manipulate and manage the people around him. His understanding was far beyond his actual age, and she sometimes felt as if she were dealing with a college student. But she had noticed that as he grew older, that particular skill was constantly growing. If he didn't have such a good heart, it could be a very dangerous talent. "I'm sure it does work, and only you can decide if it's the right thing to do. I can only tell you it's wrong when you use it with family and people you love. It might make them not trust you."

"Then I won't do it," he said immediately. "Not if you say I shouldn't." He paused. "Does that mean I have to call Cara back and tell her not to come?"

"What?" She frowned. "Why should you?"

"I wanted her to come home. I knew that you'd spend most of the week with her and not work." He added simply, "So I fixed it."

"Fixed it?" Her eyes widened. "You didn't tell her I'd been ill? I deliberately kept that from her so she wouldn't worry. And I told you not to say a word when you talked to her."

"And I didn't tell her." He was genuinely upset. "I wouldn't do that if you didn't want me to."

"Then exactly how did you 'fix it'?"

"I told her that Jock was going to be here this weekend." His luminous smile lit his face. "I knew that would bring her. She doesn't get a chance to see him very much when she's on tour."

Eve stared at him in shock. "Yes, that would bring her." But she hadn't realized that Michael would know that. The relationship between Cara and Jock Gavin had been ongoing since Cara had been only a little older than Michael's age and Jock had saved her life. It had been one of those strange, rare attachments that perhaps comes along once in a lifetime. The child who had been friendless and on the run most of her life. The young man who had fought his way from the depths of guilt and despair and was probably still fighting. Through the years, they had been best friends, almost brother and sister, and yet lately Eve had become aware something . . . deeper had emerged. "But he's not going to be here. He's still in Scotland. I haven't heard anything from him. I can't believe you would lie!"

He shook his head. "He'll be in Atlanta. He promised to bring me that family kilt that MacDuff said I could use for the show-and-tell exhibit next week. And he said that he'd bring along all the family historical stuff with it so that I could have a complete presentation. But he said that it was priceless to the MacDuff family so he'd have to be here to keep his eye on it." He beamed at her. "But it's nice of him, isn't it?"

"More than nice. Extraordinary. And why didn't I hear about this show-and-tell?"

He looked at the Dennis reconstruction. "You were busy."

"Are you trying to give me a guilt trip?" she asked sternly.

He smiled innocently. "Maybe. Is it working?"

"It is not." She pushed him away from her. "And since when have you gotten so chummy with Jock Gavin? He's not been around much in the past few years."

"I like him. Lord MacDuff might be the one everyone makes a big fuss over, but Jock is cool."

"Yes, he is." Jock was Lord MacDuff's best friend and not only ran MacDuff's Run but also handled all of MacDuff's investments, which Jock had built into a large fortune. He was totally brilliant and had a history more dark and complicated than she wanted to explain to Michael at the moment. "But how did you get to know him well enough to decide that he was cool enough for you to approach about borrowing a MacDuff family heirloom?"

"Well, Cara liked him. I knew I'd probably like

him, too. So I started phoning him whenever I felt like talking about Cara or to ask him questions about Scotland or that loch you said we liked when I was a little kid."

"You did like it." She had spent months in Scotland when she was pregnant with Michael and later had taken him to Loch Gaelkar when she and Joe had been married. The loch was a magical place of mist and legends, and it had not surprised her that he'd felt at home there. But then she had never seen a place where Michael wasn't at home. He seemed to have an affinity for everything that had to do with nature and life itself. "You could have asked me about it."

"I wanted to ask Jock. It was kind of neat having him explain everything in that Scottish accent." His smile widened. "He laughs when I try to imitate him. And I think he knows lots of other things that he didn't tell me. Maybe he will someday." He added gravely, "I didn't bother him, Mom. I think he liked to talk about Cara."

She didn't doubt it. She'd been aware Jock had been keeping his distance from Cara during these last years when she'd been completing her studies and starting to launch her career, but she didn't believe he would ever allow himself to totally lose touch. And it was possible Jock had also been caught up in the spell Michael managed to weave over everyone with whom he came in contact. "But you didn't tell me you were talking to him. Why?"

"I would have told you if you'd asked me."

"You're quibbling."

He nodded. "Sometimes secrets are fun." He made a face. "But this is one of those times you think I was using a friend to get what I wanted?"

"Isn't that what you think?"

He thought about it. "I guess I do. It didn't seem like that when I was doing it. All I thought about was you."

She tried to stifle the melting tenderness she was feeling. "And I appreciate that you were concerned. But you have to think about other people as well." She made a face. "I'm only grateful you didn't decide to bring Jane into your machinations, too. I'm surprised you didn't figure a way to have her cancel her art show in London and come winging home."

Michael smiled and just shook his head.

"Michael?" she said warily.

"Jane visited us just three months ago. It was too soon. I would have had to tell her you'd been sick. I couldn't do that, so it had to be Cara."

But he had thought about it, Eve realized. "I'm surprised that stopped you. Why not bring the entire family?"

"I promised you," he repeated. "But I would have made sure that it didn't hurt Jane. She would still have been able to make her art show. A few days wouldn't have made a difference."

"No, it wouldn't." And she knew he would never do anything to harm Jane. He considered Jane MacGuire and Cara Delaney as his sisters and he adored them both. He didn't understand the difference between blood relations and family members invited by love, and he never would. As for Jane and Cara, they had been his willing slaves since the night he was born. "But it should be her choice. So we're back at square one, aren't we?"

"Yeah, I guess we are." He met her eyes. "Do I have to call Cara back?"

She sighed. "No, that would make everything worse." The relationship between Cara and Jock was delicately balanced enough without bringing Michael's convoluted maneuverings into the mix. Besides, it had been too long since Cara had been home. Eve had missed her. "Just promise me that this kind of thing won't happen again."

He was silent.

"Michael."

"I promise I'll try not to make it happen." His expression was troubled. "Unless I get scared about you or Dad again. Then I'd have to do anything I need to do. You can see that, can't you?"

"No, I can't see—" She stopped. She'd been going to be the good mother and tell him rules were rules and there should be no exceptions. But she wouldn't lie to him. If she was frightened for any of the family, she wouldn't hesitate to do anything she needed to do to protect them. "I can understand that you'd have a problem. But we discussed persuasion and being honest. Will you promise to tell me first before you do anything else?"

"Sure." He smiled brilliantly. "Does that mean I can persuade you not to work tonight?"

She shook her head ruefully. "No, that doesn't mean you'll get your way every time. That's not how it works."

His smile faded. "Then what good is it if I still have to worry about you? How *does* it work, Mom?"

"We compromise. I might be persuaded to knock off at ten. Take what you can get, kid."

"Right!" He jumped to his feet and tossed a salute to the reconstruction on the dais. "You heard her, Dennis. Ten." He headed at top speed for the front door.

Had she just been persuaded or manipulated she wondered suddenly. Worry about it later. "Where are you going?"

"I've got to go down to the driveway and help Dad give the Jeep a tune-up. He said I needed to learn how to do it. It's going to be fun!" He slammed the porch door behind him, and she heard him running down the porch steps, and calling, "Cara's coming home, Dad. Maybe we'd better tune the Toyota, too."

"Suits me."

Of course, it did, Eve thought with amusement as she followed him to the front porch. Working on the cars was a favorite pastime for both of them. Joe because it allowed him to work with his hands instead of his mind, Michael because he had a thirst for knowledge that was positively unquenchable. But perhaps the main attraction was that they could be together and bond. She stood looking down at the driveway, where Joe and Michael were already bending under the hood of the Jeep. So different and yet so much alike. Joe in his jeans and the chambray work shirt he always wore when he worked outside on the property. Tall, muscular, lithe, but with the same brown-red hair and tea-colored eyes as his son. Michael with a child's gangliness yet brimming with vitality and the sheer joy of living in his khakis, tennis shoes, and Falcons sweatshirt. He was laughing up at Joe and saying something Eve couldn't hear. She wished she had a photo of this moment to preserve it forever. Michael's eager expression was glowing with all the love and respect that he felt for his father. Joe was gazing down at him with a half smile that was both understanding and tender. Another guy moment, she thought. For an instant, she felt a little wistful about that bond between them that she would never be able to share. Joe and Michael were constantly together. Whether it was Joe teaching Michael every skill under the sun, playing different sports, barbecuing, or fixing that darn Jeep. The envy was immediately gone. What was she thinking? She and Joe had their own special places in Michael's life, and she was grateful for every minute that he gave to him. As even her son had learned, she was something of a workaholic, and Joe's job as a police detective was equally demanding. Hopefully by sharing the responsibilities, they had managed to give Michael everything he needed.

"Want to come down and help?" Joe called up to her.

She shook her head. "Just enjoying watching the two of you slave. I have to get back to work. It seems I have a curfew."

"Curfew?"

"Ask your son." She turned and moved toward the front door. "Be sure you don't get too involved with that Jeep and skip supper."

"How about you?" Joe asked.

"I'll grab a sandwich now." She cast one more glance down at the two of them. The setting sun was casting a golden aura around them. Their chestnut hair looked almost auburn in this light. They were strong and healthy and beautiful . . . and they belonged to her.

Lord, she was lucky.

"Curfew?" Joe murmured as he glanced down at Michael. "What have you been up to?"

"She said I should use persuasion instead of . . ." He took a wrench and tightened a nut. "So I did. I wanted her to rest, but all she'd give me was ten o'clock."

"That's not bad." Joe leaned on the fender, gazing thoughtfully down at him. "Persuasion instead of what?" He chuckled and held up his hand. "Never mind. You got busted, didn't you?"

He looked up at Joe. "Did I?"

"Michael."

"I only wanted her to rest more. I didn't like it when she got sick."

"Neither did I."

"I was scared."

"So was I." He shrugged. "And I also wanted her to rest more after the doctor released her. But I've learned that's a difficult thing to accomplish with your mom. And it's something you'll have to learn for yourself. So I let you go for it. You were doing very well, but you must have gotten a little overconfident."

He nodded gloomily. "She called me manipulative."

He chuckled. "And you are. I've noticed it myself in the last year or so. I like to think it's in the nicest possible way, but Eve would be wary of it. What tipped your hand?"

"Cara."

"What on earth have you been— No, don't tell me. Eve will go into it later."

"You're laughing. Mom didn't think it was funny."

"Because she's in charge of your immortal soul and is very conscientious about it. Not my responsibility. I believe your soul is doing just fine. There's nothing wrong with you trying to take care of your mom. I would have done the same if I hadn't thought you were doing pretty well on your own." His smile faded. "Now, if I hear that you behaved in a way that I don't approve of, it will be a different matter. You realize that, don't you?"

"Yes, sir." Michael's lips were twitching. "But I thought you wouldn't mind as long as it was Mom."

Michael knew very well that Eve was the exception to every rule, Joe thought ruefully. She was the center of their universe. If she had not been that to Michael since the moment of his birth, he would have learned it from watching him.

"I do mind because she does. She gave you an alternative for what she considers unacceptable. She says be persuasive? Then do it. No shenanigans." He loosened the distributor bolt. "Now hand me that timing light and I'll show you how to hook it up to the number one cylinder . . ."

"Stop laughing, Joe." Eve scowled as she looked down at Joe's grinning face. "Or so help me, I'll push you out of this bed."

"It's funny. You have to admit it." He pulled her down into the curve of his shoulder. "I had no idea Michael was graduating to CIA status. That plan to make you rest involved a very complicated set of characters and scenarios that relied on what our son has learned about all of us."

"And you're proud of him? Don't you dare let him know."

"I'll try to restrain myself. But what can I say? I'm a police detective, and I have to admire Michael's technique. It was really very intricate. And involving Jock was a stroke of genius." He murmured. "He must have been studying the Cara and Jock dynamic for a while."

"Dynamic? You're talking as if he's one of those forensic psychologists down at your precinct."

"Am I? Ridiculous, of course. It's just interesting."

"He's a kid," she said flatly. "And he probably has no idea about any so-called dynamic. I prefer that he doesn't. I want him to stay a kid for little longer. He's already shown signs of being too—"

"Manipulative?"

"He told you? Most kids don't even know how to spell it, but I think he wrote the book. No way. I want him to forget it. As it is, I'll have to call Cara and warn her that she'll have to be on guard if he decides he has a good reason to do anything like this again. Though I did give him a lecture, and I want him to believe I have your support."

"You always have my support." His lips brushed her

temple. "And you know that Michael would never do anything to really upset you. He's just getting older, and he's feeling his way toward independence."

"Independence? He's only ten."

"And the idea scares you."

"Yes," she whispered as she put her cheek in the hollow of his shoulder. "I want to hold on to these days and not let go. You know what we've been given in Michael. I'm afraid of doing something wrong, Joe."

"I'm not," he said gently. "I think all we have to do is love him, guide him where we can, and trust him. You felt like that from the time he was conceived. Why have you changed?"

"He wanted to take care of *me*. I'm supposed to take care of him."

"It appears he's not going to allow that to happen. It's that pesky independence thing again. Perhaps you can work out a compromise."

She made a face. "I didn't do too well with the last one I made with him. I think I might have given him exactly what he wanted."

"But you learned from it. And he has lessons to learn, too."

"How magnanimous of you to admit that," she said dryly. "You're darned right he does. CIA, indeed."

Joe chuckled. "Now you're getting back to normal. I'm surprised Michael managed to shake you up like this."

"It's your fault, too."

"I beg your pardon?"

"I was standing out on the porch and looking down at you and Michael, and I thought how lucky I was."

"Without doubt."

"I'm not joking. But nothing lasts forever. Michael is going to grow up and leave me. You're in danger every day, Joe. So I have to keep Michael young and under

my wing as long as I can." She pulled his head down
and kissed him. "And I have to keep you with me, I
have to protect you from every danger." She kissed him
again. "I have to heal all your wounds. If you're lost,
I'll have to seek until I find you." This time the kiss
was lingering. "It's a great responsibility."

"But you're up to it?"

"Oh, yes." She smiled lovingly as she pulled off her
nightshirt and crawled on top of him. "The question is,
are you up to it?"

MARQUIS HOTEL

"Good heavens, Eve, why would Michael go to all that
trouble just to get me to come home?" Cara chuckled
as she kicked off her shoes and curled up on the couch
with her cell and a Coke she'd grabbed from the mini-
fridge the minute she'd walked into the hotel room. "It
sounds almost Machiavellian. You've got to be kidding.
Are you sure you didn't misunderstand?" Her laughter
faded. "Look, I talk on the phone with Michael a few
times a week, and I don't remember him even mentioning Jock more than once or twice in the last year or so.
When he told me that Jock was going to be in town
to help him with that historical show-and-tell exhibit, I
thought that maybe you might have arranged it."

"Not likely," Eve said. "Major imposition. You
should have known I'd never have encouraged Michael
to ask anyone to just hop across an ocean to help him
with a school project." She paused. "You probably did
know, but you were so excited about seeing Jock again
that you just accepted it."

Eve knew her too well, Cara thought. Only she had
not just accepted everything Michael had told her, she
had leaped at the opportunity. "Maybe not that much of

an imposition. Jock might not have been in Scotland. You know he travels all over the world."

"Including New York when he visits his investors," Eve said quietly. "Where you have an apartment that you use for a base when you're on tour. You should have been able to get together there and not have to rely on seeing him here."

Cara's hand tightened on the phone. Had she hurt Eve? It was the last thing she would ever want to do. "You're acting as if Jock was my sole purpose for visiting you. You're my family, Eve. I've been so busy with this darned touring that I haven't been able to take the time to come home very often but it's not because I—"

"Hush," Eve interrupted. "Joe and I know all that. Do you think that we don't realize how important these concert dates are when you're just starting your career? We're glad to see you whenever you can spare the time. You've worked very hard during these last years, and now everyone is going to see how really wonderful you are." She paused. "But I also know that you're very responsible, and you wouldn't have rearranged your schedule for anything but an emergency. So why is Jock an emergency, Cara? What's wrong?"

"Nothing." She tried to keep the unsteadiness from her voice. "He's fine. He's always fine. He's perfect. Not that I'd know. I haven't seen him in over eighteen months. And then it was only for thirty minutes after a concert in New York. Then he made an excuse, and he was gone." She cleared her throat. "He's avoiding me. Not that he's not done it before. I think you probably realized that's it's been going on for years. You know so much about us, Eve."

"And I've tried to stay out of your business," Eve said gently. "You and Jock have always had a very special relationship." She paused. "Do you know, the first time I saw the two of you together I had the feeling that somehow, some way, you were meant to complete each other. Over the years it was like watching Romeo and Juliet or some kind of fairy tale. It was as if you've been running toward each other all your lives. Weird, huh?"

"Yes." Cara was stunned. "You never said anything."

"And I wouldn't have said anything now except that you've been so unhappy lately. I didn't want to interfere. But it's not interfering to tell you that you're not alone, and I'll be here if you need me."

"I've always known that, Eve."

"Good. But it bears repeating. Okay, that's all; I've said what I wanted to say. I know you'll have to work it out for yourselves."

"And Jock's way of working it out would be to eliminate it entirely," Cara said jerkily. "Well, it's not going to happen. I told him four years ago that he wasn't going to get rid of me. But because of my music and his damn stubbornness, I've barely been able to see him. That has to stop." She whispered, "I miss him, Eve."

"And I'm certain he misses you, too. But he wants to give you your freedom. He thinks that being his friend isn't healthy for you."

"Bullshit," she said bluntly. "It's my being his lover that he won't accept. We've been best friends since I was twelve years old and he saved my life. That was fine, that was great, I didn't think I needed anything else. He was wonderful and he had that shining inside . . . But then I grew up, and I found out that wasn't enough. I wanted more. And *he* wants more, dammit. I *know* it. He just won't reach out and take it." She drew a shaky breath. "Listen to me. I'd better hang up. You didn't want to hear me ranting like this. I'm sorry. I guess I've been holding it back too long. Floodgates have a way of breaking. But, as you said, you guessed most of it."

"I had my suspicions." Eve hesitated. "And one of

them was that Jock had a more complex reason than the possibility that he would interfere with your life and career if he didn't step away from you." She paused. "Thomas Reilly?"

"Of course, Reilly had everything to do with it. He nearly destroyed Jock with his damn brainwashing," Cara said bitterly. "He was only fifteen when that terrorist bastard got hold of him and did his experiments to try to make him into a master assassin."

"Not tried," Eve said. "Be honest, Cara. He *did* it. Jock eventually ended up in an asylum on suicide watch. He's lived with that guilt for years. He thinks that person he was back then will never really go away. Is it any wonder he believes that supreme ugliness in his background should never contaminate your life?"

"It wasn't his fault," Cara said fiercely. "None of it. Contaminate? No one could say that my background is spotless. My parents were involved with a Mexican cartel and my mother tried to kill me just because she didn't find it convenient for me to remain alive. My grandfather is still the head of one of the most powerful crime families in Moscow. You know that. You and Joe took me away from all that horror." She moistened her lips. "And then Jock came along and saved my life. And then he made me believe that my soul was mine alone and had nothing to do with who my parents were or where I came from. Do you know what that meant to me?"

"It meant that he gave you a great gift. But he only told the truth, Cara."

"No, more than that. When I realized that my mother had killed my sister Jenny and was trying to kill me, I had nightmares about being like her. I was afraid, I was confused, and he understood. No one had ever understood how I felt until Jock. I didn't have to pretend, I just always knew he would understand. As long as we were together, nothing else mattered." She drew a long, shaky breath, and added brusquely, "And all that horrible business about Reilly and that brainwashing really has nothing to do with who we are now. I'll make him realize that."

"I hope you do," Eve said. "Jock can be very tough. I hope he gives you the chance."

"If he doesn't give it, I'll take it." Then Cara moved to lighten the conversation. It was her fault the tone had become entirely too heavy and emotional. She hadn't wanted to burden Eve. But the words had just tumbled out, a sign of how nervous and upset she was today. "But we've gotten completely off the subject of Michael. I'll have to believe you if you tell me he's remarkable enough to stage something as complicated as this. After all, it's Michael. We all know how unusual he is."

"Believe it. Hopefully, I've nipped it in the bud. I just wanted to call you and let you know the capability is there and flourishing."

Yet there was something else Cara couldn't quite understand. "But what I'm having trouble believing is that he'd miss me so much that he'd go to such lengths just to get me to come home for a visit. Not when he has you and Joe. He's probably the most self-sufficient kid on the planet, and you're all he needs." She paused. "Is something wrong?"

Silence. "What could be wrong? You'll see that everything is pretty much as you left it when you came home six months ago." She changed the subject. "Did you just arrive at the hotel?"

"Yes, I was getting in the elevator when I got your call. I'll order room service, jump in the shower, then go down to the St. Jude suite to smile and play my fiddle."

"And dazzle everyone within hearing distance."

"I hope that's true. I visited the St. Jude Hospital when

I was in Memphis, and those kids are incredible. I try to let the local fund-raisers know when I'm in a town so that they can throw a get-together for local benefactors. It's usually only one night or afternoon, but it makes a difference. That's why I won't be able to get out to the lake cottage until tomorrow."

"I believe we can wait. Joe and Michael are going to barbecue." Then she asked softly, "Jock? Can we count on him to be here?"

"Yes." Dear God, she hoped he'd be there, Cara thought desperately. It all depended how persuasive she could be when she confronted him tonight. "Even if I have to tie him up and threaten to steal MacDuff's precious heirlooms he's guarding."

Eve chuckled. "That might be difficult. As I said, he can be pretty tough."

"Not so much. I could ambush him. He's staying at this hotel. I called MacDuff last night and checked where Jock was registered. That's why I asked the St. Jude people to set up the fund-raiser here." She tried to keep the lightness in her tone. "All this intrigue and planning just to get one man to meet me face-to-face. You'd think I'd have more pride, wouldn't you? There are people who actually like to have me around. Did I tell you my grandfather wants to set up our meeting in Arizona this year?"

"No, you did not. Probably because you knew I wouldn't approve. I was hoping that Kaskov would just gradually fade out of your life. He's a dangerous criminal. You need to stay away from him."

"I made him a promise," Cara said simply. "He gave us what we needed to keep you and Michael alive when my mother gave you that poison injection while you were carrying him. But I always knew there would be a price."

"Then I should be the one to pay it."

"Why? It was my mother who tried to kill you. You were trying to save me. It was only right that I be the one to pay the debt." She added quickly to ward off any arguments, "Besides, my grandfather doesn't ask much. One month a year, and I choose the place. It's not as if he's throwing me into some opium den. He keeps me entirely separate from his activities."

"Until he decides differently. Jock *hates* it."

"But then Jock has no business having an opinion when he's trying to opt out of my life." She added gently, "Eve, Kaskov saved you and Michael. You're my family now. These little trips are nothing in comparison to what he gave me."

"It's not nothing to me," Eve said grimly. "Whenever you're around Kaskov, you're in danger. If not from him, from his enemies, who think killing his granddaughter would be great sport."

It was time to get off the phone. Cara should have known that simple sentence would lead to this upset. She was usually more careful, so smooth it over so Eve wouldn't dwell on it. "As I said, the only reason he wants me around is to play for him. Those concerts every night after dinner are the only thing he requires of me. I'm very safe when I'm with him." Then she straightened on the couch and swung her legs to the floor. "But now it's time I hit that shower. And I'd like to practice for thirty minutes while I'm waiting for room service. I'll call you when I get up in the morning and tell you when I'll— *we'll* be there."

"You do that." She added softly, "It will be good to have you home, Cara. We've missed you."

Cara could feel tears sting her eyes. "I've missed *you*. Screw this touring. I could get a job with the Atlanta Symphony. I don't have to be some kind of star. It's only the music that matters."

"You *are* a star, Cara. I've known that from the first

time I heard you play. There's no way you can get away from it." She chuckled. "You just have to be the kind of star who writes her own ticket so you can come home more often. That will satisfy all of us. I'll talk to you tomorrow." She ended the call.

Cara inhaled shakily. Talking about her mother and her grandfather had brought back all the pain and fear she'd gone through as a young child. But it had also made her remember how lucky she'd been to have Eve and Joe become part of her life. She'd never dreamed that she would be as accepted and loved and protected as she felt now. Why couldn't Eve realize what a treasure she'd given her? Cara had always tried to show her and give back from the moment Eve had taken her into her home as a young girl. Not that it had been easy. Eve seldom would admit that she needed help, and it was often necessary to—

What could be wrong?

She was suddenly remembering Eve's reply when she'd asked her if anything was wrong.

A silence, then a noncommittal question instead of an answer. And then a quick change of subject.

Eve would never lie to her. But an evasion of the truth couldn't be called a lie. Not when she'd said she would see for herself tomorrow that everything was all right.

Was she being overimaginative?

Maybe. But she was still uneasy. Had she been so absorbed with her own emotional upheaval that she'd been blind to Eve's problems?

Tomorrow. If there was a problem, she'd get to the bottom of it tomorrow. Heaven knows she had enough to worry about tonight.

Jock Gavin was here. She smothered the jolt of excitement the thought brought. Her best friend, her savior, the man who made everything right just by smiling at her. And so much more. Don't be afraid to say it, to think, to hope.

Her lover.

She suddenly couldn't breathe. Not yet. What if he didn't want her? It was all very well to tell Eve she knew that he did, but he could have changed. He was very strong, and he might have been able to cast her out of his life.

As Cara's parents had done when she was only a child. The thought came out of nowhere. Cast her out in the darkness, where there was only panic and death.

But Jock had helped save her from that terror. Why would she remember that now?

It was nonsense. Don't even think about it. That comparison had hurt too much. She couldn't allow it. She got to her feet and headed for the shower. She was feeling a restless, driving urgency now. She had to hurry through all these preparations so that she could get to her violin.

No matter what darkness, pain, or unhappiness was in store for her, the music would save her.

CHAPTER

2

Cara closed the door of her hotel suite on those last two officials of the St. Jude fund-raising committee with a sigh of relief. She'd thought they would never leave. They'd only wanted to express their appreciation and get autographs for their kids, but she'd just wanted them to *go*. The evening had been totally worthwhile, and she wasn't sorry she'd volunteered, but she was glad it was over. She'd been on edge since the moment she'd played her first selection tonight.

It was stupid and impossible, but she had imagined she could actually feel Jock here. Not likely in this palatial skyscraper of a hotel. It was just that she'd wanted it so badly. And she was so ridiculously nervous that she'd scarcely been able to make conversation with those nice people who were going to open their wallets for those kids who needed it so desperately.

But he was *here*. MacDuff had told her he was going to be here. And Michael, for some weird reason of his own, had made sure of it. All she had to do was phone Jock . . . and then go to him.

But that seemed to be a gigantic task at this moment.

Her heart was beating so hard that she could hardly breathe. Her palms were damp and cold.

Stop being a coward. This was what she had wanted. Just do it. She drew a deep breath and reached for her cell. She hesitated as she started to dial. What if he was still avoiding her and didn't answer a call from her? She called the desk, and the next moment, she was hearing Jock's room phone ring.

"Hello."

His voice . . . It had been so long . . . Yet she could see him standing before her. She'd always thought he was the most handsome man she'd ever seen, as beautiful as a concerto. All lithe grace and muscle, fair hair, those silver-gray eyes, the lean face that was almost classically perfect in contour.

"Hello?" he said again. He paused. "Cara?"

She drew a deep breath. "Expecting me? I suppose MacDuff called and warned you that I'd asked where you were staying."

"Not warned," he said quietly. "He just wanted to make sure we didn't miss each other. He was a little surprised that I hadn't already told you myself."

"And I'm not surprised at all. I want to see you. What's your room number?"

"Not a good idea, Cara."

"That's what you tell me. It's a matter of opinion. What's your room number?"

"It's 1417."

"I'll be there in a few minutes. I'd appreciate it if you don't try to duck out through the hotel kitchen. You've tried everything else to avoid me in the past year." She pressed the disconnect.

She swallowed and braced herself. First contact over, it hadn't been that bad.

The hell it hadn't. Then why was she shaking? And it would get worse the longer she delayed.

She should probably change clothes before she left the suite and went to him. She was still in the white lace gown that she'd worn for the fund-raiser. She knew how she looked in the damn thing. It would give the entirely opposite impression than the one she wanted to convey.

It would have to do. She grabbed her evening purse and headed for the door. She couldn't wait any longer.

Three minutes later, she was knocking on Jock's door.

He swung the door open. "Hello." He smiled. "I decided to wait for you. Slipping out that kitchen exit would have lacked dignity." He stepped back and waved her into the suite. "You do realize you're being very melodramatic, Cara."

He was just the same. She stood there staring at him. Black trousers, white shirt, open at the throat . . . and that smile that she had never been able to forget. "But that's who I am." She brushed him aside as she entered the suite. "What else did you expect? I *feel* things. I'm not cool and controlled like you." She whirled to face him. "I don't hide away and think everything will sort itself out. I know it won't." Her hands clenched into fists. "So when I feel myself coming apart, I have to come to the one person I know who can put me back together."

His smile faded. "And are you coming apart, Cara?" he asked thickly. "That alone should show you that I was right when I told you that you had no place with me."

"No, it only tells me I have to work this out." She lifted her chin. "And since you didn't run away this time, you must have decided that it's only fair to give me my chance. Were you waiting for me to call you?"

"I was actually waiting for you to finish your concert tonight so that I could call you."

That took her by surprise. "You knew about the concert?"

"I make certain that I know pretty much everything about what you do, Cara," he said quietly. "I was tempted to get an invitation from the St. Jude organizers so that I could come down and hear you, but I decided the venue was a little too intimate. You would have seen me."

"And heaven forbid I'd know that you actually wanted to listen to me."

"But you've always known that. I've been your biggest fan for years. That will never end, Cara."

"*Stop* it. You're being so gentle and careful not to hurt my feelings. I could just *slap* you."

He suddenly chuckled. "And I thought I was doing so well."

"You're trying too hard." She took a step closer to him. "You want to get rid of me? I'll make it easy for you." She looked him directly in the eyes. "Just say that I'm wrong, that you don't love me, that you'll never love me the way I love you."

He went still. "My God, Cara," he said hoarsely.

"Say it. I'll believe you. Because you've never lied to me."

He was silent.

"You can't say it? Then will you be as honest with me as I am with you?" Her voice was shaking. "Because it feels very lonely out here by myself."

"We wouldn't want that, would we?" he said huskily. His eyes were glittering as he looked down at her. "Though God knows I should do it." He reached out and touched her hair with exquisite tenderness. "You'll never be alone in that, Cara. Not for as long as I live."

Intense relief. She had thought she was sure, but it had meant so much. "That's what I thought. That makes everything much simpler."

"No, it doesn't." His hand dropped away from her hair. "Look, you were born with everything against you. You were hunted and terrorized and lucky to get through your childhood without being killed. No one should have had to go through what you did." His eyes were suddenly blazing into her own. "You deserve a fresh start, and now you have it. You have the whole world before you. Go for it, dammit."

"It doesn't work that way. How many times do I have to tell you?" She moistened her lips. "Four years ago I let you persuade me that I should walk away from you for a while. Though you really meant forever, didn't you? You thought I was too young. Wrong. You thought that the man you'd been all those years ago was so evil that it would hurt me in some way. Wrong. You thought that if you stayed away from me I'd forget you. Wrong." She had to stop to steady her voice. "All wrong, Jock. All these four years have done is make everything harder for me because you weren't there. You said we could still be friends, but you even took that away." She lifted her chin. "And you made me come running after you when I didn't even know if I was all alone in what I was feeling. That's a terrible thing to do to me. Because I haven't felt alone since that night when you walked toward me across that courtyard in Scotland and I thought that you looked like a prince from a Disney movie. And then I didn't care what you looked like because the only important thing was that you were always there for me." She took another step toward him. She had to make him understand. "Ever since that night there have only been two things that have been important to me, two things that made up for everything bad that had gone before. One was the music." She swallowed to ease the tightness in her throat. "The other was Jock Gavin."

"Cara." His voice was husky. "Don't do this to me."

"Why not? You deserve it. Because you're stupid and stubborn, and I'm tired of hurting. I won't *have* it,

Jock." She suddenly couldn't stand not touching him. She ran the last few steps. "So do something about it." She laid her head on his chest, and whispered, "Make it stop hurting, please."

"Oh, shit." His arms went around her. "What the hell am I supposed to do with you?"

"Anything you want," she said unsteadily. Dear God, it was going to be all right. This was *her* Jock, familiar and yet always a mystery. He felt so *good*. She could feel his heart beating fast and hard. "I thought I'd made that clear." She nestled closer. "The one thing you can't do is send me away or go off on your own and forget about me again."

"I never forget about you." His hands were gently rubbing the nape of her neck. "Not that you'd let me. I've never seen such a determined woman."

"Woman. Not girl. At least that's an improvement. Have we at last established the fact that I'm an adult woman and not the young girl you've been protecting all these years?"

"So established." His hands cupped her neck and tilted back her head. "I'd be a complete lech if I didn't go along with that considering my present condition." He smiled teasingly. "But how can I separate the two. You're the complete package."

"I see." She hesitated, then said in a rush, "Then would you like to unwrap the package? I think it would be a great idea."

He stiffened. His gaze narrowed on her face. "Are you trying to seduce me, Cara?"

"I think I am. The idea just popped into my head, so I'm not really sure."

"Then I believe you'd better be certain before you do it again. Why did it just pop into your head?"

"Because I thought how terrible it would be if I couldn't please you. I've been thinking about that a lot lately. I admit you're a little older than I am. You've had all those zillions of women through the years, and it will take me lots of time to catch up. I hate the idea of your having to put up with me while I—"

"Zillions?" His lips were twitching. "My, it's a wonder I ever managed to get out of bed, isn't it?"

"Well, maybe I exaggerated a little." She was also smiling. "When I was younger, I didn't think about it at all. But when I was older, and I realized I wanted to go to bed with you, I thought about all the other women who would want that, too."

"But not zillions, I assure you."

"Stop laughing." She met his eyes. "Because I've decided that I do mean it. I think I have to catch up. What about it?"

His smile faded. "Catch up? I think you're way beyond me, and you don't even know it. You're clean and glowing and ready for life. There's nothing more beautiful or complete. If anything could convince me that I should get the hell away from you, this could."

"No!" She grabbed hold of the front of his shirt with both hands. "If I said the wrong thing, forget it. I'm not letting you go after I went to all this trouble. You don't have to go to bed with me."

"Oh, I don't?" He leaned forward and kissed the hollow of her throat. "What a relief."

Heat. Electricity. A door opening that would never close . . .

"Unless you decide you want to," she said breathlessly.

He drew a long breath. "That's already decided. That's what this is all about." He lifted his head and pushed her gently away. "But that would be dangerous for me. I still haven't given up the fight, you know."

"I'm not letting you back away from me again," she said flatly. She tried to smile. "You've always tried to protect me. Sometime you have to realize that I have to choose who and what I want to be protected from. You're definitely not on that list, Jock."

"I should be." He held up his hand as she started to speak. "But we'll call a truce temporarily. Is that okay with you?"

"It depends on the terms."

"Would you be satisfied if I no longer try to avoid you? If we go back to what we had before. Friendship is a wonderful thing, and ours was very special."

"Yes." It had been the most special thing she had ever experienced. "But it won't be enough." She suddenly smiled. "Are you still hoping I'll change my mind? It won't happen. But it's a very good truce you're offering me. Because I found out something tonight. You do want me very much. If we're together enough, that should tip the scales for me." She whirled away from him, suddenly brimming with hope and heady exultation. "But I have to be sure that those terms are spelled out and beneficial. You said you won't avoid me, that's not good enough. I know you're a busy man, but I want you to come to some of my concerts. I want you to call me on the phone and talk to me at least once a week. If I get some free time, I want you to meet me and spend some time with me."

"That doesn't appear to be too onerous," he said gently. "Anything else?"

"Just one. If I call and ask you to come to me, you have to come." She added simply, "Because it will mean I won't be able to stand being without you for one minute more."

"Cara."

She threw back her head and laughed. "See? Look at you. I'm going to win this, Jock."

"I'm scared to death you might." He turned away.

"But in order for it not to be a runaway victory, I believe I'll send you back to your room."

"No, if you want us to be friends, you can act like one. I don't want to leave you yet." She smiled at him. "Could I have a glass of wine?"

"Why not?" He crossed the suite to the small bar. "How discourteous of me. But I do have some excuse. As I recall, you weren't old enough to drink the last time the subject came up."

"And you like to remind yourself of that." She took the glass of merlot from him. "But I'm of age for anything that comes along these days." She sipped the wine. "Though I don't have a broad range of experience in much of any of it. The music always gets in the way. Everything for the music."

"And you wouldn't have it any other way."

"Of course not." She made a face. "But I'm not liking all the froufrou that goes along with it." She looked down at the white lace gown she was wearing. "Paige Hunter, the designer my agent hired, makes me wear stuff like this. She says it looks virginal and youthful and makes the audience be more impressed when I start playing. You'd think that only the music would matter to them."

"I'm sure once you start to play, they don't care what you're wearing."

"Not if I do what I'm supposed to do." She took another sip of wine. "But I didn't want to wear this gown tonight. The last thing I wanted was to give you ammunition against me. You're probably thinking how young and dewy-eyed I look, right?"

"I always think that no matter what you're wearing."

She sighed. "But this makes it worse. And you know there's nothing dewy-eyed about me. I know how terrible the world can be. But I also know it can be wonderful if I don't let stupid men like you ruin it for us." She looked down into her wine. "But there's one thing that is true. I'm still a virgin. I'm sorry. I know no one wants virgins these days. I thought about going to bed with someone else to relieve you of that burden, but I didn't get around to it. No, that's not true. I just don't want anyone but—"

"Hush." His fingers were suddenly on her lips. His voice was thick. "I don't believe I can take any more of these confidences at the moment. You're coming very close to killing me. Whatever you are is quite perfect. Now, can we drop it?"

She nodded. "I just thought I'd get it out of the way." She turned and sat down on the couch. "Will you sit down with me and have another glass of wine and tell me everything you've been doing? I've missed that, Jock."

He smiled, filled his glass, and dropped down beside her. "I'm afraid I've been leading a very boring existence compared to your touring. No glamour at all."

"I don't really do anything but work." She curled up close to him. "Except for that one month a year I spend with my grandfather. But you know all about that, don't you? You never let me be alone with him. Were you at Tahoe last year?"

"Tahoe's a beautiful area. I imagine that you find it inspirational."

"That's a yes. I was looking for you. It was very frustrating to know that you were probably somewhere nearby protecting me from my grandfather when you'd been ignoring me all year." She gazed down at her wine. "Frustrating and totally useless. You don't have to keep such a close eye on me. The only thing about me that interests my grandfather is my music. I'm perfectly safe."

"You keep saying that. I prefer to make my own judgment about Sergai Kaskov."

"And I prefer not to talk about him at all. You get all quiet, and it makes me nervous. I was just curious." She smiled. "And I'd much rather you tell me all about your boring life. Let's see, mountain climbing, yacht racing, training with combat teams." She leaned her head against his shoulder. "Besides all you do for Lord MacDuff. Not so boring, Jock."

"If you say so." He took a sip of his wine. "But don't say I didn't warn you . . ."

She was asleep.

Jock gazed down at her.

She'd resented that dewy-eyed description, but at this moment, she looked incredibly fresh and glowing . . . and beautiful.

He reached down and traced the line of her cheek with his forefinger. So strong. So vulnerable. So completely willing to fight for those she loved.

As she had fought for him tonight.

But he couldn't let her win that battle. He was right, and she was wrong. He'd given up the right to have anyone like Cara in his life. He was still the assassin Reilly had made him, the deadly poison was always just waiting for a trigger to release it. He couldn't let any of it touch her.

But how to keep her from being hurt again? He'd hoped that she'd find someone else during these last four years. That was a lie. No hope. Just desperation.

And she'd responded by fighting back and coming after him. What they'd been together was too strong. He'd only managed to make her feel rejected and uncertain. He'd seen that hurt, and he couldn't put her through that again.

Well, he'd work it out, he thought wearily. But not now, take these hours and cherish them. He'd told her he'd go slow and give back a little of what he'd with-held from both of them during these last years. He knew she was thinking that she could change his mind completely and get what she wanted.

And what *he* wanted, God help him.

His finger touched her upper lip with exquisite ten-derness.

And maybe God would help him by letting him know how he could save her when she wouldn't save herself.

And forgive him for taking longer than he should to figure it out for himself because of how much he needed these memories . . .

Jock was carrying her.

"What are you doing?" Cara asked sleepily.

An elevator . . .

She was suddenly wide-awake. "Jock!"

"Just taking you down to your room. It's nearly morning. The hotel will be stirring soon."

"Then let me down. I can get there by myself. I'm not a child."

"You looked like one curled up on my couch all those hours." He let her slide to her feet. "But if you insist."

Wonderful hours. Listening to him talk, gazing up at his expressions, knowing that she had made chance into a slim reality. "I insist. It's bad enough I'm parad-ing through the hotel in this gown. I gave a concert for St. Jude's last night, remember? If I run into anyone, I want the focus to be about reminding them to give to the charity, not whether they caught me on a walk of shame." The elevator doors were opening, and she moved forward. "Go back to your suite. I'll be fine."

"When I see you to your door." He got on the elevator and punched the button for the twelfth floor. "Just as I'd do with all the other zillions of women that I send on that walk of shame. I wouldn't want you to feel neglected."

"Be quiet." She smothered a yawn. "It was only a slight exaggeration."

"But I'm impressed you're being so discreet. It indicates that these years in the spotlight have not only matured you, they've taught you about consequences."

She stiffened. "What's that supposed to mean?"

He met her eyes. "That you should consider that you have responsibilities, and I would definitely get in the way. You're already finding that out."

"Really?" The elevator door slid open. "You're wrong again, Jock." She strode past him down the hall to her suite. Those hours of golden contentment were abruptly shattered. She searched in her bag for her key. "Though you evidently think you've discovered a weakness that you can explore." She turned to face him, her eyes glittering. "I don't care what the media or anyone else thinks of me. It was only the kids I was concerned about. From now on, I'll handle that kind of obligation so that there won't be a problem. And as for my 'maturity,' it only tells me what I want and that I intend to get it." She punched her finger at his chest. "So it would be smart of you to take me now so that we could have a life with some dignity and grace. Because I don't care if I have to look like I have the morals of an alley cat or one of those Hollywood rock stars. But I think you would, Jock. No one is more protective than you." She kissed him hard and fast. "But I don't want you to protect me. All I want you to do is love me." She was fumbling with the key. "Come by and pick me up at eleven. I promise when we get to the lake cottage that I won't cause you any embarrassment. After all,

I'm so very mature these days." She slammed the door behind her.

She stood there in the dark, trying to recover. She shouldn't have lost her temper. It had only been a few words, but it had shown her that the path was still going to be rough and hard. She had just been disappointed and caught off guard at a time when she'd been more happy than she could remember being in a long time.

But it would be all right. She had made strides tonight. She would make more in the next few days. Go to bed and sleep and start over when she woke.

She turned to pick up her violin case and take it to her bedroom.

She stopped in bewilderment.

It wasn't on the couch where she'd set it when she'd come into the suite with the St. Jude committee.

Maybe the turn-down maid had set it on the floor or taken it to the bedroom.

But she'd put the Do Not Disturb plaque on the door when she'd left the suite, as she always did. The violin was an Amati and very valuable. She never permitted strangers around it when she was not in the room.

She was starting to panic. The violin was more than valuable, it was part of her. Just as the music was part of her.

She reached out to turn on the light. The violin wasn't on the floor.

She ran toward the bedroom.

Darkness, again.

She reached for the wall switch.

Still darkness.

But the living-room switch had worked . . .

A sound behind her.

Harsh breathing.

She whirled.

Sharp pain in the back of her neck as a needle was plunged deep!

And then the darkness disappeared into total nothingness . . .

Cara wasn't answering.

Jock had already knocked on her door three times and called her cell. It had gone straight to voice mail.

He shouldn't be surprised, Jock told himself. He had managed not only to hurt her again but make her angry. She had probably decided to go to the lake cottage by herself and let him trail along later. It was what any other woman would do in the same circumstances.

It was not what Cara would do.

She was everything that was honest, and straightforward, and determined. Even when she had confronted him in anger, she had not been anything else. If she had decided to not let him go with her to the lake cottage, she would have called him and told him. She would not have just left and let him find out when he got to her door.

Unless there had been an emergency with Eve or Joe.

He pulled out his phone and dialed Eve.

"Jock?" Eve said when she picked up. "Cara said she was bringing you here for lunch. Are you still coming?"

"I don't know. Am I? Is everything okay there?"

"Fine. Joe and Michael have just put on the steaks. When are you and Cara going to be here?"

"Cara's not there?"

"Not yet." She was silent. "I'm not liking this, Jock. What's wrong?"

"It might be nothing. I just thought I'd check in with you." But he could feel the coldness clutching at him. "There were reasons why she might not be answering her door at the hotel. It was just that she told me to be here."

"What reasons?" Eve's voice was suddenly harsh. "Listen to me. I don't care what kind of brouhaha the two of you are having, Cara isn't one to hide out in her suite unless you did something pretty damn bad. What happened?"

"Other than the usual, I have no idea. I'll let you know when I do." He pressed the disconnect.

Shit!

He stared at Cara's door for a minute longer. The coldness was growing within him. Do the civilized thing and con the desk to open that door for him? Screw it. It would take too much time. Why bother when he'd been trained to break into any stronghold to reach the target? He bent down and worked for less than a minute on the lock before he threw the door open.

The overhead light was on in the sitting room, but everything else seemed normal.

"Cara?"

No answer. He hadn't thought there would be.

She wasn't here. And the coldness within him was freezing, hardening more with every second.

He moved slowly toward the bedroom. Before he reached it he saw Cara's evening purse on the floor. He bent to pick it up and saw her phone inside it. It was still registering the calls he'd just made to her.

Shit!

There was a light on in the bedroom. He could see the bed was untouched.

Then he saw the blood.

On the carpet.

On the bed skirt.

Splashed on the wall beside the door leading to the bathroom.

No!

He was running toward the bathroom.

More blood on the white tiles.

No blood in the shower.

But there was blood on the ripped and torn pieces of the white-lace gown that had been tossed on the vanity.

Cara making a face. "I didn't really want to wear it tonight."

He felt the muscles of his stomach clench as he turned away. No body, he told himself. Hold on to that. Blood, but no body yet. It didn't have to be true. Search. Find out what happened. Find *her.*

He went back into the bedroom.

And then he saw the violin.

"Get down here," Jock told Joe curtly when he picked up his phone. "Marquis Hotel. I'm going to need you."

"What's wrong?" Joe turned away from the barbecue grill. "You upset Eve when you called before."

"And everyone knows that's a primary sin in your eyes. Too bad. I need you here. And you're going to want to be here. It might be a good idea not to bring Eve." He paused. "I can't find Cara. But I found plenty of blood."

"Shit."

"Exactly. I didn't want to disturb anything in her suite, but you need to get a forensic team down here to take it apart. And you're the only one I'd trust to make certain they do a decent job." He added with icy precision, "And to stop the hotel-security people from trying to keep me from doing what I need to do. I have to find her."

And Joe knew how dangerous it would be for anyone to get in Jock's way once he'd made that decision.
He kept that deadly talent firmly leashed these days,
but Cara would be the trigger that would loose it. No
one had any firm info about the number of people
Jock had assassinated when he'd been under Thomas
Reilly's control, but Joe regarded him as one of the
most lethal men he'd ever met. "I'll be there in thirty
minutes. The forensic team will be there in forty-five.
Don't do anything that will get in my way when I get
there." He hung up and turned to Michael. "You'll
have to finish up here. I have to go and deal with some
work downtown. Take care of your mom while I'm
gone."

"I always take care of her. Just like you do." Michael's head was tilted as he studied Joe. "Is it Cara?"

Joe had given up trying to figure out how Michael
seemed to be able to guess what he was thinking. It
was easier just to accept it. But he never lied to the
boy. "Jock thinks she might be in trouble. I'm going to
go and find out if he's right." His hand clapped down
on Michael shoulder. "But we'll bring her back. It just
might not be before dinner. So finish those steaks and
put them in the fridge."

Michael nodded. "It's going to scare Mom," he said
soberly as he turned back to the grill, "You'd better go
and say something to make her feel better."

"I'll try to do that." Joe turned, left the barbecue
area, and ran up the steps to the porch. It was all very
well for Michael to tell him to say something to make
Eve feel better, but what could that be? He didn't know
enough to tell her anything hopeful.

And she wasn't going to like not being able to go
with him to the hotel. The only way she'd accept it was
if she felt it necessary to stay and take care of Michael.

As Michael felt bound to take care of his mother.

Everyone was trying to take care of everyone else. That's what families did.

But who was taking care of Cara?

I found plenty of blood.

"It's about time you got here," Jock said roughly as he crossed the lobby to meet Joe. "The security chief won't show me the video feed from the security cameras. I wasn't going to wait any longer."

"Only thirty minutes," Joe said impatiently. "I don't have a helicopter parked at the cottage, dammit." He scanned Jock's expression as he headed for the elevator. It was every bit as grim and lethal as he'd thought it would be. The muscles of his jaw appeared leaner, more intense, his silver-gray eyes were bright . . . and eager. No, not eager. Hungry. This must be the face of that young boy who had been transformed into a relentless assassin by Thomas Reilly all those years ago. Joe could tell he was going to be a major problem. And Joe didn't need any more problems when he was worried sick about Cara. He got on the elevator. "I'll get you those videos, but I want to see her room first before forensic gets here. What floor?"

"Twelve," Jock said curtly as he punched the button. "But I need to see those videos right away. You don't need me."

"You're right, but I need to keep you from intimidating those security guards. That's not helpful. So you can stay with me until you're a little calmer." He got off the elevator. "And I'm going to have to tell Eve what I saw here or she'll come herself. You can tell me if I missed anything." He glanced at him. "Because I'm sure you didn't miss anything."

"No." His lips twisted. "I have the entire suite memorized. Every detail." He opened the door to

Cara's room. "Every drop of blood. But if you need
help, I took photos." He stepped aside and let Joe pre-
cede him. "Go in and get it over with."

Joe braced himself as he slowly toured the suite. It
was agonizingly painful to see the blood and the evidence of violence. This was Cara, who had been with
them since she was an eleven-year-old girl. Bright, gentle, and full of dreams and music, and only wanting to
be a part of a real family. He cleared his throat. "You're
right, plenty of blood."

"You haven't seen all of it." Jock went to the side
of the bed next to the windows. "This one is the most
interesting." He gestured to an object on the floor. "And
might tell us something."

It was a violin lying in an open black-leather case.

Joe couldn't even tell the wood or color of the violin because of the blood. The bridge and strings were
coated in blood and the note-shaped F-holes from
which all sound issued were filled and overflowing
with blood. He felt sick as he stared down at it. "My
God."

"That was my first reaction," Jock said. "Until I realized it isn't Cara's violin."

"What?" Joe's gaze flew to his face. "Are you sure?
All that blood . . ."

"I know her violin. Cara's grandfather gave it to her
while she was being held at his estate in Moscow. Kaskov
might be a murdering son of a bitch, but he loves music, and he gave her an instrument that was worthy of
her. When I found a way to break her out of there, she
couldn't take the violin with her." He shrugged. "So I
stole it and brought it to her later. I became very familiar
with that violin." He nodded at the violin on the floor.
"And that's not it. But I couldn't find it anywhere in the
suite either. That means wherever Cara is, the violin
went with her."

"And what is this one?" He was looking at the blood overflowing the F-holes on the body of the violin. "And whose blood is that?"

"That's the first thing you're going to have forensics check. But it's not going to be Cara's," he said through set teeth. "It won't be hers."

"I hope to God you're right," Joe said as he turned away. "Come on, I'll take you down to security." His phone rang, and he glanced down at the screen. "And there's Kimble with forensics. I'll send them up here to get to work."

"Blood type, first," Jock said.

"Even though you're so sure it's not Cara's?" He shouldn't have said that. He'd learned denial never helped, but he could see that Jock's emotions were raw, and he was suffering. But Joe was also in pain, and he was going to have to tell Eve if that blood was Cara's. "Never mind. You know I wouldn't do anything else."

"I know." Jock didn't look at him. "But I have to be certain. And you might tell them to check the left F-hole on that violin. I thought I saw an initial half covered in the blood. It might be an ID."

"Now you tell me." He was dialing Kimble back as he headed for the elevator.

CHAPTER
3

Jock spent most of the next hour examining the videos of the cameras aimed at the twelfth floor and the lobby. Meanwhile, Joe checked the register and phone records for anyone checking in or out between five and eleven in the morning.

Joe's phone rang fifty-five minutes after they'd reached the security office. He glanced at the ID. "Kimble."

Jock tensed. His gaze zeroed in on Joe's face for any hint of expression. No expression, dammit.

"Thanks, Kimble." Joe hung up and turned to Jock. "The blood in the suite is AB-positive," he said. "Cara is type O."

Jock closed his eyes. "Thank God." Then his eyes were open, and he was gazing back at the videos. "We've got a chance then. He could have just killed her in the suite and smuggled the body out of the hotel. He didn't do that, he had something else in mind. She could still be alive."

"But why the blood?"

"How the hell do I know? He wanted to confuse the issue? Make us look for a corpse instead of a captive?"

He was flipping through the video shots. "Nothing suspicious in the halls." He went rigid as he checked another area. "Wait. The stairwells. The cameras were disabled between the twelfth floor and the valet parking lot in the basement." He was quickly checking the video feeds from the basement parking lot. "Blank," he said savagely. "But only from that stairwell to the exit to the street. Nothing to trigger anyone to come down and check on it." He got to his feet. "But someone might still have seen something. I'm going down there and questioning everyone who came near that—" He stopped as his gaze was caught by something else on the video. "What the hell?" He bent over the machine, his entire body galvanized, focused on the figure in the shadows several yards from the stairwell. Then his fingers were flying over the keys, magnifying the image.

"What is it?" Joe leaned forward, his gaze narrowed on the video. "It's still not clear enough. What do you think you're seeing?"

"It's clear enough for me. You can get your experts to make the details pop even more, but I don't need it." He was checking the time on the video. "It was 6:40 A.M. And he's heading for that stairwell. Very smooth. Completely professional." Then the shadowy figure reached the zone near the stairwell where the cameras had been disabled. He abruptly disappeared.

"You know him?" Joe asked harshly. "Who the hell is it? If you don't tell me who the son of a bitch is in two seconds, I'll break your neck."

"I do know him." Jock was running the time forward on the video. "And so do you. Though not nearly as well as I do. I've had time to study him. We've had several encounters over the years."

"Who?" Joe bit out. "Now!"

"Nikolai." He'd finished running the video up to the present time and he turned back to face Joe. "The chief assistant and enforcer of Cara's loving grandfather, Sergai Kaskov."

Joe froze. "What?"

"You heard me. No one could be more loyal to Kaskov than Nikolai. He's worked for him for decades. He'd die for the son of a bitch." His lips tightened. "And I'll be glad to oblige him. As soon as I get Cara back from him."

"You think that Kaskov ordered him to take Cara?"

"I don't see him doing it without orders. That was Nikolai in that video. He went up the stairwell but didn't return that way. You should find out how he got her out of the hotel."

"I don't need you to tell me what to do." He was frowning. "But it would be much simpler for him to kidnap Cara when she goes to visit him this summer. This is . . . extreme." His lips twisted. "Though Kaskov probably knows you keep an eye on her during those little intervals. You've never made it a secret. I admit I was even grateful."

"Then you should have kept her from going," he said flatly. "She never listened to me. Now look what's happening."

"I don't know what's happening, and neither do you. You just want to go out and kill someone and get Cara back."

"Exactly." He turned away from the video cameras. "And I will. Do you know where Kaskov is, or should I tap my sources?"

"I'll check with Interpol and a few of my own contacts." He reached for his phone. "I suppose it's useless to tell you to stay out of this, Jock. Kaskov is very powerful, and there's no doubt that he's capable of performing any crime under the sun. But when I was looking at that evidence in Cara's room, it didn't look like him. Nor this Nikolai if he was the one taking the orders. That gown torn in pieces with all the blood . . . It had an element of savagery. Kaskov isn't savage."

"As far as we know," Jock said. "We do know he's head of a Mafia group who deals in practically every kind of crime known to man. He could be anything. That's what I kept telling Cara. Every time she sees him, it's a risk." He shook his head. "I'm going after her." He met Joe's eyes. "And I know you are. But you should let me handle Kaskov."

"Screw you."

"Just a suggestion." He got to his feet. "These days I've noticed you try to stop and think before you go in for the kill. Very admirable, but not efficient."

"While you tend to revert to instinct and that training that nearly destroyed you," Joe said. "Cara would hate to know that she'd caused that to happen."

His lips twisted bitterly. "Then maybe she'll finally learn her lesson and stay away from me. We'll have to ask her after I get her back." He headed for the door. "I'll be in touch. I suppose I should tell you that I'm going to stop by your place and see Eve. Cara might have talked to her about her plans to meet with Kaskov. I'll try not to upset her."

"Of course you'll upset her. It's Cara. But Eve wouldn't have it any other way." He shrugged. "But watch out for Michael. He might not be quite as understanding."

"Joe called and told me you'd be coming," Eve said as she watched Jock climb the porch steps. Her arms were crossed tightly across her breasts as she tried to control herself. Showing Jock the panic she was feeling would not do either of them any good. "I don't know what I can tell you. I talked to Cara a few times this month, but I can't remember her talking about Kaskov except that one time yesterday afternoon." She grimaced.

"And then I made her defensive, and she didn't say much." Her gaze was raking his face. "You look like hell."

"Surprised?" He'd reached the porch. "You don't look very far from that yourself. I didn't expect anything else. But I decided to face you anyway. Just in case I could jar you into remembering anything that could help."

"Face me?" Then she remembered the last thing she'd said to Jock when he'd phoned her. Something about Cara's not hiding in her suite unless what he'd done was pretty damn bad. "You thought I'd blame you for this?"

"Why not? I am to blame. I should have protected her. I knew Kaskov was a threat."

Eve stared at him in frustration and aching sympathy. Of course he would feel responsible. He'd always protected Cara from every threat since they'd first met. And she could tell he was feeling the torment of that failure now. She had seen him like this before, and she was immediately on the alert. He would be driven and reckless and totally lethal. "There's no way you should blame yourself, Jock. We don't even know what happened yet, but Cara has never expected you to be—"

"I expected it of myself." His eyes were suddenly blazing. "And I *failed* her. So don't tell me what she expected. Just help me get her back."

The demons had truly been loosed, and she took an involuntary step back. "I'll do everything I can. You're not the only one who cares about her. Stop acting as if you are. Now sit down on that swing, and I'll pour you a cup of coffee. Then we'll talk." She stared him in the eye. "I'd take you into the house, but you look like you're burning up inside, and I don't want Michael to see you like this. It might upset him."

He nodded slowly. "Which is exactly what I told Joe

I'd try to avoid with you." His lips twisted. "I'm not doing so well, am I? I'll try not to compound it by upsetting Michael." He dropped down on the swing. "But I don't need coffee."

"No, you're operating on pure adrenaline at the moment," Eve said as she sat down in the wicker chair next to the swing. She concentrated on keeping her hands from trembling as she poured herself a cup from the carafe. "But I'm not there yet. I'm still shaky and scared and bewildered." She lifted her cup to her lips. "Mostly scared, and Michael is going to sense it. He always does." She gazed at him. "So I'd appreciate it if you'd tell me something to make me less afraid." She moistened her dry lips. "Any tiny little detail will do."

"I don't believe she's dead."

"Now that's a big detail." Eve had to steady her hand as she took a sip of coffee. "Why?"

"Because it doesn't make sense that Nikolai would be ordered to eliminate her. I don't know why Kaskov had him take her, but unless he had a reason that would benefit him in some way, he wouldn't kill her. Kaskov never does anything that lacks reason or purpose."

"Unless his reason is that he's gone wacko. He's a criminal, Jock."

"Possible. Not probable. He's brilliant and very practical. I'd rather look to Kaskov for a reason." He added calmly, "Before I cut his heart out."

"And put Cara in a position where she could get killed by one of Kaskov's men? Don't you dare do that, Jock."

"I'll be careful. I can be careful, Eve. I know all the ways."

Eve shivered. "I'm certain you do. I don't want to hear about it." She added, "Now ask me what you need to know about Kaskov and let me get back to Michael. Otherwise, he'll be out here asking you questions."

"And I know how persistent he can be when he wants to know something. Where was Cara going to spend her month with Kaskov?"

"Somewhere in Arizona. She didn't say where. But that wasn't going to be for another two months." She frowned. "Kaskov wouldn't be foolish enough to take her there? He'd know she might tell me. She was always honest about letting him know that she confided in me."

"She's always honest about everything. No, he probably wouldn't take her there. But it's somewhere to start. He usually rents the properties where he takes Cara. I can usually track down what real estate he's been considering lately by using my contacts in Moscow."

"For heaven's sake, the situation isn't remotely similar. Kidnapping is hardly the same as a pleasant month in a resort somewhere."

"It's a place to start," he repeated. "She hasn't mentioned anything else he's spoken about?"

"I told you, I'm sure I didn't give the impression I wanted to cut his heart out, but she knew I didn't want her to see him. That didn't encourage her to bring him up in casual conversation." She shrugged. "She was more defensive than anything else when she spoke about him. She said they had nothing in common but the music, but she felt sorry that she had it to give and he didn't. She said it made her sad. He grew up with his mother at a *Gulag* labor camp in Siberia. She was a musician, and he wanted to be a violinist. One of the guards smashed his hands with the butt of his rifle. So he told Cara he had to find another direction."

"I've heard the story," he said impatiently. "Only Cara would feel sorry for a mob kingpin like Kaskov."

"He's her grandfather. And I think it's mostly that she knows how it would feel to lose her own music. Besides, she hasn't got any other relatives. And she's grateful to him for saving Michael and me. She can't forget it." She looked down into her cup. "Though I wish she would. She's been Kaskov's hostage for too long."

"Not after I find her. You're not going to have to worry about it again." He got to his feet. "Unless you can tell me anything else I'll be on my way. I have to contact Palik about—"

"I want to see the photos."

He froze. "What?"

"Joe said you have photos of Cara's hotel room. I want to see them."

"I don't think that's a good idea."

"I don't care what you think. Cara *belongs* to us. I have to be part of this hideous thing that's happened to her." She held out her hand. "Give me your phone."

He slowly reached in his pocket and pulled out his phone. "There's no sense in you looking at them." He handed the phone to her. "Joe can tell you what forensics says about—" He saw that she was starting to flip through the phone, and said quickly, "The blood's not Cara's. Joe checked."

"He told me," she said dully as she gazed at the photos one by one. The blood . . . The torn lace gown . . . The coated strings of the violin. "It's horrible."

"I told you that you shouldn't look at them."

"No, you were wrong. I should have looked at them." She was forcing herself to look through them again. "Monstrous. Twisted. Insane." She felt sick. "And Kaskov might be terrible in many ways, but he's not any of those things." Her chest felt tight. "He didn't do this. Whoever caused this . . . ugliness was insane."

"It was Kaskov. Nikolai was *there*."

"I can't help it. You're wrong. I wish you weren't." She sat up straight in her chair. She felt as if had to brace herself. "Because this is much worse." She looked him in the eye. "I know about insanity and monsters. I've dealt with them for years. Every time I work on one of those children who were savaged by one of them, I get to know them better. I know how they think and what horrors they enjoy and the way they react." She said jerkily, "Do you actually think I just let my sculptures go back to the police and close my eyes? I couldn't do that. I follow every case and make certain that justice is done. But that means I have to know those monsters, what they do, what they are." She added bitterly, "I probably know more than an FBI profiler by now. I've studied thousands of crime-scene photos, I can tell you what those murderers are feeling by the blood spatters on the wall." She shuddered as she tapped his phone. "This is a monster."

"You could still be wrong about Kaskov. You don't know him that well."

"I've talked to him on the phone. I've watched him with Cara. I've seen how ruthless he can be when he wants something. I've also seen that he's complicated and that he kept his word to save Michael and me when he could have broken it. I know him well enough to know that he's not a monster. Neither is Nikolai." She couldn't stop shivering. "You don't want to believe it, but it's true." She was trying to keep her voice from shaking. "And that means you have to find her soon, Jock. Because she's not with Kaskov. She's with *him*."

"You're damn right I don't want to believe you," he said roughly. "You're scaring me to death. How do you know it's not just your imagination? Nikolai was there. It's only reasonable that—" He broke off and started to swear. "But I can't count on anything being reasonable, can I?" he asked bitterly. "Not when I know you'd never tell me this if you didn't believe it. And I *trust* you, dammit. You wouldn't send me down a wrong path when it might mean Cara could die."

"No, I would never do that. You know I love her."
She swallowed. "And you're right, she could die. If you
don't hurry. Unless he has some agenda that makes
him wait. Sometimes that happens, and they live for a
while after they're taken."

"And I'm supposed to hope that this murderer has
an agenda?" A muscle jerked in his cheek. "So that he
won't kill her before I can—"

"May I come out now?" Michael was standing in the
doorway, his brown eyes enormous as he stared at Eve.
"I don't like what's happening with you. Are you okay,
Mom?"

"I'm fine, Michael." She smiled with an effort. She
held out her arms, and he ran to her. She held him
close for a moment. "There's nothing wrong with me."
She nodded at Jock. "Ask your friend here. We're just
talking. He was about to leave anyway."

"You're cold," Michael whispered. "You're shaking."
He whirled to Jock. "She's *hurting*," he said fiercely.
"Did you do it?"

"I'm afraid it might have been partly my fault."

"You shouldn't have done it." Then, as he studied
him, the anger faded. "But you're hurting, too. Why?"
He answered himself. "It's Cara." He turned back to
Eve. "Dad found out something bad, didn't he? How
bad?"

She wouldn't lie to him. "We don't know yet. We
don't know where she is. But we're going to find out.
Your dad is looking for her now." She gazed at Jock over
Michael's shoulder. "And as soon as he leaves here, Jock
will be looking for her, too. He was just going to tell me
where."

"Where do you think I'm going?" Jock asked
roughly. "I don't have any choice. We only have one
possible clue. You might not believe Kaskov is guilty,
but Nikolai was at that hotel at the same time she was

taken. That means Kaskov knows something." He
turned to leave, and added grimly, "And I guarantee
he'll tell me what he knows. I just have to find him."

"Hurry," Eve said. "You have to hurry, Jock."

He flinched. "So you told me." He headed for the
porch steps. "There's no question about that. Regardless of whether I believe you're right about this or not,
I'd never take the chance."

"But you do believe I'm right," she said unsteadily.
"Be careful. Let me know how I can help."

"Joe and I will have it covered." He cast a quick
glance at Michael. "Take care of your mom. I'll find
Cara."

"I always take care of her," Michael said gravely.
"See you, Jock."

He nodded. The next moment he was running down
the steps.

Michael watched Jock get into his car before turning
back to Eve. "He's scared." He leaned against her. "So
are you."

"Yes." Her arms tightened around him. "This . . .
isn't . . . good. We can't let Cara stay lost. I have to find
her."

"I know. Jock didn't understand that you'd have to
go look for her." He took a step back. "All he's thinking
about is how much he's hurting and that he has to get
to her."

"But you understand?" Eve asked. "Of course you
do. Cara is family. We have to bring her home. I was
the one who brought her to this house and told her that
she'd always have a home here. That makes her my responsibility. I can't sit and wait for anyone else to find
her. It has to be me."

"I understand." His hands nervously grasped her
arms. "She's my family, too. She's as much my sister

as Jane. But I don't think that's what you're trying to tell me, is it?"

"Not tell you, ask you. When your dad or Jock find out where Cara is, I have to go and help. But I can't leave you unless I know you're safe. Will you let me drop you off at Catherine Ling's place to stay with her and Luke until I come back?"

He immediately shook his head. "I should go with you."

"No, I'd only worry about you." Not that she wouldn't worry anyway. But Catherine Ling was a CIA agent who was also Eve's good friend, and trust was everything. "Please, Michael. It's my job, not yours."

"Because she's your responsibility? Isn't that what you said?" He met her eyes. "But I brought Cara here this time. She wouldn't have come if I hadn't done what I did. So she's my responsibility."

"We don't know that it wouldn't have happened." She didn't know what else to say. That monsters could attack with no warning or excuse? "Think about it. Maybe your dad will be able to find Cara right away, and I won't have to help." She got to her feet. "And now I'm going to call your dad and tell him what Jock and I discussed and find out if he knows anything more." She headed for the door. "And then I'm going to try to keep myself busy and work on that reconstruction of Dennis. I hope you're not going to raise any objections about my working today?"

"No," he said soberly. "I think Dennis might help you."

She wasn't sure he was right, she thought wearily, as she went into the house. She gazed at the skull on which she had spent hours repairing the bullet hole in the right temple. It had been clear Dennis was the victim of one of the monsters she had told Jock about. Had the bullet come without warning or had the monster taunted the little boy? Ordinarily, she didn't torture herself with painful questions until the reconstruction was complete. She just went about doing her job with gentleness and compassion to bring them home. It was after she sent them back to whatever law-enforcement office had requested her services that she let herself think about the monsters.

She went slowly over to her worktable and touched the skull. Was it hard for you? I hope it came quickly.

Did you know your monster?

Were you frightened, Dennis?

She closed her eyes as the tears stung.

And are you frightened, my Cara?

Darkness . . .

Music . . .

Cara's heart was pounding so hard it was hurting.

She couldn't breathe.

She wanted to scream, but there was something in her mouth.

She tried to move her arms, but her wrists were tied.

But she could move her legs, and she began to kick out.

"Stop it." It was a man's deep voice, filled with impatience. "I knew you'd be this disturbing. I could tell you'd have no sense of dignity."

She tried to speak, to ask him to take out this damn gag. She kicked out again and connected with something.

Swearing.

Then he was tearing the blindfold off her eyes.

A stinging blow to her cheek!

Her head jerked back and hit the floor.

Dizziness.

"Behave. I don't want to have to kill you yet." He slapped her again. "You have duties to perform."

What was happening to her? Cara kept her eyes closed to buy time until she could gather her senses and try to think. Whatever it was that was happening, it was terrifying. All she could remember was the darkness of the bedroom, then the sharpness of a needle in the back of her neck. A sedative . . .

Why?

And who? She wasn't going to learn that by playing possum.

She opened her eyes.

A man was sitting in an easy chair only a few yards from where she lay on the floor. "Good evening." His voice was smooth, the tone sounded modulated and educated with just a hint of an accent of some kind. "Are we ready to begin?" He was not a young man; his skin was firm but crinkled at the corners of his slanted dark eyes, his hair pure white but elegantly barbered. His thin, spare body also possessed a certain elegance in the beige trousers and silk shirt set off by a dark paisley vest. "I do hope so." He took a sip of his whiskey. "You've been terribly boring. I thought you'd regain consciousness much sooner. Though I didn't expect all that disgusting kicking and grunting."

She made another disgusting grunt behind that gag.

"Oh, very well. You can't be expected to be very entertaining if I can't talk to you." He reached down and jerked down the gag. "If you scream, I won't put the gag back, I'll sew your lips shut."

She believed him. His eyes were gleaming catlike as he stared at her. He *wanted* to do it. She felt the fear ice through her as she realized what kind of man this was. Careful. She had to be very careful. "I won't scream. I won't do anything that you don't want me to do. I only want you to let me go."

"I'm afraid that would be impossible. I chose you very carefully. I need you to perform for me."

"Chose me? I've never seen you before."

"But I've seen you, Cara." He reached down and stroked her cheek. "And I know how you manage to charm all those people who listen to you. You have no real talent, but you've found ways to fool them. Even I have to fight it."

His touch was delicate and those cat eyes . . . It was like being stroked by a jaguar that was probing before the strike. Keep him talking. Find out everything she could about him. "I've never wanted to fool anyone. I've just wanted to play for them." Where was she? What could tell her what she needed to know? Her gaze flew around the room. Not large. It looked like the interior of a cabin. A fireplace, easy chair, a kitchenette. A huge TV on the far wall.

And the music . . .

The strains of the Mendelssohn violin concerto.

She vaguely remembered the sound of that music when she'd been regaining consciousness.

"You're looking for a way out?" He laughed as he studied her expression. "It will be amusing to watch you try to find one."

"It can't be very amusing when you have my hands tied like this. Not amusing and not brave. It's not as if I'm much of threat. Just look at me."

"It's true you appear very fragile. But your guardian is a police detective. Surely he's taught you to protect yourself."

He knew about Joe. Not good. Everything he knew about her made her position weaker. But she'd already decided he was not going to be easily fooled. "Naturally, but I'm a musician, not a ninja."

"But I believe you may be very intelligent. So the ropes will remain for the time being, Cara."

"You know my name, but I don't know yours."

"How rude of me. I should really level the playing field as much as possible. I'm John Svardak." He took another swallow of his whiskey. "Now you have a name to tell your Joe Quinn if you happen to run into him on one of your strolls."

"Strolls?"

"Just a bit of whimsy. You'll understand later." He bent down and took off her gag. "I find whimsy comforting when the world sometimes seems very dark. Would you like a drink of water? You haven't had anything since I took you from that lovely suite in Atlanta." He frowned. "I had to wait a long time for you to come back that night. I was beginning to get annoyed. You looked so pure and innocent in that gown. I should have known that you'd show yourself to be the slut you are once you got away from an audience. Who did you fuck before you staggered back to your room?"

Then he didn't know about Jock. "No one. I was just out with a friend."

"You're lying. Oh well, it's not important. But you made me angry by keeping me waiting. I'm afraid I did serious damage to your pretty gown."

She looked down and realized that she was no longer wearing the white lace gown. She had on a pair of khaki jeans, tennis shoes, and a loose white shirt. Why would he go to the trouble of changing her clothes? It was on a par with the rest of his bizarre actions. "It doesn't matter. I didn't like it anyway."

"How kind of you to absolve me of blame. But I really think I have to show you why you mustn't irritate me. Actually, I've been looking forward to it." He got to his feet. "One has to know where one stands in the scheme of things."

"And where do you stand? Svardak? Is that a Russian accent?"

"I was actually born in Estonia. And I ask the questions, Cara." He reached down and pulled her to her feet. As she swayed, he caught her by the waist to steady her. "Definitely not displaying any ninja qualities. Perhaps you were telling the truth." He clicked a button, and the TV on the wall began to glow. "Now watch closely."

Her suite at the Marquis.

Blood.

Everywhere.

He was moving around the bedroom slinging it from a large vial. The bed, the carpet, the wall. Then he moved to the bathroom. Her gown lying on the vanity was torn and barely recognizable.

She inhaled sharply as she watched him hurl the blood on the lace. It wasn't the damage but the force of his action that frightened her most. She could believe he'd been angry with her when he'd destroyed this room. Angry . . . and unhinged.

She had to take a moment before she could speak. "So now you've shown me." Her gaze was still fixed on that blood-spattered gown so that she wouldn't have to look at his face. "You've destroyed a perfectly nice gown and caused the hotel housekeeper at the Marquis a good deal of extra work with all that blood. Since I was unconscious, who were you intending to intimidate with such a useless action?"

His hand tightened on her waist and an unexplainable expression flickered over his face. For an instant she thought it was rage, but then he smiled. "You have courage. I might enjoy our time together." He tilted his head. "Who would be intimidated? Who would go over this scene with an entire team to find some trace of you? Joe Quinn. Don't you believe he would be filled with fear and rage?"

"Joe is tough. He wouldn't be afraid of you." But

Joe would be afraid for her she knew. She had been so shocked and bewildered since she had regained consciousness that she still couldn't put everything together yet. It was the second time Svardak had mentioned Joe, and she was definitely uneasy. "And he's used to blood. It won't take him long to find out it's not mine. Even if it's the same type. There's DNA these days." She stiffened as her gaze flew to his face. She had to ask him. "Whose blood is it?"

"I might have stolen it from a slaughterhouse." His gaze was watching her expression maliciously. "Or I might have broken into a Red Cross blood bank," he murmured. "But I needed so much. You haven't seen all of it." He turned the video back on and was leading her back into the bedroom. "And this was most important of all."

The violin.

Blood coating the strings.

Blood gushing from the F-holes.

Shock.

She felt as if that blood was smothering her as it was smothering any music that violin could ever produce. She was struggling to keep from gagging.

"I thought that might disturb you a bit," Svardak said. "But you can see how I needed so much blood. It was necessary to impress not only you but your devoted guardian."

She shook her head to clear it. "It's not even my violin."

"No, I couldn't bear to use that beautiful Amati for the demonstration. Besides, I needed it for you." He enlarged the image of the violin. "And after all, it's only right she have her tribute."

She moistened her lips. "She?"

"Marian Napier." He nodded at a black-and-white

photograph on the wall portraying a young woman holding a violin. "It was Marian's violin." He turned and smiled into Cara's eyes. "So was the blood."

He wanted to see the shock and horror. She could see the hunger and anticipation. Don't give it to him. Whatever he wanted, don't give it to him. "You killed her?"

"That's obvious, isn't it? You mustn't be too upset. She was even less worthy than you." He tilted his head as he punched a button on the remote, and the music of the violin concerto flooded the room. "Just listen to her." He grimaced. "A total amateur. Her string work was abominable. I tried to guide her technique, but she couldn't grasp the proper way to do it. Of course, she was under stress when she made that CD for me."

The music was surrounding Cara. Now that it was louder she could hear the faint vibrato as the artist tried to perform the concerto. But the technique was terribly stilted. The shakiness of the bow strokes . . . the agony of trying to create beauty out of sheer terror.

"Why?" she choked. "For God's sake, why?"

"I gave you a hint. Perhaps you're not as clever as I thought you might be." He smiled. "It's all about tribute, Cara."

The music was swelling and so was the agonized sadness Cara was feeling as she listened. "Will you turn off that CD? It's making me ill."

"Oh, I wouldn't want to do that." But he didn't turn down the volume on the CD. His gaze was fixed hungrily on her expression, drinking it in. "Perhaps we'll only use it as dinner music."

"Dinner? You mean you intend to keep me alive for a while? Why?"

"The same reason that I had to discard Marian. Tribute. I've only been able to offer Anna inferior gifts of late, but you're very special for many reasons."

"Anna?"

"Questions." He smiled. "You're full of questions. You're hoping to turn questions into answers that might save you. I might even answer them sometime. It depends on how cooperative I find you."

"I'll keep asking," she said. She couldn't stand that music any longer, and she added recklessly, "And I think you'll answer because you're egotistical and a little crazy and you want someone to think how superior you are."

"I'm not crazy." His lips thinned. "But I'm superior to you in every way. Or I'd slice your throat right now and cheat myself of the pleasure later."

The chords were grating unbearably on Cara's nerves. She should be able to ignore it, but she couldn't. The concerto was controlled, painfully disciplined, and the young violinist's fear seemed to be rising as the music rose. Cara couldn't stand it. "Turn off her music," she said through set teeth. "Please."

"Such a sensitive soul." His eyes were glittering with malice. "Are you feeling close to poor Marian?" He was pulling her toward the front door. "Let's get you a little closer." He opened the door and pushed her outside. Cold wind was suddenly pulling at her hair and plastering her shirt to her body.

Night sky.

No stars.

Mountains. Hills. Wilderness.

Trees.

He was dragging her forward. "Come along. She's waiting for you."

Through the veil of pine trees she saw that she was on the edge of a huge canyon looking down at an abyss hundreds of feet below.

The wind whipped her face, and she thought any minute it would sweep her down into the abyss.

"Do you hear her call you?" Svardak asked softly. "Perhaps if she still had her violin, she'd play for you. She's probably lonely. She's only been down there two days."

She couldn't take her gaze from the darkness below. "You threw her down there?"

"Why not? She was dead, wasn't she? I'd already taken the blood, and I had no more use for her."

"Why not? She was *innocent*."

"She was an unskilled amateur who stole the glory from those who deserved it." He scowled. "And I don't like you criticizing me. You will *not* do it." He shoved her against a pine tree, untying her hands, looping the rope around her body and tying her to the pine. "See how you like keeping Marian company out here." He was standing before her, the wind blowing his thin hair back from his face. He gestured to a shadowy figure in an anorak standing watching a short distance from the cabin. "Don't bother thinking Abrams will help you. You can scream, but my guards know better than to interfere. It's really only you and Marian alone together. It's cold and windy, isn't it? It's always windy here. You'll probably be stiff and frigid by morning. If you beg me, I might let you come back inside."

"Or you might not." She was already shivering. "Did you offer that option to Marian Napier?"

"Perhaps. I don't remember. I had her for more than a month, and it was difficult to keep track of what I did to her." He smiled. "But I do know it wasn't on the first night. I knew you would be special." He turned and started back toward the house. Then he stopped and glanced over his shoulder, his dark eyes gleaming maliciously. "Do you remember I mentioned you might run into your beloved Joe Quinn on one of your strolls?" His gaze shifted to the canyon. "I was thinking of that place that Marian makes her home now."

She went rigid. "Joe? Why? That doesn't make sense."

"It makes perfect sense. I've been making plans. If I'm to keep you as long as I intend, I can't have him interfering. Policemen can be so bothersome." He opened the front door. "Just another thought to keep you warm through a long, cold night."

The next moment, the door had slammed behind him, and he was gone.

No, not quite gone. He had turned up Marian Napier's violin CD full blast so that it was loud enough to reach her and once more make the music a painful assault.

She was alone.

She didn't feel alone. She was surrounded by that sharp wind, nightmares of blood and horror, and the knowledge that Svardak was just beyond that door. He was probably waiting for her to call out to him so that he could prove to himself how weak and vulnerable she was.

And there was no doubt she was vulnerable, she thought wearily. But that didn't mean she had to bow down to this Svardak when he was probably going to kill her anyway. She had come close to dying many times during her early years, and she knew that men as evil as Svardak couldn't be stopped unless you had weapons to fight them. They just went on and on, re-creating themselves like one of those monster transformers in the comic books.

And she had no weapons or skills. She wasn't Jock, who was trained as an assassin, nor Joe, who was an ex-SEAL. She was only a musician.

A musician who sounded so sorry for herself that she was suddenly filled with self-disgust, she thought. There was nothing "only" about being a musician. It was magical. It had purpose. It merely had certain drawbacks.

Like the ability to stay alive.

She was getting colder. She couldn't be sure how low the temperatures would dip tonight. It was April, but she must be somewhere in the mountains, and that could mean that the weather could plummet to below freezing. The wind would make it even worse. These clothes she was wearing wouldn't ward off hypothermia. She just had to pray the temperatures didn't plunge that low.

First, make certain the ropes that bound her were secure. He'd tied her so quickly that there might be a way to free herself. She began wriggling, struggling against the confines of the ropes around her body. They gave only a little, allowing only very limited movement. No possibility of freeing herself. Though she might be able to keep her circulation going if she moved frequently.

But she had to accept that she was going to remain here until Svardak freed her. It might be wise to surrender now and live to fight another day. But she had an idea that it might not be wise at all. For some crazy reason, Svardak wanted her to be a worthy adversary. And she had no doubt that he was totally insane after what she'd experienced tonight.

But he must be able to hide it well if he'd been able to get past hotel security and into her suite to do that horrible damage. And then there was that poor girl Marian, whom he'd kidnapped and killed. None of it would be easy unless he was able to appear normal on occasion. Cara felt again that terrible sadness she'd experienced when she'd first heard Marian play that Mendelssohn concerto. She had been trying hard to do what that bastard had wanted her to do. Yet he had found Marian boring and inadequate and had no compunction about killing her. She was not proper "tribute."

Tribute. Cara didn't even know what that meant. But if she didn't find out and use it to escape Svardak, then she'd probably die.

And Joe might also die. She knew Joe would be searching for her. It was clear Svardak knew that as well. Joe might be caught in a trap as she had been swept up at her hotel.

Or Jock could be at risk. Svardak didn't know about Jock, but that didn't mean he was safe either.

The thought sent a bolt of frantic fear through her.

No! Both of you stay away. Let me fight this alone.

Last night, she had been full of hope because she had thought that all she had to worry about was convincing Jock they could have a life together. How could it have changed this quickly?

Well, life *had* changed, and she had to change with it. Her mind was suddenly brimming, full of Svardak's words and images. Think about them while she was trying to fight off the cold.

Tribute.

A violin with blood pouring from it.

Anna, a woman Svardak had not wanted to talk about.

Marian Napier, that poor frightened, young violinist who Svardak had tormented and eventually killed.

All terrible visions, but she had to remember so that she would be able to put this picture together when she confronted Svardak again.

It's really only you and Marian alone together.

Her gaze was drawn helplessly to the darkness of the abyss a few yards away. Marian was down there, lost in the darkness. Had he taken her music from her when he'd used her violin in that horrible way? No, Cara had to believe the music went on even though what people called life did not. Nothing else made sense to her. Beauty and nature and the sounds of all heaven and earth had to continue.

"Did you find that, Marian?" she whispered. "I hope you did."

No sound but the wailing of the wind through the canyon.

What had she expected? It must be because she was feeling so desperate that she wanted to believe this horror could not be totally without some kind of hope. She leaned back against the tree, huddling to retain what body heat she had left. "He's a terrible, terrible man. I wish someone had been here for you. But I'm here for you now. Neither one of us is alone."

Just the sound of the wind whipping through the deep gorge.

But she could still hear the strains of Marian's Mendelssohn concerto pouring from the house.

Why was she feeling that the heartbreaking pain and fear in Marian's music that had previously torn Cara apart had vanished? The notes were there, the terrible vulnerability was there . . . but she was no longer feeling the woman's pain.

An answer? Imagination?

No way of telling.

She was just feeling that she was not as alone as she'd been only minutes before.

"He wants to hurt me as he did you," she whispered. "He might do it. But maybe we can fight this part of it. I'll think about you, not about the horror, but about the music, because in the end that's what both of us are about. Okay?"

Did the wind in the abyss sound a little less sharp and cruel?

"I want you to know that in spite of him, you performed the Mendelssohn very well. The beauty was there beneath everything that he made you do. That's why it was hurting me so much. I don't believe I do justice to Mendelssohn. Tchaikovsky seems to suit me more."

Was she talking to herself, or Marian Napier, or just the music itself?

What the hell? It could be that she was starting to experience the first signs of hypothermia.

If she was, then she would fight it off as long as possible. She started to shift, to move, to open and close her hands. She would do what she could and hope to make it through the night.

And it would not be so bad to have the company of someone else who loved the music as much as she did . . .

CHAPTER

4

W hat have you found out?" Jock asked, when Joe answered as he was driving away from the lake cottage. "Any word from Interpol about Kaskov's present location?"

"Not yet. He doesn't appear to be at his Moscow estate."

"Appear? I need definite." He paused. "Has Eve called you yet?"

"No. Should she?"

"Don't get protective. Yes, I upset her. But she upset me as well. She made me show her the photos."

"I knew she would." He paused. "What did she say?"

"She said she didn't believe it was Kaskov."

"Anything else?"

"Monster. I suppose I don't have to explain to you what she meant."

"No."

"Well, she had to explain it to me. And I didn't like what she said. But I'm still going after Kaskov because I have no other choice." His hands clenched on the steering wheel. "And Interpol just struck out. I have to get someone who can find him now, not later."

"By all means. Choice?"

"Dima Palik. He has his ear to the ground in half the countries in Europe and particularly Moscow and sells that information to the highest bidder. I've worked with him a number of times before."

"I'm familiar with his work," Joe said harshly. "Do what you have to do. But notify me as soon as you hear anything. Do you hear me, Jock? You don't go off on your own."

"I hear you. Have you been able to run anything down about that violin?"

"It's only been a few hours. They have to be careful not to destroy any forensic evidence from the blood as well as the violin itself. But you were right, there seems to be something inscribed inside the left F-hole when they can manage to safely clear the blood away."

"Safely?" Jock swore beneath his breath. "There's nothing safe about any of this. Get them to do their damn jobs."

"That's what they're doing," Joe said quietly. "Just not the way we want it done. I'll give them just a little longer; and then I'll go in and see that it's done our way." He didn't wait for a reply. "Now, I'm going to hang up and call Eve and make sure you didn't do any damage. I'll call you when I find out about the violin." He ended the call.

More nothing, Jock thought with frustration. Blind alleys all the way. But it couldn't go on. He couldn't permit it to go on.

He pulled over to the side of the road and accessed the number for Dima Palik.

Palik answered in three rings, and he did not sound pleased. "I don't wish to be involved in this, Gavin. I deal in information, not services. Find someone else."

"Really?" Jock stiffened. "It seems you might already be involved if you refuse a job before it's offered.

Which means I have no intention of finding someone else. What's happening, Palik?"

Silence. "You're a good customer, but I won't be made a go-between for anyone. The man in the middle invariably gets chopped. I intend to lead a long and prosperous life."

"You won't live more than the very short time it will take me to get to you," Jock said softly. "If you don't tell me what the hell you're talking about, Palik. I don't have much time, and I'm not going to waste a second of it. I do hope you don't make the mistake of thinking that I'll allow you to survive if you cause me a problem in this."

Another silence. "I shouldn't have answered the phone. I just wasn't certain how you'd react later if I didn't."

"Palik."

"Okay, but you keep me out of it from now on. He's not going to care what happens to me, but you protect me." He added harshly, "Go ahead, you want to know. Ask the question."

"There's only one thing I want to know, and evidently I'm not going to have to ask. Only Kaskov could intimidate you to this extent. Did he tell you to set a trap for me?"

"No, I dealt with Nikolai, and he's intimidating enough for me. He just called today and told me to expect a call from you very soon. He said that if you offered me a job, I was to take it." He paused. "And if part of that job was to find Kaskov, that I was also to accept it."

"And you're saying that's not a trap?"

"Nikolai said that Kaskov had assured him it was not. He just wished to facilitate your finding him in the least amount of time. And in the safest manner for Kaskov possible." Palik added sourly, "Nikolai was most adamant that Kaskov remain safe. It surprised me since Kaskov is probably more protected than Putin. What did you do to Kaskov?"

"We've had a few encounters. We have a mutual acquaintance that brings us together."

"I don't want to be present at the next encounter. You're on your own after I text you the address Nikolai gave me. It's not really an address, just a general location. Nikolai said that they'd get in touch with you when you arrived."

Jock pulled up the text with the address. "Coal Town, West Virginia? Not what I expected."

"Nor I," Palik said. "I checked it out when Nikolai gave me the address. Less than three thousand people. Most below the poverty level. Not exactly up to Kaskov's standards. The entire area would fit in that opera house he patronizes in Moscow."

"He must have a reason," he said absently. "He always has a reason." And if Kaskov was still in the U.S., then that reason must be important to him. "Did he give you any other message for me?"

"Isn't that enough?" Palik asked. "I expect you to pay me, you know. I might not have had to do the work, but the risk is there anyway."

"Aye, the risk is there." The risk of dealing with Kaskov was always present, and he couldn't blame Palik for backing away from him. "But I'll need you anyway. Purely on the fringe . . . but when I call for information, I want you to be ready to give it to me."

"I thought it was going to end up that way," he said, disgusted. "As long as you don't pull me into Kaskov's world. It's a bit too nasty even for me."

"I need you close. Where are you?"

"Paris."

"Too far. I want you in New York by tomorrow."

Palik sighed. "I'll be there." He hung up.

Coal Town, West Virginia. Jock gazed down at the

text. It was as unusual a location for Kaskov as Palik had said. When Kaskov wasn't conducting his very criminal activities, he was a complete sophisticate. He was a patron of the symphony, the Bolshoi Opera, and various other cultural organizations in Moscow. He would have no business in a small town in West Virginia. So why was he there?

Because it was probably within six to eight hours driving time of Atlanta?

Guesswork. But it was also guesswork why Kaskov wanted to draw him to that small town. He had chosen to use Palik to do it because he knew as much about Jock as Jock did about him. He'd realized that Palik would be Jock's choice when he was on the hunt.

And he'd wanted to be sure that Palik would have the answers immediately, so that Jock would be able to reach him with top efficiency and speed.

But Kaskov had not been the only one to push Jock to look deeper, to go faster.

Hurry, Eve had said. *You have to hurry, Jock. He's a monster . . .*

"What a fool you are," Svardak said roughly. He untied the ropes binding Cara to the pine tree and jerked them off her. "Look at you. You're nearly frozen. You could have spoiled everything. I don't even have the tribute yet."

"You're the one—who is—a fool." Her teeth were chattering and she could barely speak. "You—tied me—to that tree." So cold . . . She was shaking. She didn't know how long she'd been out here, but it had been many hours. She didn't think it had gone below freezing, but she couldn't be sure of that either. She'd only been aware of the night, and the wind, and the need to force herself to move. "But nothing is your—

fault? No, of course not. Did you blame Marian, too?"
He was pushing her toward the house, and her feet
were so heavy and cold, she could barely keep her foot-
ing. "Why didn't you just let me stay out there for the
rest of the night? I could have done it. Marian and I are
both stronger than you." She was so dizzy, she wasn't
sure what she was saying, but she had to let him know
that he couldn't destroy her as he had Marian. It didn't
matter any longer to her if she could figure out a strat-
egy that would save her or not. She just couldn't let him
win. "And if you decided to pitch me down into that
canyon, I would still be stronger. Because there's the
music . . . There will always be the music."

"Shut up." He shoved her into the house, then toward the fireplace across the room. "Get closer to the
flames. I won't have you dying on me." He pushed her
to the floor. Then he was kneeling beside her, taking
off her shoes and socks, then rubbing her hands. "And
what if you'd done damage to your hands? Look at
them. They're stiff and cold as icicles. And you have
to play . . ."

The circulation was returning, and her fingers were
beginning to throb. She'd thought she'd been exercising
them enough to keep them warm enough during the
night, but perhaps not . . .

Then he was standing up and grabbing a fur throw
from the easy chair. "All you had to do was call me."
He threw the fur over her. "Stubborn bitch. All you had
to do . . ."

"And beg you?" She looked up at him; he was only
a dark blur against the firelight. "You said Marian
begged you. How could I do that? I'd lose if I let you do
that to me. Marian and I would both lose . . ."

"Are you crazy? Marian's dead."

"How—do you—know? She had a soul. She had the
music . . ."

He was muttering curses, but she could no longer bear to look at him. Later. When she was stronger . . .

She closed her eyes.

A stinging slap! "Don't you die. I won't have you die."

The words were harsh yet desperate. That desperation might give her a weapon. She slowly opened her eyes. "I'm not going to die. I'm just tired. I had to keep my muscles flexed and moving . . . Let me sleep." Test him? "But first give me something hot to drink to take away the chill."

He didn't move.

She closed her eyes again.

He was growling something beneath his breath. And then she heard movement.

A few minutes later, she felt a cup being pressed to her lips. Heat. Coffee. Black and thick, but hot. He was spilling it down her chin, forcing her to take it. "Wait." She opened her lips and took a few swallows. The coffee did help. And the fire was performing its magic, and she was slowly becoming warmer. Over his shoulder, she could see the black-and-white photograph of Marian staring down at her from the wall. Pale, glowing skin, light eyes, shining brown hair curling beneath her chin. One lovely, graceful hand holding her violin . . .

You were so young, Marian. You had so much to live for. Thank you for keeping me company tonight. It was good to have a friend . . .

She pushed the cup away. "That's enough. I'm better now." She closed her eyes again. "Go away and let me sleep."

She could feel him staring at her. "I don't obey your orders, bitch," he said roughly. "I'll do what I please." But he was tying her wrists again. Not too tightly, she noticed. Heaven forbid he damage her hands, she thought bitterly. He'd been in a panic at the thought she wouldn't be able to play again. And now he was going away, so he had obeyed her after all.

That interchange had taught her a few things she hadn't known before. She had won the first battle of wills. She was going to be safe until Svardak got what he wanted from her. He was confident that he could do that, but there was a slim chance she might be able to manipulate him and the situation. Though it wasn't as if she had any talent in that direction. Jock always said she was too honest for her own good. She should have Michael here to teach her, she thought ruefully. Eve said he was fast becoming an expert.

Eve, Joe, Jane, Michael, Jock . . . memories of them were surrounding her, banishing the cold and fear, veiling the terror she would feel in a few hours. Hold them close until she drifted off to sleep, and perhaps they'd linger and keep the nightmares from coming.

Did you have people you loved help you through those last days, Marian?

COAL TOWN, WEST VIRGINIA
5:40 A.M.

"The violin belonged to Marian Napier," Joe said the instant that Jock answered the phone. "Twenty years old, born and raised in Toronto, Canada. She was studying music at Fleming Conservatory. The violin had no real monetary value, but it belonged to her grandfather, and she wanted to protect it, so she had that tiny gold ID plaque inserted inside the left F-hole."

"But she couldn't protect it, could she?" Jock said grimly. "You're all past tense, Joe. Where is she?"

"They don't know. She went hiking in the mountains over a month ago and never came back. There was a search, but the police never found anything. She lived with her grandfather, and she didn't have any really close friends. The report was that she was only obsessed with her music. They haven't ruled out an accident in those mountains."

"But they will now since you sent them the photo of the violin. That was more than self-explanatory. Anything else?"

"Her teachers said she was very promising. I gather not on the level of Cara, but very good. The school had featured her in their last student concert. They said she was totally dedicated to her music. Sound familiar?"

"Aye." And that familiarity was chilling. "But Marian Napier disappeared over a month ago. We have no proof she's dead."

"And neither of us want there to be proof." He paused. "But the blood all over the suite was the same AB type as that Canadian girl's. I'm trying to avoid telling Eve about her until I can balance it with a little hope. What did you find out from Palik?"

"It's debatable whether it's hopeful, but at least I'm not standing still. According to Palik, I've received what amounts to a royal summons from Kaskov. He's in West Virginia."

"What? Why didn't you tell me?"

"I didn't want you to descend on him with guns blazing. I want information from him first."

"Where in West Virginia?"

"I'll let you know after I talk to him."

"Damn you."

"If it's any comfort, I had to scout an entire town to find him before he finds me. I have it narrowed down to two areas, and I should be able to give you a location soon."

"If the bastard doesn't kill you. It could be a trap."

"Eve will say it isn't. If you're right, then just get in touch with Palik and squeeze him until he tells you what he told me. You're exceptionally good at squeezing. Must be that SEAL mentality. I have to get moving. I'll call you when I can." He broke the connection.

He sat there for a moment gazing at Spruce Knob Mountain in the distance. The tallest mountain in the Allegheny range, it was beautifully majestic. This entire area was mountainous except for the flat riverbeds. Both the Blue Ridge and Allegheny ranges met here in West Virginia to form deep gorges and rugged wilderness and matchless beauty.

A completely foreign environment for Kaskov.

However, a terrain like this would make it easy to hide a young woman like Cara in those mountains.

Yet give him just a sign, any indication, and Jock would still find her.

But first he had to track down Kaskov. He doubted if Kaskov would make a great effort to hide from him since he'd practically sent him an invitation through Palik. It was probably just part of the hoops Kaskov wanted him to jump through. That being the case, he would choose a place where he could indulge his taste for luxury and still be able to station his guards with maximum efficiency. Jock has already found that there were only two locations in the Coal Town area that would meet those criteria.

He got out of the car and moved into the brush. The plateau or the riverbed? He'd already done the calculations and the psychological reasons for either choice. Time now for instinct.

The river bed . . .

"Open your eyes. I know you've not been sleeping," Svardak said roughly. "Stop trying to play me for a fool."

"I was sleeping," Cara said as she opened her eyes

and stared coolly up at him from her nest of throws in front of the fireplace. "I slept for hours. Until you came stumbling into the room and woke me. And I didn't have to try to play you for a fool. You did that very well on your own." She struggled to sit up as she spoke. "Either a fool or a madman. Are you going to hit me again? Or maybe you'd rather toss me out in that gorge to be with Marian. I really don't care. But I do want to go to the bathroom and clean up. If you prefer to deny me that simple courtesy, I'll learn to live with it. Though you might not be happy with the result."

He was frowning at her. "You're like him," he said slowly. "Last night, I thought that you were just out of your head. But you're like *him*."

"Like whom?"

"Kaskov." His lips twisted. "You're like that son of a bitch Kaskov. You look like an angel from heaven, but you're as bad as he is. It's no wonder he cares about you."

She stiffened as his words hit home. The reason why she had been taken? It had always been a possibility in the back of her mind. It wouldn't be the first time she had been targeted. Her grandfather had many enemies, both in the criminal underworld and all the victims he'd left in his wake. Which was Svardak? "Kaskov doesn't care about me. I've never lived with him. Hardly ever seen him. We're almost strangers. Can't you tell? I've never even called him grandfather. If you know anything about him, you should know Kaskov cares only about himself."

"I know a great deal about him," he said bitterly. "And I realize that there might be one other thing that he cares about." He reached down, tore the throws off her, and tossed them aside. "But by all means, we must make you both comfortable and presentable before I

show you to Kaskov. Before-and-after contrast is everything." He pulled her to her feet. "Come along. I'll take
you to see Marian's quarters. I'm certain she wouldn't
mind you using them. You seem to have formed such
a rapport with the poor woman in this short time. I
shouldn't be surprised. After all, I intended her death
to send a warning to Kaskov that tribute was required."
He was dragging her across the room toward a door
to the left of the fireplace. "However, I should tell you
that side of the house butts up against the canyon, and
since you're a musician and not an acrobat, you'd find it
impossible to get out the one window without falling to
your death. That would make Kaskov extremely sad."
He threw open the door. "And it might make me even
sadder because I would have failed." He shoved her
into the room. "But that won't happen, Cara."

She was in a bathroom, she realized. A simple ivory-
tiled shower at the far end of the small room. A toilet.
A vanity with a double mirror reflecting both her and
Svardak.

A mirror that was broken and splintered in one
upper corner . . . with a smear of blood caught in the
splinters.

Svardak met her eyes in the mirror. "No, it wasn't
me. Marian became quite desperate and depressed toward the end and did it herself. I just didn't get around
to cleaning it before you came." He smiled. "Oh, that
did upset you." Then he was pulling her into a small
anteroom, where there was only a small cot and the
window he'd mentioned. He opened the window and
stood aside. "As I told you, even Marian wouldn't have
been depressed enough to try to escape this way."

She might have tried it if she'd lived another few
days, Cara thought. She stared down through the veil
of pine trees to the twisting depths of the canyon that

plunged only a scant six to eight inches from this window. Anything to get away from this man who must have made her life hell.

He added, "And if she had, she would only have run into the guards I have stationed down the trails."

"Down the trails?"

"The mountain and the cliff trails. Did you think I only had those few guards you saw up here in the thicket? I wouldn't take a treasure like you without having adequate protection. I've been planning this for too long." He slanted a look at her. "I was sure that it would not only be Kaskov who might be interested in you. I knew Joe Quinn was going to be tracking you, and that would require me to be ready. It's much easier to set traps than go on the defense."

"It would be even easier to take me somewhere Joe wouldn't be able to find me. Why bother with him? Joe doesn't have anything to do with Kaskov."

"But you're very fond of him, and that could be a weapon if I choose to use it. Besides, I'm very happy here. I've become accustomed to this little shack. It's quite homelike." He nodded at a tan duffel on the floor under the window. "I brought a few more items of clothing for you. Put on the red blouse after your shower. It will photograph beautifully."

"Photograph?" She immediately thought of the photograph of Marian on the wall of the other room.

"You heard me. I need a photo of you."

"To put up beside Marian's? A gallery of victims? That just shows how sick you are."

"I've been thinking of taking the photo of Marian down. It's served its purpose."

"To shock and horrify me?"

"Yes, it worked beautifully."

"It won't anymore. I think she's strong and beautiful, and so was her music. You just couldn't see it."

"And you can?" His lips thinned. "She was as soft and weak as you are. I broke her, Cara. Just as I'll break you."

"She probably only pretended."

"I *broke* her." His eyes were glittering with anger. "When I finished, she did anything I wanted. And when she played, she did it in the proper way. *My* way."

"Stilted and afraid?" She lifted her chin, glaring at him. "And you don't even see that you didn't break her at all? She couldn't stand what you were doing to her music, so she just went away."

"I killed her."

"She beat you. She didn't want to let you take that part of her, so she just stopped fighting. But she kept her music."

"Liar!" He hit her in the stomach with his fist.

Pain.

She staggered back against the wall.

He was breathing hard. "Stop doing this to me. I don't want to hurt you yet. I have to follow the plan." He straightened. "You will do what I told you to do. I want that photo. And I'm sure you'd prefer to get yourself ready. Marian always thought I was too rough." He pushed her back into the adjoining bathroom. "Now I'll get you out of those ropes." He pulled a length of chain with a set of double handcuffs out of the top drawer of the vanity. The handcuffs were linked with a footlong length of the same chain that was fastened to the vanity. He slipped two handcuffs on her wrists that were linked with an eight inch chain and locked them in front of her. "The principal chain is fastened to the wall in back of the vanity, and it's very secure. The length of the chain will allow you to use the shower and facilities and barely reach the cot in the next room."

She looked down at the chains and handcuffs on her wrists. "And Marian lived like this for over a month?"

"No, it was much worse for her. I told you, I became very bored with her. I had to find ways to make her amuse me. Perhaps you can keep me entertained without my exerting myself."

"But it's not about me, it's about Kaskov, isn't it?"

"No, it's also about you. Anna wouldn't want me to leave you out. She wasn't left out."

"Anna?"

"My sister." He turned and headed for the door. "He didn't leave her out, Cara. Now clean up and change, and I'll give you something to eat. Then we'll discuss what else you can do to entertain both me and Kaskov."

The door closed behind him.

She stood there gazing at it for an instant before she turned around to face the mirror over the vanity. The splintered glass, the smear of blood. Had Marian taken her fists and pounded it and tried to smash it? Depression and frustration? Or had she wanted to break off one of those splinters to cut her own wrists? Cara had tried to lead Svardak in that direction because she couldn't bear the thought that he'd believed he'd completely destroyed Marian. She would probably never know the truth, but Cara didn't believe it was the latter. Marian had held on so long, she didn't think she'd give up at the end. Maybe she'd wanted to retrieve one of those mirrored splinters to cut Svardak's throat, Cara thought fiercely. She only wished Marian had managed to do it.

Should she try to clean the blood from the mirror?

No, she didn't want to erase the signs of the battle Marian had waged. It would hurt her every time she looked at them, but she did not want that battle ignored as if it hadn't existed.

"I'm finding out things, Marian," she whispered. "And he might be even more terrible than I thought. I doubt if you even knew anything about Kaskov. You might just have been a piece in his puzzle."

As he intended Cara to be a pawn.

He wouldn't do it. Marian hadn't been able to escape him, but Cara would search until she found a way. She couldn't permit him to hurt her or any of the people she loved. "He thinks I'm weak because all he sees in me is the music. He thinks that I won't be able to fight hard enough to bring him down. He's wrong, isn't he? I thought that might be true in the beginning, but now I know the music just makes us stronger . . ."

She gave one last glance at the web of splintered glass, then turned to the shower and began to awkwardly take off her clothes.

RIVER'S END, COAL TOWN, WEST VIRGINIA

"I need answers, Kaskov," Jock said coldly from the doorway behind the luxurious granite dining table where Kaskov was having his breakfast. "And I didn't appreciate having to run across three states to find you without a definite address or a current phone number."

Kaskov didn't look up from his eggs Benedict. "Stop complaining, Gavin. You would have had to come here anyway. And it always amuses me to offer you a challenge. It took you practically no time to locate me once you were in the area. You didn't damage any of my men, did you? I might need them." He finally turned his head and studied Jock's expression. "Ah, what I expected. Actually, what I wanted." He added quietly, "I'm almost certain she's not dead, Gavin. Would you care to sit down and have a cup of coffee while we discuss it?"

Jock gazed at him, weighing his words. Kaskov hadn't changed since Jock had last seen him. Late fifties, gray-streaked dark hair, strong, fit body. Total confidence, no fear, no hesitation. "Almost isn't good enough. If I find you're wrong, I'll kill you first, then go after Nikolai. I couldn't locate him on the grounds. Did you send him away?"

"It seemed the prudent thing to do since I knew you'd probably know he was at the hotel."

Jock shrugged. "It's only a delay." He walked toward the dining table. "I'll find him."

"I know you will. You have that talent." He pushed aside his plate and poured himself a cup of coffee. "You're quite superb. Probably the most exceptional hunter that I've ever run across." He took a sip of coffee. "And reputedly the best assassin though you haven't let me test your abilities in that area."

"That was a long time ago."

"But it's something that never leaves you," he said softly. "Does it?"

"No." He poured himself a cup of coffee from the carafe. "Which is why you should answer me very quickly. You don't want me to become impatient."

"Why not? It's sometimes very entertaining to watch you go into orbit. Though I admit I'm not in the mood at present." He gestured to the chair across from him. "Sit down, I need to get this over. I had trouble getting rid of Nikolai, and I don't want him bursting in here and trying to protect me before you realize you have no reason to kill him."

Jock hesitated and dropped into the chair. "Convince me."

"I sent him to the hotel to get Cara and bring her to me."

"Not convincing."

"I'd been told that Cara might be targeted by a very nasty individual and that I needed to remove her very quickly. I sent Nikolai because she knew him and might not be afraid of him. I didn't want to alarm her."

"But alarm or not, you were going to take her."

He nodded. "He's very dangerous, Gavin. I needed to get her out of there."

"But you didn't get her out." His lips tightened. "Why not?"

"Nikolai was too late. Her schedule said that she'd be in Charlotte for another night. She changed it at the last minute and went to Atlanta. By the time Nikolai found that out, he'd lost almost the entire day." His lips twisted. "Don't blame Nikolai. I imagine it was your fault she changed schedules. You were there in Atlanta, weren't you?"

"Aye." Jock stared him directly in the eye. "I was there."

"But not close enough to do Cara any good?"

"That's also true."

"And now you're blaming yourself for not being able to keep her safe. Good. It will make it all the easier for me."

"I don't intend to make anything easy for you. On the contrary. Why am I here?"

"I needed you. I have excellent men, but none on your level. You're totally unique. How many times have I asked you to come to work for me?" He lifted his hand. "Never mind. I know that would be dangerous for both of us. I have rules, and you're a loose cannon. But one can never be sure when circumstances will change, and I'm content to use you at present."

"Who took Cara if it wasn't Nikolai? I suppose it was one of your long list of enemies who wants to strike a bargain with you?" His hand clenched on the cup in his hand. "This isn't the first time that it's happened. I tried to tell her it was a risk just being around you. She wouldn't listen to me."

"Because she has that peculiar idea that honor still exists in this world." He shrugged. "When we both know, it does not. But I found it very convenient when

I decided she was offering me something that I wanted very much."

"You son of a bitch."

"Absolutely. But after that episode a few years ago, when Cara was nearly killed by one of the people in my circle whom I'd . . . offended, I made sure it would not happen again. I vetted everyone with whom I came in contact, I had any suspect individuals watched. And she *was* safe, Gavin."

"The hell she was. Then where is she?"

"That's what you're here to find out." He added quietly, "And you'll have to do it quickly. I don't know how much time she's going to have. I might be able to stall for a short time, but I believe he's erratic."

"I want a name."

"John Svardak."

Jock leaned forward. "Will he negotiate?"

"Not in good faith." He smiled faintly. "Were you planning on offering him my head if he gave you Cara?"

"It was a possibility. Or money. I have plenty of money. If he wants more, then I'll take some of yours."

"Oh, will you?"

"Or anything else he'll accept."

"I'm afraid it's not going to be that simple. The first option would probably be his preference, but he'd want my death later rather than sooner. And he'd almost certainly kill Cara in the most painful way possible before he let it happen." He met Jock's eyes. "He's quite mad. He was diagnosed with schizophrenia in a hospital in Estonia over thirty years ago. He was incarcerated in a mental hospital for almost twenty years before he escaped. He's high-functioning and brilliant. He'd earned degrees in law and pharmaceuticals while he was in the hospital, and it was probably easy for him to disappear off the radar once he escaped. In the last ten years, he's evidently been very busy acquiring money and making plans how to best make my existence totally miserable."

"Thirty years," Jock repeated. "No one can say you don't leave an impression on those around you. What the hell did you do to him?"

"Nothing." He shrugged. "Not that I wouldn't have done a good deal to him if I'd found him. But he'd been placed in the hospital under a false name, Fedor Petrov, and he slipped through my fingers. I thought he might have committed suicide or something equally pleasant. I didn't know he was still alive until I received the first photo."

"Photo?"

Kaskov got to his feet and went to the buffet sideboard against the wall. "Five months ago I received two photos in the mail." He took a large manila envelope from a drawer and handed it to Jock. "You might call them Before and After. The envelope was postmarked in St. Petersburg. Then the next month I received another two photos with the envelope postmarked in Ireland. Then the next month two photos postmarked in Bermuda. The last one I received was two days ago from Charlotte, North Carolina."

"Shit!"

"That was my thought. Much too close to Cara's concert event." He was leaning back against the buffet with his arms crossed. "And after you glance through those photos, you'll understand why I sent Nikolai to gather her up and bring her to me."

Jock already had the envelope open and was pulling out the photos.

ST. PETERSBURG—KATYA TARVONA

The first photo was of a young girl in a white blouse and black skirt, her brown hair pulled back in a ponytail. She was holding a violin.

The second photo was the same young girl, her throat slit, still holding the violin with bloody hands.

"My God," Jock said.

"It doesn't get any better," Kaskov said.

DUBLIN—MOIRA REARDON

Dark, curly hair, rosy cheeks, blue eyes. No more than eighteen or nineteen. She was wearing a green-plaid jacket over a white sweater. She was holding a violin.

Second photo. Eyes wide open. Blood was pouring out of a wound in her breast and she was holding the violin frantically in front of her as if to ward off the fatal blow.

"They're all like this?" Jock asked hoarsely. "Same composition?"

Kaskov nodded. "Before and After."

HAMILTON, BERMUDA—GILLIAN HALEY

Tanned, sun-streaked hair, a little plump, wearing a pink sundress and sandals, holding her violin.

Jock only glanced at the second photo. The sundress was no longer pink, it was bloodstained. But the violin was there in the forefront.

"I don't have a name on the last photo I received from Charlotte, North Carolina," Kaskov said. "We've been doing a search, but Nikolai hasn't been able to find any violinists missing in the area with her description."

"I think that I can furnish you with the name." Jock pulled out the last photos. "Marian Napier. You should have been checking Toronto, Canada. Svardak must have snatched her there while she was hiking. Because it was in Canada, the hunt and publicity would be confined to Toronto. Evidently he was being more careful the closer he got to Cara and didn't want to tip his hand." He looked at the second photo. It was what he expected. Blood pouring from the woman's wounds to saturate the violin. He felt a sudden burst of rage as he tossed the photos back at Kaskov. "But why weren't *you* being careful? Violins? Young women being slaughtered. Don't tell me you didn't think about Cara. I could *kill* you."

"I thought about it. I told you I had her under strict protection, and the first killings were nowhere near Cara. The Bermuda death was too close, but I was already moving to take care of the situation." He shrugged. "And you can't kill me, you're going to need me. You're right, it would have struck an immediate chord with me if I hadn't had a frame of reference other than Cara in the back of my mind. That first killing at St. Petersburg hit too close and threw me off balance. I started to look for a dead man."

"What? With a damn violin?"

"He could have regarded it as a symbol. I told you he was crazy."

"But you didn't tell me nearly enough about him." He was shooting questions, "Where is he? Why does he have Cara? Do you know how I can get to him?"

"I don't know where he is. I might have an idea how you might get to him. I paved the way." He paused. "Why does he have Cara? Pure revenge, I'm afraid." He put the envelopes back in the drawer of the buffet and closed it. "My fault. I shouldn't have stopped searching for him. But I'd eliminated the rest of them, and it was a busy time for me." He added sardonically, "I was a young man, and I hadn't learned the value of being thorough about tying up loose ends yet."

"And just who had you eliminated?"

He silently held up his hands. Four fingers on each hand had been smashed and were now crooked and malformed. "Did you think I'd allow that to happen to me without returning in kind? I'm sure Cara told you about it. She was very upset. She loves her own music so much that she couldn't imagine how I could bear it. But she's so very young and soft, isn't she?"

"Not so soft. She did tell me that you grew up in a *Gulag* prison labor camp in Siberia and that you wanted to be a violinist. She said that a prison guard smashed your fingers. You told her that you could no longer play and had to go in another direction. Should I guess the name of that guard?"

"Ivan Svardak. He was John Svardak's father. He also had another son, Boris, and a daughter, Anna. Anna was also a violinist. Technically excellent but no magic. But she was very ambitious. We were all very ambitious in that labor camp. The bastards who ran our *Gulag* graciously permitted the younger prisoners to work from dawn to dusk in the mines but gave us the hope of escape if we spent any free time working in their 'social' program. Being a musician and sent to Moscow to a prestigious school was one of the only ways to get out." He looked down at his fingers. "And Anna's father was ambitious for her. Anna convinced him that I wasn't worthy to enter the competition that might get me a little too much attention. She said that I had no technique, but I was able to evoke an emotional response that might get in her way. So Boris and Ivan took care of that for her. They cornered me in a hallway. It turned out to be a family affair. Anna was there watching to make sure they did a good job. And I remember her younger brother, John, laughing as my bones broke. It was the longest ten minutes of my life."

"Evidently they believed you were a threat to this Anna. You were that good?"

"I was superb." He added, "But I was also pragmatic. Dreams are for children. Power is for adults. So after my hands healed, I found my way to a group in the labor camp who dealt in power. I was out of the prison in a year, then I was on my way."

"Svardak?"

"I'm getting there. It took me three years to rise to a position in the organization where I could allow myself to take back those ten minutes of torture in that Gulag. I went after Ivan and Boris first. Anna saw me do it and took off with brother John in tow. She disappeared from view and probably thought I'd forget. I never forget. Years later, I located her and sent a man to take care of her."

"But you lost John Svardak."

"I told you I did," he said roughly. "I searched for years, but I couldn't find him. Anna hid him very well in that mental hospital, and she died before she could be questioned. I lost him, and I'll pay the price."

"If Cara doesn't have to pay it for you."

Kaskov shook his head. "Oh, you won't allow that."

"No, I won't. It's too bad it won't help those other women Svardak butchered. You should have been on top of this from that first killing."

He shrugged. "I told you that it spiraled me back to another time, another Kaskov. As far as I knew, that first victim was murdered by a madman who was killing randomly and was no real threat to me. I didn't know his potential."

"But you suspected it was Svardak."

"Of course I did," he said impatiently. "The family had dominated and changed my life. I immediately started an in-depth search again. It was easier since we had a new victim and I have many political contacts these days." His lips twisted. "Perhaps too easy. At one point, I wondered if Svardak was deliberately leaving clues to lead me to him. We found the mental hospital in Narva, Estonia, where Anna had placed him, and I was given a few lessons on what I was going to have to deal with in John Svardak. The surrounding village had a long list of missing and murdered citizens. You might be interested."

"Right now, my only interest is finding the son of a bitch. You said you might know a way to find him, that you'd paved the way. Who did you use to pave it?"

"Ron Edding. One of Svardak's men he'd hired in the Bahamas to help get him off the island after he killed Gillian Haley. It was more difficult to arrange a murder on a small island with the strict policing of Bermuda. But Edding managed to do it, and Svardak was impressed enough to hire him for his regular crew . . . which he told Edding was occupied at that time with doing guard duty in this area of West Virginia."

"And how do you know all this?"

Kaskov's brows lifted. "The police might not have been able to track down Svardak's accomplices on Bermuda, but do you think Nikolai would have had problems? He knew the importance. Edding was already gone when he arrived, but Nikolai found out he had a mistress, Malia Basteau, he visited twice a week in Nassau. After in-depth questioning, Nikolai found out Edding had called her after he left Bermuda but told her that he'd have to wait until he got back to Bermuda to call her again. He must have trusted her because he was foolish enough to tell her that he was in this general area. But he said that Svardak was watching everyone, and he'd be a dead man if he found out Edding had called her."

"But he didn't even have Cara then."

"But he might have had Marian Napier. Her body hasn't been found. And if he'd already set up a safe place to dispose of a body, why not use it for Cara?"

Jock could feel the tension tighten every muscle. "Why not, indeed. Can you force his mistress to call Edding back and pump him for more information about his exact location?"

"I could, but she's frightened now, and she'd probably make slips. You don't want that. It would be dan-

gerous for Cara. The best I can do is text you a photo
of Edding. Why do you think I didn't go after Svardak
myself? The minute he thought I was on the hunt, he'd
kill Cara. It was better to let you dispose of him."

"How kind of you. You're right, I'll find him on my
own." He turned toward the door. "And I'd better get
started. Send those photos to Joe Quinn, will you? I'll
call him and fill him in on this location. But he needs
to have the complete scenario of what's going on with
Svardak. I won't have him kept in the dark. I might
need him."

Kaskov nodded. "Use him if you wish. But understand I deal only with you, Gavin. But I'll send him the
photos with omissions about my previous association
with Svardak and his family. He'll get everything else."

"Protect yourself all you please," he said curtly. "I
don't give a damn about what they did to you or what
you did to them. All that matters is getting Cara away
from him. I'll find him. I'll kill him. If I need you, I'll
call you."

"As you like." He watched him head toward the
door. "However, I believe we should discuss one other
possibility. Svardak has probably been anticipating
taunting me for a long time. He won't miss the opportunity of showing off Cara and his power over her. I'll
get a call or, more likely, a Skype." He paused. "No
doubt it will be painful to watch. Should I invite you to
his little party?"

Just the thought was making the anger pound through
Jock. Anger and pain. Kaskov would have known that
would be his response and wasn't above being pleased.
He hadn't liked having to send for Jock. Nor the orders
Jock had been issuing since he got here. He couldn't
blame him, and it didn't matter. He'd brought Jock here
where he at least had a chance of saving Cara. "Aye,
call me. But don't let either him or Cara know I'm here

watching. If it's going to be a party, let's have it be a surprise party."

He walked out of the room.

He had handled the situation just right, Kaskov thought. Well, as right as you could manage to handle a man as dangerous as Jock Gavin.

He went to the window and watched Gavin stride down the driveway. He'd had to be very careful not to give up any control while he'd revealed that nightmare of over thirty years ago. He must *always* retain control. After all this time, it shouldn't have been this difficult.

But time hadn't seemed to matter today, perhaps because Jock Gavin's fire and passion reminded him of that boy he'd been himself on that day in Siberia . . .

LABOR CAMP

Pain!

The butt of Ivan Svardak's rifle struck Kaskov's temple as he entered the hallway, stunning him. He staggered as the rifle struck him again. "What in hell is—"

"Grab him." Kaskov realized dazedly it was Ivan Svardak, one of the guards, speaking to his son, Boris, who was behind him. "I've seen him fight in the yard. He's a tiger. Put him down!"

"I've got him." Boris was behind Kaskov, his arm around his neck. "Hit him again!"

He was already hitting him, whipping the barrel across his shoulder with full force.

More pain. Get rid of the sons of bitches. Kaskov broke free, whirled, and karate-chopped Ivan's neck. Then he head-butted his son in the stomach.

But Ivan was there again, beating him with the butt of the gun. He brought Kaskov to the ground.

Darkness.

He was barely conscious as he struggled to his knees and heard Svardak call, "Anna, come over here and give me your scarf so that I can gag him." He kept hitting Kaskov again and again. "You wanted this done. Now come and help."

"Why else am I here?" Anna smiled as she crossed the hall and handed her father the scarf. She looked down at Kaskov. "He's bleeding. We won't get in trouble if he dies?"

"He won't die. And I'll tell the sergeant I had to smash his hands when I caught him stealing."

"He was stealing," Anna said. "He was trying to steal away my prize from all of us." She stared down at Kaskov with a vicious smile. "It was mine."

Smash his hands . . .

Only those words were clear through Kaskov's pain and dizziness.

Smash his hands? Take away the music? Take away everything he was?

"No!" He started to struggle again. "You can't do it. I won't let you do that to me." He got an arm free and hit Boris Svardak in the groin.

But his father immediately struck Kaskov again, this time in the belly. Then he pulled out his pistol and whipped him with it until the entire room and all their faces were only a blur of pain. "Stop fighting. I was going to knock you out first," he hissed. "But you hurt my son. Now you're going to feel every single bone splinter." He gagged him with Anna's scarf and turned to Boris. "You get the first hit. Index finger." He handed him the rifle. "Go slow. Make him feel it."

"I want to do it." John, Svardak's youngest son, was

stepping forward. "He tried to cheat Anna. Can't I do it?"

"Maybe later. It's your brother's treat now."

Kaskov tried to move, to stop them. He couldn't do either. He could only watch as they spread the fingers of his right hand and lifted the butt of the rifle. It was going to happen. They were going to take everything away from him. They were going to take what had kept him sane in this hellhole of a camp. They were going to take the music.

He could see their faces above him, all eager, like hungry vultures, waiting for the first scream.

He would not give it to them.

The butt of the rifle was coming down . . .

But, oh my God, he would make them pay . . .

"Gavin has left the property, sir." Nikolai had come out of the kitchen and was standing behind him. "Am I allowed to resume my duties?"

"Why not?" He turned away from the window to face Nikolai. "If you can overcome your irritation with me for ordering you to stay away from him."

"It's not my place to question you. But I saw no reason. I would have obeyed your orders."

"But Gavin would not. He saw the video of you at Cara's hotel. It was best to avoid conflict in this case. Everything went very smoothly without your interaction." He went back to the table. "The only thing that went amiss was that my breakfast was interrupted. Would you tell the chef to make me another eggs Benedict?"

Nikolai nodded and started to turn away. Then he turned and looked back at Kaskov. "He did not hurt you?"

"What? Why would you think that?"

"You've been flexing your hands since I walked into the room." He repeated, "He did not hurt you?"

Kaskov looked down at his hands. It was lucky that it had been Nikolai who had noticed. It was only an instant of loss of control, but he would have to watch it. He smiled and shrugged. "Of course, he didn't. My hands are perfectly fine, Nikolai. Now see about my breakfast."

CHAPTER

5

LAKE COTTAGE

I don't want you to see these," Joe said as he climbed the steps to where Eve was standing on the porch. "It's only going to upset you. We're not going to let it have anything to do with Cara."

"Jock looked at them. So did you." She took his tablet. "And everything that man did has to do with Cara." Yet she didn't open the tablet. Joe had told her what she would see, and she had to brace herself. "And there are things I don't like about this either. Do you think I want to stay here while you go hunting with Jock? I should be there. When are you leaving?"

"As soon as I show you those damn photos and say good-bye to Michael. Is he home from school yet?"

She nodded jerkily. "He's doing his homework. I told him that you were going after Cara. He wanted to go with you." She turned into his arms and buried her face in his chest. "I told him I did, too. He didn't like it when I said I might have him go visit Catherine Ling for a few days." Her voice was muffled. "But I said we'd discuss it later since we didn't exactly know where Cara was and we have to wait until you and Jock tell us."

"You mean until Jock tells us," Joe said dryly. "He's

been out in those mountains all day trying to locate Svardak's base camp. I'm just hoping he'll find it before I get there." He grimaced. "Or maybe I'm not. Because he'll probably not wait for me before going in after Svardak." His fingers were tangled in her hair as he rocked her back and forth. "We'll find her, Eve."

"That's what I keep telling Michael." She gave him a quick kiss. "Now you go tell him. He took my lecture entirely too much to heart, and he's feeling responsible for bringing Cara to Atlanta." She took a step back. "And I'll take a quick glance through those photos while you're doing it. I don't want Michael getting curious."

"Right." He headed for the door. "I guarantee those photos are considerably different from your reconstructions he's become accustomed to seeing." He looked back at her. "I still don't want you to look at them."

"Go say good-bye to Michael."

He shook his head and went in the house.

She gazed down at his tablet. Then she forced herself to open it.

ST. PETERSBURG—KATYA TARVONA

She inhaled sharply as she was assaulted by the sheer brutality of the photos. Youth and eagerness, then death and destruction.

She had told Joe she would glance through the photos, but she was held, horrified into sluggish inertia. She went through each one, digesting each sick detail. Then it was done, and she could close the tablet. She drew a deep breath and stared out at the lake, which was clean and blue, trying to forget the faces of those young girls who'd had their lives cut short by a monster. Trying to forget how close Cara must be to that monster.

"Okay?" Joe was standing in the doorway behind her with Michael at his side.

She nodded and handed Joe his tablet. "I was just

thinking that it's likely Michael and I will definitely pay that visit to Catherine."

"I was afraid of that. Call me so that I can talk you out of it." He looked down at his son. "Walk me to the car?"

"Phone as soon as you make contact with Jock." She kissed him and held him tight for a long moment. "Be safe."

"Always." He was walking beside Michael down the steps. "And I don't have to worry about you. Michael and you are a great team."

"You bet we are." She watched him hug Michael a final time and knew he was whispering something in his ear. Guy stuff, again? Then Michael was waving good-bye to him as he drove out of the driveway. Then Michael was running up the steps. He nestled close to her as they watched Joe drive down the road until he was out of sight as he turned the corner.

"What did he whisper to you?" She smiled down at him. "Or do you have to keep it a secret?"

"Nah, he just told me not to be a pain in the neck and make sure you don't worry."

"You're supposed to make sure I'm not worrying? That sounds like your dad. I'm not the one going away. Next time, tell him he should be the one you worry about."

"He wouldn't like that." Then his smile faded as his gaze went back to the point where Joe's car had disappeared around the bend. "But you're right, he's the one I should worry about . . ."

The red peasant-style blouse Cara had put on after her shower was one of Michael's favorites, Cara remembered as she gazed in the mirror. He thought it made her look happy and not so serious as her usual neutral-tone shirts and slacks. But then Michael was always about being happy. She reached up to touch the simple low neck. She usually wore it with a gold cross Jock had given her years ago, and she felt strange without it.

Jock . . .

"Very good." Svardak was standing in the doorway behind her. "I knew it would be perfect." He was gazing critically at her hair. "Not quite perfect. Your hair is still wet. I can take care of that." He went to the vanity and pulled out a blow-dryer. "I thought I'd bought one of these for Marian . . ."

"No!" She jerked away from him.

"Oh, you don't like the idea of using Marian's possessions?" He was staring at her maliciously as he turned on the dryer. "She only used it the one time, when I had to make her presentable for her photo. She didn't complain. By that time she knew better. Now stand still and let me dry your hair, or I'll be forced to beat you with this very expensive dryer. That would leave nasty bruises. Much worse than the ones I've already given you. You don't want to upset Kaskov when he sees the photo. The first photo is always serene and happy. Contrast."

She gazed in revulsion at the nozzle of the hair dryer. In his hands, the dryer looked like a small snake. But she didn't want to argue and give Svardak any other weapons. She unclenched her hands. "It wouldn't upset Kaskov. I told you that he doesn't care anything for me." She had to raise her voice as he brought the hair dryer closer as he blew through the long strands. "You must know that my grandfather's occupation doesn't lend itself to being either tender or loving. Life is all about him."

"Shut up. I'm concentrating. It has to be just right." He added softly, "This should make you feel even closer to Marian. Don't you feel the intimacy?"

She did feel an intimacy, but not the way he meant. He wanted her to feel helpless that he was repeating this act that had preceded Marian's death. She didn't feel helpless. She felt angry and sad, together with a growing recklessness that surprised her. She didn't *care* that he held the power. No one should be permitted to do what he'd done to Marian Napier. No one should be permitted to hurt Eve and Joe the way Cara knew they'd be suffering by now. She could take whatever he'd do to her. He had to realize that in the end it wouldn't matter, *he* wouldn't matter.

"That's the way you should be," he murmured. "Meek and compliant." He held up a strand of her hair. "See how it shines now. And look how rosy your cheeks are from the heat of the dryer."

"Maybe not from the dryer." She held up her wrists. "Are you going to take the chains off me? You promised me something to eat. Unless you just want to throw me some bread and water?"

"I wouldn't think of it." He unlocked the cuffs from the chain. "What good is surface polish if you look like you're starving? Before and After." He pushed her toward the door. "I have a bowl of stew for you on the bar. Be sure not to spill anything on that blouse. You look like a gypsy, much better than that insipid gown you wore at the concert."

"What concert? I know you weren't at the charity concert at the hotel."

"Don't be ridiculous. I would have been nauseated to see them all fawning over you as if you were some angel of mercy. No, I had a box at the concert in Charlotte. That way I could ignore your lack of skill and concentrate on what was going to come afterward."

"You mean this horror you've dreamed up?" She sat at the bar and looked down at the unappetizing stew in the bowl in front of her. "What a completely useless life you must lead to have to depend on slaughter to keep you amused. You might think I have no skill, but I don't destroy." She began to eat the stew. Cold and lumpy. Yet she had to keep up her strength. "And you're wrong, I'm actually very good. I've been taught by experts, and I've worked hard." She forced herself to take another bite. "And Marian Napier was also good. You just don't have the judgment to appreciate anything that's outside your own narrow viewpoint. Whoever taught you about music must have been extremely limited and without any sense of—"

"Bitch!" He knocked her off the stool. She fell hard on the floor, striking her temple. It took her a moment to recover. She shook her head to clear it of the waves of pain. The blow had come so swiftly, she'd had no time to brace herself. He was standing over her with clenched hands. "Limited? Anna was superb. It's the rest of you who know nothing. You have no discipline or control."

There was something here that she might be able to use . . . She slowly got up on one elbow. "Anna? Your sister?"

"Of course. Anna had no limits. She was so perfect, everyone was jealous of her skill and tried to crush her."

"She played the violin?"

"Of course. So much better than you."

"Then I would like to hear her." She paused. "But you're speaking past tense. She's not alive?"

"No." His face was twisted with pain. "He killed her. She didn't think he'd find her, but he did. She told me she'd come and get me, but she didn't. He hunted her down and shot her and she never came back to get me at that hospital."

"Who did it?"

"You know who shot her." His face was flushed, his eyes glittering. "You know who killed them all."

"I have an idea it had to be Kaskov. But I don't know why. Tell me."

"No." He was suddenly smiling recklessly. "I'll let him tell you. But not now, it has to be the right time." He reached down and jerked her to her feet. "And he has to have the Before photo to prepare him. So that he'll know what's coming next." He slung her into the chair in front of the fireplace. "But you'll not insult my sister again, or I'll use that fire poker to scar that pretty face."

"I didn't know I was insulting her. I don't insult other artists. I was just remarking on your lack of judgment. I didn't realize she had taught you. How could I? I don't know anything about you."

"You'll learn very soon." He was backing away from her, his head tilted as he studied her. "Yes, that chair is perfect for you." He went behind the bar and got his phone. "And I knew the red top would show you off beautifully." He was clicking photos with his phone camera. "Now the violin . . ." He went to the kitchen pantry and pulled out her violin case. He set it in front of her. "Open it, I know you've missed it. Such a wonderful instrument. Anna should have had one like it."

"There's no other instrument like it. Each Amati or Stradivarius is unique and individual. If your sister was as clever and talented as you claim, she'd know that." She took the violin out of the case, her palms unconsciously caressing the fine wood. "Even if you don't." The violin felt so good in her hands. Just touching it made her feel that wonderful sense of belonging, bonding to something that was part of her and yet part of the world around her. "But any violinist would appreciate this Amati."

"And you love it." His eyes were narrowed on her face. "Kaskov gave it to you, didn't he?"

"Yes. But I don't love it because it came from him. I love it because it makes beautiful music." She looked down at the strings. "We complete each other. We make beautiful music together."

He scowled. "You don't, you know. You're mistaken."

"I won't argue with you." She glanced up at him. "Take your photo."

"You don't give me orders. I want you to look perfectly natural." He came forward, unlocked her handcuffs, and took them off. "I want you to look the way you did at that concert." He smiled mockingly. "Play for me, Cara."

"Why?"

"Because it's the Before photograph, the one to cherish and remember."

She looked up at the photo of Marian Napier on the wall. No smile, but all the glow of youth and courage was in that face. Cara wished she'd had a chance to know her. The longer she was here, the closer she felt to Marian. "That's her Before photo? Who has the After?"

"I'm sure you can guess. Kaskov, of course. But you really wouldn't want to see it. Play, Cara. I'm becoming impatient."

She was tempted to refuse, but he would only force her, and the violin might be damaged in the conflict. It didn't really matter. She *wanted* to play. It would release a little of this poison that he'd injected every minute she'd been with him.

She tucked her violin beneath her chin and began to play the Tchaikovsky.

"No," Svardak said instantly. "Something else. Maybe the same Mendelssohn as Marian played."

She paused. "I'm not Marian. You want me to play? I'll play what I like and how I like. You shouldn't care, you said we were both amateurs, didn't you?" She started to play the Tchaikovsky again. "You want me to look the way I did at the concert? I played the Tchaikovsky."

Just try to get away from him. Let the music take her to that magic place that had always been her joy and her solace. She could see how tense and resistant he was. She half expected him to step forward and strike her again.

It didn't happen. She didn't look at him, but she was vaguely aware that he was just standing there, listening. Then she wasn't aware of him at all, he vanished as the music swept her away.

Tchaikovsky, Mozart, Dvorak. Then, exquisite, exciting Vivaldi. The music rose, fell, surrounding her, completing her . . .

Then she went back to the Tchaikovsky and began again.

"Stop it!" Svardak stepped forward and tore the violin away from her and threw it on her lap. "It's ugly. It's an abomination."

"Is it?" She was breathing hard, she could feel the heat in her cheeks as she stared defiantly up at him. "What a liar you are. You know it's not ugly. I can see it in your face. You *liked* it."

"I was only letting it go on to get what I wanted from you," he said hoarsely. He was taking photo after photo of her at top speed. But Cara saw with shock that his hands were shaking. "But I couldn't let you do that Tchaikovsky again. You're too . . . flamboyant and personal. She would have hated it."

"Anna?" Her gaze was watching him, assessing. "Then she was also a liar. Music *is* personal. Music is supposed to reach out, raise the spirits of those listening, not glorify the artist."

Her head snapped back as his hand lashed out and

cracked against her cheek. "She didn't lie. He was the one who was wrong. We were right to do what we did."

She ignored the pain but had to wait a few seconds until the dizziness disappeared. "Really?" She had to be careful now, she told herself. She might have gone too far. He was very close to losing control. She had just been caught up in the exhilaration of the moment and the knowledge that Svardak might not be quite as committed to his weird fantasy as she'd thought. But if he wasn't, the idea that he'd already killed Marian to serve it was even more terrible. "Would you like to tell me about it?"

"Why should I? You're *nothing.*" He was putting the handcuffs back on her. "You'll know soon enough. I've decided to let Kaskov see more than a photo tomorrow." He jerked her across the room, then outside. "In the meantime, I don't even want to be in the same house with you. Just looking at you I'd hear that hideous music." He was dragging her toward the pine tree overlooking the abyss. "You can stay out here today and commune with Marian." He'd already rigged a chain around the tree, to which he fastened the cuffs. "While I go through those photos and choose the best one to send Kaskov tonight. It has to be just right."

"It's still daylight. Aren't you afraid someone will see me out here?"

"Not at all. The trees are so thick on this cliff that you couldn't be seen from a plane. I've leased the lands all around here and, as you've seen, I have guards stationed here and also along the paths down to that canyon. No trespassers allowed." He looked back over his shoulder with a malicious smile. "Unless I choose to permit it. Did I forget to tell you that I gave the guards a photo of Joe Quinn and told them he'd be my special guest if he stopped by to see me?"

"Yes, you must have left that out." Don't let him see the shock and fear. "But you said you weren't worried about my being seen by anyone, so I won't worry about Joe."

He didn't like that she could tell. His smile didn't waver, but there was a flicker of impatience on his face. "Worry about him. Arrangements can always be made."

He disappeared into the cabin.

Terror. Breathe deep. Look straight ahead and don't let him see the fear. She could tell he was feeding on every sign that the torture he was inflicting was working. She allowed herself a few moments before she relaxed and sank back against the tree in case he was still watching her. She must not show weakness, or it would destroy anything she'd accomplished in establishing herself as an equal foe to him. She could take the punishment as long as it made him believe he still had a battle to win. Once he thought that she'd capitulated and was no longer worthy of him, it would become much more dangerous for her.

And dangerous for Joe, Svardak would search for more entertaining ways to make her to come to heel, and he thought he already had one in Joe Quinn.

For God's sake, stay away from here, Joe.

"Where the hell have you been?" Joe said as he saw Jock striding across the parking lot of the Mountain Stream Diner toward his rental car. "I've been waiting half the day for you."

"Be quiet, Joe. I was busy. I decided not to stop in the middle of it." Jock opened the car door and dropped down in the passenger seat. "I might have found her."

Joe tensed. "Cara? Where?"

Jock was taking out a map from his jacket pocket.

"The general area is a canyon about fifteen miles from Coal Town. Mountains all around and very rough country. The canyon sits in the middle of a mountain on one side and a cliff that curves in a half circle on the other. Svardak would need privacy if he held Marian Napier there for over a month. Not an area where hunters and climbers would be permitted." He pointed at the canyon, and then the mountain and steep cliff shadowing the valley below. "I called Palik and had him check out real-estate transactions in the Coal Town area for the last six months. While I was waiting, I took a hike to look at the canyon myself. It was definitely a possibility."

"What did Palik say?"

"A six-month lease on the entire canyon and mountain area was taken out three months ago, supposedly by a Canadian real-estate company that wanted to explore setting up a tourist and spa resort. Palik said it was going to take him at least a week to dig up the true leasers because the paperwork is buried very deep." He smiled bitterly. "He suggested my expertise might prove more effective than his to get it done. I told him that he'd have it for me tomorrow morning together with a complete map of that canyon, or I'd pay him a visit."

"I imagine that will make it happen," Joe said. "But are there any other prospects we can check out in the meantime?"

"Not ones that are nearly as likely." He folded up the map and stuck it back in his pocket. "And how do we know the deadline I gave won't be too late? I'm going back and doing some more reconnoitering tonight. I just came back to get you."

"You could have told me where this canyon was located and have me meet you."

"I was afraid you'd do some exploring on your own. You're almost as hungry as I am to get your hands on the son of a bitch. There are supposed to be guards watching Cara."

"And you want to be in control," Joe said. "No way."

"I *will* be in control," Jock's said coolly. "Svardak will be in touch with Kaskov, and Kaskov will be in touch with me. He's refused to deal with anyone but me. Which means that I could disappear and leave you out of it entirely. I didn't choose to do that, Joe. I didn't have to call you and tell you where to come. I did it because I thought you'd be of value. You're good, and you're smart. I'm a loner, but I would rather have you beside me than anyone else. I'll listen to you, I'll respect you. But I have to know that you won't do anything that will ruin my play. The minute I see a sign of it, I'll walk away from you."

The bastard meant it, Joe could see with frustration. "You know I won't let you walk away from me. Did you consider that if you're not right about the canyon, it might be too late for Cara."

"Yes," he said hoarsely, "she'll die. It will be entirely my fault and no one else's. But that's the way it's been from the beginning."

"Bullshit. It will be Svardak's fault. But if you want the blame, you'll have to stand in line. Even Michael is thinking that he might be responsible. Which makes me want to kill Svardak even more if that's possible. Michael's only ten years old."

"Why would Michael—" Jock broke off as his cell phone rang. "Kaskov." He pressed the access, then the speaker. "Talk to me, Kaskov."

"You talk to me," Kaskov said. "I'm beginning to lose faith in you, Gavin. Have you located her?"

"Maybe. I might be close."

"Which for you means that you're very close."

"But I'm not sure, and I should be sure. Do I have time to verify before I go in? Why are you calling me?"

"Because I received a photo tonight. Not in the mail, as usual, but on my computer. He's evidently in a hurry."

Jock's hand clenched on his phone. "Then I don't have time."

"You might, he's not in enough of a hurry to not twist the knife. He's going to let me talk to Cara tomorrow night on Skype. I told you I thought he'd probably do that. He's been waiting a long time for the opportunity." He paused. "If you still want to monitor the Skype, you'll have to come back here. I'm sure that Svardak thinks of me as a huge tarantula sitting in my luxurious office in Moscow. If I came to you out in the mountains, it would spoil the illusion, and he might take alarm. Seven tomorrow night."

"I'll be there unless I locate her and find a way to take her before that time." He added harshly as he had another thought, "But the asshole has had her for two days, and we've all agreed he's a monster. I don't even know if she'll be well enough to travel."

"Oh, I'd be very surprised if she wasn't able to travel," Kaskov said dryly. "I'll send you the photo." He hung up.

The next moment, Jock's phone pinged as the photo was transmitted.

Joe looked over Jock's shoulder as he pulled up Cara's photo. "Holy shit . . ."

Cara was sitting in a chair in front of a fireplace. Her hair was slightly tousled, and she was wearing a red blouse that echoed the vibrance of the flames. There was a violin lying across her lap that he recognized as her Amati. Her chin was lifted and she looked more beautiful than he'd ever seen her. Beautiful . . . and different. There was usually a gentleness, a warmth, that illuminated her features. He didn't see that now. She looked totally defiant and challenging as she stared up at the camera. Her cheeks were flushed, her eyes glittering, and she appeared ready to leap out of the chair on the attack.

"I see what Kaskov meant," Joe said slowly. "She doesn't look like a victim. Svardak hasn't done too much damage."

"Yes, he has," Jock said, his expression frozen as he stared at the photo. "He's done a hell of a lot of damage. He's hurt her. He's made her—" He broke off and drew a deep breath. "But you're right, if nothing else happens to her before we get to her, she'll be able to travel through those mountains." He scanned the photo. "There's a bruise on her left temple that appears fairly recent, and she probably has others that we can't see. Her wrists seem to be chafed; he probably keeps her tied when he doesn't want to show her off. That's all that's on the surface. Everything else is buried inside."

"Naturally, she's under severe stress, Jock," he said quietly. "That doesn't mean she won't bounce back once we get her away from him. She's very strong."

"I know how strong she is." He added jerkily, "But he's *doing* something to her. No one knows better than I do how a soul can be twisted and tortured until you can't recognize it as belonging to you. I won't have it happen to her."

"He's not Thomas Reilly, Jock. He might be a monster, but he doesn't possess the drive and focus of your particular demon. He's crazy, not a ruthless sociopath."

"Sometimes it's hard to tell the difference. Sometimes it doesn't matter. Either way, I have to keep him from touching her again." He jammed his phone in his pocket. "Start the car, Joe. We're heading for Lost Canyon. Svardak is giving Kaskov a brief reprieve, but we don't how long that will last after that Skype tomorrow night. We've got to know everything there is to know about how to get to her and what kind of obstacles we're going to have to face to take her away from him. Edding told his mistress there were at least half a dozen other men on Svardak's payroll in this area, but there may be more. We'll have to verify numbers and locations."

Joe said grimly, "And find out if you're even right about Lost Canyon." He took out his phone. "But you'll have to wait a few minutes before we take off. I promised I'd call Eve the minute I knew anything, and I've already had to keep her waiting all day. I need to give her some kind of progress report that sounds hopeful if I'm going to keep her at home and not running here at top speed. Right now, it could go either way." He started to dial. "So I'm going to tell her that we received the photo and, no matter what you think, Cara looks relatively unharmed to me. And I'm definitely not going to tell her that this trip to Lost Canyon could be a wild-goose chase."

"Tell her what you like," Jock said curtly. "Your opinion. And we won't know if it's a wild-goose chase until you get us to Lost Canyon. So make your call, dammit."

LAKE COTTAGE
4:35 A.M.

"Where are you?" Eve asked, when Joe answered his phone later that night. "I've been worried. You said you'd call when you got to Lost Canyon. No call. And I haven't been able to get through to you for hours."

"I told you I'd be in the mountains, and I'm getting lousy cell reception. I was going to call you when I got to a clear area. I'm heading down the mountain now." He paused. "Is everything all right?"

"Why shouldn't it be?" Eve asked. "I'm not the one

climbing mountains in the middle of the night. Why are you doing it? Tell me it's Cara."

Silence. "It could be Cara. I hate to admit that Jock may be right again, but it looks like he might."

Eve felt a rush of relief. "Thank God. You found her?"

"We're not near that far along. We split up when we got to the canyon, I took the mountainside, and he took the cliff. I've found signs of three recent camps being struck next to the trail leading up the mountain. Plus one cigarette butt near the last campfire together with a shoe print, size eleven. Whoever has been up here has been moving camps frequently and trying to clean up after themselves."

"Could Cara have been in the camp?"

"Possibly. But there would probably have been more signs. And I found only the one shoe print. It looks more like sentries or lookouts keeping a sharp eye on the canyon for intruders. But that's not entirely discouraging."

"What did Jock find?"

"I have no idea. Before my cell cut out, he was saying that he was sure he was onto something. I guess I'll find out when I get down." He added grimly, "Providing he shows up where we agreed to meet. There's no telling with Jock. If he found a lead, he might have decided to follow it and leave me trailing behind. No one could call him a team player."

She could tell that he was tired and frustrated. "But no one could say that he isn't extraordinary at what he does. Give him a break, Joe."

"I'd like to break his neck." He paused. "It's probably better we're at the opposite sides of the canyon. But don't worry, I won't throw him off a cliff until we find Cara."

"He's probably thinking the same about you. Two alpha males should definitely give each other space."

She was silent, then said, "Or call in a referee to strike a balance."

"No, Eve."

"I agree, I'll have to find a much more useful role to play, but I know I belong there with you. Things are starting to happen now. I won't get in the way, but get used to the idea, Joe." She went on quickly, "I told Michael that I was hoping that we'd get Cara back before I had to take him to drop him off with Catherine, but that was wishful thinking. I knew it when I said it. We'll leave for Catherine's when Michael wakes up this morning."

"Shit!"

"I have to be there for her. You know I do. I've waited as long as I can."

Silence. "She wouldn't want you here. She wouldn't want you near Svardak. And I sure as hell want you to stay away from him. There's no way I can talk you out of it?"

"I don't want you there either. Neither one of us is going to get what we want." She didn't wait for him to reply. "Make a reservation for me at the nearest hotel to Lost Canyon and text me the address. I'll call you as soon as I know what time I'll be arriving. I'll probably be driving from Louisville. It's not that far, and it will be quicker than trying to get a flight to a town somewhere near Coal Town."

"You know I'd rather you took all the time in the world. I'm tempted to call Catherine and try to persuade her to keep you with her."

"She wouldn't do it."

"I know. Okay, I'll make your reservation. I haven't checked in anywhere yet. Jock is pushing so hard I'm not even sure he's slept since Cara was taken. I thought I'd end up in a sleeping bag in the mountains or curled up in the car for a quick nap."

"And I might go along with that, but let's try for a hotel room." She had to end this call. She had made him worried and unhappy, and she hated it. "An occasional shower would be nice." She paused. "I love you, Joe."

"Then stay home." Then he sighed. "I love you, too. I'll let you know if we find out anything else." He ended the call.

Done. She slipped her phone into the pocket of her robe and stared out at the lake. She had been wrestling with the decision since Jock had told Joe that Kaskov had given him a solid lead to where they could find Cara. Everything had been so much easier before Michael had come into their lives. It had become a balancing act to care for him yet do her duty to Jane and Cara. But in this case, she had no choice but to put Michael behind Cara. The stakes were too dangerously high.

The decision was made. Stop brooding about it and start preparing to put it into motion. She turned and headed across the porch for the door. Pack a bag for Michael and her own duffel. Make a pot of coffee to get enough caffeine in her system to help get through a sleepless night and the journey to come.

She opened the door and headed for the kitchen.

"Is Dad okay?"

She stopped short as she saw Michael curled up on the couch in the living room. He was barefoot and wearing his blue-and-white-striped pajamas. His hair was tousled, and he looked younger than he usually did, but his expression was grave.

"What are you doing up, Michael?"

He swung his feet to the floor and straightened as he said quietly, "I kept thinking about Dad. I knew you were trying to call him after I went to bed. Is he okay?"

"Sure, your dad is supertough." She smiled. "It would really take something major to even faze him. He's just searching very hard for Cara." She dropped down beside him and slid her arm around his shoulders. "But they may have found a clue to where she might be. That's good, isn't it?" She brushed a kiss on the top of his head. "I thought you might have been lying awake worrying about Cara."

He shook his head. "I do worry about her. But mostly about Dad."

"Why?" she asked gently. "Did you have a nightmare or something?"

"No, I don't usually have nightmares. Not scary stuff. Most of my dreams are just puzzles to help me figure things out."

"Really? I didn't realize that." But she should have, she thought. It was her duty as his mother to question everything concerning him. She couldn't remember when she'd had to cuddle him when he woke in the middle of the night. When he woke, it was usually with a question. "Then why are you worrying about your dad?"

"I don't know. I just am. You were worried about him tonight, too. I could feel it. You said he was somewhere in West Virginia?"

"Yep, it's a fairly small state. He should be able to whip right through it looking for Cara."

"I looked it up, and it's really pretty. Mountains and streams and lots of mist, and all the trees are wonderful in the fall. Is Dad liking it?"

"I think he's too busy to notice scenery right now."

Michael nodded. "I think you're right. He'll notice it later, when it's all over. It will be better then." He looked up at her. "But you should tell him to be careful, Mom."

She went still. "Why, Michael?"

"Sometimes he forgets to think about himself. He thinks about you and me and Cara and Jane, but he doesn't think about himself." He laid his head against her arm. "You should remind him that he's important, too."

"Next time I see him I'll be sure and do that." It was an opening she couldn't ignore. "Which may be soon. I told your dad that I'm—"

"You're taking me to Catherine and Luke," he finished for her. "That's why you were sad when you came in from the porch. You knew he'd be scared for you." He gave her a mischievous glance from beneath his lashes. "Honest, I didn't eavesdrop, Mom."

"I wasn't about to accuse you." Her gaze narrowed on his face. "No arguments?"

He shook his head. "I'd only upset you and make you more sad. I'll work it out. When do we leave?"

"After breakfast. I'll call your teachers and get advance assignments. Will you pack, or do you want help?"

"I'll do it." He got to his feet and headed for the bathroom. "It will be nice to see Luke again. He's cool." He stopped at the doorway. "But you'll remember to tell Dad what I said?"

She felt a little frisson of uneasiness. "I'll tell him."

"Good." He started to turn away again.

"Michael."

He looked back over his shoulder.

She had remembered Michael's words that had so startled her. "I'm glad you don't have nightmares, but I'm a little surprised. Are you sure there's nothing you'd like to tell me?"

He started to shake his head, then stopped. His smile faded. "I always like to tell you things. She says it's better for you if I don't this time. But I can't lie to you."

She stiffened. "She?"

"She says that she knows you'll never forget her, but there's a time to move on, and I have to help you."

Her hands clenched at her sides. "She?" Eve repeated.

"Bonnie," he said gently. "Our Bonnie, Mom. You told me all about her years ago, how much you loved her and that she was taken away from you when she was only seven by one of those bad men who hurt children." He smiled. "But you didn't tell me that she has hair the same color as yours, but it's all curly and stuff. Or that she's really, really cool."

"Bonnie is a little hard to describe," she said shakily. "Apparently, you've found out for yourself." She paused, then said carefully, "Just how would you describe her, Michael? A dream?"

He shook his head. "Maybe. Whatever she wants to be. But mostly my friend. And sometimes she teaches me stuff." He tilted his head curiously. "Why do you ask? You know all about Bonnie."

And clearly so did Michael, she thought. He accepted Bonnie as a spirit and thought no more about it than if she were Cara or Jane. She should really not be surprised. Michael himself was something of a mystery. "Different people have different viewpoints. I wanted to make sure you weren't confused. How long has she been coming to see you, Michael?"

"A long time. I think . . . from the beginning."

She remembered the night Michael was born, and she had been certain that Bonnie was there. "I think that's very likely. But she hasn't paid me a visit for a long time. I believe I'm jealous. I'll have to have a word with her."

"She only wants you to be happy, Mom."

"I *am* happy." It was true. The idea that Bonnie had always been present, easing Michael's way in the world, was comforting. But Eve had missed those visits, dammit. "But Bonnie might be trying to manipulate me the way you were trying to do. How do we know just because she's a spirit that she knows everything? And she should realize that being happy doesn't necessarily mean forgetting about her."

"Are you angry with me?"

"No, I'm happy for you that you've been able to get to know Bonnie. I just wish that you'd shared the experience with me."

"Okay, I'll talk to her about it next time," he said gravely. He gave her his luminous smile and disappeared into the bathroom.

She ruefully shook her head as she turned away from the door. She was still trembling with shock, she realized. She had never expected, nor dreamed, that the answer she'd get from Michael would be about Bonnie.

First, that weird insistence about cautioning Joe. Then the acknowledgment that Bonnie was very much in Michael's life. Not that one had to have anything to do with another, she thought quickly. Probably no connection at all. She was the one who had brought up the subject of nightmares. As far as Michael was concerned, it was all about Joe.

Therefore, there was no reason to be uneasy. Michael had been absolutely no trouble about her going to be with Joe, given her nothing but cooperation when she'd asked.

I'll work it out.

What was he going to work out?

And why had he been so worried about Joe when the threat was to Cara?

Just accept that he was just being Michael, and she would eventually know all the answers. She wasn't about to try to cross-examine him at the moment. She was too worried about Cara to delve into what Michael was thinking or planning. She just had to trust that his basic goodness of heart would keep him from causing her problems at this crucial time.

So stop fretting and just get ready to go.

But first grab a strong cup of coffee and say a couple prayers. The way she was feeling now they might both be needed to get her through the day.

CHAPTER

6

There were two men at the camp nearest the top of the cliff . . .

Jock crawled closer on the ridge above the encampment. One guard was curled up in a sleeping bag, the other leaning against a tree, with his automatic on his knees, staring into the fire. He was awake, but just barely. It would be no problem at all to maneuver close enough to cut his throat without waking the other guard.

There had also been two guards at the other encampment he had spotted from the twisting trail sixty feet below this ridge. Svardak evidently didn't trust single guards on watch, which meant he was smart and wary. Not wary enough. The guards at the first encampment had been even less alert than these two.

But there had been no sign of Cara at either encampment.

Was there still another encampment higher up on the cliff? His gaze searched the twisting path that led to the brush-and-tree thicket that started forty or fifty yards from the ridge where he was lying. Entirely possible. Svardak might have set up a series of barriers to keep rescuers from approaching or Cara from escaping.

It would take him only minutes to reach that thicket and get his answer.

But it was getting light, and he'd be exposed on this ridge in another fifteen minutes. He needed to get down into the heavier pine brush on the lower plateau unless he wanted to start the action now.

Wanted? He *craved* it.

He closed his eyes as he fought the hunger that had been devouring him since he'd found that first camp. Cara had to be close if Svardak had set up these guard posts. It would be so easy to take them out and interrogate . . .

But it might be a trap. He didn't know enough yet. He couldn't take a risk that could get Cara killed.

He would think of another way.

But he had to verify that the sleeping guard was who he thought he was. He lifted his binoculars to his eyes again and waited for a clear look. He had caught a quick glimpse a few minutes ago before the guard had burrowed his face in the blanket. Not enough. He had to be sure. He waited.

One minute.

Two.

Three.

The guard stirred restlessly.

He saw his face.

Yes!

He put the binoculars away.

He hesitated. It would be so easy . . .

He took one last longing look at the two guards.

No! He couldn't do it.

He started to crawl down the ridge.

"You're sure that guard was Ron Edding?" Joe asked eagerly, his gaze on the cliff. "No mistake?"

"It was Edding," Jock said impatiently. "I showed you the photo Kaskov gave me of the man Svardak hired to get him out of Bermuda. I went up there looking for him, and I double-checked before I came down. I had to make certain we were on the right track." His lips twisted. "Besides, you're such a doubting Thomas that I had to put your mind at ease."

"Which was the intelligent thing to do. I like to be sure there's a fire before I bring out the hose." Joe's gaze was fixed on the cliff, which was still wreathed in early-morning mists. "Let's go back up there. We'll take the camps one at a time at time, then—"

"And what about the encampments on the mountainside that you ran across? All it would take would be a casual glance from someone with binoculars, and Cara's dead. And maybe she's being held on the mountainside."

"But you don't think that's true," Joe said. "Neither do I. Those camps I ran across were moving camps, the men there were scouts, whose aim was to make certain no one came too close and to know about it if they did. The ones you described were permanent. They're set up and ready for action. You said that you believed you'd have seen her if she was there."

"Aye, but I'm going to be damn sure. Any move we make has to be a surprise." He added grimly, "And not for us. We'll go in tonight, and we'll know everything we need to know."

"That means he'll have Cara for another full day. I don't like it."

"Do you think I do?" Jock said savagely. "I came within a heartbeat of—" He turned away and moved down the trail to where they'd hidden the car in a dense forest off the access road. "We'll catch a few hours' sleep and come back and take another look in the afternoon. You need to get close enough to those camps

on the mountain to make sure Cara's not there instead
of in that thicket at the top. I'll go up the cliff trail and
see if there's any possible way I can get her out of this
canyon without being target practice from three directions."

"You'd have to strike it very lucky to be able to do
that." Joe paused. "I talked to Eve while I was on the
mountain. She'll probably be on her way here today.
She told me to get her a room at a hotel."

"Why aren't I surprised? Your responsibility, Joe."

"I wish it was. This is Eve."

"I repeat, your responsibility. I'm going to be too
busy today to worry about anything but that cliff. I
need every minute to—" His cell phone vibrated and
he glanced down at the ID. "An email from Palik. It's
not six yet, evidently he took me at my word." They
had reached the car, and he got in the passenger seat.
"You drive. I need to read this." He accessed the email.
"The Canadian real-estate company that handled the
lease on the canyon was acting on behalf of a company in Estonia. That's information we no longer need
now . . ." He was scrolling down the email. "But we do
need this info. He sent us several maps of the canyon
and surrounding terrain." He was flipping through the
maps. "I need to see that thicket on top of the cliff. I
couldn't see anything through those trees. But it doesn't
seem to be—" He broke off as he flipped to a new page.
"*Yes.*"

"It's pretty crude." Joe was looking over his shoulder. "Just some kind of basic structure and a road leading down through the thicket on the other side of the
cliff."

"It's what I needed to know," Jock said. "He has an
escape route if he needs it. That road disappears into
the forest on the north side of the cliff, and we might
have a hell of a time tracking him." His finger was

tracing the curve of the cliff close to the canyon. "And there's another trail here that would allow those guards from the mountain to come running if Svardak called. He must have been planning this for a long time. He was doing everything he could to keep from being surprised. Two separate trails down to the canyon and a convenient back door."

"We'll find a way to get around it."

Jock looked up at the thicket on top of the cliff. Cara was there, and all he had to do was to get to her. All? There was also the small matter of getting her out alive. "We'll get around it." He was flipping through the other maps. "It's just going to mean that the day is going to be even busier than I thought."

"But you're still going to go to Kaskov's at seven to take a look at Svardak's Skype?"

"Did you actually think I'd change my mind?" he asked harshly. "Like you said, he's going to have a full day to do more damage to her. I have to know if he's taken advantage of it."

LOUISVILLE, KENTUCKY

9:10 A.M.

"You're sure you don't mind, Catherine?" Eve asked as she took Michael's duffel out of the trunk. "I'm feeling guilty about just tossing my son at you. You're usually so busy, you don't have that much quality time with Luke." Catherine Ling had been a CIA operative since she'd been a young girl, and she managed to balance a career and motherhood effortlessly, but Eve still felt a bit guilty giving her any additional burden.

Catherine smiled. "Toss away. It will be good for Luke to have Michael here. He gets impatient with most of the kids his own age. He led an unusual life for his first eleven years, and it's always been hard for him to bond. Michael may be younger but he's . . ." She hesitated. "Different."

Eve laughed. "Very delicately put." She looked at Michael, sitting on the front steps talking with Luke. No, it was clear the two had no problem bonding. "Though I'm certain Luke also has to be very patient with Michael. Michael tends to have an insatiable curiosity. I'll call you when I get in and check on him."

"If you like." Catherine's smile disappeared. "But it sounded to me like you might be busy. I'll take care of Michael, Eve. You do what you have to do."

"Thank you." She turned and gave her a quick hug. "I'm praying I won't be long."

"So am I. I'd like to go with you. I'm sick about Cara."

"I know. We're all practically out of our minds." She looked back at Michael. "But it helps to know that he's being well taken care of."

"Our pleasure." She gave her another hug. "Now get on the road. I know you're anxious."

She nodded. "That I am." She called to Michael, "Come and say good-bye to me."

Michael jumped to his feet and ran over to her. "You're leaving?" He went into her arms. "Will you call me tonight?"

"You know I will." She gave him a bear hug. "I have to check and see if you're giving Catherine a hard time."

"I won't." He grinned at Catherine. "She might turn me in to the CIA."

Catherine smiled back at him. "It depends on what you and Luke have been planning. I saw that you had your heads together."

"Nothing scary. Luke's just going to take me over to Hu Chang's lab and show me the stuff he's been working on."

"That could be very scary," Eve said. "Some of Hu Chang's experiments aren't for general consumption." She was joking. Catherine's friend Hu Chang was brilliant, and his philosophy was far from the norm, but he would never do anything that would harm anyone close to Catherine. "Don't let him lure you to the dark side."

"I like him," he said simply. "So do you."

"Yes, I do." She pressed a kiss on his forehead. "Be good. Don't give Catherine any trouble."

"We'll be fine," Catherine said. "And Hu Chang will keep both of them busy."

Eve gazed down at her son. "Michael?"

He nodded gravely. "It's okay, Mom, don't worry about me. There's still time." He gave her another hug, and when he lifted his head, he gazed up at her with those shining amber eyes, and whispered, "Dad." Then he was gone and running back to Luke.

She stared after him.

Joe, again.

He was not permitting her to forget her promise in this last moment.

"He's handling it well," Catherine murmured. "So stop frowning, go do your job." She opened the driver's door for Eve, gave her a quick kiss on the cheek, and turned away. "Bye, Eve. I expect to hear the minute you find Cara." She turned and walked back toward Luke and Michael.

Eve hesitated for an instant, and then got in the car. Most people would have the same response as Catherine to Michael's behavior. On the surface he was being a poster child of obedience and cooperation. But she could never be sure what was whirling beneath that surface.

However, he had said she didn't have to worry. That was something, wasn't it? Well, it had to be enough. Follow Catherine's advice and go do her job.

She started the car, set her GPS, and pulled away from the curb.

LOST CANYON
7:10 P.M.

"Come out here." Svardak had thrown open the door of Marian's quarters and was glaring at Cara where she was sitting curled up on the floor, leaning against the vanity. "What are you doing? I haven't heard a sound from you since I put you in there after dinner."

She braced herself. More punishment? Svardak had been savage most of the day. Cat and mouse. Then when she responded, he would strike her several times with vicious force before he'd let her alone for a while. But she *had* to respond, she couldn't let him believe he could toy with her emotions or make her afraid.

She glared back at him. "What could I be doing? My choices are limited." She got to her feet. "But when your choices are limited, it doesn't mean that you're defeated. You just concentrate on what you have and what you are. I was sitting here remembering how I loved sitting by Lake Gaelkar in Scotland when I was there for Eve and Joe's wedding." She looked him in the eyes. "And suddenly I was there again. So you couldn't take that away from me. I wonder if Marian did the same thing with her home in Toronto. Did she ever mention it?"

"She was too frightened of me." He disconnected her cuffs from the main vanity chain and shoved her through the door into the living room. "So I did take that away from her. Just as I'll take everything away from you when I get a chance to concentrate more fully on you."

"It won't happen," she said quietly. "I'll just go away from whatever you do, and you won't be able to bring me back. You take away one joy, I'll find another one." She looked at the computer that he'd already hooked to the giant TV on the wall and set up for Skype. "Oh, it's time to show me off for my grandfather? I know you've been eagerly anticipating it." She smiled mockingly at him. "Would you like me to play a concerto for him? What about the Tchaikovsky?"

"Shut up! I won't have you spoil this for me." He pulled her in front of the TV. "You'll be quiet until I tell you to talk. All you speak is lies anyway."

"I speak the truth. It was Anna who lied. It must have been easy for her to get you to believe her. Children are gullible, and you never really grew up, did you?" She inhaled sharply as he twisted her wrist. "Is that going to be the rule of the night? I guess I'll have to go back to my lake in Scotland."

"If you don't shut up, I'll send you straight to hell." He pressed the Skype button, and Kaskov suddenly appeared on the screen in front of her. He was sitting at a desk in what appeared to be a library. "How nice of you to join us, Kaskov," Svardak said. "Cara has been wondering if you care whether she lives or dies. I've been trying to reassure her."

Kaskov ignored him. "How are you, Cara? I'm sorry you've had to go through this."

"So am I." She grimaced. "More than you know. But what can you expect? His crazy sister brainwashed him until he doesn't know any better." Her teeth sank into her lower lip as Svardak twisted her wrist again. "He said you killed her. She probably deserved it."

"I thought so at the time."

Svardak's curse was low and vehement. "Both of

you stop lying about Anna. This bitch is just like you, Kaskov." Svardak's lips were tight. "I was right to take her. None of the others were this bad. She won't listen and nothing I do—"

Cara stiffened. "None?" She had suddenly caught the meaning of that one word. "None of the *others*?" She whirled to face Svardak. "Marian Napier wasn't the only one you killed before you took me? How many others were there?"

"Oh, that shook you." His eyes were narrowed with pure malice. "I never said she was the only one. I was keeping the others for a surprise. You'd become so fond of Marian. Why don't you ask Kaskov? He has all the photos." He paused. "Except one."

She turned back to Kaskov. "How many?"

"Four. He wanted to make a statement and impress me."

She felt sick. "All of them so young and talented like Marian?"

"Very close," he said quietly.

She was having trouble comprehending it. "Because you killed this Anna?"

"He had a little more reason. I also killed his father and brother. Unfortunately, I missed ridding the world of you, Svardak. You'll be glad to know I've been profoundly sorry I was so careless. I was hoping to make it the same type of family affair that you created for me."

"What are you talking about?" Cara asked.

Kaskov held up his hands. "Ten minutes to change a life. They all found it both satisfactory and amusing. When my turn came, I preferred to put an end to your family and not just change it as you did mine, Svardak."

She stared at those scarred, crooked fingers. "It was them? They did that to you?"

"He deserved it," Svardak spat out. "Anna had to win that competition and get us all out of that labor camp. My father might have been a guard, but he was only a step above being a prisoner, and do you know how they treated us? They threw us in with the children of the prisoners for most of the day and let us fend for ourselves with that vermin. Kaskov was like you, he would have been able to fool the judges into thinking he had some kind of special talent. So we showed him he couldn't do that to us."

"By trying to destroy him?" Kaskov had mentioned the event that had changed his life to her almost casually, and it had still shocked her. Now, facing the sheer ugliness of the act itself, it was filling her with horror. "He did nothing to deserve that kind of treatment. He was only a young man trying to survive in that place."

"He deserved to be destroyed," Svardak said. "He killed Anna, he killed my father and my brother."

"After you did that hideous thing to him. Yes, killing should not be excused, but evil begets evil." So much evil that it was smothering her. Her gaze went to the photo of Marian on the wall. Not alone. Four innocent lives. "And you're such a coward. You didn't go after him. You chose to find four young girls to torment and kill who had done nothing to you. They had their entire lives before them, and you took them away."

"Not four. Five." His lips drew back in a feral smile. "You've forgotten yourself, Cara. And they didn't matter, they were only tribute for Anna and a notice to Kaskov of what was coming."

"Tribute?" The word suddenly triggered the rage that had been simmering since she had learned of those other women who had suffered at his hands. "Lives to be laid on the altar of your sister who had so little talent that she had to cheat to even be considered a decent musician?"

"One more word, and I'll break your neck," he said hoarsely. "That's not why I wanted to bring you to

Kaskov." He twisted her to face the TV again. "Look at her, Kaskov. Your granddaughter, your blood. I might let her live for a week or two if she amuses me. But I'll more than likely kill her before that time. She's really the best tribute of all because she's such a complete bitch. But I promise I'll give you a daily report on what I'm doing to her."

"I suppose you wouldn't accept ransom for her? That would be a form of tribute."

Svardak chuckled in disbelief. "Not the kind I have in mind." He lifted Cara's cuffed hands to display them to Kaskov. "I've been thinking about doing the same thing to her hands as we did to yours. That would be a true tribute to Anna."

Kaskov stiffened. "That wouldn't be—"

"You *monster*." Cara couldn't believe it. He was reaching out, searching for the ultimate way to make her his victim. Then the anger exploded, she could feel the heat burning in her cheeks as she jerked her hands free and whirled to face him. "You'd do it just to hurt Kaskov? Because it wouldn't hurt me." She thrust her hands at him. "Go ahead and do it. Take away the music. I'll find something else to make life worth living. I told you that whatever you take from me, I'll find a way to cheat you. I won't let you win." She glared into his eyes, feeling as if her entire body was blazing as she said softly, "Not one victory. Not one damn tribute. Go ahead and try to—"

His hand had shot out and struck her across the mouth with all his strength. She fell to her knees, but she was still glaring up at him.

"*Damn* you." He fumbled at the remote and turned off the Skype. He kicked her, and she crumpled backward onto the floor. Coppery taste. Blood. Her lip must be split, she realized dazedly. He kicked her again.

Pain.

His face was contorted above her as he dragged her toward Marian's quarters by the chains of the cuffs around her wrists. He threw her into the bathroom. "You made a mistake. You'll *never* win." His voice was shaking with fury. "I'll show you later tonight how much you can hurt. But I can't touch you right now, or I'd kill you. I won't spoil my pleasure of having Kaskov watch how far down I can take you. He has to *see* it."

He slammed the door.

She lay there, breathing hard, the anger still searing through her. She had gone too far. She had lost control. But when she had been told about those other women, the shock and fury had been too great to suppress.

Those poor women he had broken and killed. Victims. All of them innocent victims. And that's what he had considered her. A victim. But isn't that what she'd considered herself? She'd fought him, but she'd never thought she'd be able to overcome him. She'd just wanted to stay alive.

Calm down. Breathe deep and regain control.

It was several minutes before she was able to obey that self-admonishment. But the time allowed her to think. She must never lose her temper like that again. She had to be clever and begin to plan and watch for the right time. Because as she lay there, she had realized that Svardak had to be stopped any way possible. He couldn't be permitted to ever do this again.

She was done with being a victim.

It was time to go on the hunt and kill the bastard.

The instant the Skype disappeared from the screen, Kaskov spun toward Jock who was sitting in the far corner of the library. "My God, you'd better be able to get her away from him soon. She was on the attack

from the minute he turned on the Skype. I wasn't expecting her to be the problem."

Neither had Jock. Cara had been all flame and bold-
ness and reckless defiance. It had scared the hell out of
him. When she had held up her hands and dared Svardak to try to destroy her, it had been his worst nightmare. And when Svardak had struck her, he had nearly
exploded. "We don't know what she's gone through.
We've just got to hope that she won't challenge him
like that again until I can get to her." He jumped to his
feet and headed for the door. "You be ready if I need
you," he said harshly. "I'll probably need reinforcements at some point. I don't know what I'm going to
run into tonight."

"You're sure that she's in that canyon?"

"I saw Edding in a sleeping bag at that second campfire on the cliff trail. Why else would he be there?"

"Then I could send Nikolai and some men with you
now."

"No way. If Svardak feels overwhelmed, the first
thing he'll do is kill Cara." If he hadn't already done
that after the screen had gone blank, Jock thought desperately. The memory of her falling to her knees with
Svardak standing over her was chilling him to the
bone. "I'll take Joe Quinn. I spent the afternoon on that
ridge and cliff, and I have an idea how we can work
it if Svardak doesn't have too many men stationed in
that thicket at the top. I need him to either be totally
surprised or feel he has a chance to escape with her. Or
both." He looked over his shoulder. "I'll take anything
I can get. What I won't take is your screwing up if I
call you."

"If I didn't need your services, I'd make you pay for
that insult," he said with silky menace. "I don't screw
up, Gavin."

He opened the door. "The hell you don't. You left Svardak alive."

"True." The threat was gone. "I stand corrected. It won't happen again."

"You won't get another chance," Jock said as he strode down the hall. A moment later, he was out of the house and heading for his car. He called Joe as he reached it. "I'm on my way to pick you up."

"Is she okay?"

"No. But she was alive when the Skype ended. It depends on how angry she makes him whether she stays alive. We have to get her out of there tonight." He pressed the disconnect.

Ten minutes later, he pulled up in front of the Holiday Inn Hotel and jumped out of the car. Joe was walking toward him across the parking lot. His expression was not pleased.

Shit.

Eve was two steps behind him.

"No, Eve," he said flatly, as they reached him. "Go back inside."

"Go to hell." She got into the backseat. "I'm not arguing with you, Jock. I've done enough of that with Joe since I got here. I'm not going to be crawling all over that canyon and risk getting in your way. But I am going to be sitting in this car if you need a driver to get Cara away while you two are busy trying to keep that monster at bay." Her lips thinned. "And from what you told Joe, it sounds like you don't have time to do anything but say yes and thank you."

Jock muttered a curse and got into the car. "You don't move from this car once we get to the canyon." He glared at Joe, who was getting in the passenger seat. "And you concentrate on Cara and what we have to do and forget Eve's here."

"Not possible," Joe said. "But she'll keep her word,

and we might need her." He made a face. "Either way, we're stuck with her. I did everything I could. She won't budge."

"Stuck with me?" Eve said coolly. "I won't address that at present, but I will later. Right now, it doesn't seem as important as getting to Cara. Suppose you focus on doing that, Jock."

But he was already backing out of the parking space and driving off the hotel parking lot. "No, nothing is more important," he said curtly. "Remember that, Eve. I like you, I don't want anything to happen to you. But I'm not going to let you get in my way."

"Fair enough. Now tell me what to expect so that won't happen. Joe said that you're almost sure she's being kept in some kind of shack or cabin in the thicket at the top of that cliff bordering the north end of the canyon. How do you get her down?"

"I go up the cliff trail and take out the guards at the first encampment, then I move on to the second. That's where Edding is located. I take out his partner, but I make sure I keep Edding alive to get information about the number of guards in that thicket and exactly where Cara is being held. Joe is going up the mountain trail to locate the two camps there." He paused. "Then, depending on what Edding tells me, Joe will either cause a major diversion on the mountain to draw Svardak away from Cara while I take her down the cliff trail, or I'll go in and get her while Svardak is still there."

Eve's gaze flew to Joe. "What kind of diversion?"

He smiled. "Stop worrying. Nothing close-range. Jock managed to get a few very powerful and efficient explosives from Kaskov that should do the trick. Explosives are never a problem for me."

"I know they aren't. But it sounds to me like a problem however it's handled," Eve said curtly. "Can't you delay it just a little longer and find another way?"

"Not a chance," Jock's voice was clipped. "Not after what I saw on that Skype tonight. I have to get her away from him."

"That bad?" she whispered.

Jock eyes were fixed on the canyon looming ahead. "Aye, every bit that bad."

Cara slowly sat up and pushed the hair out of her face. She took a deep breath as she leaned back against the vanity. She had to prepare herself. She might be able to talk her way out of the punishment Svardak was going to inflict, but she doubted it. She could force herself to endure it, but she wasn't sure that she might not break and say something to make it worse. The fury inside her was violent and still seething.

The only other way out was to take the route that she'd already chosen. He had to die.

She had never realized she could be that calm and cool about a decision to take a life. Even when she had been hunted and growing up with danger around every corner, the idea had never occurred to her as an option. Life was too precious a gift to destroy it.

But the thought was here before her now. And Svardak's life was not too precious to destroy. Marian and his other victims would have had no problem if they'd had the opportunity.

But how to do it? He was far stronger. She had the basic skills Joe had taught her, but he was keeping her cuffed. She had no weapons.

But neither had Marian Napier. She had taken his punishment until she could take it no longer. Then she had made her move.

Cara looked over her shoulder at the splintered corner of the mirror. Suicide? Or weapon? She still couldn't be sure of Marian's intent. But she knew what her own intent would be. "Help me out, Marian," she whispered as she got to her knees and pulled herself to her feet. "You got that splinter started, I'll take it the rest of the way . . ." She grabbed a washcloth from the shower and climbed awkwardly onto the vanity. Balancing on her knees, she could just reach that shattered corner. She used the bracelet of the handcuffs to work at the broken lower edge of the glass.

A small piece abruptly broke off and fell into the sink!

She froze.

Had he heard it?

She waited. No sound from the other room.

She started working with the handcuffs again.

So damn awkward . . .

She finally managed to get the edge of the cuff bracelet under the broken mirror again.

She pulled up . . .

And it broke again! She frantically tried to catch the jagged piece with the washcloth as it fell, but she wasn't in time and had to grab it with her hand instead.

Pain. She inhaled sharply as the jagged glass sliced her palm.

But she managed to hold on to the piece until she could slip it into the washcloth.

She was bleeding . . . Forget it. Worry about it later. Was that sliver of glass large enough to use as a weapon or would she have to try again? She looked down at the triangular glass reflecting up at her. It was about four inches long and two inches wide. Not perfect, but it might be okay. It was too dangerous risking another attempt. She carefully wrapped the glass in the washcloth again and put it on the sink. Then she turned on the cold water and ran it over her hand. It stung, but the bleeding had stopped. The cut was little more than a scratch.

Relief. After years of taking care of her hands to make sure she would never hurt them, she had broken the cardinal rule tonight. Worse. She had risked the end of her music when she had taunted Svardak earlier. And she wasn't sorry. She couldn't let him win because she wasn't brave enough to risk what was most important to her.

"We did it, Marian," she murmured as she looked up at the corner of the mirror. "But I made a mess of it. There's no way that he's not going to notice that chunk out of it. I'll have to do something to distract him . . ."

Jock silently pulled the knife out of the guard's back and let him fall to the ground. One down.

But where was Edding?

Then he saw him standing on the edge of the trail several yards away, looking down at the canyon below. He had his automatic weapon cradled in the crook of his arm. "I'm bored as hell, Nelson," Edding said without looking away from the canyon. "When do you think we'll get out of here? I have a woman waiting back in Nassau. Money isn't everything."

Jock moved silently forward. The gun first, there couldn't be any noise.

Then Jock was on him. The next instant, he karate-chopped Edding's wrist, then followed it with a blow to the back of his neck.

Edding's knees buckled as Jock grabbed his rifle. "Quiet and you may live." He dragged him over to the campfire where he'd killed the other guard. "But the chances are slim. They'd be nonexistent if I had more time. I'd much prefer torture to bargaining." His knife was at Edding's throat. "But I do keep my word, so you might be lucky."

Edding's stunned gaze was on the glassy, staring eyes of the dead guard only two feet away from him. "You killed Nelson."

"He was in my way. So are you. But if you talk, I might forget it. Though I don't know why I should. You helped Svardak get away after he killed that girl in Bermuda."

"It was only business." He moistened his lips. "Was she a relative or something? I didn't do nothing to her. It was all Svardak. He's kind of crazy."

"Only business? I'm more interested in what you did here. Tell me about it."

"He'd kill me."

"No. I'm the one you have to worry about."

"You can't get away with it. We weren't the only guards, and this isn't the only camp. There's another one farther down the trail."

"Not anymore. That's where I came from." He pressed the blade and drew blood. "I want to know about the other woman, the one you've been guarding here." His gaze went up to the top of the cliff. "She's still there, right?"

"As far as I know. I've only heard talk from the guards on the hill when they brought me up there to relieve them. I haven't seen her."

"How many guards?"

"Four."

"Where are they?"

He was silent.

Jock pressed down harder. Blood spurted.

Edding said quickly, "Two guarding the mountain trail. One patrolling the area around the cabin. One watching the back road."

"Vehicles?"

"A Jeep parked by the back road."

"How close are the guards to the cabin?"

"The man on patrol, fifteen to twenty feet. The others, within view, but at least thirty or forty feet.

"You're being very precise. You're sure?"

"It's boring up here in the mountains. The guys talk, I'm probably pretty close to correct." He added defiantly, "And why should I protect Svardak? I want to live. The first thing the bastard did when I got here was have me and Nelson bury some woman he tossed off that cliff. I didn't hire on to be a gravedigger."

"No, you'd rather keep another woman penned up until he got ready to do the same thing to her," Jock said softly.

"I never even saw her. I didn't have anything to do with what went on at the cabin. The chances were that I'd never have seen her. The guys up there said that they didn't think she'd make it past the first night when Svardak put her outside all night."

Jock went still. "Really? But no one did anything about it, did they?"

Edding didn't answer, his gaze on Jock's face. "You're going to kill me, aren't you?"

"I'm thinking about it. No one in that house but the woman and Svardak?"

"No."

"Do you know anything about where that back road leads?"

"How could I? No one but Svardak is allowed to use it." His voice was shaking. "I don't want to die. How can I save myself? I'll do anything."

"I think you've done it." He sheathed his knife, pulled out duct tape, and taped Edding's mouth. "At least a reprieve from me. But that doesn't mean you're home free. I'm very irritated that you closed your eyes about what he was doing to her." He bound his wrists behind him. "So I'll give you to Kaskov to decide what he wants to do with you. Warning. He's not likely to be lenient." He got to his feet. "And that suits me fine." He heard Edding grunting and struggling behind him as he turned and walked away.

He called Joe as he headed up the trail toward the thicket at the top of the cliff. "Use the explosives. There are guards within ten or fifteen feet of the cabin where they're keeping Cara. I can't get that close without risking Svardak's knowing I'm there and killing her. Give me fifteen minutes to get into position and take out at least one of the guards. Then blow the hell out of that encampment on the mountain."

"You've got it. Fifteen minutes." Joe cut the connection.

Fifteen minutes. Jock could feel the blood pounding through his veins. It was going to happen. Fifteen minutes, and he'd have Cara back and Svardak would be dead. He started up the trail at a dead run.

CHAPTER

7

Svardak was coming.

Cara stiffened as she heard his footsteps. She felt an instant of panic before she controlled it. She'd done all she could. She'd tried to wash all the glass and blood off the sink. She'd wrapped her makeshift glass dagger in the washcloth and tucked it in the waistband of her pants. Then she'd pulled the bottom of her red blouse out to cover it. There was no bulge that she could see. It might not be enough, but Svardak's rage at her might make the difference. At any rate, it was the best she could do.

The door was opening.

Showtime.

She jumped to her feet and was there immediately in Svardak's face, confronting him. "I've been waiting for you." Her hands clenched into fists. "I've been thinking about your sister and how ashamed she'd be of you. You weren't man enough to kill Kaskov, so you took me. And I'm nothing to him. He hardly changed expressions during that conversation, did he?"

His face flushed with anger. "She wouldn't be

ashamed. She'd be proud of me. He wanted you back. He offered me money for you."

"Money means nothing to him. He probably has billions. That's another mistake your family made." She took a step closer. She had to make him keep looking at her face so he wouldn't glance up at that mirror. "You took away his music, but you gave him more power and money than he would ever have made on the concert stage. So your stupid sister cheated herself more than she cheated him."

That was the insult that tipped him over the top. "She wasn't stupid. *You're* stupid." He slapped her, hard. "Or you wouldn't insult her. Don't you ever learn? Every time you do, I'll hurt you."

"Like you hurt Marian and those other women? But Kaskov hurt your Anna, didn't he?" She was only inches from him now, and her words spat at him like bullets. "How long did it take her to die? Do you know, or were you cowering in that mental institution she stuck you in? She must have really hated you to put you in that place."

"She loved me. She said I was too careless, and Kaskov would find me. She wanted me to get well and be safe."

"She made you believe that? You were in her way. What a fool you are."

That was enough. He made a sound deep in his throat, and his hands closed on her neck. "Bitch. Liar."

She couldn't breathe. "It's—true," she gasped. "Fool."

He leaned forward and jerked her cuffs free of the vanity chain. Then he was whirling her out the door and into the living room. His face was almost the deep red of her blouse and his eyes were wild. His grip tightened on her throat. "Why are you doing this? I didn't want it to happen yet."

"I don't want you to have anything you want." Her eyes blazed up at him. "I won't be your damn tribute."

He slapped her again, then backhanded her other cheek. "You will, Cara. You won't win. I'll win. Because after you're dead, I'll erase every trace of you from the earth. Your Joe Quinn and Eve and that kid will all be tribute." He leaned forward, and hissed, "Look at me. Did you hear me? I promise you. Tribute." He hit her in the stomach.

She crumpled to the floor and rolled over on her side, holding her abdomen.

"Hurt? Get up on your feet. I'm going to do it again."

She didn't answer, she just rocked back and forth, clutching her stomach.

"I said get up!" He fell to his knees beside her. "I've only just started." He grabbed her shoulders and started to pull her. "You're going to take back every word you said to—"

He *screamed*.

He stared in dazed horror down at the jagged glass sticking out of his abdomen. "What did you—"

She pushed him off her. "Tribute, damn you." She jumped to her feet and ran toward the door. "To Marian and all those other—"

Kaboom!

She staggered against the door and grabbed it to keep from falling. An explosion? The cabin was shaking, and she heard Svardak cursing on the floor behind her.

She must not have hurt him enough. She had to get out of here . . .

Then she was outside in the night and the cold. The sharp wind whipping her hair into her face.

Fire. She could see leaping flames halfway down the mountain. The guards who usually guarded the cabin were running toward the trail leading down the mountain.

Kaboom.

Another explosion shook the earth.

She turned in the opposite direction from the mountain and started running through the trees toward the cliff.

"Cara!"

Jock's voice!

But it couldn't be Jock. She was just dazed and bewildered. Or it could be some kind of trick. She kept on running.

"Dammit, Cara. Stop!"

Closer. The voice was closer,

"Cara! I don't want to—"

She fell to the ground. Tackled. She'd been tackled. Svardak?

She started to struggle.

"Cara, I can't let you—" He was holding her shoulders pinned to the ground. "Look at me!"

She had no choice but look at him. Not Svardak. Silver-gray eyes, those wonderful features twisted in agony. She stopped fighting. "Jock?"

"Thank God." He got off her and pulled her to her feet. "We've got to get out of here. I don't know how long Joe's explosions can keep those guards occupied." He looked down at her cuffs. "I don't have time to get these off you right now. Later." He was pulling her across the thicket. "We're going down the cliff trail. I'll hold on to you. It's not too bad. We'll be down to the canyon floor in a heartbeat." He was leading her down the winding trail even as he spoke. "It's going to be fine, Cara."

Fine? She didn't believe him, but it was good to have Jock here and trying to comfort her. And he was so smart and he might be able to keep Svardak from getting to her again. But he had said something disturbing. Her gaze went to the mountain trail that was still in flames. He had said Joe had done it . . .

Joe!

She stopped short. "Joe's here? Joe started that explosion?" Panic was racing through her. "No, it can't be Joe. He can't have anything to do with Svardak. It will make him—" She was trying to pull away from Jock. "I have to go back to the cabin. Right now. I shouldn't have run away. I should have finished him."

Jock's grip tightened on her shoulders. "You're not making sense. We have to get out of here." He drew a deep breath. "Look, you're hurt. I can see it. And you're not thinking clearly. We don't know what kind of reinforcements Svardak might pull out of his hat. I have to get you out of here. Then I'll go back and take care of Svardak."

"I'm thinking clearly." She was staring desperately up at him. "He can't win, Jock. He can't kill anyone I love. I'm almost sure I didn't kill him. I tried, but I only had that piece of glass . . ."

"He won't win." His hands tightened on her shoulders to keep her still. "I'll take care of it. I promise you. Now come with me."

"Promise me?" She shook her head. "But Svardak made me a promise, too. He didn't know about you, but he knew about the others." She was struggling. "I have to go back and—"

"Cara." He held her still, his eyes holding her own, his face contorted with pain. "I have to get you down," he said hoarsely. His hands moved to her throat. "Come with me, or I'll have to do it the only way I can."

He didn't understand. She was so dizzy and scared for Joe, she wasn't making it clear why she couldn't do what he wanted. "Let me go, Jock." She kept struggling. "He'll hurt them. I can't let him—"

"Shh." His thumb had slid to her carotid. "Relax. I'll take care of everything. Trust me . . ."

His hands were tightening.

"Jock?" What was he doing? Her eyes widened in bewilderment. He looked so strange. His eyes were moist and glittering.

"Trust me . . ."

Darkness.

Someone was coming!

Eve jumped out of the car as she saw Jock's shadowy figure coming through the trees. Panic flooded her as she saw he was carrying someone over his shoulder in a fireman's lift. "Jock!" Then she saw the flow of silky dark hair of the woman he was carrying. "Cara?"

"Don't panic. She's not badly hurt." He muttered a curse. "No, that's a lie." He was striding toward her. "But it's not physical, and we'll handle the rest. Open the passenger door."

She ran around the car and opened the door for him. "What do you mean, she's not hurt. She's unconscious. Did Svardak do it?"

"No, I did. She'll come out of it in an hour or so." He put Cara gently on the seat and worked a few minutes at freeing her of the handcuffs. He tossed them in the backseat and fastened her seat belt. "Get her out of here. You should be safe. I called Kaskov when I was halfway down the cliff and told him to send Nikolai and men to meet you on the road. He should be almost here. Tell him to take you to the nearest ER and have her checked out." He started to turn away. "Get going, Eve."

"Stop right there, Jock," Eve said. "You don't give me bits and pieces of an explanation, then walk away." Her gaze lifted to the mountain trail that was still blazing. "Joe. Dammit, what happened to Joe?"

"He's okay. I called and told him I'd gotten Cara out, and he was fine at that time. I haven't been able to reach him since then." He was already moving toward the mountain. "I'm going to take the mountain trail to get back up to the thicket, so I should run into him when I reach the point where he set off the explosives. I'll call you when I make contact."

"You're going back to the thicket? Why?"

"Svardak's still alive. I made Cara a promise."

"Are you crazy? I'll bet there are probably still Svardak goons alive and lethal up there. Yes, I'm worried to death about Joe. Cara wouldn't want you to run a risk like that."

"I don't know what she'll want. But I know what I want." He looked back over his shoulder. "Kaskov will be sending more men up that mountain to finish what Joe started. We'll keep Joe safe, you just get Cara out of here. That's what you said you came with us to do. Now do it."

Her hands clenched as she watched him start up the trail. She'd been frantic about Joe as well as Cara while she'd been waiting here. She wanted to follow Jock up that trail to see for herself if Joe was all right. Lord, she was tired of being this passive.

But it wasn't what she wanted to do that was important. She had to get Cara out of here or risk her being captured again. She ran around to the driver's seat and jumped in the car. The next moment, she was driving out of the forest, and two minutes later, she reached the road leading back to Coal Town.

She glanced at Cara in the dim light cast by the control panel. She inhaled sharply as she saw the bruises, the cut lip, that delicate throat that was swollen, red, and badly bruised. Heaven knows what other wounds she'd suffered that weren't immediately visible. And

Jock had regarded these physical wounds as relatively unimportant? She knew how he would have reacted to them when he first saw Cara. It meant that he expected something worse had happened to her.

The monster must have struck deep.

She reached over and gently touched Cara's knee. But Cara was strong, and monsters could be defeated. "It's over. And we'll be here for you . . ."

Headlights ahead!

She stiffened, her hands clenching on the steering wheel.

Then her phone rang.

Kaskov.

"Stop the car," he said curtly. "We're coming toward you. I want to take a look at Cara."

"I didn't expect you. Jock said Nikolai was going—"

"I chose to come along. Pull over."

She pulled to the side of the road but didn't get out of the car.

Kaskov got out of the passenger seat of the Mercedes and strode toward her car. "Roll down your window."

She pressed the control for the passenger seat. "She's unconscious, but Jock said she was probably all right."

Kaskov was playing the beam of a flashlight on Cara's face. "That's what he told me, too. I had to be sure. I didn't like the idea that she might have a concussion. Is he certain she doesn't?"

"Only a doctor can be certain, but he thought she was . . ." She hesitated, then shrugged. "And it wouldn't be because she's unconscious now. Jock said he did it. He said she'd wake up on her own in about another hour."

Kaskov stiffened. "Why?"

"He didn't go into it. He was too busy getting back up that mountain to go after Svardak. Evidently, he left that minor item undone."

"Careless." Kaskov's gaze was still on Cara. "I don't like this development."

"Neither do I," Eve said bluntly. "But I'm not going to argue with him when there are still important things to do. Have you sent men up to the mountain to help Joe?"

"Would I dare not do as I was told when Gavin warned me not to screw up?" he asked mockingly. "They should reach the canyon in another five minutes."

"Then you've already screwed up. They should be climbing that trail by now. Joe's still up there." She started to roll the window back up. "Now get back in your car and let me get Cara to that ER. We don't know what other damage has been done to her. Your Nikolai is supposed to be acting as an escort to see that I get to a hospital with her. They should have left you at home to make sure that everything else got done."

Kaskov frowned; and then he chuckled. "Honest to the point of extreme pain as usual, Eve. You're probably quite right." He turned toward his car. "We'll get her there safely. There's a hospital on the other side of Coal Town, and I've already sent one of my men to pave the way."

"Great." Eve made a face. "All Cara needs is to have the medical staff too terrified to treat her." She pulled back out on the road. "Now you definitely have to come with us to run interference, Kaskov."

LOST CANYON

"Shit!"

The Jeep that Jock had seen parked near the back road when he'd been up here at the thicket before was gone.

"Problem?" Joe came up the trail behind him.

"Unless the car that was here was stolen by one of Svardak's men, we have a big problem." He went to the edge of the cliff, where the winding back road appeared to disappear around a curve halfway down. "Fresh tire prints. I was afraid of this." He knelt as he saw something else. A minute drop of blood caught in one of the ruts at the top of the road. He got to his feet and turned back toward the cabin.

The front door of the cabin was wide open.

"Cover me." Jock ran toward the cabin. He paused to the right of the doorway, then dived in and rolled to the left. Then he was on his feet and dodging behind the kitchen bar.

No shots.

Silence.

The room was empty.

A long smear of blood on the floor in the middle of the room and another sprinkle near the front door.

Joe was suddenly in the room. "I'll take the door to the left."

Jock went to the other room. "Clear," he called to Joe. "Svardak's quarters. Still luggage here and a rifle in the corner." He came out of the room to see Joe standing in the middle of a bathroom. He was staring down at a length of a chain in his hand that had been affixed to the vanity.

"This is where he must have kept Cara." Joe's hand tightened on the links of chain. "Chained like an animal." He threw the chain on the vanity. "He's not here." His voice was hoarse. "God, I wish he was. I *want* him."

Jock's gaze was wandering over the small room, the splintered mirror, the faint trace blood on the drain of the sink, then back to the chain.

Control.

Don't let the rage take over yet.

Save it. Nurture it. Let it become part of him.

He turned on his heel and strode toward the door. "Then don't just talk about it. Let's go hunting."

Eve . . .

Cara could hear Eve's voice talking to someone, but she couldn't make out the words . . .

But if Eve was here, Cara had to know if she was safe, if they were all safe . . .

She forced her lids to open and saw Eve's face. She was frowning. Something must be wrong, Cara thought in a panic. "Eve!"

Eve's gaze flew to her face. "Hey, don't be afraid." She was immediately beside her, holding her hand. "It's over. You're fine, Cara. Go back to sleep. You're in the hospital, and we've just gotten you settled into your room. The doctors say that you're not badly hurt but that you need rest and sleep. They gave you a shot to make sure you'd get it. Don't fight it."

Drugs . . . That was why she was so blurry . . . "They shouldn't have done that. I need to keep awake. Svardak . . ."

"You're safe. He can't get to you here."

Eve didn't understand. "But I can't get to him . . . either. He's . . . not dead yet, is he?"

"Not yet. He'd disappeared when Jock and Joe got back to the cabin. They're still searching for him."

Joe!

"But Joe's safe?" Her hand clutched Eve's. "Svardak didn't know about Jock, so he should be okay. But Joe . . . he knew about Joe and you and Michael. He knew . . ."

"Shh. Calm down. Joe's safe. We're all safe."

"No, you're not. And it's my fault. I didn't do what I was supposed to do." She could hear her voice slurring. "They shouldn't have given me that drug. I keep drifting off. What if he does something . . . while I'm sleeping . . ."

"I won't let him," Eve said gently. "Trust me."

"That's what Jock said." She could no longer hold her eyes open. "Trust me . . ."

The hospital room was dark.

But Cara knew that Jock was there as soon as she opened her eyes. He was sitting in a chair no more than three feet from the bed, and she could *feel* him. But it wasn't enough, she wanted to see him. "Turn on the light, Jock."

"I promised I'd call the nurse when you woke. I'm not supposed to touch you or talk to you."

"Turn on the light."

He reached over and turned on the light. "Satisfied?"

"No." She desperately wanted to reach out and touch him. There had been times when she had wondered if she'd ever see him again. Now he was here before her. He looked strong and beautifully, vibrantly alive. "But it will do for right now. I just wanted to make certain you were okay. Eve said you and Joe were searching for Svardak."

"I assure you that he would have been no danger to either one of us."

"I couldn't be sure of that." She shivered. "He's so evil, Jock. I believe evil is always dangerous. The poison seems to spread everywhere."

"I have a very potent antidote for that particular poison. Don't worry about me."

"Don't be ridiculous. I'll always worry about you."

She held up her hand as he started to speak. "Eve said that Svardak got away. How did that happen?"

"I took too long getting you down the cliff. By the time I got back up to the cabin, he'd taken that Jeep parked up there and escaped down the back road. Joe and I tracked the car until it disappeared into the trees. It looked as if the road led down toward the next mountain over. He knew exactly where he was going." His lips tightened. "But it's only a postponement. I'll keep my promise to you. I'm sorry, Cara."

"Sorry? It's my fault, not yours. I should have stayed and finished it." She whispered, "I was hoping I'd at least hurt him enough so that he wouldn't be able to get away. I stabbed him, you know."

"No, I didn't know. You weren't too coherent. But I gathered you'd done something to him. There was blood on the floor of the cabin and a few drops near the back road where the Jeep had been parked."

"But he still got away. I didn't think I'd killed him. He was cursing . . . I stabbed him in the stomach, but I only had that jagged glass I'd pried from the mirror." She rubbed her temple. "I should have been more careful, Jock. But I knew I only had the one chance to—"

"Hush. Stop apologizing," he said hoarsely. "You're driving me crazy. Forget it. You shouldn't have had to face any of this. I should have been there to do it for you."

She drew a deep breath. He was right, it wasn't the time for looking back. It would get her nowhere. She smiled with an effort. "That would have been difficult since you weren't the one to get an invitation from Svardak. It was me or no one. You'll have to make sure I do a better job next time."

"You don't have to worry about that. There's not going to be a next time for you."

"That's the second time you told me not to worry," she said quietly. "I can't help but worry. Particularly now." She moistened her lips. "He promised me that he would erase everyone I loved. I told Eve that he didn't know about you, but he might now. You were probably very visible and effective when you and Joe were destroying everyone in sight."

"I admit I wasn't shy and retiring." He smiled grimly. "But I intend to keep him too busy hiding from me to plan an assault."

"He won't hide. He's crazy. He'll want to strike out as soon as he's able. It's my fault. He hates me now as much as he does Kaskov." Her hand clenched on the sheet. "Maybe more. That's okay as long as it's just me. But he mustn't touch anyone else. I can't let him do that."

"Will you shut up?" He was suddenly beside her, his hands cradling her cheeks. "Look at you, dammit. Bruises on your face and body. Split lip. Eve said they even found a cracked rib. No telling what kind of other emotional and mental trauma. He *hurt* you." His eyes were blazing down at her, his mouth drawn back from his teeth. "And he's never going to touch you again. Not ever. So don't give me that bullshit about keeping everyone else safe from the son of a bitch. He's not going to live that long."

"But you didn't find him yet," she said quietly. "He got away from the canyon. He's still out there."

"I'll *find* him." His hands gathered her two hands in his own. He said through set teeth, "But I have to know everything he did to you. So that I'll know how long I keep him alive and in agony before I put him down like a rabid animal."

"Do you think I'd tell you that?" She pulled her hands away from him. "The last thing I want is for you to torture and kill for me. One thing I found out from all this is that I've let myself be a victim all my life. I let my friend, Elena, protect me when I was a little girl on the run. Later I let you and Eve and Joe protect me and fight for me. I can't let it happen again. When I get out of this hospital, I'll be the one who goes after Svardak."

"Wrong."

She looked deep into his eyes. "No, Jock. It stops here. If you won't accept it, walk away from me. Svardak made me a victim, and I'm taking it back. And I won't let him make a victim of anyone else in my name." She closed her eyes. "You can turn off the light now."

He didn't move.

She could sense his frustration . . . and his pain.

She didn't open her eyes. "I'll tell you three things about my time with Svardak; and then I'm not mentioning it ever again. One, it became a battle between us, and I won as many as I lost. Two, those battles did not involve rape. Three, I have to win the final battle, and no one else can win it for me. I owe it to Marian and all those other women he called his damn tribute." She turned over on her side. "Good night, Jock. Will you turn out the light now?"

He slowly got to his feet, and she heard the click of the light switch. She could sense him just standing there in the dark, staring at her. He finally asked jerkily, "Why did you mention that he hadn't raped you?"

"Because I thought it would bother you not knowing. You would have been afraid it would mean too much to me."

"Aye," he said thickly. "You could say that. Imagine me worrying about a tough little cookie like you. I'll see you tomorrow morning, Cara."

She heard the whoosh of the door as he left the room.

Tough little cookie? She didn't feel anywhere near that description, she thought wearily. Those last minutes had been terribly painful. She had been hard and firm when she had only wanted to go into his arms and be held and comforted.

But that had been necessary in this new world she found herself in, the world Svardak had created for her. A world where every emotion was deeper, stronger because she had learned she had to fight to hold on to them. She had not thought she could love Jock any more than she had before. But as she had lain here and watched his face and heard him speak, it had been the difference between a lazy river and a deep ocean. She knew it would be the same with all the other people she cared about.

She wasn't sure that Jock had understood, and it hurt her, because he always understood everything about her. But she would work until he did understand and begin to accept her as she was now. She had to do it no matter how long it took.

Because there was no way on earth she would lose that battle to Svardak.

6:10 A.M.

"How is she?" Joe asked Eve as he strode down the hospital corridor toward her. "I talked to Jock, and all he'd say is that we have to find Svardak." He took her in his arms. "As if I didn't know that." He kissed the top of her head and held her close. "I've been up in the mountains trying to find someone to question about his whereabouts. I'll know more when we interrogate some of the prisoners Kaskov's men took there. The bastard seems to have just disappeared."

"That doesn't mean he won't reappear," Eve said as she held him close for another instant and stepped back. "Cara thinks he will." Her lips twisted. "And who should know better? She's terrified of him."

"She didn't let him see it. She stabbed the son of a bitch."

"I know. Completely foreign to anything our Cara would normally do." She shuddered. "She's not afraid for herself. Jock said she's afraid for us. And that's worse, Joe. I'd much rather we could count on her hiding out and cowering in a cave somewhere."

"It will get better. We don't even know what kind of hell she's gone through." He looked down at her. "But I know what kind of hell you've gone through." He gently touched the dark circles beneath her eyes. "When did you sleep last?"

"Probably about the same time you did," she said impatiently. "And you can't wait to get back out there and go hunting with Jock again. Do you think I'm going to leave Cara? She's never been more vulnerable in her life."

"I beg to differ." Kaskov was walking down the corridor toward them. "Cara doesn't impress me as being that fragile at the moment." He glanced at Eve. "Neither do you, but you appear to be very tired and stressed." His gaze shifted to Joe. "Why don't you take her away from here and stay with her until she's better?"

"Go to hell," Joe said coldly.

"That's no doubt my eventual destiny, but I don't appreciate your giving me orders." His tone was deadly soft. "But I'll forgive you since the suggestion that I gave you was not mine but Cara's." He turned to Eve. "I received a call from Cara an hour ago on my number routed through Moscow. Naturally, I picked up since it was only five in the morning, and I was concerned."

Eve's gaze flew to the door to Cara's room. "I returned her phone to her the moment that we got her settled. But why would she call you?"

"I'm about to go in and find out. But she gave me orders to make certain that you and Quinn were doing well and resting before I entered her presence."

"Orders? You?" Joe echoed skeptically.

"I admit I was a bit surprised," Kaskov said. "And intrigued." He turned back to Eve. "But I believe she really meant that she wanted me to be sure that I was keeping you both safe while she bothered with talking to me." He gestured to Nikolai, who was standing near the elevator. "So Nikolai has taken over guarding her hospital room so that you'll be free to get some rest. I think you can trust him."

"No," she said succinctly. "He belongs to you. He's your man and your man alone."

"True. And he has my orders that no one is to come near Cara." He said to Joe, "Didn't I do everything possible to help you in the canyon last night?"

Joe nodded slowly. "I could have used a few more prisoners to interrogate. You were a little too efficient."

"Well, you can't have it all ways. I was annoyed that I'd not been able to get to Cara sooner. And several of them escaped before we even got there. Your fault, not mine. But we still have a few left. Did you find out anything from the ones you captured?"

"Not yet."

"Then give it up and rest for a few hours. You probably won't lose anything. No doubt Gavin will still be working on it now that he knows Cara is safe. But we all realize what drives him." He sighed as he studied their faces. "Or go and stand guard over Cara and have her waste her energy arguing when she only wanted a few minutes to talk to me. Why should I care?"

But he had cared enough to send those men to the mountain to try to help Joe, Eve thought. And they would never have found Cara if he hadn't involved them in the search. She was still furiously angry that it had been his initial fault that Cara had been taken, but she couldn't deny he'd done everything he could to get her back. "Joe?"

"Four hours." Joe was gazing at Kaskov. "She'll be safe with him. And you need the rest. I promise I'll have you back here before the doctors give her permission to leave."

She felt a flash of instant rejection followed immediately by frustration as she looked at Joe. She wasn't the only one exhausted. Joe had been climbing all over that damn mountain for two days. "Four hours." She turned and started down the hall. "I need to call Michael and let you talk to him. He was worried about you and Cara when I phoned him last night. So you stay with me, Joe. Got it?"

"I really need to go back to—" Then he shrugged as she gave him a steady look. "Got it. Four hours." He glanced at Kaskov. "But I need to know what Cara wanted with you. I'm not going to be left in the dark."

"That's entirely up to Cara. You'll have to ask her. If you'll recall, I'm the outsider in your cozy family picture." He turned and headed toward Cara's room. "For some reason no one wants to let me come closer than the fringes. Imagine that . . ."

"It took you long enough." Cara quickly straightened in the bed as Kaskov walked into her room. As usual, she felt the instinct not to show weakness to her grandfather. In some bizarre way, it was a little like the defensiveness she had felt with Svardak. Strange, when one had been trying to save her and the other to destroy her. "I've been waiting."

"What a pity," Kaskov said. "You'd have had my presence sooner if you hadn't acquired two such protective guardians. I had to bother myself with persuading instead of commanding since I knew you'd be upset if I followed my ordinary manner of dealing with obstructions." He crossed the room to stand by her bed. "And I didn't wish to upset you since your call completely intimidated me."

"Stop mocking. This is difficult enough without your making fun of me."

His gaze was narrowed on her face. "You could wait a day or two. You don't seem to be in top shape."

"No, I can't wait. *He* won't wait." She looked him in the eye. "And I might be in better shape than Svardak is. I don't know. Maybe not. I probably did everything wrong. I've never stabbed anyone before. That means I have to count on his being able to reach out and hurt them."

"One can't expect to be an expert at mayhem and murder on your first attempt," he said sardonically. "You probably did as well as could be expected. Would you like to explain whom you mean by 'them'?"

"You know. He tried to do it with you. He wants to make me hurt by using the people he thinks will be able to do that." Her lips twisted. "He was wrong about my being able to hurt you, but he still wouldn't admit it. But he spelled it out to me just before I stabbed him. He wants to erase me. That means Eve and Joe and Michael. He didn't mention Jane, but I'm sure that he wouldn't leave her out. She just hasn't been on his radar."

"And did he mention Jock Gavin?" Kaskov asked softly.

She tensed. "No. I was hoping to keep Jock away

from him. There was no reason for him to know about Jock. It's not as if he— There was no reason."

"Except for the fact that Gavin was the most likely person in your world to appear and draw and quarter Svardak." He murmured. "A trifle naïve, Cara?"

"Perhaps," she said wearily. "But I thought if I managed to escape from Svardak, then I might have been able to keep him from knowing about Jock."

He chuckled. "Truly naïve. Jock's not going to give up until he kills the son of a bitch in the most painful way possible."

"I would have found a way to keep Jock out of it." She met his eyes. "Believe me."

He studied her face. "I do believe you." He shrugged. "I might not have believed you six months ago, but something has definitely changed. I thought that had possibly occurred when I saw you on that Skype. You were . . . explosive."

"I wonder why? Just because my life had been torn to pieces by a monster who you'd just told me had killed not one but four innocent women?" Her smile was bittersweet. "You might say it was a game-changer, Kaskov. I'd told Jock that I was all grown-up, but that was my diploma. But you know about diplomas, don't you? You received yours in that labor camp."

"How clever of you to pinpoint the exact time and place of my coming of age." He tilted his head. "And I assume that mention was intentional?"

"Yes, that's where this all started. I have to get you to listen to me, and I figured that might be something to build on."

"I'm listening. That's why I'm here. But you mustn't bore me, Cara."

"Perish the thought. I realize that my only entertainment value for you is connected to the violin."

"Not 'only.' You've furnished me with a good deal of excitement during these last years. You seem to have the facility to draw a whirlpool of interesting people and situations around you."

She looked at him in disbelief. "You're incredible. I'm the lightning rod that caused the bolts to strike?"

"No, I caused them to strike. Fate just made you the most attractive target."

"Fate? You're my grandfather, my blood, don't blame it on fate, Kaskov. All of this is your responsibility." Her hands clenched on the sheets. "You made your choices. A terrible thing happened to you, and you let it twist you into the man you've become. I don't know what else happened to you on that road, and I won't ask you. But when you killed Svardak's family, it started the dominos falling all around you." Her eyes were suddenly blazing. "Including those poor, innocent women who would never have died if they hadn't been caught up in this ugliness." Her voice was shaking. "It was *wrong*, Kaskov. Svardak was hideous and a demon. But you were wrong, and you have to help me keep him from doing any more damage."

"Oh, do I?" His face was without expression. "I believe you're overstepping the bounds of our relationship, Cara. I don't take orders from anyone, certainly not from a child."

"No, we're back to my entertainment value again. But I'm no longer a child. And it's to your advantage to help me because that way you won't run the risk of losing the one thing that you find worthwhile in that relationship."

He was silent. "An intelligent argument. How wise of you not to rely on my affection or humanity."

"Don't be silly. You're careful not to show anyone those qualities. I think you might have felt some affection for my mother, but I've never been sure."

"But you're sure you might find me useful? And how am I to help you?"

She drew a deep breath. She had not been certain she would get this far with him. "The most important thing is to keep my family safe."

He chuckled. "Really? I believe we've discussed the problems I have dealing with Joe Quinn and Eve. I hardly think they'll willingly put themselves in my hands for safekeeping."

"I don't care. Just do it. You're very smart. There aren't many things you wouldn't be able to do if you put your mind to it."

"That's accurate, but it depends on whether I think it's worth my while. And I'm curious to see what else you have planned for me."

She took a deep breath. "You have to find Svardak for me. He was hurt. He'd have to have a doctor. And you have contacts. You can find out where he's hiding."

"Or where he's making plans to launch his next attack on you," he said softly. "That's far more likely with a man as crazy as Svardak."

"You're right. Far more likely." She braced herself. "Will you help me?"

"I'm considering it." His gaze was probing her face. "You're not going to want me to discuss any of this with Quinn or Eve, are you? You want to go after him on your own."

She nodded. "They'd take it out of my hands. They'd want to protect me. I'd have to go away to do it, and that would hurt them." She leaned toward him, every muscle in her body burning with intensity. "You're the only one who would accept my doing what I need to do. It would make sense to you. You'll want it to be me."

"Will I?" He gazed thoughtfully at her. "Because you intend to finish what I failed to do all those years ago? I admit there does appear to be an intrinsic blood justice connected with you killing Svardak. However, it really doesn't appeal to me. I would much rather kill him myself. I found myself very annoyed when I was watching him with you."

"But don't you see? He'll go after me." Her words came fast and hard, tripping over each other. She had to convince him. "You're still paramount on his list, but when I stabbed him, it became personal. I put everything about my time with him on a personal level. I was like a constant thorn jabbing at him. He's crazy, and he can't handle that kind of treatment without responding."

"Did it occur to you that you didn't show the greatest judgment yourself to taunt a madman?"

"It occurred to me, but I couldn't let him win." Her gaze was eagerly searching his expression. "And you also understand that, don't you? You're going to do as I ask."

"Perhaps. We'll take it step by step. I'll see to it that your family is protected. I'll search for Svardak, but I would have done that anyway." He tilted his head. "Whether I give you information that might bring you and Svardak together again will be determined at a later date."

"You'll do it. Svardak beat you. It was a terrible defeat in your eyes. It brought back memories of that day at the *Gulag*. You'll do anything you can to erase that defeat." She tapped her chest. "And that's me. You'll have to use me to get to him."

"I don't appreciate being thought predictable, Cara."

"You're not predictable. You intimidate me, and you sometimes frighten me. But I have to try to understand you because this is important to me." She lay back down on the pillow, drained. "And there are two other things that I'm going to ask you to do. They're also very important to me."

His lips turned up at one corner. "By all means, don't hesitate to state your demands. I find I'm becoming accustomed to it."

"Not a demand. A request. Marian Napier's body is probably buried somewhere in that canyon. I don't know where. Svardak told me he'd thrown her down there, but he wanted to shock and frighten me. He wouldn't just leave her body out in the open for anyone to find. I think he buried her. Maybe one of Svardak's men might be able to tell you." She was having trouble keeping her voice steady. "I'd like you to find her and send her home to her grandfather to bury. Will you do that?"

He was silent. Then he said quietly, "That doesn't seem to be an unreasonable request."

"Thank you." She cleared her throat. "I believe she'd like to go home. That canyon was . . . lonely."

"And the other request?"

"Don't tell Jock Gavin what I've asked you to do for me."

He chuckled with genuine amusement. "Why on earth would I do that? Regardless of my final decision, it would be the quickest way to sign my death warrant." He turned to leave. "I'll leave Gavin entirely for you to handle. You seemed to have developed a variety of new attitudes and skills while you were at Lost Canyon. Perhaps that will help you with Gavin."

She watched the door close behind him.

Kaskov was wrong. Everything she had learned at that cabin in the thicket had merely complicated her relationship with Jock. The best she could do until this nightmare was over was to keep him away from Svardak.

And she might be able to accomplish that if Kaskov cooperated with her. There was never any way of being certain what he would do in any given circumstance, but she might have guessed right about him.

If she hadn't, then there was still the chance that she could manage this alone. She just had to know what to expect. Because she had told Kaskov the truth.

Svardak would be coming after her.

All she had to do was wait.

CHAPTER

8

He had started to bleed again, Svardak realized furiously as he got out of the Jeep and made his way toward the three-story, A-framed cabin/office several hundred yards away. He'd managed to stop the bleeding after he'd first gotten away from the canyon, but now it was starting again. Was he dizzy? Maybe a little. If he didn't get this knife wound stitched and take an antibiotic, that bitch, Cara, might claim she'd done him serious damage.

But he couldn't take a chance on going to even an urgent-care hospital. Too many questions. He didn't know enough about what had happened when those explosives had gone off on the mountain. Not yet. Joe Quinn? Kaskov? He'd know soon. Any of his men who had gotten away would contact him and be begging for money and a way to escape. In the meantime, he had to protect himself, so he'd driven north, deep into the Appalachians, to recoup and hide and get this damn wound taken care of so that he could function.

"May I help you, sir?" A sandy-haired man in a brown uniform who looked as if he was barely out of college was coming out of the cabin. "Have you had an accident?" His concerned gaze was on the blood on Svardak's shirt. He hurried down the steps. "Let me help."

"Thank you." Svardak leaned against him as he slowly went up the steps. "Quite a place you have here. I thought I was seeing things when I saw that third story that looks like a tree house."

"My partner and I get bored in the winter. It's a work in progress. Maybe next year we'll finish it. Anything to keep busy." He was frowning as he gazed at the wound. "Have you lost much blood?"

"I don't believe I have. It was stupid of me." He looked at the ranger's ID tag. "Ranger Billings. I only ran into a sharp branch. For it to hurt this bad, you'd think I could at least have been attacked by a bear. Do you have a first-aid station here?"

"Yes, but I'd rather run you into you into Charleston to a hospital unless it's an emergency." He grinned. "Since we don't have a doctor on the premises, I wouldn't want you to sue me. All I've had is a six month course in basic first aid."

"That might do. Anyone else here?"

"Just my partner, Bob Duggan, but he's out checking on a possible fire hazard today. He won't be back for the rest of the morning. Besides, he has the same training as I do. I'll take a look at your wound, but we'll almost certainly be driving you to Charleston." He opened the door with the red cross imprinted on it. "No broken bones? Anything else I should know about it?"

Not a perfect situation, but it would have to do, Svardak thought. One young punk kid on the premises who could be easily controlled and then disposed of.

And by the time the other ranger returned, Svardak would be ready and waiting for him.

"What else should you know about my wound?"

Svardak repeated. "Well, there may be glass in it. You might have to take bits of it out before you stitch it."

"Glass? From a tree branch?" He was frowning. "And I won't be stitching it. I told you that we'd have to go—" He broke off, stiffening, his gaze on the switchblade knife that had appeared in Svardak's hand. "There's no need for this, sir," he said quietly. "I only want to help you."

"There's every need." He pressed the blade into the center of the ranger's back. "And I'll explain the glass and the bitch who stabbed me while you do help me." He added mockingly, "It's important you realize who's responsible for what's going to happen to you, Ranger Billings."

BLUE RIDGE GENERAL HOSPITAL

"The head nurse says you've been causing massive waves about getting out of here," Eve said as she came into Cara's room. "The doctor just released you an hour ago. Give me a break, Cara. Do you know how long it takes someone to be sprung out of a hospital?"

Cara smiled. "Sorry. I wanted *out*. And they weren't massive waves. Hardly a ripple. Actually, I was thinking of turning Kaskov loose on administration. But I was afraid they'd throw me out in the street." She tilted her head. "Come to think of it, the nurse was looking very uneasily at Nikolai while I was talking to her. Maybe he supplied her with the definition of 'massive.'" She got to her feet and picked up the canvas duffel containing the phone, clothes, and vanity items Eve had brought to the hospital for her. "Ready to go. So I'm officially sprung? Can we leave now?"

"After you tell me why you wanted to talk to Kaskov," Eve said. "Joe didn't like it." She paused. "Neither did I."

Cara met her eyes. "I told him that what he'd done was wrong and that he had to protect my family from Svardak. He said you'd argue. Don't argue, Eve. Look at it this way—if you're safe, then I have a better chance of being safe. The family is the only weapon he has as far as I'm concerned."

"We can take care of ourselves." She frowned. "We don't need your damn grandfather."

"He'll have his people be unobtrusive. Think of Michael. Think of Joe. Just don't fight it. Please." She moistened her lips. "I didn't tell you, but he kept mentioning Joe while I was with him. He said he'd made special plans to keep Joe from taking me back. He seemed to think of Joe as a challenge."

Eve's eyes widened in shock. "Joe *is* a challenge. That's why he doesn't have to have a major criminal like Kaskov babysit him."

"But it scared you when I told you that just now," she said soberly. "It scared me, too. But I knew Joe would ignore it. So let him ignore it. But just do me a favor and let me do what I can to keep from worrying about you all."

"And then have you owe Kaskov again?" Eve's lips tightened. "No way."

"It won't be like that this time. I promise you."

Eve hesitated, then slowly nodded. "Okay. I guess you've gone through enough trauma. Do what you like as long as it doesn't cost you." She gave her a quick hug. "Now let's get out of here. I want to pick up Michael at Catherine's and be home by midnight."

Cara had known this confrontation was coming. "You go ahead. I'd rather stay at a hotel here in town until Svardak is caught."

"No deal," Eve said flatly. "Joe and I both want you out of this area. It's not safe for you. We're going back to the lake cottage, and Joe is going to arrange with the precinct to give you protection."

"Svardak could find me anywhere." She turned and was heading for the door. "You know Joe won't be leaving these mountains until he's sure that Svardak is no longer here. He's out there looking for him now, isn't he?"

"Of course, he's a cop, and Svardak is a mass murderer. Not to mention what he did to you. Joe's contacting all the county sheriff's departments for help with the locals. And he's trying to track down some more of that bastard's goons to squeeze them for information."

Cara grimaced. "And you're trying to tell yourself that he'll be fine, and you're not at all nervous."

"It's his job," Eve said. "And it's my job to accept that sometimes it does scare me. At least you're safe now, and that makes Joe safer."

"Well, it's not *my* job," Cara said quietly. "I'll check into that Holiday Inn where you said you stayed the first night. I'll move on when Joe moves on." She looked over her shoulder and smiled faintly. "Don't worry, I'm not going to be trekking along after him. That would draw Svardak's attention to Joe. But I have to be close to him."

"The hell you do."

"Yes, the hell I do," she said quietly. "All the years he took care of me, and now I have a chance to try to take care of him. You know how much I owe him, Eve. How much I owe both of you."

"You've always had that idiocy about owing us," Eve said shakily. "It's crazy."

"It's right. And you're not going to talk me out of this. So you go home and take care of Michael and let me keep an eye on Joe. No one is safe from Svardak, and who is more vulnerable than a child? You know Joe would say the same thing." She opened the door and looked back at her. She made one more attempt to convince her. "Stop worrying, Eve. Look, there's no current sign of any threat to Joe. Maybe I'm paranoid. There's a threat to me, but that would exist anywhere until Svardak is caught. Besides, Kaskov will probably have Nikolai watching me. Even Svardak would have trouble getting past Nikolai." She was closing the door. "Call me when you and Michael get home. Okay?"

She didn't wait for an answer as the door clicked shut behind her.

She drew a deep breath and started swiftly down the corridor toward the elevators. She didn't know if she'd pulled it off or not. Eve's first instinct would be to either yank Cara back to the lake cottage or stay with her here. But Michael's safety was a powerful magnet and always Eve's and Joe's paramount concern.

She would just have to see if she'd made a good enough case to persuade Eve to get in that car and head back to Catherine's to pick up her son.

HOLIDAY INN
7:40 P.M.

Cara stepped out of the shower, dried off, and slipped on the white terry-cloth robe Eve had stuffed in the duffel she'd given her.

She looked like a drowned rat, she thought ruefully as she gazed in the vanity mirror. Bruised, thinner than she remembered, far too fragile, with that sopping-wet hair hanging around her face and down her back. At least she was flushed from the shower. Maybe she wouldn't appear like such a damn victim once she got rid of that drowned-waif look.

Okay. Stop putting it off. She drew a deep breath and braced herself. Then she took the portable hair dryer from her makeup bag. She was being stupid. It was a tool. Nothing to dread about using it.

She forced herself to raise the hair dryer.

Only a tool.

Her cell phone on the nightstand in the bedroom was ringing.

Cara stiffened. Coincidence. Stupid to be so jumpy. He wasn't reaching out to her. She shouldn't panic, only Eve knew she was here. But she lowered the hair dryer and found she was almost running to the nightstand to pick up her phone. "Eve?"

"No," Jock said curtly. "She's probably well on her way to pick up Michael. Where you should be."

"Hello, Jock." It wasn't really a surprise. Eve had not wanted to leave her alone. She knew Jock would be one of Eve's choices to fill the gap. "Eve phoned you? She shouldn't have bothered you. There's nothing you can do. I don't need you."

"That's obvious. Or you would have told me when you decided to leave the hospital. I'm only grateful that Eve decided to tell me that you'd opted to disappear into the depths of Coal Town instead of getting the hell out of Dodge."

"She didn't have many options. She knows I'm trying to make Kaskov help me, and she could have gone to him, but she doesn't trust him. She does trust you, Jock."

"Which is more than you do."

"I trust you." She sighed. "You're just going to be difficult."

"You're right about that. Stay where you are. Now it's my turn to tell you not to slip out the back way. I'm less than five minutes from you." He cut the connection.

She slowly put away her phone. He was angry, and he

would be more than difficult. She automatically started to brace herself for what was to come. It always hurt her when she knew all was not right between them.

Then she shook her head as she realized what she was doing. Not this time, Jock. There was too much pain in her world right now. She desperately wanted to see him, but it had to be her way. Easy to say, she thought ruefully. Not so easy to accomplish when he was already storming the gates and giving orders.

He was knocking on her door in four minutes. She threw open the door. He was just as high-impact as she'd thought he'd be. Dark jeans, black shirt with sleeves rolled up to the elbow, and that magnetism casting out sparks in every direction. She tried to smile. "Hi, stop looking so grim." She stepped aside to let him come in. "I would have let you know I'd left the hospital . . . eventually. I just didn't want to deal with you for a while." Then her eyes fell on the object he was carrying, and she inhaled sharply. "The Amati?" She grabbed the violin case from him and set it on the bed. "I was afraid to ask about it. I thought he might have taken it with him." She was unfastening the latches and throwing open the lid. "Or smashed it . . ." She gently took out the Amati and was stroking the bridge with caressing fingers. "It could have gone either way."

"I should have told you I had it." He was leaning against the door, watching her face. "I brought it down on that second trip, but when I saw you in the hospital last night, you blew my mind." His lips tightened. "And we weren't talking about music. When I was watching that Skype Svardak had with Kaskov, I wasn't certain we'd ever be talking about it again. You took a hell of a risk."

She nodded. "I had to risk everything. I couldn't hold anything back. I had to show him that no matter

what he did, I was strong enough to survive him." She
tucked the violin beneath her chin. It felt so *good*. She
closed her eyes, luxuriating in the textures, the deep
wood scent, the knowledge that the music was still out
there, still part of her. "You have no idea how strong the
evil in him is, Jock." She opened her eyes and looked at
him. "But evil can't win all the time. I believe you think
it might, that your experience with Thomas Reilly made
you think that. That's why you're so afraid for me."

"You're damn right I am," he said hoarsely. "Look
at you. You're sitting there, huddled in that terry robe,
with your hair clinging all around you, bruised and cut
and still lecturing me about worrying about you?"

"If you'd given me time to repair a little of the damage, I wouldn't look like this. I'm fine now, Jock."

"Damage?" His eyes were blazing in his taut face.
"Nothing was supposed to happen to you, but it did.
And I couldn't do anything to stop it, to help you. Do
you know what that did to me?"

She did know, and she was melting as she looked
him. She could see all the hurt and the helplessness
because she knew it would have hurt her terribly in the
same circumstances. "You came to help me. I could
have died if you hadn't been there. You shouldn't have
done it, but you came."

"Do you actually believe I could do anything else?
That wasn't enough," he said jerkily. "I saw that photo
and the Skype, and I realized what that bastard was
doing to you. He was twisting and changing you, and
I wasn't there to stop it. And now you're telling me
that you're fine and only need a little time to repair the
'damage.' Don't lie to me. I saw it, Cara. I could *feel* it."

Of course he could. Just as she would be able to feel
his pain. And she was hurting him even more by trying
to close him out and hide what Svardak had done to
her during those days. She had to stop it. "I won't lie to

you. But I can't talk very much about it because it was mostly inside. I know that will bother you, but I'll share what I can." She met his eyes. "This is hard because I don't want to show you that I'm not as strong as I want to be. But you said that you couldn't help me while I was with him. That doesn't mean that you can't do anything now." She carefully put the violin back in its case. "The memories . . . are bad, Jock. Maybe you can make some of them go away. Will you do that for me?"

"I'll do anything for you."

"Then will you come here?" Don't hold it in. Don't back away from it. She got to her feet as he came across the room. "I didn't know that it might be the little things that would bother me." She said unevenly, "It may seem foolish, but they might stay with me. I don't want them to be hanging around getting in the way. It would be like *him* being there." She pushed Jock down in the chair beside the bed and then dropped down on the floor in front of him. She reached up and took the hair dryer from the nightstand where she'd thrown it when she'd answered the phone. She handed it to him. "I don't want to be a bother, so it's all right if you say no."

His eyes were narrowed on her face. "What are you asking, Cara?"

"I told you, it's . . . pretty silly." She settled back down on the floor between his legs with her back to him. "I was having trouble . . . drying my hair before you came today. Svardak insisted on using Marian Napier's hair dryer on my hair at the cabin, and he kept talking about her while he was doing it. It made me sick. I . . . liked her. I felt as if I knew her, Jock. It hurt me. The memory still hurts me." She looked over her shoulder at him, and whispered, "All the years we've been together, all I've had to do was come to you, and you'd make everything that was bad good again. Can you make this go away, too?"

He went still. Then his hand reached out and touched her cheek with the most incredible tenderness.

"Aye," he said thickly. "I'll make certain you won't remember him." His eyes were glittering as he looked down at her. "You'll only remember what you choose to remember." He turned the dryer on low so it was like the purr of a cat. "Or what I choose for you to remember. Will that be all right?"

"I think so." She leaned her head back on his knee. "I know you'd never make me remember anything that would make me unhappy."

"I've been fighting to avoid that for years. You wouldn't listen." His fingers were winding themselves in her thick black hair, separating it to reveal her nape. "This is a really beautiful part of your neck. Silky . . . vulnerable." The stream of gentle warm air was blowing on the naked skin of her nape. "I've always loved your hair, but it's a shame to cover it." His fingers were now gently massaging that skin as he pushed the strands of her hair back and forth with the rhythm of the dryer. Revealing her soft skin to the blast, then covering it, then repeating the action. Over and over and over. And always his touch, guiding, stroking. She swallowed and moistened her lips. She was finding that rhythm incredibly erotic. "Jock . . ."

"A little more heat?" He pressed another button. "Not too much, just enough to make you know it's there waiting for you."

Heat surrounded her. *He* surrounded her. His voice, his words, his scent, his essence. "It makes me feel . . ." She didn't know how it made her feel. It was like nothing she'd ever felt before. "Waiting for me?"

The heat was gone. He had turned off the dryer. "Why not?" His fingers were running through her hair now. "You're quite perfect, you know." He bent forward, and she could feel his breath on her ear. "You should have anything you want or need. I've always thought that, Cara." She felt his lips brush her earlobe. Then his tongue rimming the edge of her ear . . . She inhaled sharply and went still.

"Turn around," he said softly. The hair dryer was on again. "I have to do the front." But the tips of his fingers were still running up and down the sides of her neck with an exquisite sensual sensitivity that was breathtaking. "I'm finished back here."

She closed her eyes as sensation after sensation tingled through her from that stroking, teasing touch. "Are you? I'm not sure that I am." But she wanted to see his face while he was touching her, that face that was like a beautiful concerto . . . She got up on her knees and turned to face him. And his face was as wonderful as she'd thought it would be. His lips fuller, the shape still clean and defined yet infinitely more sensual, his eyes glittering and intense. "You might know better than I do."

"But you've always been a quick learner." He took a strand of hair at her temple and blew it gently with the dryer. "Sometimes too quick. It's been the bane of my existence. Now close your eyes again, you're distracting me."

"Why? I don't want to close my eyes. I want to see you."

"Close them." He bent forward and his lips brushed one lid and then the other. "Who's running this show?"

She reluctantly shut her eyes. "I should still have something to say about it."

"Wrong. You shouldn't speak at all." His hands were on her hair again. "You should only feel." He was shaking her long hair around her shoulders, blowing, then pulling it back entirely to bare her neck and shoulders. "The hollow of the throat is so very sensitive . . . I can see your pulse beating . . ." Then she could feel the seductive warmth of air touch the hollow of her throat. She leaned back with a cry, her neck arching. "And now it's beating faster," Jock said. "Is it the heat again? Then let's give you more . . ."

The air became warmer, harder, focused, but it was no longer on her throat. It was moving down to the curve of her breasts at the robe closure. Shock. Her nipples were swelling, tautening, pushing against the terry material.

Her pulse leaped crazily. She reached out blindly and grabbed at his knees to steady herself. "What . . . are you doing?"

"Only what I told you I'd do," he murmured. "Now keep your eyes closed . . ." He pushed the robe open. "Beautiful," he said thickly. "Do you know how beautiful you are?" He was taking the long strands of damp hair from her shoulders to drape them over her breasts and nipples. The faint coolness made her gasp, and her fingers dug into his thighs.

"Shh, it will be gone soon."

Heat that was almost hot.

Cool wetness that was pure sensual provocation.

His hands moving the strands of hair teasingly over her breasts and nipples, rubbing, waiting, then rubbing again. "Did you know that if you take one single strand from the rest, it has a kind of strength and friction that can be . . . exciting." He ran the strand back and forth over her nipple. "What do you think?"

She couldn't answer. She was biting into her lower lip to keep from screaming. The friction was mind-blowing.

"I believe you agree. Then let's continue as we've started."

Softness, sharpness, heat, dampness . . . friction.

The muscles of her stomach were clenching.

"Jock, I . . . can't stand this."

"Aye, you can. I know you. You can stand anything."
He slowly brushed the strands of hair away from her
breasts. She could feel his breath on her nipple as he
licked the swollen tip. "But I'm not sure about myself.
I'm not as strong as I thought." Then his mouth was on
her breast, sucking, biting, holding.

She made a sound deep in her throat. She couldn't
breathe. She wanted *more*. She tried to get closer to
him.

"No." He held her still. "Just this." His teeth bit down.
"Let it come, Cara. Let it come, love."

It went on and on.

His hands. His mouth. His *teeth*.

She was trying not to cry out. But after all the teasing and intimacies that had gone before, she was helpless, wild. She didn't know what she was doing. What
difference did it make? She didn't *care*.

"Jock, I'm . . . burning up."

"But you'll never remember anything but this when
you reach for that dryer, will you?" he murmured. "Or
any dryer. It's your will, your pleasure. That's the only
thing that's important."

"No, not the only thing." She threw her head back as
shudder after shudder racked her. "I'll remember you . . ."

"That's definitely allowed. Now just a little more . . ."

More? How could she take any more? Something
was happening, and she couldn't stop it.

"Jock, I don't know . . ."

"Shh. Ready? It's fine." Then Jock's hands were cup-
ping her buttocks as he pulled her up onto his lap and
into his arms. The scent of him . . . The rough denim
of his jeans against the softness of her hips and belly
against his hardness as he held her tightly to him as
he moved her back and forth so that she'd feel every
sensation.

Fire.

Hunger.

Need.

Convulsion.

Her back arched, and she grabbed his shoulders and held on to him as wave after wave poured through her. Like the heat. Like his mouth. Like the feel of him against her. "Jock!"

"You're fine. You're beautiful." And all the time he held her, rocking her, his hand tangled in her hair. Not speaking, just there for her.

It was several minutes before she could manage to lift her head to look at him. "I wasn't . . . expecting that, Jock."

"You asked me to perform a service for you." He kissed her lingeringly. "And it was my pleasure. I considered that it was up to me how I would do it. Did I succeed?"

"Oh, yes." She was still shaking from the aftermath. She laid her head back down on his shoulder. "But I don't believe anyone would consider that fair to you."

"Then they'd be wrong. It was a little like being stretched on a rack at times, but no one could say I didn't receive certain benefits." He kissed the tip of her nose. "But right now I believe that you should get off me and put that robe back on. The benefits aren't as obvious with you naked."

Naked.

She hadn't realized that the robe had somehow completely disappeared. "I'm sorry." She saw it in a heap on the floor at their feet. "I didn't notice." She slid out of his arms and picked up the garment. "I didn't mean to make you feel uncomfortable."

"You didn't notice?" He watched her slip on the robe and tie it. "Only you, Cara. It's not as if I've ever had the chance to see how beautiful you are naked. Some stupid individuals would even think that you might be uncomfortable."

"Why? I belong to you. I always feel comfortable with you. It doesn't matter if I'm naked or not." She met his eyes. "No, that's not true. If you're looking at me, then it would matter. Everything is different then. That's why I didn't want to close my eyes. I was afraid I'd miss something."

"Cara."

"And I did miss something. I missed being able to give you what I should have. I took, but didn't give." She sat down on the bed. "Before you arrived, I was thinking how difficult you were going to be, and I was right."

He smiled. "You missed quite a bit else actually. You must know that was only the start. A small gift that wouldn't hurt you."

"Then we should start over."

He shook his head ruefully. "Never satisfied."

"You know better." She looked down at her hands, her arms. "My skin feels as if it's glowing," she said wonderingly. "And my body is singing. I can hear it. Is it always like that?"

"No, only when it's someone as special as you. The rest of us mortals have to be content with lust and just a damn wonderful time."

"I'm sure that's good, too." She thought about it. "For everyone but you. You have that shining inside you. You should have everything that means." She suddenly jumped to her feet and ran back to him. "I bet you could hear it if I showed you." Her face was luminous with eagerness. "If you forgot all that nonsense you have stored up inside you about taking care of me. I knew we could be wonderful together, but now I know we can be magic." She reached out to touch him, and said softly, "I want you to be with me and hear the music. It's important, Jock."

He shook his head. "That's not going to happen." He looked down at her hand on his chest. "Someday, you'll realize I'm right. I'll guard you, I'll see that Svardak is out of your life, I'll be your friend. I won't be your lover."

She felt a ripple of shock. She'd been so full of hope that it jarred her a little. But only a little, just another battle to fight.

She took her hand away from him. "You're already my lover, Jock. Can't you feel it? And next time, I won't let you get away with anything but total commitment. I'll take you as a friend and a companion. But I'll guard myself as everyone should do." She leaned forward and kissed him. "Do we have that straight?" She turned away. "And now I have to get dressed and let you take me out to dinner. We have things to discuss." She headed for the bathroom. "But first I have to brush my hair. A dryer only does so much." She glanced over her shoulder with a sly smile. "Unless you'd like to do it?"

"Actually, I would," he said thickly. "I like the feel of your hair touching my hands. I . . . spark. But then I want my hands on you any way that I can. Which is why there's no way I'll do it."

"Unless you think it will save me from pain or hurt . . ." She shook her head. "You'll do it someday, and it will only be because it's part of what we are together. But I'd really rather do something wonderfully erotic for you. However, you might have to help me with that. Think about it, Jock."

"There's no doubt that I'll do that," he said dryly.

She smiled. "I thought you would." She started to close the door behind her. "Give me twenty minutes."

"Make it thirty." He rose to his feet and headed for the front door. "I'm going to need at least that long to cool down. Maybe longer."

"Really?" She tilted her head, her eyes gleaming with curiosity. "You have such wonderful control that I would never have guessed. That's very interesting. How close were you to—"

"Get dressed." The door slammed behind him.

"I like this place." Cara's gaze wandered around the red-leather booths and black-and-white-tile floor of the Lost Canyon Diner after the waitress had taken their order. "It looks like something from the fifties."

"Let's just hope the food is substantial," Jock said. "You look like you've lost a pound or two."

That's what she had thought, but she hadn't wanted Jock to notice. He was too protective as it was. She smiled. "It isn't as if Svardak didn't feed me. The cuisine just wasn't to my liking. The hamburger I ordered will be much better." She made a face. "And you look blade-sharp and very trim. I bet you haven't been eating much either."

"You'd lose. I always eat exactly what I need to keep me going when I'm on the hunt." He watched the waitress set their coffee in front of them. "It's part of my training, and I have been very much in Reilly mode since the moment I found out you were gone." He smiled at the waitress. "Thank you. Do you suppose you could hurry up that order? My friend here probably forgot to eat today."

"Sure." She smiled back at him, and Cara could see the slightly dazzled expression she had come to expect on any woman who came in contact with Jock. "Anything you say. I know how to take care of my customers." She disappeared in the direction of the kitchen.

"Not necessary, Jock," Cara said. "You made it sound as if I was fading away."

"Then you did eat all your meals in that hospital today?"

"I ate a little of my breakfast. I was busy later."

His lips tightened. "Arranging your escape. Then it *was* necessary, and the waitress didn't mind."

"She wouldn't have minded if you'd asked her to cook the orders herself," she said. "And if she'd thought it was *you* who was fading away, she'd have been in this booth trying to resuscitate you. She barely saw me."

His brows rose as he leaned back in the booth. "Are you including her in my 'zillions' of women?"

"No, just a hopeful candidate." She grinned at him. "Like me. But I have a much better chance than she does."

He stiffened. "No you don't." He lifted his cup to his lips. "No chance at all."

"Stop saying that. I can't believe it. It would hurt too much." She took a sip of her coffee. "Actually, I think I've made good progress. You said that from the minute you knew I was gone, you were in Reilly mode. What was your first thought in that moment when you came to pick me up at my suite?"

"What do you think? That it shouldn't have happened. I should have been able to protect you."

"And, did it occur to you that if you'd taken me to bed as I wanted you to do, that you'd have been beside me and not outside knocking on that door?"

He was silent. "Of course it did."

"And it will keep coming back because you have that protective gene going on." She frowned. "It's not something that I want to use, but I might have to go that route. The reason you came tonight was that you were afraid that I was doing something that was out of your comfort zone."

"Comfort zone? You're damn right. You should be with Eve at the lake cottage. And she knows it, or she wouldn't have called me."

"Maybe. Eve's almost as protective as you are. I wasn't certain if she was going to leave me here." She lifted her cup to her lips again. "But she's also very clever. I told her I was going to stay and keep an eye on Joe until Svardak is captured. She didn't like the idea, but she doesn't like the idea of any danger getting near Joe either." She was thinking about it. "She might not believe I'd be any real help to Joe, but she knows you would be. By sending you to me, there could be a double benefit in her eyes."

"What are you talking about?" he said impatiently. "She didn't mention Joe. Just that you were staying until Svardak was caught."

"She knew I'd tell you. She's walking a fine line and doesn't want Joe to think that she'd doubt him in any way."

"Doubt?" He was frowning. "Why the hell should she doubt Quinn? And what the hell does he have to do with you staying?"

"Svardak will try to kill anyone I love," she said quietly. "He told me he would. And he zeroed in on Joe while I was at the cabin. I asked Kaskov to guard them, but Joe will be almost impossible since he'll be putting himself in the line of fire." She met his eyes. "Just as you would, Jock. I don't have much hope of keeping him away from you now. You were too visible."

"What a pity." He leaned forward, his eyes intent. "Let me understand this. You're staying because you want to keep Svardak from killing Joe Quinn." He snapped his fingers. "Oh, and maybe me as well? Did I forget that?"

"Yes, you did. And don't make fun of me. I can be of value. As long as I keep close to Joe or to you, I'll be a constant distraction." She could tell what was coming as she looked away and put her cup back in the saucer. "Because as much as he'll want to kill you, he'll want to kill me more."

"Tremendous value," Jock said. "Why should I make fun of you? It's a masterstroke. Anyone who saw that Skype could see how much he hated you."

"It *is* a master stroke." She was still looking down at her cup. "I worked hard to make him consider me a threat and a prime enemy while I was with him. I can use that now."

"No!"

"Yes." She raised her eyes and inhaled sharply as she saw Jock's expression. "That's the way it has to be. I'm not going to run to Eve and hide at the lake. I know I can't stop you if you decide to go after Svardak. That's probably what you've been doing since you left me at the hospital. But when you do, you'll know you're leaving me here and that I'll find Joe and stay close to him . . . until Svardak finds us."

She could see the myriad violent emotions flitting across his face—anger, desperation, frustration. "And what if I go after Joe myself and watch out for him," he said through clenched teeth. "God, Joe would strangle me if he heard that. This is all crazy. But would you go to Eve then?"

"No. I won't give you up to Svardak either. I told you, he'll know you're someone important to me now."

"So you're keeping both me and Joe tied to you in hope that we'll be able to reel in Svardak when he goes after you."

"No." She had to explain it, though he wasn't going to like this either. "I wouldn't use you like that. That would defeat my purpose. It's in hope that *I'll* be able to reel him in. I tried to make that clear to you in the hospital. It seems a reasonable way to go about it."

"Son of a *bitch*." He was gazing at her in disbelief. "Reasonable?" He said flatly, "It sucks."

"It has to be me," she said quietly. "I was almost able to do it before, and I was more helpless than I've ever been in my life that day. I won't be that helpless this time. I'll see that I have weapons and a plan. It could work."

"If neither Joe nor I cared if you're going to come out of this alive," he said savagely. "We do care. *I care*."

"I know." Her lips were trembling as she tried to smile. "I find that special and wonderful. But that's what this is all about, taking care of the people I love." She swallowed. "And making certain that I give Marian and those other victims their own tribute."

"No, for me it's about keeping you alive." He was clearly fighting for control. "And finding a way to get around this idiocy."

"You're upset. Why don't you cancel dinner and just take me back to the hotel?"

"Because I can't be sure what you're going to do at any given minute right now. I have to work through this. That means you have to work through it with me." He drew a deep breath, then said, "We are going to have dinner, and you are going to eat well. We'll have another cup of coffee, then I'll take you back to the hotel."

She nodded. "And all the time your mind will be clicking and you'll be figuring out how to get your own way." She added quietly, "I can't let you do it this time, Jock."

"You don't know that. It might turn out to be your way, too. Stay and have dinner with me, and we'll talk about it."

He'd tamped down the anger and that charisma was back in full force. He was smiling that smile that she could never resist, and this was no exception.

"Why not?" She smiled back at him. "I always enjoy being with you regardless of whether or not you're plotting anything that might worry me. I just had to warn you."

"Duly noted." He hesitated, gazing at her face, then he reached out and covered her hand with his own. It felt warm and strong, and she found herself clinging to it. "And, as usual, you managed to disarm me just when I was ready to go on the attack. I'll try to keep my plotting to a minimum. But I can't deny it will be happening. You're not helping me keep this ship on an even keel." He released her hand and took out his phone. "But you'll excuse me if I have to initiate the first phase of the plotting. I have to call your hotel and make a reservation. I checked while you were getting dressed, and there weren't any connecting rooms available, but I'll be able to get the room next door to you. I'll have to rely on you to lock your door and keep me on speed dial. I should have booked it then, but I was hoping you'd be reasonable."

"And that you could persuade me to pack up and follow Eve. We both realize how persuasive you can be."

"Evidently not persuasive enough."

"It depends." She smiled. "You'd have absolutely no trouble persuading me to share my room with you."

He shook his head. "And that could result in a great deal of trouble." Then the hotel answered, and he was talking to reservations.

She sat there and listened to him, watching his expressions. He was going to fight her, and she had to accept whatever that meant. She couldn't expect anything else from him. She hadn't wanted him to be a part of this nightmare, but now there was no choice. At least they'd be together for a little while longer. Life was too short not to reach out for every bit of happiness that came your way. The only thing she could do was to enjoy the moment and try to keep him safe.

And to do it, she might have to do a little plotting herself before this was over.

CHAPTER

9

Somebody's following us, Mom." Michael was looking over his shoulder out the back window of the Toyota. "It's the blue Subaru that stopped at that same gas station we did outside Louisville."

"Maybe. There are a lot of Subarus on the road these days." She looked up at the driver's mirror. It *was* the same Subaru, and it was too damn close. "Probably because of all their mushy TV commercials about love and families and such."

"You like those commercials," Michael said absently, his gaze still on the Subaru. "But it's the same car. Two people in the front seat, and the passenger is a man wearing a Jets baseball cap. I noticed the last time it slowed for that traffic light."

And Michael always noticed entirely too much, she thought. "It's the South, and people travel from Louisville to Atlanta all the time." But he was still looking at her, and she couldn't leave it at that. "Are you worried about it?"

"Only if you're worried about it," Michael said soberly. "I just thought I'd tell you. Dad told me to take care of you."

"And you're doing a fabulous job. Eyes like a hawk." She looked at the rearview mirror. "No, I'm not worried. They *are* following us. They've been following me since I left Coal Town. Cara wanted us to be sure we had a safe trip, so she had her grandfather send a couple of his employees to make sure of it. I called Kaskov about fifty miles into the trip and verified who they were. They were supposed to be unobtrusive, but I guess they're trying to impress him." She paused. "You might see them again during the next week or so. Cara's been a little nervous since that terrible man took her from us. It makes her feel better to know we're safe."

"It will make Dad feel better, too."

"Yes, it will. Though I haven't had a chance to tell him about it since we got on the road. There isn't decent cell reception in those mountains. I got through a couple times, but then I lost him. I'll try again once we get closer to the cottage." She glanced at him. He'd been far too quiet since she'd picked him up at Catherine's a few hours ago. "I'll let you talk to him again as soon as I reach him. It's not that he doesn't want to talk to you. He's just very busy. We got Cara back, but we have to make sure that man doesn't try to hurt anyone else. Your dad will do that, it just takes time."

"I know he'll call as soon as he can," Michael said. "It's just that he's getting so close to . . ." He was staring out the window. "I was hoping Cara would come with you. She could be wrong. I don't know if she can help him."

Her hands clenched on the steering wheel. "What are you talking about?"

"He's a very bad man." His gaze shifted to her face. "He hurt Cara. We're going to have to stop him before he hurts Dad."

"It's your dad who's hunting Svardak. He'll be fine,

Michael." She hoped desperately she was telling the truth. "And I'll let you talk to him as soon as I reach him. It will be another couple hours before we get home." She tossed the lap robe to him from the back of the seat. "Why don't you cuddle down and try to nap for a while? I promise it's going to be all right."

He gazed at her a moment, then he took the lap robe and leaned back against the headrest. "I didn't mean to scare you." He closed his eyes. "I forget sometimes. I know your way is best . . . But it's the truth, Mom. He's too close. We'll have to stop it . . ."

She didn't answer.

He *had* scared her.

She was hundreds of miles from Joe, and Michael's words had made her feel alone and helpless. She had wanted to turn the car around and race back to West Virginia.

Keep calm.

She had always known that Michael was special, but she had deliberately not probed below the surface. She wanted him to grow up happy and as normal as possible. But she couldn't ignore those words he'd spoken tonight because the threat had been to Joe.

She pressed her quick dial for Joe.

No connection.

She drew a deep breath. That lousy cell reception again.

Give it another fifteen minutes.

No connection.

It was almost an hour before she got through.

And Joe answered in two rings.

"At last," she said, relieved. "I've been trying to reach you all day. Where are you?"

"Somewhere near Wheeling, I think. I'm moving north. I stopped at the local police department and asked questions. No real answers about Svardak. But there was a carjacking and killing of a farmer in the area earlier today. A handyman was also shot, but he might live. He said that it was done by two men in their thirties who left their Chevy when it ran out of gas and took the farmer's truck. They were heading north, farther into the Appalachians."

"You think that they were connected to Svardak?"

"I think it's likely it might be two of the men who managed to get away from us at Lost Canyon. I told you that there were a number that we lost after the explosion. I ran the fingerprints the police took from their car and sent it to Interpol high priority. I should be getting an ID anytime now."

"They might not be going to join Svardak."

"They're rats fleeing a sinking ship, and Svardak represents a very lucrative lifeboat. If he called them, they'd probably be there for him. And they're careless, they've already given me a track to follow. It's my only lead, but I have a hunch it's a good one. I'm getting close, Eve."

He's too close. She felt a chill as she remembered Michael's words before he'd drifted off to sleep.

"How are you?" Joe asked. "Are you and Cara on the road yet?"

"I'm almost home." She paused. "Cara didn't come with me. She's still at the Holiday Inn. She didn't want to leave until you could come with her. She thinks Svardak will zero in on you." She could hear him swearing. "I agree. But I couldn't budge her. She said Kaskov would keep an eye on her."

"And you accepted that?"

"I told you, she thought Svardak would go after her family. She used the Michael card on me." She paused. "That's why I've been trying to reach you. You might be the only one who can convince her to get out of there. I think she'll come home if you come with her."

"I *have* to find Svardak."

"I know." Don't push. Though it was getting harder every minute. "It's your decision. I thought you should know."

He was silent. "If I don't get him now, he might slip away."

"Your decision."

"I'll call her and see if I can persuade her." He had a thought. "Jock. Did you call Jock?"

"Naturally. He dropped everything and said he'd take care of it. But it might not do any good. She's . . . changed. I think it has to be you."

"I'll call Jock, too. And I was planning on calling the precinct and arranging protection for the lake cottage. That will have to stay in place regardless of what Cara does."

"Don't bother. Cara took charge of that. Anyone they'd send would be stumbling over Kaskov's men. Now she's only worried about you." Don't ask him to come home. Don't tell him to get the hell away from those mountains and come back to her. "We're fine. I'll take care of everything here. You take care of yourself. Let me know what you decide after you talk to Cara."

"You know I'll call her right away."

"Not right this minute. I promised I'd let Michael talk to you when I finally got a connection. Heaven knows when I'll get through again. I love you. Be safe." She gently shook Michael, and he was instantly awake. Had he even been asleep? "Your dad," she whispered as she pressed the speaker on the dashboard. "He's okay. No problem."

"Hi, Dad." Michael sat up straighter in his seat. "Mom is fine. I'm watching out for her. I had a great time at Catherine's, but I'm glad I'm going home. When are you coming?"

"Not right away. I have a few things to do here first.

So you'll have to take care of your mom a little longer."
He paused. "And take care of yourself, too. That's important to me. I know you're doing a good job. I promise things will get back to normal soon."

"I think they will, too. But things change, don't
they? I heard Mom say Cara had changed. Maybe normal won't be the same."

Joe was silent. "Maybe it won't. But then it would be
up to us to make it even better than before. I believe we
could think of ways to do that if we tried hard enough,
don't you?"

"Sure. We can do anything. It's just easier to do it if
we're together. Come home soon, okay?"

"Absolutely."

"And Dad . . ." Michael hesitated. "Are there any
churches up there in the mountains?"

"There are churches everywhere. One in almost every town. When people are near all this natural beauty,
they tend to want to express their appreciation. Why?"

"Churches have crosses. I can't think of anywhere
else that has crosses."

"So?"

"Nothing. I just don't like you being near any
crosses. It . . . bothers me."

Joe chuckled. "Weird. Then I'll be sure to skip any
church services while I'm up here in the mountains.
I wouldn't have the time anyway. Bye, Michael. Love
you." He cut the connection.

"Churches?" Eve asked.

"Maybe not a church," Michael said as he covered
up with the lap robe again. "It could be . . . something
else. I'll think about it."

"Why would it bother you anyway?"

"It just does." He closed his eyes. "I don't know why.
But now maybe he'll think about me when he sees it,
and that might help. It could be enough . . ."

His words were frustrating, but she wasn't going to interrogate him when that vagueness was obviously sincere. "Or maybe it won't matter if your dad leaves there right away and brings Cara home to us."

"No, it wouldn't matter then."

But Eve knew the odds were against that happening, and she had an idea that somehow Michael did, too.

"No," Cara said precisely. **"I hear you, Joe, but I'm** staying here until Svardak is caught and we can go home together. No arguments."

"Bullshit. Of course, I'll give you an argument. There's no reason for you to be here. I told you that I have a firm lead, and I'll be able to wrap this up in no time."

"Good. Then that means we'll be able to go home all the sooner . . . together. Did Interpol come through with those names yet?"

"Yes," he said curtly. "Liam Lacher, Liverpool, and Simon Abrams, Toronto. Both with very nasty records for the last decade or so. No obvious proof they worked for Svardak, but then Svardak had only minor offenses before he was put in that mental hospital. And he kept his record pristine clean after he escaped and started gathering a crew around him. But Lacher's and Abram's travel documents show that they were in the same cities as the victims when the killings took place. The connection to Svardak seems clear."

"Abrams . . ." There was something familiar about the name. She'd heard it before. Then she remembered where. "He was one of the sentries guarding the cabin. I didn't see his face, it was cold, and he always had his hood pulled up. But it was when I was tied to that pine tree on the first night and Svardak said that it wouldn't do me any good to call out to Abrams. That no one could help me . . ."

"Charming," Joe said harshly. "With memories like that, why aren't you running like hell to find a cave to crawl into?"

"Because I do have memories like that," she said quietly. "And maybe they can help. They did this time, didn't they? I was able to verify Abrams as one of his men."

"Yes, but that's as far as I'd want you to go. Go home, Cara."

"When you're ready to go with me. You and Eve saved my life and gave me that home. I'll wait for you."

"Cara."

"No, Joe," she said gently. "Search for Svardak, try to find him. But don't expect me not to be here if you need me."

"I'm not going to let this go."

"I know you won't. You'll probably call Jock and ask him to bully me. You'll call me again, and you may even sic Eve on me. But I won't leave you. You wouldn't leave me."

"Sure I would. I don't want you here." He added deliberately, "You'll get in my way."

She knew he had only said those blunt words as a last resort. "Maybe. Or maybe I'll find another way to help. Good night, Joe."

"It's *not* a good night. I'll get back to you." He cut the connection.

She set her phone on the nightstand and settled back on her pillows. She felt overpoweringly sad at having to refuse him. Joe was as close to a father as she had ever had. Father and wonderful friend and the self-appointed guardian of their family.

But Svardak had taught her that sometimes roles had

to be reversed. She couldn't always be the child running to Joe to save her. If you cared about someone, you had to take responsibility for them. If sacrifices had to be made, you didn't question them.

And sacrifices might have to be made. She had been careful not to mention that possibility to Joe, Eve, or Jock. But it had been in her mind since she had opened her eyes in that hospital. Svardak had to be destroyed before any of them would be safe. She wanted desperately to live, but not at the cost Svardak might demand. Some prices were too high to pay. Marian Napier had taught her that truth.

Don't think about it now. It might not happen. Address the present problems, not future ones. Start plans in motion. She reached for her phone again.

"Complaints?" Kaskov said when he answered her call. "What do you want now? I assure you that I put my best men on protecting Eve and the child. I contacted an associate in London, and Jane MacGuire will be absolutely safe. I haven't been able to find Joe Quinn yet, but as soon as I do, I'll have him—"

"He's somewhere near Wheeling, West Virginia," she interrupted. "Moving north. He's on the track of Liam Lacher and Simon Abrams, who evidently escaped the explosions on the mountain. They killed a farmer and took his truck and were seen heading into the Appalachians." She paused. "Possibly to meet with Svardak. I need you to send someone up there to find them and help Joe if he needs it."

"Help Joe Quinn who's an ex-SEAL and probably could mop up anyone I sent after him?" Kaskov asked mockingly. "Not an intelligent distribution of my resources."

"I don't care about your resources. I want Joe safe. He *has* to be safe. There's a small chance that he'll come back here and try to get me to go to Eve before he goes after Svardak. But it's too small to count on. He'll probably talk Jock into standing temporary guard over me while he goes after Svardak. That means that the odds will be three against one even if Svardak isn't able to gather anyone else. Get him help, Kaskov."

"Orders, Cara?" He thought about it. "But you're probably right. From my reports, Jock is already hovering over you, and Quinn will probably guess that's happening."

"Your reports? Oh, I forgot for a moment how important it is to you that Svardak not get the best of you again. Of course, you're keeping an eye on me. I even told Eve that you would."

"Very wise. I'm sure it added enormous points to your arguments for her to leave you."

"Not particularly. She doesn't trust you. But I had to take what I could get."

Silence. Then he chuckled. "Always honest. But you were far more polite before. It's interesting how you've changed."

"I don't mean to be impolite," she said wearily. "I've always thought good manners were important, like the opening movement of a concerto. They prepare the way for what comes next. It's just that there doesn't seem time right now. And I believe that everything between us has to be very clear. It never really was before."

"No, it wasn't." He paused. "Not unusual when one realizes that you could never trust your mother, and I was only a stranger standing on the outside who used your talent to amuse me."

"But it didn't really matter. I didn't matter. You were there when Eve needed you. And Michael lived. Jock never realized that was all that was important."

"I wonder why," he said mockingly. "When it appears to be crystal clear to you. Anyone should be able to see where his priorities lie. But perhaps Jock doesn't wish to see too deeply in this situation. What do you think?"

There was something in his tone. "What do you mean?"

"What could I mean? When we're being so honest and clear with each other." His voice lowered silkily. "I take it that Svardak hasn't called you yet?"

She inhaled sharply. "Why would he do that? There's no reason. My family is safe. He could threaten, but he couldn't follow through."

"Yet you've been expecting it. You have a relationship with him. You believe he'll go after you no matter what the circumstances. I was wondering if you'd be tempted to assure the safety of your family by striking first. I would."

"But I'm not you."

"No, you're not. But you took a step closer when Svardak raised his serpent's head. I found it interesting, but for some reason, it disturbed me."

"It didn't disturb me. I'm not like you or my mother or any of my family. Jock told me once that I have my own soul and my own choices. I wouldn't choose your way."

"But I believe your choices might disturb Jock even more than the possibilities that I found interesting. I always suspected you might prove to be an idealist." His tone turned hard. "Idealists have the stupid habit of falling on their swords. I find the idea unacceptable. It would rob me of something I value." He paused. "I'll send men to make certain that Quinn is safe, but you'll not play Svardak's games. Do you understand?"

"I understand. Thank you. Send Joe help, and perhaps there won't be any games to play."

"You don't believe that."

No, she didn't. Svardak would never give up until he killed her. She had realized on that last day that nothing else would satisfy him. "I want to live. I'd like to believe it. Please let me know when your men make contact with Joe." She pressed the disconnect.

This seemed the night for her to hang up on brilliant, forceful men who wanted to dominate her, she thought bitterly. Even Kaskov had been giving her problems toward the end of the conversation. Amazing.

She didn't bother to set the phone back on the nightstand. Jock would probably be calling her soon to reinforce the wisdom of Joe's admonishment to go home.

Another forceful man wanting his own way.

No, another unique, wonderful man wanting to save her from Svardak.

She stared into the darkness. Svardak was out there somewhere, a beast filled with hate, waiting for his chance to attack again. She could almost feel that vicious malice she had grown to know so well.

But there's so much goodness in the world, so many wonderful people. *No one will let you survive for long. We're waiting for you, too.*

But right now all she could feel was that hate reaching out to her in the darkness.

LAKE KEDROW RANGER STATION
WEST VIRGINIA

"More coffee?" Svardak asked Abrams. "I believe there might be some frozen dinners in the freezer if you're hungry. Evidently those rangers didn't like driving all that distance to town for groceries."

"Maybe later," Abrams said. "We picked up some burgers in Wheeling."

Both Abrams and Lacher were acting distinctly wary, Svardak thought as he poured himself a cup of coffee. He didn't blame them. When Lacher and Abrams had driven up to the ranger station an hour ago, he had forced himself to be almost cordial. It probably wouldn't last long. He was already losing patience. He'd thought that it might be expedient since he was wounded, short of men, and needed them, but they were not and never would be his equal. Abrams was barely tolerable. Lacher was shallow and stupid. "Suit yourself. I just wanted to offer you something after your long trip."

"Maybe we should leave this place," Lacher said awkwardly. "One day's drive, and we could be over the Canadian border. It's not safe here."

"Is that your opinion?" Svardak asked. "How kind of you to share it with me. But I make the decisions, Lacher. Your job is only to listen and do what I say. Understood?"

"Of course." Lacher immediately backed down. "But you didn't see what we went through on that mountain. I didn't want anything to happen to you. It seems smarter to lay low for a while, then come back and hit them later."

"Smarter? Thank God I don't pay you to have even a modicum of intelligence." He turned to Abrams, who'd had the sense to keep silent. "What's safer than hiding out here in the middle of this wilderness with the United States National Forest Service as a cover? Canada? I won't let Kaskov and that bitch think they've got me on the run." The mere idea was making his temper rise. "I'll go after them as soon as I can. How many of my men can I still count on?"

"Seven. Maybe eight," Abrams said. "They'll contact me, and I'll arrange to bring them here. I was able to contact Laidlow after we got away from Coal Town. He was with two others, but they didn't have a vehicle, so I don't know how quickly they can get here. He said that he hadn't been able to reach any of the camps on the cliff trail before he went on the run. He thinks they hit them first."

Svardak was swearing. "How did Kaskov's men get that close without any of you fools spotting them?"

"Kaskov's men didn't show up until later," Lacher said. "It was that Detective Joe Quinn, whose picture you gave us, who set off those explosives."

"Quinn?" Svardak stiffened. "Are you certain?"

"Hell, yes. You offered us a bonus for him if he showed up. I memorized his damn face," Lacher said. "The bastard was picking us off from the trees after the blast."

"And he was alone?"

"At first, then there was someone else with him. After Kaskov's men came, we didn't stick around to check IDs."

"The other man's name was Gavin," Abram's said. "I heard Quinn call him when he was running up the trail toward the thicket. I can ask Laidlow if he knows anything more about him."

"Do it." But Svardak was only slightly interested in anyone beside Joe Quinn. The fury was searing through him. He had been right to be wary of Cara's guardian. He didn't know how the son of a bitch had managed to pull this off, but he'd found a way to not only humiliate him but give Cara grounds to hold him up to scorn. It was totally unbearable. He could still see the triumph on her face after she'd stabbed him. That look had been more painful and infuriating than the wound itself. All the time he'd been here recovering and planning, he'd thought of little but how he could make her pay. Now that time was almost here. "Find out anything you can about him. But it's Quinn I need. It's Quinn I have to have."

"More than the woman?" Abrams asked.

Svardak was tired of pretending that these men were anything but servants. "For God's sake." He got to his feet and headed for the door. "One will lead to the other. Quinn will give us Cara Delaney. And, after I've punished her for making me go through all this hideous trouble, she will give me Kaskov. But first I need Quinn." He looked over his shoulder at them. "And Quinn will feel that he needs me. He won't like the idea that I mistreated his sweet little ward. It will hurt his pride. He'll want revenge."

"He'll come after you?" Lacher moistened his lips. "But that might be another reason for us to go to—"

"If you don't shut up, I'll tell Abrams to cut your throat, you yellow hyena," he spat. "Listen carefully, and I might let you survive. Quinn will try to hunt me down. Your job is to hunt him down. He'll expect my wound to hamper me and that I'll be on the run. But we're going to sit here and wait for him."

"Wait for him?"

"There are two rangers that I disposed of in the shed in the back. Go bury them and put on their uniforms. Then go to neighboring towns and leave signs that will lead him here. Use the truck that you stole from that farmer. Talk to the merchants and police and tell them that you'd had tips that that the truck had been seen somewhere in this lake area and ask if they knew anything about it. Point them in this general direction because that's where they'll point Quinn." His lips twisted. "You will be friendly and wholesome and smile a lot. Everyone will look at your uniform and be sure that you represent all that's clean and environmentally correct in America."

"It might not work," Abrams said slowly.

"Make it work." Svardak went out on the porch. "You really don't want to disappoint me."

HOLIDAY INN

"Wake up, Jock." Cara pounded on his door. "I want to get out of here. I've waited for you long enough."

"It's only 6 A.M." He opened the door. "And I don't believe we had an appointment." He was fully dressed, and his hair was slightly damp from the shower. "Of course, I could be mistaken."

"But you *know* me. And you knew I'd be waiting for you to call me after you talked to Joe. Why didn't you do it?"

"Would it have done any good?" His lips tightened. "I told Joe that I was done with trying to talk you into anything. I'm strictly into damage control from now on. It's hardly my fault that you expected anything else. Did you have a bad night?"

"Yes. You probably knew I would. Everything you do and say has an effect on me. I can't dismiss it. I tend to worry. Was it supposed to be punishment?"

"Perhaps. Though I wasn't aware of it. I've been a bit frustrated lately. I had a few things to do and thought I'd be better served doing them than arguing with you."

"What things?" Then she made an impatient gesture. "Never mind. Later. I have to get out of here. Are you coming with me?"

"Certainly. Damage control is impossible long-distance." He came out of the room and locked the door. "And where am I supposed to be going?"

"Just away from this hotel." She was crossing to her rental car, parked in front of the door of her room. "I was *smothering*, and I knew that if I took off on my own, you'd be tracking me down like Joe's doing to Svardak. So I thought I'd just take you with me."

"Wise decision. It saves so much time." He glanced at her violin case on the backseat of the car. "And I see you invited another old friend to come along. I'm sure the Amati is considerably more welcome than I am right now."

"Well, it doesn't cause me as much trouble." She opened the driver's door. "Though I couldn't play last night. Violin music is generally not welcome in the middle of the night in hotels. Particularly not old hotels with walls as thin as this one. I *needed* to play, and I couldn't do it."

"Obviously I'm not the only one who was feeling frustrated last night." He got into the passenger's seat. "Those other guests don't know what they missed. Where do you want to go?"

"You tell me." She backed out of the parking spot. "I don't know anything about this place. You might say I've had limited access up in that canyon. You must have explored the entire area while you searched for me. Just somewhere I won't bother anyone." She shivered. "And that's not anywhere near Lost Canyon."

"Not too difficult. Go straight down this road for a few miles and turn left on Patriots River Road until you get to the riverbank. It's fairly deserted, and no one but the birds will object to a little Tchaikovsky." He leaned back in his seat. "And, if they do, you can refer them to me." He snapped his fingers. "Oh, that's right, you'd prefer to handle all that yourself. I'll be sure and remember."

"Don't be sarcastic. I can't take it today." She paused. "I don't object to us helping each other. That's natural and right. I just don't like it to go only one way." She changed the subject. "What did Joe ask you to do last night?"

"I think you can guess. He asked me to take care of you. He said for me to give him two days, and he should be able to find Svardak. If he didn't succeed, he'd come back and take my place here so that I could have my chance at him."

"Wonderful," she said dryly. "Babysitters, incorporated. You're right, I did guess. I just didn't realize Joe had given himself the two-day limit. I suppose that's the only way he thought you might not give him too much of an argument. Joe's always been clever."

"Very," he said grimly.

"But you resented not being able to go after Svardak, particularly when you found out about Lacher and Abrams heading up there."

Jock was silent.

"And since you were chained to me here, you immediately started to make plans on how to try to find a way to capture Svardak when you got your chance. That's what you were doing instead of wasting your time talking to me."

"I didn't consider myself chained to you," he said quietly. "I never said that."

"But you thought it," she said quietly. "And chained is the right word. I know about chains, Jock. I learned a lot about them in that cabin."

"I know you did," he said hoarsely. "I saw them. I *hated* it."

"So did I. And I would never want to do that to anyone. I won't do it to you." She paused. "But you're doing it to yourself, and I can't stop you." She shrugged. "All I can do is try to be part of the process and help where I can."

"I've hurt you."

She didn't want to admit it even to herself. "No, you're being too sensitive. I know you would never intentionally do anything to make me sad or hurt me. You're just driven by the events that made you who you are. You're a hunter, and you resent being in a cage yourself." She added, "Now what were you doing after Joe hung up?"

He shrugged. "It seemed clear that Svardak was

trying to scramble and gather an effective force again. If there was a potential manhunt, he'd need more than two men to defend himself. He probably sent out an SOS to anyone who managed to escape Lost Canyon. I needed to know how many that would be and if I could possibly intercept a message from Svardak to one of them."

"To find out his location," Cara said. "But first you'd have to track them down before you could do that."

"Tracking is far easier than digging out an entrenched enemy." His lips twisted. "And you've just told me how naturally hunting comes to me these days. I've never lost the skill nor the mind-set. Which is something I've been trying to tell you for years."

But because she had been the one to say it, she could see it had hurt him. Why were they constantly hurting each other, she thought desperately. "And how will you find out how many of Svardak's men escaped that canyon and where to find them?"

"I'm already working on it. I called Nikolai and started questioning him last night. He's very efficient, and every man who was not killed but captured on that mountain would have been questioned so that Kaskov would have a complete picture of Svardak's operation." He shrugged. "It took me most of the night while Nikolai gathered information from his men." He added grimly, "And then got permission from Kaskov to tell me everything. That probably took the most time since Kaskov doesn't have to worry about you any longer and will want to go after Svardak himself."

"But Nikolai gave you the information?"

"Eventually. No doubt Kaskov was afraid I'd be bothering him directly rather than going through Nikolai if he didn't. Eight men escaped the explosions and Kaskov's attack and disappeared before they could be caught. Kaskov also has another prisoner, Ron Edding, who I handed over to him. But he hasn't started questioning him yet."

"He wouldn't be able to tell him anything," Cara said. "Svardak is a loner. I think he chose Abrams to head his team, but that was as far as he'd go. He'd use the men who worked for him, but he'd never confide in them."

"You can never tell when someone will prove a gem of knowledge . . . if encouraged. At any rate, I know more now than when I hung up from talking to Joe last night." He gestured to the road. "Turn here. Then go a mile and turn at the next curve."

She did as he instructed. She could see the gleam of green-blue water through the trees. "No houses. It's pretty remote."

"Not as remote as you might think. Kaskov's rental estate is about ten miles down this road." He raised a brow. "But I assume you don't want to go for a visit? Though he probably does have a music room, and he wouldn't throw you out."

"No, thank you," she said dryly. "I'm in no mood to perform, and we weren't on the best of terms the last time I talked to him. We had a disagreement."

"I won't ask what about. I can make a guess. You appear to be having disagreements with all of us these days." He pointed to a willow tree by the river's edge. "That's a pretty place, and no one will argue with you for at least the next few hours. After that, I make no promises."

"It takes two to make an argument." She parked off the road some distance from the willow tree. "And I refuse to argue with you, Jock. The sun is shining, you've brought me to a beautiful place, and I refuse to let you spoil it." She jumped out of the car and grabbed her violin case. "So you just sit there and plot and plan like Machiavelli and ignore me." She darted him a challenging glance as she took the violin out of the case and strode away from him down toward the river. "If you can manage to do it . . ."

"Machiavelli? I'm sure he never had anyone like you with whom to contend. And I've never been able to ignore you. It's a mental and physical impossibility to—"

She was no longer listening.

Tchaikovsky. She attacked it with her entire heart and soul.

The music . . .

The melody . . .

I'm here.

Listen to me.

Share with me.

Grieg.

Crystal lakes. Reflections of beauty. Wind moving through the trees.

Heartbreaking.

Enchanting.

Mendelssohn.

Heavier.

Complicated.

Innovative.

I told you I wasn't as good at this as you, Marian. I can't make it sing . . .

But it shouldn't sing, she realized suddenly. Why hadn't she understood that before? It was so clear to her now. It should travel from movement to movement, not standing out, but letting the artist become one with the melody. Is that what you tried to do, Marian?

Help me make it come alive . . .

Mozart.

Swagger and elegance.

Teasing the cadence.

Tchaikovsky.

She had to have more of the Tchaikovsky.

The sheer lyrical excitement, make the canzonetta warm and sensuous to balance it. That was the way it should happen. It had been out there, just waiting for her to see it.

It was all new and fresh and different. She had thought she knew the music, but she'd known nothing. It was teaching her as she went along.

Explore.

Experiment.

Break every rule.

Throw open every gate.

Dear God. The music . . .

CHAPTER

10

I'll be damned," **Kaskov murmured to Jock, his** gaze on Cara playing beneath the willow tree some distance away. "What the hell is going on here?"

"You took your time." Jock was sitting beneath an oak tree near the road and didn't shift his position as he watched Kaskov walk toward him. "I was losing faith in Nikolai's sentries. We showed up here on your doorstep over four hours ago."

"Nikolai was told five minutes after Cara parked her car here," Kaskov said absently, his gaze never leaving Cara. "But since you were with her, I told them to adopt a wait-and-see policy until we saw what you were up to."

"But then curiosity finally got the better of you. I thought it would." His eyes went back to Cara. "Though I had no idea that this would happen. She said she wanted to play and to find her a place to do it. Some of Svardak's men are still on the loose. She had to be safe."

"So you brought her to me? That's a first."

He shrugged. "I knew you'd have sentries watching the property. I could take advantage of your security and not have her deal with you. It was a win-win situation."

"You could have brought her to the house. I wouldn't have contaminated her."

"Wouldn't you? I wasn't sure, and I didn't like the idea of the two of you being in any more contact than necessary. Though I actually did offer. She said she wanted to play, not perform."

"I'm not sure what she's doing is either one." He never took his eyes off Cara. "It's . . . different. I've never heard her play like that before. I've never heard anyone play like that. My God . . ."

"Aye, I thought the same thing," Jock said. "I'm not an expert on music like you, Kaskov, but I'm an expert on Cara. But I learned something new about her today." His lips twisted. "And I wish that I hadn't chosen to bring her here today. It's only going to make it more difficult to keep you away from her now."

He nodded slowly. "You might be right."

"I know I'm right." He grimaced. "Now get the hell out of here. I don't think there's any chance that she'll notice either one of us for quite a while, but what's going on with her is only *for* her. No audience. I don't want her to know you were even here."

"You're being very selfish."

"Damn straight." Then he wearily shook his head. "It means something to you. You'll do what you please. I can't stop you." He met his eyes. "Or maybe I don't want to stop you. But I don't want you to steal this moment from her, and I will stop you from doing that."

Kaskov was silent. "It would be interesting to see you make the attempt. You're always so innovative, Gavin." He gave one last long look at Cara and turned away. "Stay as long as she wishes. She'll be guarded as a member of my family should be guarded."

He stopped and turned as he reached the woods.

"You do know I envy you, Gavin? It's most disconcerting. I don't remember the last time I envied anyone. I always considered it a sign of weakness." He glanced back at Cara. "But I do envy you these next hours with her."

He turned and disappeared into the woods.

Someone was standing in front of her, Cara real-ized vaguely. He was saying something but she didn't have time to pay attention. "Go away. I'm busy now."

"Easy." His voice was low and soothing. "Slow down, Cara. It's time for a break. It's been over eight hours. You're on fire. You need to rest and eat. I can practically see the calories burning."

Jock, she realized dazedly. It was Jock with his hands on her shoulders. But it was too soon, she couldn't stop now. There was too much happening inside her, happening all around her. She had to tell him that so that he would understand. "Jock, I never knew that there were so many ways. It's wonderful . . ."

"I can see that." He cradled her face in his two hands and looked down into her eyes. "I could tell something special was happening to you. But now I think it's time for you to take a break and recharge. It's not going to go away, is it?"

"No, that's what's wonderful about it," she said eagerly. "It's just keeps opening and showing me more. I never realized it was all there inside me."

"But you're exhausted, and you need to eat. Eight hours, Cara. I know you could go longer, but it might not be good for you. Pace yourself. You're hungry, aren't you? Think about it."

She was ravenous, she realized in shock. "Starved."

"I thought you must be." He kissed her forehead,

and his hands dropped away. "As I said, you were on fire. You need to replace some of those nutrients Tchaikovsky took away from you. Okay if we go and get something to eat? Then you can come back here and play if you still want to do it."

She suddenly smiled brilliantly. "Don't be so gentle and soothing. You're treating me like a child, Jock." She hesitated, then sighed and reluctantly put her violin in its case. "I told you it wasn't going to go away. But I suppose you might say I got carried away and forgot about that." She looked at the late-afternoon rays of sun shining on the river. "Eight hours? You've been very patient. I'm sorry."

"I'm not." He smiled. "It was an experience that I'll never forget. You were extraordinary. Maybe like watching someone climb Everest or seeing an eagle being born."

"What?" She laughed. "Ridiculous. What a comparison."

"Well, I could see something momentous was going on for you." He held out his hand. "But I believe I'll drive if you don't mind. You're still on the top of Everest, and you need to come down a little before you deal with mundane traffic. You've been on pure adrenaline for too long. Exhaustion might hit anytime now."

It was already hitting, she realized. She was suddenly feeling a little light-headed and weak. "Food should take care of that." She took her keys out of her pocket and put them in his palm. "Let's go to that place we went to last night. They were quick, and I loved the hamburger."

"As you command." He took her violin and put it in the backseat. "But no one can say I'm trying to impress you with fancy cuisine." He opened the passenger door for her. "Relax. You might not get all the way down from Everest by the time we get to the restaurant, but maybe that's good." He got into the driver's seat and started the car. "Do you want to talk about it?"

"I think I do. I want to share it with you. But I don't know what to say." She was frowning, puzzled as she watched him drive out onto the road. "It was confusing at first. I so desperately wanted to play, Jock. I hadn't played since I was at the cabin with Svardak, and that was almost more of a battle. But even then I could feel something was changing, it wasn't quite the same."

"You couldn't expect it to be."

She gestured impatiently. "I realized that, but I didn't know what was happening. Everything was moving too fast. I was facing things that I'd never faced before."

"That you should never have had to face," he said harshly.

"But suddenly they were there, and I had to deal with them. That's what life's all about. Accepting and dealing. I was so afraid and angry and bewildered while I was with Svardak. Because it wasn't only about the fact that every emotion and depth of feeling was exaggerated more than I could have dreamed, somehow it was all tied up with the music. Marian Napier and what she went through, the cruelty of Anna Svardak and what she did to Kaskov. Those other three women who died as tribute to Anna. The music was all part of it."

"What are you trying to say?" he asked quietly.

"That when I got away from Lost Canyon, I realized that what I felt for you and everyone else I loved had changed and grown and deepened. And I knew I would never be the same." She added simply, "I just didn't have any idea that it would do the same for the music, that it would open new doors there, too."

His eyes narrowed on her face. "Explain?"

"I see more, I hear more, techniques that I never

thought about are occurring to me." She leaned forward, her eyes shining. "No limits, Jock. Isn't it wonderful?"

"Wonderful," he said softly. Then he chuckled. "And wouldn't Svardak be pissed off to know that he'd accidentally given you a gift that you treasure."

"He'd *hate* it. It's all innovation and creativity and everything that Anna taught him was to be despised." Her smile faded. "But I believe Marian would like the idea that he couldn't ever really stop the music and that everything he did only made it better." She paused, thinking. "And if anyone gave me a gift, then it might be her."

"You know, some would say that it could only be the jump-start maturing of your own God-given talent."

"And isn't that a gift?" She leaned back in the seat. "Stop being practical. I had a wonderful day, and magic happened." Her eyes were suddenly gleaming with mischief. "And I bet that you didn't have one Machiavellian thought while I was playing. Admit it."

"No bet. You had me completely mesmerized and totally helpless."

"You're never helpless." She added contentedly, "I'll settle for mesmerized. I'm glad you were here and I could share it with you. It's hard to share when you're fighting me all the time. I have to work at just keeping you from throwing away what we have."

"Wrong. I'm only trying to keep you from throwing what *you* are away." He said gently, "You took another giant step today. You should protect what you learned, what you could be."

"What do you think I'm doing?" She reached out and lovingly touched his arm. "You haven't been listening. How I feel about you is part of the music. It's part of who I am. It was like that from the first moment I met you, and it's getting stronger and stronger all the time."

"Then find a way to—"

"Hush." She gave his arm a mock pinch. "No more of this. I won't let you lecture me. And I won't let you talk about Svardak either. Not today. Today, there's no ugliness in the world. I want to go back to that last night at the Marquis when we sat and talked and drank wine. Do you think we can get wine at that diner?"

He smiled. "If we can't, then we'll go somewhere else."

"Oh, I think you'll be able to arrange something." She leaned back in the seat. "You can send that waitress who wanted to jump you to pick up a bottle at the local liquor store."

"No, that would be illegal. Besides, then I'll be obligated to return favor for favor." His eyes were twinkling. "Is that okay?"

"No, but I'd handle it." She loved to study his face when it held that hint of mischief. So different from the Jock who was all driving intensity. But then she loved all the complicated facets that made Jock who he was. Yet she was glad that he was deliberately giving her what she wanted from him when she was soaring high. She said lightly, "Watch me. Today I can handle anything, Jock Gavin."

"Go to bed." Jock set her violin case inside her door and handed the key back to her. "I believe you're a little giddy."

"By giddy, you mean drunk?" She shook her head. "On two glasses of wine? It just made me feel . . . sort of floating."

"You were floating already." He turned on the light switch and checked out the room. "And giddy was the right word. Not drunk, but a bit tipsy? The combination might have been a little overwhelming. You told me you aren't used to drinking."

"But it was a celebration, and it was a good wine, wasn't it? I told you that waitress would make certain you had whatever you wanted. She was pitifully obvious tonight." She smiled mischievously. "That's why I had to drown my sorrows. I had to find a way to cope."

"Brat."

She threw back her head and laughed. "There's no way of pleasing you." She suddenly threw herself into his arms and hugged him. "And I'm so willing to try. Stop stiffening. I'm not going to spoil my day by risking another rejection. I've just wanted to be close to you all evening. It would have made a perfect day." She gave him another hug, then backed away from him. "But it was almost perfect, wasn't it? I can't expect to have everything. It was a good evening for you, too. I could tell."

"It was a fantastic evening," he said softly. "Thank you for letting me share it with you. It was a pleasure just watching you . . . glow." He took a step closer and took her back in his arms. "And if you feel like playing again, go ahead and do it. I'll handle any and all repercussions. Just send them to me."

His arms felt so good, strong, gentle. She closed her eyes, drinking it in. "We might both get kicked out."

"Then I'll take you back to the river. There will be moonlight. You'll have whatever you need." He pressed her closer for an instant, gave her a quick kiss, and pushed her away from him. "Anything you need. But you might try to sleep a little before you explore that option. I'll still be available if you pound on my door at the crack of dawn again."

"That's comforting to know." She smiled as she watched him walk toward the door. "But you're always comforting, and controlled, and supply every need. I'd think you'd get bored by the role."

"Bored?" He looked over his shoulder, and for a second, she saw those silver eyes flicker. "This time you've got the wrong word. Good night, Cara. Lock the door behind me."

She stood there after the door closed. There had been something in those last words that had been . . . different. But she was always searching for promising or different when it came to Jock's attitude toward her. But she didn't want to analyze his every word tonight. It had been too good a day, and she wanted only to remember it and forget anything that wasn't positive and hopeful.

She crossed the room and locked the door. She glanced at the violin case on the floor beside it. Tempting. But she was tired, and crack of dawn had sounded good to her. She would shower and get to bed and think of Jock's face as he had looked while they had been talking at the restaurant. No, while she had been talking, she ruefully corrected herself. She had been chattering and excited, and he had sat there watching and smiling and giving her all his attention. Which had made a great day even more wonderful for her. Selfish. She'd have to make it up to him, but right now, she only wanted to remember that he had taken the trouble and that it also had meant something special to him. That was more than enough for one day.

She grabbed her robe and headed for the shower.

Two hours later, she was lying in bed and staring into the darkness. She'd thought she'd be so exhausted that she would have no trouble going to sleep but that hadn't been the case. Maybe it was merely that she was still wired and excited from the day, but she was wide awake.

Think about Jock.

Think about the music.

Though neither was soothing to her right now. They were exciting and challenging and completely—

Her phone was ringing.

She went still. Jock?

She reached for the phone on her nightstand.

No ID.

She pressed the access. "Hello."

"You still have your same phone number," Svardak said mockingly. "I thought you'd be afraid to keep the number since you'd realize I probably knew it."

She inhaled sharply. She felt as if she'd been kicked in the stomach. She was suddenly ice cold. Somehow she felt as if he knew it, that he could actually feel her shock and terror. Hide it. "Why should I be afraid of you, Svardak? You're no one to fear. The last time I saw you, I left you bleeding on the cabin floor."

Silence. "So you did. I haven't forgotten one second of it." His voice was suddenly ugly. "And every now and then I get a twinge in that damn wound that reminds me, you bitch."

"I was hoping you wouldn't feel anything by now. I thought you might have bled to death. Evidently, I didn't do a very good job. I'll do better the next time. I won't have to rely on a makeshift dagger. Who patched you up, Svardak? Any chance of blood poisoning?"

"No chance at all. That fool who stitched me was a bungler, but I'm pumped full of antibiotics. And I'll be able to function well enough to do what I have to do. I'll take care of arranging an expert job later . . ." He paused, then added maliciously, "After I finish with Joe Quinn. I'm planning on taking a long time with him."

She felt the panic ice through her. "Wishful thinking. Joe made a fool of you. He and Kaskov made a shambles of your damn canyon. I'm safe, and so is Joe. You don't have a chance of doing anything to him."

"I have every chance. I'm sure he's hot on my trail as we speak. I'm just waiting for him to get close enough. He's practically in my hands right now."

"Liar. You're not stupid enough to stay around here when Kaskov and Joe are on the hunt for you."

Silence. "Here. You said here. Are you so eager to see me dead that you stayed close enough to see it happen? I'll have to check that out. Very foolish, Cara. I might even decide to bypass Quinn and go straight for you again."

"Neither is a safe bet for you. But by all means try."

"I'll think about it. But I really have my heart on using Quinn as a path to you. I could tell how much that would hurt you. At one point, you were ready to plead for him." He paused. "That's when I decided that I had to think of something really special and painful for him. Would you like to hear a few of the things that I plan on doing to him?"

"Not particularly. I'm not interested in fantasies."

"No, it's because you know it will hurt you. Such a tender heart. I might even tell you a few other things I did to Marian. Perhaps they wouldn't be extreme enough, but they would hurt you. Though I prefer to go the route of the tortures of the inquisition. I studied those in depth while I was preparing for Kaskov. They'll do just as well for Quinn."

"I might as well hang up now, Svardak. This conversation is going nowhere."

"That's not true. I'm getting a great deal from it. I can tell how frightened you are."

"I'm not frightened. What you did to me is over. You can't hurt me or any of the people I care about."

"Yes, I can. I've already started. I'm reaching out to all of them. Quinn, first. Then Kaskov, after that, I'll go down the list." He paused. "But I've been told I might have to expand my list. Abrams said there was someone else at the canyon. Who is Gavin, Cara?"

Her heart lurched. She felt sick. She had known that there might be a possibility that he'd learn about Jock, but she'd hoped desperately that he wouldn't.

"You're not answering. Did I miss someone?" he asked softly. "Let me guess. Was it the same man you spent the night fucking while you kept me waiting at the hotel? I was very angry with you for doing that, remember?"

"Because you're crazy. I was supposed to rush back to my suite, so I wouldn't keep you waiting to kidnap me?"

"Who is he, Cara?"

She tried to make her tone without expression. "How should I know? Perhaps one of Kaskov's men."

"I don't think so. I can tell he means something to you. Never mind. I'll find out. Perhaps a lover would be even better than Quinn for my purpose." His voice turned low, silky, and vicious. "No, I won't cheat myself. I'll have it all. And you'll see me butcher everyone who's ever been close to you."

"You'll have *nothing*." Her voice was shaking. "I won't let you hurt anyone. You're just a hideous, senseless man on the run. We'll catch you, then you'll never be able to—"

"Ask Kaskov if he was able to catch me all these years," he interrupted. "And I've already stopped running, and I'm the one who is going to spring the trap. I'll call you again when I have Quinn ready to talk to you. Did I tell you how angry this damn wound is making me? I think I need to start Quinn off with a broken bottle shoved into his belly. And be sure to look up those other clever tortures I mentioned. I'll use every one before I'm done." His voice was soft and venomous. "Look around every corner, try to protect and keep them all safe. It won't do you any good. Someday, I'll be there."

He cut the connection.

She lay there, frozen, trembling. God, she was grateful he had seen fit to hang up. She had been losing control from the moment he had mentioned Jock. The other poisons he had been spewing had been expected, but Jock had been a shock.

She was still in shock. Still caught up in the horror that she'd believed she'd escaped that night in the canyon. Only hours before, she'd been so happy, so sure that life was not the nightmare that Svardak had shown her, that even out of the darkest evil some ray of goodness could be found.

But he was alive and as full of hate and bitterness as ever. More than bitterness, she thought with panic. He would never stop hunting, never stop seeking revenge. And soon he would know everything there was to know about Jock, too. And there had been no goodness or hope in any of the words with which he'd battered her tonight.

Ugliness. Total ugliness.

And she couldn't stop shivering.

Look around any corner. Someday, I'll be there.

No!

Someday, I'll be there.

She tossed her covers aside and staggered to the bathroom. She splashed water in her face and drank a glass of water.

It was a mistake. She threw it up a moment later, along with her dinner. Her knees gave way, and she sank to the tile floor. This was all wrong. She was being weak and letting the monster terrorize her. Why was she permitting it to happen now, when she'd been strong before?

Because today had been so intensely wonderful it

had brought home once again how much she had to lose.

Someday, I'll be there.

And what would she do if he was? Crawl into a bathroom and huddle on the cold tiles until he went away? Let him ruin her life as he had tried to do at that cabin? She couldn't do that because now the stakes were so much greater.

Stop shaking, dammit. It was just another battle she had to win. *Take deep breaths, and try to think of a way to do it.*

Someday, I'll be there.

12:38 A.M.

No more hesitation, Cara thought as she stared at the clock on the nightstand. She shouldn't have had to lie here in bed, tense and on edge as she'd done for the last few hours. The decision had been made, and now she only had to execute it.

Only?

Just do it. She sat up in bed and swung her legs to the floor. She slipped on her terry robe over her nightshirt, and she was dialing Jock as she crossed the room to the door.

"Cara?" he answered immediately. "Okay?"

"No." She opened her door. "But we have to make it okay. I'm leaving my room now, and I'll be at your door in just a moment. A welcome would be appreciated. I thought I'd give you warning. I didn't want to have to pound on it as I did before." She cut the connection.

She left her room, locked the door, and by that time Jock had thrown open the door of his room and was standing in the doorway. The light from the lamp behind him silhouetted his body, which appeared to be naked except for a towel draped about his hips. "What's wrong?" He asked warily, "Are you ill? Too much wine?"

"Not now." She shook her head. "I was sick earlier, but that wasn't the wine either." She went past him into his room. "You sleep naked. I didn't know that. But then you wouldn't let me know something that intimate. You'd consider it encouraging me." She dropped down in the chair beside his bed. "Too bad. You're as fantastic-looking as I always knew you'd be. I feel a little cheated."

"Why were you sick?" His eyes were narrowed on her face. "And what the hell is wrong with you now? You were fine when I left you. Right now, you're barely holding it together."

"I'm doing considerably more than holding it together. Don't sell me short. I'm just having trouble bracing myself for more difficulty from you after what I've already gone through."

"And what have you already gone through?" he said through his teeth. "*Talk* to me."

"Svardak."

He stiffened. "What's that supposed to mean?"

"His wound was bothering him." Her lips twisted. "He wanted to share it with me. Along with a few other thoughts and comments. He was so glad I hadn't changed my cell number."

"Son of a *bitch*." Jock was swearing softly, vehemently. He was across the room, dropping to his knees beside her. "When?"

"A few hours ago."

"Why didn't you call me then?"

"I wasn't in terrific shape for a while. He caught me off guard, and you might say I was in shock." She tried to smile. "Hence the sickness that had nothing to do with the wine."

His hands grasped her shoulders. "What did he say to you?"

"Mostly what you'd expect. But as I said, he caught me off guard and I didn't expect anything. Every word he said was like a fresh cut. Later, I had to think and sort things out to make sure he hadn't told me something that might be important." She reached up and rubbed her temple. "It was ugly, and it took me longer than I thought to get past it. But I knew that there might be something I could use. I should have recorded the call, but I didn't think of it. Silly. You would have thought about it. I should have—"

"Stop rambling." He shook her gently. "You shouldn't have done anything but survive the bastard. No one could expect anything else of you."

"Of course they could. And I remembered most of it after I had time to pull myself together. One of the things was that he said that he was almost ready to gather in Joe. He was boasting, but it could be the truth."

"Or a blatant lie. I'll try to contact Joe and make sure he's still okay."

"I already called him, but I couldn't get through. These damn mountains . . ."

"I'll try him again. What else?"

"I believe Svardak is still in the mountains and won't leave the area until he gets what he wants. He's already made contact with Lacher and Abrams, so they must have definitely been on their way to him when they killed that farmer. That might help us zero in on his location." She paused. "But I made a slip, and he knows that I may still be in the area."

"Then we get you out of here," he said grimly.

"Why? One intimidating phone call doesn't alter anything. He's fixated on Joe right now." She moistened her lips. "But that may change. One of those men told him you were on the mountain, and he asked me questions about you. He thinks that you might be my lover." She smiled crookedly. "I'd shout that from the housetops if it were true. But he's the one person I'd never want to know it. He's totally unpredictable. He's already trying to decide if killing you or Joe might hurt me more."

"Neither of those options are going to happen," he said impatiently. "What else?"

She tried to think. "Wherever he is, he didn't get conventional medical care to patch up his wound. He said he couldn't trust the bungler who tried to sew him up. He's on heavy antibiotics, but he said he's waiting to have his wound stitched until after he takes care of his list. That means we can't trace him through an urgent-care or local hospital."

"But who tried to sew up that wound and patch him up?" he murmured. "We might have to explore that question. No name?"

"Svardak isn't stupid. Insane, yes, but not stupid. I was upset and probably revealed a hell of a lot more than he did." She wearily shook her head. "But that's all I can put together from what he said tonight. The rest was just . . . poison. He only wanted to hurt me."

"And he did it," he said hoarsely.

"Of course he did." She gave a half shrug. "I was happy. I was . . . floating. He couldn't know, but he chose the perfect time. That's why it took me so long to get over it and decide what to do."

"It shouldn't have taken you long at all. I told you what you had to do."

"I realize what you *want* me to do," she said wearily. "That was a given. Go home, be safe, let you protect and build a wall around me that would leave you outside. But I knew it was never going to happen. So I had to think of a way to make certain that you admitted it to yourself."

"Really." He sat back on his heels. "And just how do you intend to do that?"

"By not being patient and trying to convince you that you're wrong. It doesn't matter if you're right or wrong in your own eyes. All that matters is that I'm going to get what I want. I'm so tired of fighting you. I want to fight *with* you."

"It does matter, Cara. It has to matter."

"Then you should know that I'm not waiting to be traded off to Joe when it's your turn to go after Svardak. Whatever made you believe I'd allow it?" She paused. "Tomorrow, I'll go looking for Joe, and I'll stay with him until we catch Svardak. I can't let him get his hands on Joe."

"The hell you will!"

She shook her head and stared him in the eye. "I'm going to do it. Nothing is going to stop me. Accept it, Jock. You're welcome to go with me though I'd prefer you don't. Svardak scared me when he was talking about you. But you're very clever at hunting, and I'd be foolish to refuse your help."

"How kind of you to consider me an asset." His eyes were blazing. He added sarcastically, "You'll forgive me if I don't return the compliment. You'd be a total disaster. Don't even think about it."

"Of course I have to think about it. You're perfectly right, I'm not qualified. But I wouldn't be a total disaster. I have one asset you don't have, Jock."

"And what's that?"

She said simply, "Svardak wants me very badly. I might not have to go to him, there's every chance he might come to me."

"Son of a bitch." He didn't speak for a moment. "Why am I even surprised?"

"I don't know." She smiled sadly. "You're so clever that you're always two steps ahead of everyone. It's probably that you didn't want to think about it. Like I didn't want to think about Svardak knowing who you are. Because it hurts too much."

"It won't hurt. I won't let you near him."

"I leave in the morning. I think you'll be with me." She got to her feet. "In the meantime, I'm going to go to bed. It's been a rough few hours for me." She untied her robe and slipped it off. She thought about taking off the sleep shirt, then decided against it. Provocation wasn't why she'd come here, and Jock was on edge already. "But I'd like it very much if you'd hold me until I go to sleep. Which side of the bed do you usually sleep on? I don't want to intrude."

"Intrude?" He slowly got to his feet. "What are you doing, Cara?"

She answered herself. "The right side, the pillow is mussed." She lifted the cover and slipped into the left side. "Turn out the light, Jock. I've told you what I'm going to do, and there's no use arguing about it right now. I just want you to hold me."

He was staring intently at her expression. "You're frightened? You don't want to be alone?"

"I don't want to be alone," she repeated. "Hold me."

He reached over and turned out the lamp. "We're not finished talking, Cara. And this isn't a good idea."

"Hold me."

And then he was in bed beside her, his arms pulling her close. "Better?"

She exhaled slowly as she cuddled closer. The scent of him . . . The feel of him . . . "Much better. You didn't have to panic. It's not as if I was going to attack you. This isn't easy for me either."

"I assure you, panic isn't what I'm feeling," he said thickly. "And you should go back to your room."

"*This* is my room." She nestled her head in the hollow of his shoulder. "Wherever you are, that's where

I'm going to be from now on. That's another thing I decided after I hung up from Svardak. I won't risk losing what we could be together. When I was at the canyon, I had to force myself not to think of you because I was so sad at all we'd missed, what we might have had." She had to steady her voice. "So get used to having me in your bed. It's not going to change. I'm not listening to you any longer." Her lips brushed his shoulder. "Feel free to ignore me, but I don't believe you will. Because I've got a wild card. You'll always remember that if I'd been in your bed that night, Svardak wouldn't have been able to take me."

He was silent. "It's something that I won't easily forget. That doesn't alter the basic argument."

"Hush. No more of this. Just hold me and tell me you want me here. Do you know how difficult it is for me to act this aggressive? I don't have the experience for it."

"Oh, are we back to those zillions again? I assure you that you're doing very well."

"I know I should be better. But I figure until I learn all the tricks that you won't mind putting up with me, because you do love me, Jock."

His hand reached up to stroke her hair. "That's quite perceptive of you. One always has to know one's limitations and how to overcome them."

"I don't regard it as a limitation. It will be a challenge. You've always liked showing me new things." She got up on one elbow and looked down at him. "Your body feels . . . hard. I like it. Is this how it starts?"

"I've gone way beyond the starting gate."

"Good." She laid her head back down on his shoulder. "Then I don't have to be aggressive anymore. What do I do next?"

"Nothing." His hand was gently stroking her throat. "Lessons aren't what you asked of me when you came to my bed tonight. You wanted me to hold you and tell you that I wanted you here. You said you needed it." His fingers were mesmerizingly gentle. "Do you still need it, Cara?"

"I always want to know you want me with you," she said unevenly. "And it's not what I need all the time. I don't ever want to cheat you again."

"You didn't cheat me." His arms tightened around her. "I'm holding you. Do I want you here? Aye, there isn't a moment I don't want you with me." His hands tangled in her hair. He whispered, "You're not going to give up, are you?"

She shook her head.

"What am I going to do with you?"

"I'm sure something will occur to you. But words will help."

"You want words?" he asked. "You're the only thing in life that makes it worth living to me. I value everything about you. Your smile, your humor, the way your eyes light up when you see me, how much you care for everyone around you, your honesty, your stubbornness. I don't know why we were brought together, but I thank God we were. Is it any wonder that I want to keep you happy and safe?" He brushed his lips across her cheek. "It's purely selfish on my part." He kissed the tip of her nose. "Are those enough words for you?"

"No," she added huskily, "I want more. But that will do for now. Words can only go so far. Because I've been thinking about it, and I believe I'm the one who's being cheated." She tucked her head beneath his chin. "And if you love me that much, then I deserve more from you. You're just a little confused with all that highfalutin honorable nonsense." She kissed his throat, then closed her eyes. "But I'm willing to forgive you if you come to your senses soon. I'm going to go to sleep now.

Thank you for holding me, and making my world come right again, and for that beautiful declaration."

"My pleasure," he said thickly. His arms tightened around her. "Anytime."

"No, not anytime." She cuddled closer. "It has to be soon. We deserve it . . ."

CHAPTER

11

He was gone.

His warmth, the golden strength of his body, the scent of him that had surrounded her through the night.

Gone.

Sadness.

Loneliness.

Cara reached out in the darkness for him. "Jock . . ."

"Shh, I'm here." His hand grasped her own, warm strong . . . "I just wanted to sit here and watch you sleep."

She opened her eyes. It was still mostly dark in the room, but there was enough light so that she could see him sitting in the chair beside the bed. "That's not fair. Did I snore or anything?"

"Nary a snore. Just a kind of purr, like a kitten."

"I think you're lying to me."

"Never. Not even for your own good. I've been a total failure."

"You don't know how to fail." She paused. "But why were you watching me?"

"I was having trouble not waking you. Putting distance between us was one solution."

"Not a good one." Her hand tightened on his. "Because you woke me by not being here for me. I missed you."

"It seemed the thing to do at the time. I had a few things to think about, and you were getting in my way." He reached forward and gently touched her cheek. "You always get in my way. You're always there. I tried so *hard*. Why wouldn't you listen to me?"

She went still. There was something in his tone . . . Suddenly, she couldn't breathe. "Because you were wrong. But maybe you aren't now?" She pushed herself to a sitting position, her gaze searching the darkness. "Turn on the light. I want to see your face. What were you thinking about?"

He made no move to turn on the light. "I was thinking that there was no way I could go through what I did that morning at the hotel again. I don't care if I'm a selfish bastard or ignoring the greater good. I can't *take* it."

"I believe the greater good isn't all it's cracked up to be. It's all in the eye of the beholder. Go on. What else?"

"What else? Isn't that enough? You told me that you'd never give up on us. That you'd always be in my life. But I can't be sure of keeping you safe unless I'm with you." He paused. His next words were unsteady. "So I *have* to be with you." He was silent again, then he asked, "Will you let me share your bed until you find out how wrong you are about me?"

She closed her eyes as the waves of relief cascaded over her. "Thank God."

"Is that yes?"

Her eyes flicked open. "It wasn't perfect, but yes.

Your other declaration was much better. This one was full of mistakes and false assumptions. You will never control me just because we're having sex. It has to be because I believe it's important to make you happy in that way. And it's you who will find out how wrong you are." She got up on her knees on the bed. "But on the whole, I'm grateful that you've come this far. We'll go into the rest later." She pulled her sleep shirt over her head and threw it on the floor. "Now will you turn on the light? I really want to see you when we're having sex. You were so wonderful-looking when you opened the door tonight. Like one of those beautiful Greek statues."

Silence. "Who said we're going to have sex now?" he said silkily. "Aren't you taking too much for granted?"

She stiffened. "Am I? You don't want me? I told you I was afraid there might be a problem. I'm sorry. I didn't mean to push you. We don't have to—"

"Hush." He was suddenly on his knees on the bed facing her. "I was teasing you. I'm feeling a bit over-whelmed and out of control. Do I want you?" His hands were suddenly on her breasts, his thumb's flicking back and forth on her nipples. "I've been sitting here trying to keep myself from jumping back into bed and com-ing inside you. Aye, you might say I want you, Cara." His mouth was on her throat and then moving down to her breasts. He was cuddling her breasts in his hands, lifting them to his mouth. "If you want to completely understate what I'm feeling." He was licking her nip-ples, sucking delicately, then nibbling with tiny, sharp bites.

Scorching heat.

He bit harder.

Her back arched. "Jock!"

"Shh." He was pushing her back on the bed. "And

the reason why I don't want the damn light on is that I can't keep control of myself right now. I'm burning up, and I have to be careful with you." He was pushing her legs wider, then his fingers were rubbing, plucking, massaging. "And all I want to do is push up and in you."

His fingers . . . Her stomach was clenching. He wasn't the only one burning . . . She gasped. "Then do it."

"I will." His mouth was on her breast again. "Soon."

His fingers again, but moving slowly now, but deeper. Not deep enough. Not fast enough.

She couldn't *stand* it.

Her nails bit into his shoulders. "Now!"

"No." He was breathing hard. "Easy, love. I have to be careful to—"

"No, you don't." Why was he talking instead of *moving*? She was pulling him over her, in her. "I can't *stand* it. You don't have to do anything but this." She lunged upward.

Pain. She cried out and froze for an instant.

"Dammit," Jock's voice was harsh, agonized. "See? Why wouldn't you listen?"

"Because it wasn't important. This is the only thing that's important." She started to move again. "You. Me. This. Help me, Jock."

Fever.

Heat.

Her heart was beating so hard she could scarcely breathe.

"No." His teeth were clenched. "*You're* important. Don't do—" He broke off as she lunged up to meet him again. He closed his eyes. "Shit!"

Then he was going deep, holding her hips immobile as he plunged. He was swearing softly as he moved. "Cara, this isn't what— I should have known I'd—"

"Shut up." She pulled him down and kissed him. "I *love* you. I've been looking forward to this for a long time. If you want to worry about something, worry about not disappointing me."

He gazed down at her, and she could see the moisture glittering in his eyes. Then he stroked the side of her face with the most incredible tenderness. "I believe it's too late for anything else," he said unsteadily. "So I promise you won't be disappointed." He kissed her, slowly, sensuously. "But I think we'll slow down a bit, just a little because I can't bear anything else. But teasing is always good." His fingers were rotating, plucking, pinching, pulling. "What do you think?"

She cried out.

His heat. His fullness. Surrounded by the erotic motion of his fingers.

She thought if he didn't stop, she was going to scream.

Then his fingers moved again, and she knew she'd scream if he did stop.

"Jock . . ."

"Soon, love." His face lean, intense, his lips curved in a purely carnal smile. "There's so much more . . . I'll make the wait worth your while." He added another finger. "After all, I made you a promise."

She gasped, her muscles clenching. "I don't . . . believe I can wait. Can't you postpone this until later? I . . . think . . . that . . . we should—"

Then she did scream as he made still another movement. "Jock, dammit, *now*."

"Shh. Okay. You're right. Definitely later." He was over her, gathering her still closer. "No way I can take any more of this . . ." He kissed her, and whispered, "Hold on to me, Cara." He kissed her again. "And I'll hold on to you. I'll never let you go again."

Never let you go. Sweet words. Glorious words, she

thought dazedly. Words she had wanted to hear from him for all the years they'd been together, through deep friendship and the first bewildering tendrils when friendship had turned to love. Had that love always been there waiting to be born? Eve had thought that it had.

It was as if the two of you had been meant to complete each other.

What a beautiful thought. As beautiful as Jock, as beautiful as this moment.

Then she couldn't think at all because he was deep inside her, and the world was exploding around her.

Never let you go . . .

"Are you all right?" Jock was frowning as he sat up in bed and watched Cara come out of the bathroom. "Did I hurt you?"

"No, I'm not all right." She took off her shower cap and tossed back her hair before tightening her robe and crawling back in bed. "I'm perfect. I'm no longer an anachronism. Thank you very much. And you were *almost* not turned off by the fact that you had to do the deed."

"Shut up," he said gruffly as he pulled her close. "You are perfect. But you were perfect before, and I was not turned off by anything. You're totally magnificent."

"I'm totally magnificent when I'm playing my violin. I'm a mere amateur at playing this kind of game. But I'll get better with practice." She tucked her head in the hollow of his shoulder. "And, admit it, you *were* intimidated at the idea of despoiling my virgin body. You were backing away so quickly, I thought I was going to lose you for a minute."

"I was not intimidated. I was worried about hurting

you, but that wasn't my problem." His lips twisted bitterly. "But it might as well have been because I managed to put you at risk anyway. So much for protecting you. I was a total failure. Nothing was going right. I was an ass. I went up in flames."

"Thank God." But he was clearly upset, and she did not want anything to spoil this night. "And I saw no sign you were a total failure. You were entirely too good. Why were you being an ass?"

"You probably haven't had time to think about it. I didn't protect you. I was intending to do it, but it was you, and I'd wanted you for so damn long and—I'm making excuses and there are no excuses. Please . . . forgive me."

She stared at him in bewilderment. "What on earth are you talking about?"

"I told you that you hadn't thought about it. Dammit, for all I know you could be pregnant. I didn't protect you, dammit."

"And that's why you're ready to cut your throat? For heaven's sake, I didn't give you a chance." She started to laugh. "And I didn't protect me either. Which means I didn't protect you. That's far worse on the scale when you think about it. I know how responsible you are and what kind of burden a child could be on you. Because with you, it would be a lifetime commitment whether or not you wanted to be a father. So who's most to blame, Jock?"

"Me." He was scowling. "Because you're young and brilliant and shouldn't be tied down by my selfishness. Don't try to be generous. I screwed up."

"I don't remember it quite like that. I seem to recall I was being very aggressive trying to overcome that damn virgin stigma. But, of course, you wouldn't take that into consideration." She suddenly scooted away from him, sat up in bed, and crossed her legs. "So I'd better clarify this point before it takes on a life of its own." She giggled. "Actually, that's pretty funny, but you're not laughing."

"You bet I'm not."

"Then let's go back to square one. Poor little virgin victimized by an irresistible cad and unable to defend herself from the lustful fiend." Her smile faded. "First, I was a virgin, and I do find you irresistible, but I had to fight to get you to seduce me. And I've made it plain I'm grateful you went to the bother of doing it. In addition, I welcome and delight in that lust. If I'd wanted to defend myself, I would have had no problem." She tilted her head. "You're still frowning, I'm not convincing you. Okay, I should have known that the pregnancy idea would scare you on my behalf. You persist in thinking that I'm too innocent and inexperienced to consider the consequences and was just carried away." She shook her head, and said bluntly, "I thought about it before I went to you that night at the hotel in Atlanta. I didn't know what was going to happen when I saw you again. All I knew was that I loved you, and I had to make it work somehow. Sex was always a possibility, and I'm not an ignorant child." She leaned forward, her gaze holding his own. "I didn't *care* if I got pregnant, Jock. Not then, not now. It was always my choice. I thought of it as a win-win situation. I knew if it did happen, and everything else went wrong, I'd at least have your child." She added softly, "And what a wonderful gift that would be to me."

"Oh, shit." His silver-gray eyes were glittering with moisture as he reached over and pulled her back into his arms. "You're crazy," he said thickly as he tucked her head into the hollow of his shoulder. "Completely out of your mind."

"No, don't you see? Win-win."

"Maybe for me." His voice was uneven. "But not for you. You'll forgive me if I hope that wonderful 'gift' is put on delay for a considerable time. I won't have you cheated."

"You still don't understand." She lifted her head to look at him warily. "And does that mean you're not going to want to have sex with me again tonight? There's such a thing as closing the barn door too late, Jock. I don't want—" He was kissing her, deeply, hotly. She could feel the muscles of her belly clench. "Yes?"

"Not until we get you protected, which will be the first thing in the morning. I don't give a damn about barn doors. No more taking chances." He was leaning over her, looking down at her. "I went nuts before, I won't make the same mistake this time." He kissed her again. "But there's sex; and then there's sex." He opened her robe. "Let's experiment. There are so many ways . . ."

LAKE COTTAGE 2:10 A.M.

"There you are." Eve breathed a sigh of relief as she saw Michael curled up on the porch swing. "And what are you doing out here at this hour?"

"Just listening to the wind in the trees." He sat up as she came toward him. "I was thinking that Dad might be listening to the wind in the trees where he is now. But it's probably a different sound from here. When we were on that last camping trip, Dad told me that different elevations and lakes make sound travel thinner or fuller. He's in the mountains, isn't he?"

"You know very well he is. You spent hours going though those West Virginia maps before you went to bed tonight." She sat down beside him. "And then you scoot out here at two in the morning without saying a word to me? Not good, Michael."

"I didn't want to wake you. I didn't think you'd worry." He looked down at the blue Subaru and black Lexus parked a short distance away beside the lake. "You knew Mr. Kaskov's men wouldn't let anything happen to me. You said that's why they're here, to keep us safe."

It was true she was growing a little more confident about the two Russians she'd reluctantly permitted to keep an eye on Michael and her. They were like unobtrusive shadows, and Cheknof seemed very conscientious about staying close to Michael. He'd even insisted on taking Michael to school in the morning and waiting all day to bring him home.

"I'd still prefer you let me know when you decide to wander." She slid her arm around his shoulders. "Why can't you sleep? Are you worried about your dad?"

"Sort of." He looked thoughtfully out at the lake. "Maybe not yet. I just keep thinking about him. I feel as if I'm *with* him. I know he's in the mountains, but maybe he's *near* a lake? Not a medium-size lake like ours, bigger, and there are woods all around him."

She was silent, then said carefully, "Of course he could be near a lake. After all, he's in the middle of a wilderness. And it's natural that you would associate his location with elements that you and your dad have in common." Her words were entirely practical as a mother's should be when grounding an imaginative ten-year-old. But who knew how much was imagination and how much was pure mystic Michael? "But it's nice that you feel that you're with him. I wish I could feel like that right now."

Michael frowned. "But you're always with him. Whenever I'm with him, I can feel you there. Didn't you know that?"

"Yes." But she hadn't realized that Michael was aware of the strength of the bond between them. "But that's kind of an always thing, much vaguer than what you were talking about."

"It doesn't feel vague. It feels . . . warm." His gaze was still on the lake. "I don't want him to be alone. I want to be with him."

"You said that you felt like you were with him," she said gently.

"No. *Really* with him."

"You know that's impossible."

"Is it? He wouldn't say that if I were out there alone." He glanced at her face. "Or you, Mom. He'd never leave you anywhere alone. He couldn't stand it."

"I hear what you're saying." She made a face. "You have to realize he doesn't want us with him. It's his job. We have to try to understand." Though she was not having much success. She hadn't been able to reach Joe more than twice in the last day as he moved in and out of cell-tower reach. She was distinctly on edge. "He's smart and tough and better at what he does than anyone I know. We have to trust him."

"I trust him." He was still frowning. "But it's not enough. Not this time. Maybe I'll be able to figure out something so that we can help him out a little."

"Maybe you will." She got to her feet. "But how about coming back to bed and getting a little sleep before you have to get up to go to school? You have soccer practice this afternoon." She smiled. "You said you never have nightmares, but perhaps this will be one of those times when you get a little help figuring out stuff."

He smiled. "Okay." He followed her to the door but stopped abruptly to turn and look at her. "He's tired, Mom," he said softly. "He's missing us. He wants to come home. But he thinks he's very close now. He's excited, and he's looking at a funny-looking house across the lake and wondering if that farmer's truck might be in woods near there."

She went still. "Really?" She tried to smile. "Maybe you don't need help figuring out anything tonight. You appear to have everything under control."

He shook his head. "It comes and goes."

She put her arm around him as she drew him into the house. "Be sure you let me know if anything interesting comes your way," she said lightly as she locked the door. "I miss your dad, too."

"He's safe right now, Mom," he said quietly. "Like you said, he's very smart." He looked back at her as he headed down the hall to his room. "I won't let anything hurt him."

"Not your job, young man." She was turning out the lights. "I took on that duty when you were two years old on that day in Scotland when your dad and I were married. Leave it up to me."

"But how can I?" His smile was suddenly luminous. "When Dad said that I had to take care of you? It's all one, isn't it?" He turned away. "Night, Mom." He disappeared into his room.

She shook her head as she went past his door to her own bedroom. It had been a strange several minutes, and she still wasn't sure what had occurred. Could it be that Michael was in some kind of psychic contact with Joe? He had never indicated before that it had ever happened, but she and Michael had possessed such a bond for the first few years of his life. It had gradually disappeared, and she had thought that it was because the contact was no longer necessary. Admit it, she had never been certain about anything concerning Michael except that he was special and beloved. That was enough for her; anything else would set him apart, and she feared the loneliness it might bring him.

But if Michael was in contact with Joe, it might mean that her son felt the bond might be necessary to protect his father. The thought sent a chill through her. It was a bizarre idea, but maybe some force out there was trying to find a way to keep Joe alive and with them.

What force?

"Bonnie?" she whispered. "I don't like the idea of being closed out of this private club you seem to have with Michael. But I'll take it if that's how it has to be. Just please stick around and give Michael and Joe a hand now and then . . ."

LAKE KEDROW, WEST VIRGINIA
5:45 A.M.

Joe slowly lowered his binoculars after gazing across the lake at the forest on the other side.

No sign of anyone in those woods. No sign of that farmer's truck on which he'd been getting tips on sightings for the last two days.

Are you out there, you son of a bitch?

Every instinct was telling Joe that he might be very close. But instinct was never enough. The only approach to those woods and the ranger station was the road around this lake or a canoe. Either would be clearly visible from the opposite bank. He'd have to leave the car here and go the rest of the way on foot or risk being spotted. That would take him several hours and put him near that forest in midday but he could always wait for darkness to strike if there was an obvious threat.

He put on his knapsack and started to walk down to the overgrown path that led around the lake. His eagerness was growing with every step after only going a quarter of a mile.

It felt *right*.

Yet he knew instincts could fail you and prove deadly so he needed to be very careful. Even if he didn't feel like being careful. All the stored-up energy and bitterness of the hunt was streaming through him as memories of what Cara had been put through by Svardak flowed through him. His pace unconsciously quickened.

I'm coming for you, bastard. Just a little longer . . .

HOLIDAY INN
11:55 A.M.

So far, so good, Cara thought as she moved silently from the bathroom toward the door of Jock's room. Jock was lying on his side, his eyes closed just as they'd been when she'd left his bed ten minutes ago. Now all she had to do was get out of here and to her own room before he—

"And where do you think you're going?"

Busted.

She sighed and turned to face him. He still hadn't moved from his position, but his eyes were now open, and he had a faint smile on his face. She grimaced. "I should have known that I wouldn't get away with it. You're looking entirely too smug. How long have you been awake?"

"Since you slid out of bed." He held out his hand to her. "I missed you. I'm sorry you found me so unsatisfactory that you decided to skip out on me. Come back to bed, and I'll try to do better."

Unsatisfactory? She could still feel her body throbbing with heat just looking at him. The tan skin, that tousled fair hair and teasing smile . . . He knew very well what those hours of erotic experimentation had done to her. She wanted nothing more than to run to him and jump back into his bed. "I thought I'd go to my room to shower and get dressed."

"Later," he said softly. "I've just thought of another way to prove myself to you. You have to let me try to redeem myself. It's only fair."

"I think I should go now. It's almost noon. I meant to leave much earlier and you know it. I was lying there beside you and I thought how hard it was going to be the longer that I—" She stopped short as she caught a flicker of expression cross Jock's face. She suddenly stiffened. "And that's what you meant to do, isn't it? I believe you're the one who's not being fair. Isn't that true? You're taking advantage of the fact that you nearly drove me crazy last night, to use it to delay what I told you I had to do."

He was silent. Then he shrugged and sat up in bed. "Guilty. You weren't the only one who went a little crazy last night. And I went a little more insane when I saw you heading for that door. I'd been waiting for you to come back to me, then I saw you leaving, and I remembered you'd told me you were going after Joe this morning. The rest was pure instinct." He met her gaze across the room. "I won't lie to you, it might happen again. I'll use any weapon I have to keep you safe. And I would have made certain that particular weapon would have pleased us both."

That would have gone without saying. How could she be angry with him? Wouldn't she do the same to keep him safe? She thought helplessly. "It still wasn't fair. I told you what I had to do, Jock."

"And I tried to distract you from doing it. Aye, it wasn't honorable, it was only expedient." He asked warily, "What are you going to do now? Am I going to have trouble with you?"

"I believe there's no question you are. You have to realize that I'm very vulnerable where you're concerned, and you have to be honest with me. I've trusted you all my life, and I can't lose that just because of all this sex stuff."

His lips twitched. "All this sex stuff? You weren't treating it so casually an hour ago."

"I'm serious, Jock."

His smile faded. "I know you are. Come over here."

She hesitated, then slowly went to stand beside the bed.

He took her hand and lifted her palm to his lips. "You can trust me forever, and I won't use sex again. But you'll have to keep an eye on me with anything else that's involved in keeping you alive. Consider it a challenge."

His lips felt warm and soft on her palm, and she felt the beginning of a sensuous tingle in her wrist. It was starting again. "You're always a challenge." She forced herself to pull her hand away. "But I guess that will have to be good enough for the time being." She turned and headed back toward the door. "And you asked what I'm going to do now? I'm going to my room to shower and pack. I want to get on the road in the next hour or so." She turned to look at him as she opened the door. "I invited you to go with me. You never answered me."

"You knew I'd never let you go alone."

She smiled faintly. "But you hoped you'd never be forced to do it, that you'd be able to send me home so that you and Joe could team up again."

"Absolutely."

"Sorry. You're stuck with me. I'll see you in forty-five minutes."

"Make it an hour. I want to give Nikolai another call and check on how many of Svardak's men they'd managed to capture and interrogate." He got out of bed and strode naked toward the bathroom. "Then I need to see if I can reach Joe so that I can see where the hell we should be heading." He stopped and glanced over his shoulder. After those last curt, brusque words, his mischievous grin came as a surprise. "Would you consider that I was using sex as a weapon if I asked you if you wanted to share the shower with me? We haven't done that yet."

The words were solemn, the sexuality tamped down, and the humor like a gentle nudge. This was a cross between Jock, the best friend, with all the knowing intimacy of Jock, the lover. She knew he meant it to make her fully at ease with that relationship. She grinned back at him. "It would come very close."

He sighed. "I was afraid you'd say that." He closed the door behind him.

LAKE KEDROW
12:10 P.M.

Joe lifted his head and breathed in the scents of the forest, mentally separating out the scents. Nothing suspicious, it could be hunters or campers. Or it could be someone very suspicious. He hoped to hell it was.

He went a few yards farther, then stopped beside a brook and knelt as he'd been trained to do when tracking prey in an open area. It was best not to announce his presence until necessary.

He sniffed the air again. A campfire burned nearby, perhaps two miles away. He couldn't see a smoke trail in the sky, but judging from the wind, the campsite was probably due west. Not a bad place to start. He bypassed the trail and headed into the dense forest, keeping his eyes peeled for any sign of human life. Aside from a couple long-overgrown campsites, there was none.

The fire's odor came and went with each turn of the wind. The air was increasingly damp, and the clouds darkened as he pushed farther into the woods. A misty rain began to fall. After about two and a half miles, he stopped. The trees had abruptly thinned, revealing a large cedar structure with a flap pole on one side of the large porch.

"Can I help you?" The deep, craggy voice came from within the structure. In the next instant, a tall man stepped out onto that sizable front porch. He was wearing the uniform of a U.S. National Forest Service ranger.

Joe nodded. Of course. He'd run smack into a ranger substation. That must have been the rather peculiar structure he'd noticed from across the lake. "Just out for a hike," he said.

The man looked at him doubtfully. "Going off the beaten path, aren't you? We recommend hikers stick close to the trail."

Joe shrugged as he glanced around. "I know what I'm doing."

The man smiled and adjusted his ranger hat. "The last time someone said that to me, I ended up loading him onto a medevac with a pair of broken legs."

"That won't be me."

"Confidence isn't always a good thing, especially out here." He waved his hand back toward the door.

"Come inside and have a cup of coffee. I'll give you some good maps that'll save you a lot of problems."

"Sounds great." Joe cocked his head back toward the forest. "I left my backpack on a rock back there. I'll go get it and be back in ten or fifteen—"

"I'll go with you," the man interrupted. He walked down the four short steps and joined Joe in the clearing.

"That's really not necessary."

"It's easy to get lost around here, especially if you're going off path. I need to stretch my legs anyway."

"Sure." Joe walked alongside the man, slipping the strap of his canteen off his shoulder. "It's just through here."

"Lead the way. I'll be right behind you."

"I appreciate your taking the time." Joe surreptitiously unclipped the strap. An instant later, he let the canteen fall to the ground. "Oops."

The man bent over to pick it up for him. "I got it. Trust me, you don't want to lose this if . . ."

Joe spun around and snapped his canteen strap around the man's neck!

As the man writhed and tried to reach the gun tucked into his belt, Joe kneed him in his lower back and pulled the handgun away. Joe punched him in the back, and the man's legs simply ceased to work. He slumped over as the strap closed off the last of his air.

"You have about thirty seconds before you lose consciousness," Joe whispered. "Death will come about ninety seconds later. If I choose to revive you, I can probably do it within a couple minutes after that."

The man desperately clawed for air.

Joe smiled.

"You might have a few extra minutes if I can find a defibrillator in that ranger station, but that seems like a lot of work to me."

Joe let him fall to his knees, easing the pressure on his throat. The man leaned back and looked at him with eyes that were suddenly bloodshot. He still couldn't talk.

"Where's the ranger you took the uniform from?" Joe said. "For your sake, he'd better still be alive."

The man's lips quivered as he struggled to form a single word. "How . . . ?"

"The uniform gave you away. The hat brim is supposed to be two fingers above the eyebrows. This one was slightly too small for you. Plus, your socks are gray. Brown socks are regulation." He deliberately twisted the strap tighter. The man gagged. "And every ranger knows undershirts aren't supposed to be visible. You were careless." Joe shrugged. "I went through SEAL basic training with a guy who was studying to go into the forestry service until all the rules and regulations drove him nuts. He thought he might as well join the SEALs if he had to go through all that."

The man tried to stand, but Joe pushed him down by the shoulders. "Stay where you are. What's your name?"

"You think I'll just tell you that?"

Joe tugged at the canteen strap, once again constricting his captive's airway. "I think you will."

The man hesitated before speaking. "Lacher."

"You work for Svardak?"

Lacher nodded.

"Where is he?"

Lacher hesitated, and Joe once again tugged at the strap. "In a camper . . . a few miles from here," Lacher rasped. "He's waiting for my call."

"After you kill me?"

"That was never part of the plan. He just wanted you immobilized."

Joe thought for a moment. "Okay. Slowly, and I mean slowly, pull the phone from your pocket. You're going to call your boss."

"And tell him what?"

"Tell him I'm unconscious and tied up in that ranger station. If you say anything else, I'll have no choice but to terminate the conversation immediately. And that means terminating you. Understand?"

Lacher reached into his pocket with thumb and forefinger and slowly pulled out his phone.

"Be convincing," Joe said. "Your life depends on it."

A bullet plowed into the pine tree next to him!

Joe instinctively whirled and raised Lacher toward the sound, using him as a human shield. Using the canteen strap as a leash, Joe jerked him behind a thick clump of brush. "Who's your friend?" Joe whispered. "Abrams?"

Before Lacher could reply, another shot was fired. "You want to kill your buddy?" Joe shouted. "No problem. One more shot, and he's a dead man."

Joe finally made out a figure in the trees. The man was taller than Lacher and appeared to be holding a rifle.

"Drop the gun, and you may survive the day," Joe called out.

The man didn't drop the gun. Instead, he walked toward Joe, still holding his rifle in front of him. Was the son of a bitch crazy?

And then Joe recognized him.

Svardak!

Then he felt the white-hot agony as a bullet tore into him from behind!

"You fool, Abrams! Stop *hitting* him." Svardak tore Abrams away from Quinn. "You shot him, you didn't have to start pistol-whipping him. If you've killed the bastard, I'll cut your heart out." Svardak bent over Joe Quinn's body, shoved him over on his back, and tore open his shirt. He was unconscious and bleeding from a wound in his upper right shoulder, but he was breathing. "He's alive, and he'd better stay alive. Get him inside and stop that bleeding, Lacher." He straightened and moved up the steps to the porch. "Why the hell couldn't the two of you obey orders?"

"He was too damn fast. I was lucky to get a shot at all," Abrams said sourly as he watched Lacher start to drag Quinn up the steps. "Lacher was supposed to either take him out or set him up for me. Blame him."

"I do." He was scowling at Lacher, who was trying to take himself out of view with Quinn as quickly as possible. "I couldn't believe how easily Quinn took him down. He forced me to go after him myself," Svardak said. "Amateur."

"He took me by surprise." Lacher was now dragging Quinn through the office toward the first-aid room. "It won't happen again."

"No, it won't. I'm tempted to let Abrams make certain of it. But I need you, so you're going to get another chance. I never know when someone will decide to come here and check on those rangers. I think the blood's almost stopped. He didn't lose much." He watched Lacher lift Quinn onto the exam table. He took a step closer and examined the wound. "The bullet's still in there. Leave it. Just clean him up." His lips twisted. "It looks like you lucked out, Abrams. Because if you'd robbed me of the pleasure of putting that bitch through hell as she watches what I do to Quinn, I'd have to do it to you instead."

"I did what you said." He moistened his lips. "It's Lacher who screwed up. He almost lost him."

"You both almost lost him," Svardak said with

disgust. "He's only one man and you couldn't even spring the trap. I can't trust either—"

"Svar . . . dak . . ."

Svardak's gaze flew down to Joe Quinn's face. His eyes were open and focused on Svardak's face. "Oh, you're back with us? Good. How nice that you recognize me. May I say I'm delighted that you'll be around to help me teach Cara that I always keep my word?"

"Cara . . ." His eyes were suddenly sharp and fully aware. "You don't have Cara, you son of a bitch."

"No, not yet. Only her dear friend and guardian. But that makes me at least halfway to the final goal." He bent closer, and his voice was silky-soft. "She is so fond of you. It would hurt her very much to see you suffer." He reached out and pressed the bullet wound with his thumb. Quinn jerked and bit his lower lip. "You didn't scream." He pressed down again, grinding harder. "Amazing. I'm tempted to keep on until you do scream, but I want the pain fresh when she sees it." He turned and headed for the door. "But that doesn't mean I won't allow myself to enjoy myself a bit while I'm waiting for her."

"By all means." Quinn's voice was hoarse but still strong. "It's all the enjoyment you're going to get. You won't have another chance at Cara. Gavin has her now, and there's no way he'll let you get close to her."

"Gavin . . . I've heard that name before. I've been trying to check on him. He appears to be a threat." Svardak looked back at him. "But then, he may not be a danger to my plans at all. I got to know Cara so well when we were together. She's a poisonous mixture of bitch and soft sentimentality. Do you really believe she'd let anyone stop her if she thought you were being tortured?" He chuckled in delight as he saw Joe Quinn's expression. "Now that scared you, didn't it? You're not as certain of Gavin's ability to keep control of her as you tried to make me believe. We'll see who's right." He turned to the door. "Get him cleaned up, Lacher. And make certain that you cuff him afterward. If he escapes, you're a dead man."

CHAPTER

12

I still couldn't get hold of Joe," Jock said as he pulled out of the hotel driveway. "Not surprising, but it means we'll just have to travel to the last place from where he contacted us and try to get in touch with him on the way. That was Wheeling for me night before last. You?"

"The same. Eve and he try to stay in touch every day. I'll call her and see if she's heard anything from him more recently. He also tries to check in with the captain of his precinct daily, but I'd bet on Eve."

"You always bet on Eve." He glanced at her with a smile. "And so do we all. By all means, phone her. Even if she hasn't talked to Joe, she'll be glad to hear from you. I'd call her, but I've proved myself a complete failure where she's concerned. She was counting on me to persuade you to join her at the lake house."

"If anyone had been able to do it, you'd have been the one. She knew that I'd do whatever you wanted . . ." She darted him a glance as she added, "If I could."

"If you chose," he murmured. "That's a major difference. As I said, I've been a failure where that's—"

Cara's cell was ringing.

No ID.

She stiffened. Her hand clenched on the phone as she stared down at it.

"Easy," Jock said quietly. "It doesn't have to be that son of a bitch."

But it could be him. He'd called her only last night. "I know." She couldn't take her eyes off that ID. "And if it is, it may not mean anything. He likes to toy with me." She reached out and pressed the access. "Hello."

"It took you long enough to answer," Svardak said. "I'll have to teach you to jump when I snap my fingers the way Marian did. As it happens, I've found just the way to do it."

"You're lying, Svardak." She saw Jock stiffen and pressed the speaker button. "Everything you told me about Marian I chalk up as one of your delusions. You're insane, and you've been lying to me since the moment I woke up in that cabin."

"Have I? You like to believe that because it hurts you to admit how she suffered. I suppose I'll just have to prove that I don't lie to you, Cara." His voice lowered to deep malice. "Or perhaps I'll ask someone you trust to convince you. That would please me much more."

She inhaled sharply. "What are you talking about?"

"I told you last night that I was almost ready to put a noose on your Joe Quinn as I once promised you I'd do. You didn't believe me then."

"And I don't believe you now. He's too smart for you. Joe was able to find you before and put you on the run. He'll do the same thing this time."

"Really? I'd be angry if I wasn't so amused." He raised his voice. "What do you say, Quinn? Are you too smart for me?" He laughed. "He's not answering. I've found he's quite the stoic. I wasn't even able to get a response from him when I experimented with that bullet wound in his shoulder. I don't know many men who could take that degree of pain."

Shock after shock. *Don't believe him. He only wants to hurt me. No proof.* "Another lie," she said unsteadily. "You don't have Joe."

He sighed. "Oh, but I do. I'm tempted to make him scream for you, but as I said, he's tough. It might take too much of my time, and I don't want to upset you . . . yet. I suppose you'll have to see for yourself. I need a minute to display him properly. I'll call you back on FaceTime." He cut the connection.

Cara pressed the disconnect. "He sounded so certain, Jock," she said numbly. "What if he does have him? And he said something about a bullet . . ."

"Don't panic until you know for sure. Then we'll deal with it."

Her gaze flew to his face. "But you think it might be true?"

"I think he knows more than I'd like him to know about Joe's reactions."

And Cara had thought the same thing. "But he's researched him, he'd know what—"

Her phone was ringing again. Jock pulled off the road and stopped the car.

She quickly punched the access. A request for FaceTime. She punched the accept button.

"That's right," Svardak said. "Now let me point my phone at your dear guardian. Are you ready, Cara?"

No, she wasn't ready. She was terrified.

"Well, I'm ready," Svardak murmured. "I've been waiting for this for a long time." He swung the camera toward a chair across the room. "Don't be rude, Quinn. Say hello to her."

Joe!

Her heart lurched. She felt sick.

Blood. Joe was bleeding, and he was so pale. He was handcuffed and tied to a chair across the room. "Joe." She swallowed. "How badly has he hurt you?"

"Minor," he said curtly. "I'll be okay. Don't let him use me against you. Do you understand? That will be what he wants. Don't let him have it."

"But she'll find that so hard to do," Svardak said. "He still has the bullet in that wound. I can make it hurt him, Cara. You know how good I am at causing pain."

"What do you want from me?" she said unsteadily.

"I believe you know the answer." He moved the camera over Joe's face, then to his bloody shoulder. "I want you. I deserve you. You're the key to bringing Kaskov to his knees. And I owe you much more pain than I had the opportunity to inflict on you. Quinn is my opportunity to rectify that omission."

"You want a trade."

"Exactly. You have such a tender heart, and you must realize that you were destined to die. You were tribute. It was only wild chance that allowed you to escape me."

"It was also a dagger of glass shoved into your stomach. Does it still hurt?"

"Yes. And you'll pay for it." The camera suddenly was focused again on his own face. "You'll pay for all of it." His mouth was tight and ugly. "And Kaskov will watch you do it. I'm going to call him and tell him that the game is on again."

"You're so confident that I'd give my life for Joe? When I don't even know if you'd keep your word to let him live?"

"That's the chance you'll take. Could you stand the thought if you didn't take it?"

"I couldn't stand the thought that you'd made a fool of me. I wouldn't let you get hold of me again without getting something in return." She took a deep breath. "You haven't won yet, Svardak."

"Don't let him win at all." It was Joe's rough voice in the background. "For God's sake, back off, Cara."

"I am backing off," she said. "Svardak, give me proof that you'll let Joe live and we'll talk again. Or let me decide the terms I'll accept."

Silence. "I'm not going to let you dictate to me." He smiled. "But I find I like the idea of giving you an ex-cruciatingly painful period to dwell on what I intend to do to Quinn. You're so sensitive that would be a tor-ture in itself. And come to think of it, I suppose I do need a bit of time to arrange to bring in enough guards to keep you from being stolen from me again. That's never going to happen, Cara. Once I have you, you're mine. And it will be a long, long time before I decide I've had enough." He added silkily, "Yes, perhaps I'll see how you feel after twenty-four hours of worrying about what I'm doing to Quinn. I believe you'll be much more amenable." He cut the connection.

"No!" Jock's voice was clipped, his gaze on her face, as he took the phone out of her clenched hand. "Hell, no." He took her in his arms. "Don't even think about it."

She clutched frantically at his shoulders. "I *have* to think about it. I don't have anything else." She buried her face in his chest. "It's Joe. He was . . . bleeding, Jock."

"He said the wound was minor."

"He'd say that anyway," she said shakily. "You know it as well as I do."

Jock didn't deny it. "It could be true. They had him cuffed, they still perceived him as a threat. Svardak had been torturing him, and it hadn't fazed him."

"Stop it." She pushed back and looked up at him.

"I'm imagining enough without you analyzing every detail."

"You're not imagining enough to keep you from jumping in to play Svardak's dirty game," he said grimly. "No way. Joe told you to back off. You're going to do it."

"Do you think I want to go back to that monster?" she asked fiercely. "I have you, I have the music, I have family. I won't let them be taken away from me without a fight." She swallowed. "But he will make me fight. I could see it. He feels humiliated that I got away from him. He thinks he's failed his Anna. He'll want to make it up to her."

"He can make it up to her when I send him down to hell to join her," Jock said. "And I won't let him touch you." His hands tightened on her shoulders. "Now stop telling me that you'll fight to keep him from doing it. Say it's *not* going to happen. Say it."

She couldn't say it. She looked up at him. "It's Joe," she whispered. "That's why we've got to find a way to bring him home. I have so much to lose. I'll do anything I can not to let Svardak win."

"Joe wouldn't want this. He told you no."

"But he didn't tell me what to say to Eve and Michael if I let him die," she said simply.

He muttered a curse. "Damn you." Then his hands dropped away from her, and he started the car. "He won't win. Forget it." He pulled back on the road. "We have at least twenty-four hours. If it takes longer, we'll find a way to extend it."

"We're still going to Wheeling?"

"Until we find somewhere else more likely. Get on the phone and call Eve and see if she can tell us anything more. We need to know everything she knows about where Joe was in those mountains. Maybe we can GPS his phone." He frowned. "Though I'm sure that Svardak would have destroyed it by now."

Cara was already dialing. "I don't want to do this. Dear God, I'm dreading telling her about Joe."

"You'll have to do it."

"Of course. I have to be honest with her. I'd want to know myself even if it terrified me." And it did terrify her. She was still having trouble keeping from shaking. "Eve has to face the possibility of Joe's being in danger every time he walks out the door in the morning. It doesn't make it any easier for her." She shook her head. "And it doesn't make it easier for me that I brought this threat to her."

"Bullshit. Kaskov hand delivered this one on our doorstep. No one is going to blame you."

"The poison was there, but I increased the venom a thousandfold while I was with Svardak. I made him hate me. I just have to find a way to keep it from hurting Joe. I need to—" She broke off as Eve answered the phone. She took a deep breath. "Hi, Eve, Cara. I'm sorry, but I have to ask you a few questions about Joe. When was the last time you talked to him?"

Silence. "Yesterday evening. I talked to him twice yesterday, but I lost the connection on the first call." Another silence. "Why are you asking? What the hell is wrong?"

She should have known that Eve would pick up on her disturbance immediately. She'd been awkward and stiff, and it had almost spelled out her panic. "Too much. That's why we have to track him down." She briefly told her about the call from Svardak. "But we'll find him, Eve," she added quickly. "We're on our way right now. We just have to get some idea where he was traveling." Eve wasn't speaking. Cara could sense the terror she was feeling. "Eve?"

"You bet we'll find him." Eve drew a harsh breath.

"I'm sorry. Let me pull myself together. What did you ask? You have to know where he said he was when I talked to him? It's hard to think right now. Saltor, I think he said. He mentioned the Saltor River. And Ruell Falls. And there were several other places . . . I'll text you the ones now that I can remember. I'll call you back with a complete list. I'll have to go over Michael's notebook when he gets home from school to make sure I don't forget any of them."

"Michael?"

"Michael always wants me to tell him where Joe is and what he's doing. He has a notebook in which he charts where Joe is every day. I think it's a healthy outlet for him and makes him feel closer to Joe and less worried."

"I can see that it would," Cara said. "When can you call us back? The sooner we get that complete list, the better."

"Do you think I don't know that?" Eve said jerkily. "But I'm not thinking straight. I won't wait for Kaskov's guard to bring Michael home after soccer practice. I'll go pick him up myself as soon as I pack."

"Pack?" Cara had been afraid this would be the inevitable result the instant Eve knew Joe was in danger. She could hardly blame her. "You do realize that Jock and I are going to find Joe and bring him home."

"I realize you're going to do everything you can. But you're not going to do it without me." She drew a deep, shaky breath. "Look, I have to get moving, and I'm not in great shape right now. As soon as I get off the phone, I have to call Catherine Ling and ask her if she'll take Michael again. Then I'll send you that first text before I throw a few things in my duffel. I'll call you from Michael's school the minute I pick him up and go over his notes." She was silent an instant before she added unsteadily, "Maybe not the first minute. I've got to tell him about Joe." Then she cleared her throat. "But right after that, I'll be in touch, Cara. I promise." She cut the connection.

"Okay?" Jock asked, his gaze on her face as she put down her cell.

Cara slowly shook her head. "No." There was nothing okay about any single part of this, and Eve was already being hurt in all kinds of ways. The sound of her voice before she'd hung up had almost broken Cara's heart. "How on earth is she going to tell Michael?"

How was she going to tell Michael? Eve asked herself for the hundredth time as she drove into the athletic parking lot two hours later. The tension was causing the muscles of her back to lock at the mere thought. Or maybe it wasn't the dread of telling Michael about his father but just the sheer terror she was feeling about Joe. It was hard to separate her feelings when they were all the stuff of nightmares.

Stop whining. Just do what has to be done.

She parked her car beside the blue Subaru where Kaskov's guard was sitting waiting for Michael to finish his practice. Cheknof nodded politely but didn't roll down the window. Evidently, both guards had orders to be virtually invisible and seldom spoke. That was fine; all she cared about was that one of them was always with Michael. Cheknof would never leave the parking lot of Michael's school until he brought her son home. She supposed should have remembered to call him to tell him she'd be here to pick up her son, but that had been the last thing on her mind after Cara's call.

And she wasn't about to worry about it now. Her gaze was focused on the soccer field and the boys in their navy-and-gold uniforms. She had to find Michael and get through that dreaded talk without breaking down.

"Good afternoon, Mrs. Quinn." Coach Eastman was striding across the field, his brown face lit with a warm smile. "It's good to see you. Beautiful day, isn't it? What can I do for you?"

She forced a smile. "Beautiful. I just came by to pick up Michael. I'm afraid we've had an emergency, and he has to leave early." Her gaze was back searching the field. "I don't see him. Where is he?"

"What?" The coach frowned. "There must be a mistake." He checked his clipboard. "Michael was never here today. He's on the absentee roster. Maybe another of his relatives picked him up. Mix-ups happen when there's an emergency."

Eve froze. "Not here? Yes, definitely a mistake. He *has* to be here." Her gaze was frantically searching the young boys on the field. No copper-haired Michael running toward her. "Call the office. Only one person had my official permission to pick up my son, and he's sitting in the parking lot waiting for him. There was no mix-up."

"I'll call right away." Eastman was punching numbers. "But I'm certain we'll find there's an explanation. It's not as if Michael is ever a problem."

An explanation. But the only explanation that was occurring to her was causing her to shake with terror. Svardak. First, Joe. Now, Michael. Two people who were the center of Eve's life and who Cara also considered as beloved family. The bastard would consider it a coup to take not only Joe, but his son from both of them. "Yes, you check." She turned and started to run. "Come to the parking lot when you finish."

She tore across the field. It didn't have to be Svardak, she told herself desperately. Yes, he'd regard it as a double triumph, but it would be difficult to coordinate taking her son as well as Joe. Perhaps it would be too difficult from where he was in the mountains. Hope, and look in another direction.

She skidded to a stop in front of the Subaru. "Get out of that car, Cheknof. *Now.*"

Cheknof hesitated, then got out of the driver's seat. He was a bearded young man who had the strength and build of a wrestler. But he was looking at her warily. She couldn't blame him. She could feel the heat in her cheeks and the wildness pounding through her. She probably looked as fierce as she felt. "You have a problem?" he asked.

"You may have the problem. Where is my son?"

He stiffened. "Soccer." He nodded at the field. "I wait for him."

"He's not there. His coach said that he hasn't been at school all day. What did you do to him?"

His eyes widened in alarm. "I did nothing. I did what I always do. I let him out at the front door, then waited outside. He knows to call me if there is a problem. He told me to pick him up here at the soccer field."

"And he didn't call you?"

He shook his head. "I stayed here. I watched all entrances. I did nothing wrong."

She reached for her phone to make the call she should have made if she hadn't gone into a tailspin. She punched in Michael's number.

Answer me.

Five rings.

No answer.

It went to voice mail.

The panic was tearing through her.

Her eyes were blazing as she looked back at Cheknof. "Last chance. Tell me who paid you. Tell me what happened to my son." She started to dial. "Or I won't be the one to whom you'll have to answer."

"Who are you calling?" Cheknof's scowl was menacing. He took a step toward her. "Hang up that phone."

"The hell I will." The phone was ringing, but she took a step backward as Cheknof took another step forward. "Tell me what happened to Michael."

"You will *not* tell Nikolai I did not do my duty."

"No, not Nikolai, Kaskov." She held up her hand as the cell call was answered. "And you stop right there, Cheknof. He's on the line."

"What are you doing, Eve?" Kaskov asked curtly. "I answered your call because Gavin just phoned and told me about Joe Quinn. But now it sounds as if you're using me. I don't permit that from anyone."

"Too bad. I am using you, and I might not have to do it if you didn't hire scumbags who would sell anyone to the highest bidder."

Silence. "I believe that you might be referring to one or two of my employees who I sent to you at Cara's request. You're finding them unacceptable? What did they do?"

"Michael's gone," she said harshly. "I thought at first it might be Svardak, but it would be difficult for him to pull off without help. And you supplied me with two dirtbag criminals who I'm sure would fill his bill."

"Don't be rude. You're making assumptions. To which dirtbag are you referring?"

"Cheknof was on guard."

"And he was the one you were telling to stop when I answered the phone. Stop what?"

"Mayhem. Murder. Whatever he could get away with. Tell him to give me back my son."

"Speaks the ferocious mama bear. I'm sure he's already intimidated, but I'll speak to him. Give him the phone."

She took the phone to Cheknof and handed it to him. "Kaskov," she said curtly. "Talk to him."

He was still scowling with menace as he took the phone. But he was actually pale, and his hand was shaking, she noticed, as Russian words began to tumble from his lips. The power Kaskov wielded was blatantly evident.

She stood there, tense, glaring at him, waiting as Cheknof stuttered and mumbled his way through the conversation. Then he sighed with relief and thrust the phone back at her. "You should not have done that. I told you I would never betray him."

She knew he was talking about Kaskov and not her son. But she hoped it would come down to the same thing. She lifted the phone to her ear. "He's looking too relieved. What if he's lying to you?"

"He's not lying. He knows that's not safe, and he has a good sense of self-preservation."

"I don't doubt it," she said dryly. "He was ready to murder me to keep me from unleashing Nikolai on him."

"You made a mistake threatening him. You should have called me right away."

"Mistake?" she said fiercely. "I can't find Michael, and Joe's been shot. There are no mistakes, no right or wrong, until I can put my life back together again. Your errand boy should have kept Michael safe. You promised Cara."

"Yes, I did," he said quietly. "I thought I'd done what she wanted, but somehow I failed her. Now I have to find out what went wrong. I've told Cheknof that he's to make certain that nothing happens to you and to discover exactly how Michael disappeared on his watch."

"I don't want to know how, I want to know who." She saw Coach Eastman running toward her. "And if you aren't able to tell me that, I'm going to call Joe's captain and see if the police can find out." The coach had reached her, and she said curtly, "I have to hang up now. I'll call you later." She whirled to face Eastman. "What did you find out from the office? Who checked him out of school?"

"No one." The coach's expression was sympathetic. "It's as I said, Michael never showed up for homeroom. So he was placed on the absentee list. If you don't believe there was a mistake, the principal is willing to contact the authorities to investigate."

"Willing? I'm going to call them myself."

"I was not to blame," Cheknof said harshly. "No one took the boy. I would have seen it. I would have known."

"He's not here," she said, through set teeth. "You didn't know. No one saw him. He's not Houdini. He didn't just disappear after he walked through those—" Her phone was signaling a text.

Michael!

Dear God, a text from Michael.

Just two words. THE LOCKER.

Michael's locker? A ransom demand or message from Svardak?

She whirled on the coach. "I need to get into Michael's locker right now. I don't have the combination. Can you get it from the office?"

"Not necessary." Cheknof took the coach's arm and propelled him back toward the building. "I'll do it. Tell me the number."

Eastman checked his sheet. "It's 1531. But it would only take me a minute."

But Eve wasn't about to delay even another second. "Let him do it." She was hurrying after Cheknof. She *had* to know what was in that locker.

But when Cheknof swung open the metal door of the locker, it was only to reveal schoolbooks, a pair

of tennis shoes . . . and Michael's notebook. He might
have left the other items, but he wouldn't have left
that notebook. She took out the notebook and flipped
through the pages.

Dad . . .

Notes. Maps. Descriptions of areas . . .

And on the last page an envelope.

Her hands were shaking as she opened it.

A note in Michael's familiar scrawl.

*I'm sorry, Mom. Dad told me to watch out for
you, but I think we have to watch out for him
now. Last night after I went to bed, I could feel
something bad coming toward him. I knew you
wouldn't let me go with you, so I decided to go on
ahead. I'll call you when I reach the mountains
and meet you there. Don't worry, I'll be fine, and
we'll find him together. That's how it should be.*

Love,
Michael

"Shit," she whispered. Her hand clenched on the pa-
per. This was almost more terrifying than what she had
feared before. Michael alone, trying to make his way
hundreds of miles into the mountains in search of Joe.
It was crazy and she was getting panicky at the thought.

"Bad news?" Coach Eastman asked. "Anything I
can do? Will we need the authorities?"

"Yes." She slammed the locker shut. "But I'll contact them. It isn't what I thought. Thank you, Coach."
Her head was whirling. She had to get back to her car,
where she could sit and think and try to make a decision what was best to do. She walked quickly down
the hall and out into the parking lot. She wasn't aware

that Cheknof was trailing behind her until she'd almost reached her car. "You don't have to come with me. I won't need you."

He shook his head. "Kaskov says nothing must happen to you."

She gazed at him incredulously. Joe might be on the verge of death, she'd lost Michael, but nothing must happen to *her*? It wasn't worth arguing about. She got into the Toyota and slammed the door.

Her hands clenched on the steering wheel as she gazed blindly out the windshield. *I don't know what to do, Joe. Michael's really done it this time. But how can I blame him? He loves you, and he's fighting the same fight I am. I won't let you die, and I have to keep him safe. Help me, love.*

Help her? Joe was the one who needed help, and she was whining and trying to lean on him. *Think.* She had to work it out for herself. Smother the panic and handle one thing at a time. Michael was exceptionally clever, and they had taught him to protect himself from any ordinary threat. That should bring her some small measure of relief. Very small. But if any child could develop a coherent plan to get himself safely out of the city to those mountains, it would be Michael. She would try to think how to follow his steps until she found him.

First, see if Michael had even been able to accomplish what he'd set out to do. He'd been gone for most of the day, so time was on his side. But it wasn't easy for a young boy to travel unaccompanied without running a gauntlet of questions. She needed help in tracking him down, and it had to be fast. She reached for her phone and started to dial the number for Joe's captain, Ezra Campbell, at the precinct.

TENNESSEE–KENTUCKY BORDER
FOUR HOURS LATER

Eve's cell phone was ringing.

She glanced down at the ID on her phone. Cara. She braced herself. She hadn't answered it when Cara had called before because she had been caught up in tracking Michael. But she knew she had to answer now. It wasn't fair not to involve Cara even if Eve's first instinct was to protect her from worrying about Michael. Cara loved him, and she was family. Eve pressed the access. "Hello, Cara. I meant to call you back, but there were . . . complications."

"I thought there might be," Cara said gently. "I wanted to give you a little time to recover, but I was worried about you. I did receive the text you sent a few hours ago listing the other towns from Michael's notebook." Cara hesitated. "It took you a little longer than you thought it would to get back to me. How badly did Michael take the news about Joe?"

"I didn't get a chance to tell him," Eve said bluntly. "Though it wouldn't surprise me if he already knew. Something spooked him. He seemed to know something bad was going to happen to Joe and took off to the rescue."

"Took off? How could he do that? What do you mean?"

"Exactly what it sound its like. When I got to Michael's school, I found he'd flown the coop and left me a note."

"What? Eve, what did you do?"

"You mean besides have a nervous breakdown? I called Joe's captain and set him to trying to find Michael. Thank heavens he and Joe have known each other for years, and he hopped right on it. He's smart, and runaways aren't that rare to the police. The first thing he asked me was if Michael had money. The second was if his school was anywhere near a train or bus station. Michael did have the allowance he earned for chores. The second answer was that there was a Greyhound bus station several blocks from the school."

"And you found him?"

"I didn't get that lucky. But I do know that he's not being held by some pervert and that Svardak doesn't have him. Michael slipped out of school and hiked to the Greyhound station. At 10:40, he was on a bus for Wheeling, West Virginia. Which coincidentally stops in Coal Town on the way."

"Oh, my God." Cara voice was hoarse. "They let him on the bus by himself? He's only ten years old."

"And he wanted on that bus," Eve said grimly. "He had no problem at all. You know he can charm the birds from the trees. The police tapped the video-surveillance tapes, and it showed Michael at his best. The captain showed me the videos. Michael had his savings so he had the cash for his ticket. He made friends with a family in the waiting room who had three children, and he just let them sweep him on the bus with them. If he'd had more time to do his magic, they probably would have wanted to adopt him."

"It was definitely Michael?"

"Cara." But she knew why Cara was questioning it. The idea was bizarre that Michael would be hopping on any bus. He should be at home and safe. "It was Michael. He knew the video cameras were there, and he looked up and smiled at me." And she had known that smile was for her. It had been filled with love and understanding and glowing comfort. It had nearly torn her apart when she'd seen that smile. "No doubt. The minute I saw it, I knew that Michael was on his way to West Virginia. I jumped in my car and headed out after him."

"Of course you did. But just the thought scares me," Cara said. "It seems as if Michael is heading straight toward Svardak, and there's nothing we can do about it. When is the bus supposed to get to Coal Town? Can't they have the police meet it?"

"They could if he was on it." She added shortly, "He wasn't. It arrived over an hour ago and no Michael. He must have slipped off the bus at the stop before Coal Town. It's a little town called Clearwater Creek. I'm about three hours from there. I'll stop and start asking questions soon."

"Do you want us to drive back and meet you? You shouldn't have to go through this alone."

"Don't you dare." She had known that would be Cara's first instinct. "Every minute is precious right now. There's no telling what Svardak is putting Joe through. I'll handle Michael." She added wearily, "He doesn't really want to run away from me, Cara. He just didn't want to be left behind when I went to help Joe and took matters into his own hands. He said that he'd call me once he reached the mountains. I believe he'll do it. Or answer my calls. He says it's important we find Joe together."

"I don't want you to be alone."

"Joe's alone. He's the only one we should be thinking about now. I'll head up to join you as soon as I pick up Michael. Where are you now?"

"Saltor. But we're heading toward Ruell Falls."

"Right. I'll call you when I'm on my way . . . with Michael. Be safe, Cara." She cut the connection.

It had been difficult to be positive when she was this tired and still worried sick about Michael. But she couldn't afford to be anything else right now. Think positive, say a prayer, and maybe everything would go their way.

Maybe . . .

No, not maybe. Do you hear me, Michael? You're going to be safe, your father is going to be safe. Count on it. Now call me, and we'll start making it happen.

"It's crazy, Cara." Jock's lips tightened. "There's no way that Eve should be anywhere near Svardak. If she's caught, it will just give that bastard more leverage against you. She should find Michael and go home."

"Which she won't do," Cara said flatly. "I can see her putting Michael into police custody to protect him, but now that she's here in the mountains, Eve won't leave without Joe. So don't even suggest it to her. Just find a way to use her and keep her safe." She glanced soberly at him. "Like you have to do for me."

"I know what you have in mind for yourself," he said grimly. "And I don't believe you'd want me to use *her* as bait when we find where Svardak is keeping Joe."

"I hope that we don't have to think on those terms for me either. It all depends on our finding Joe." She gazed out at the rocky, steep twists and turns ahead of them. "And I wish we had daylight so that we could see where we're going."

"I don't. That would cut down the time we have before we have to deal with Svardak. We might need that time." He suddenly pulled over to the side of the road. "Let's see if we can move a little faster." He took out his phone and punched in Kaskov's number. "We'll make Kaskov do some of the heavy lifting."

"Make?" Cara murmured.

"You object?"

She shook her head. "Only if you aren't careful the way you do it. He's unpredictable. I can't have him hurting you."

His brows rose. "I'll try to remember that restriction. Sometimes it's difficult with Kaskov." Then he was speaking into the phone as the call was answered. "I need you to do something, Kaskov," he said mockingly. "And Cara says that she wants me to be polite. I thought I'd warn you to keep you from going into shock."

"How refreshing." Kaskov's tone was dry. "On both counts. If it has anything to do with Eve and the child, I already have men tailing her. As soon as she makes contact with Michael, they'll both be safe."

"It's not about Eve. Nikolai said you had two prisoners from Lost Canyon. One of them was Edding."

"Whom you left tied up as a welcome present for us. How kind. But he doesn't appear to know anything of use about Svardak. We started preliminary questioning, and he squealed but didn't talk. He said that he was new to Svardak's team and wouldn't know how to contact him. We'll continue of course."

"All he has to know is Abrams's or Lacher's phone number. Svardak is obviously gathering what's left of his crew together. Edding can try to find out where."

"If he's new, they might not want to risk trusting him."

"Persuade him to be very convincing. Or send him to me, and I'll do it. You might say Edding and I formed a rock-solid understanding in our short acquaintance."

"I can imagine. I believe that I'll be able to take care of getting what you need." He paused. "How is Cara?"

"Stubborn."

"Don't let her do anything foolish. She's on the edge. Consider it extremely self-destructive on your part to let her fall. I would be very unhappy if anything of that nature happens."

"And your happiness is always my prime concern." Jock's sarcasm was biting. He added roughly, "Just do what I need you to do, and maybe we'll get through this with the least amount of damage. Call me back." He pressed the disconnect.

"You weren't polite," Cara said quietly.

"But we both survived it. That's a victory in itself. He caught me off guard. I didn't realize he could read you that well." He glanced at her. "Did you?"

"Yes." She smiled faintly. "But he's brilliant, and I'm pretty easy to read. I don't try to hide anything. I was just surprised he went to the trouble. But, of course, there's the music. That has to be it."

"Does it?" He was frowning, his gaze on her face. "Maybe . . ." Then he turned on the car and pulled back out on the road. "But at least we agree on the concept of no falling on swords for you. Now, if he does what he's supposed to do, we might be able to work toward a more productive ending to this hellish mess."

"So now we have to wait for Eve *and* Kaskov," Cara said. "What do we do in the meantime?"

"We follow this road until we get to the next town and try to find any bars or convenience stores or diners with anyone able to answer questions about seeing Joe or Abrams or Lacher or that farmer's truck. Then we go to the next town . . ."

CHAPTER

13

You haven't seen him?" Eve thrust the photo of Michael closer to the waitress. "Are you sure? Take another look. He's hard to forget."

"Yeah, I can see he would be." The waitress regretfully shook her head. "But he never came in here with the rest of those passengers from the bus. There was one woman and her little girl and a man of about sixty. I remember all three of them, and there was no boy." Her gaze was sympathetic. "Maybe he just used the bathroom at the gas station and got back on the bus?"

She was trying to be helpful, but Eve was getting frustrated. "No, that didn't happen. Thanks." She turned and walked out of the restaurant. But what did happen? She took a deep breath, her gaze searching the street that only offered a tavern and a Kroger grocery store a block away. Try the grocery store?

What if he hadn't gotten off the bus at this stop? She didn't believe he would have exited the bus at the stop that was over fifty miles before this one. She was beginning to get panicky again, and she tried to subdue it.

Where the devil are you, Michael?

She started walking toward the grocery store.

She'd only walked half a block before she got the call.

She snatched out her phone.

Relief tore through her.

Michael!

She punched the access. "I just might strangle you, Michael."

"Hi, Mom. Sorry."

"Sorry?" She drew a deep breath. "Lame. Very lame. Where are you?"

"I'm at the church on the street across from the grocery store. I was going to come to you after you left the restaurant, but then I saw you start down this way. Do you want me to wait for you?"

"Don't move a muscle. You might disappear again. I'll be right there." She could see the Methodist church now. It was a small, vine-covered, brick structure set back from the street, with a white neon cross glowing over the arched doors. It appeared to be totally dark and deserted except for that sign. How had Michael even managed to get inside? What did it matter? He was *here*. Her pace increased as she got nearer to it; and then she was running up the steps.

The door swung open as she reached the top. "Hi, Mom." Michael smiled at her. "Come in and sit down. You look tired. Those pews aren't very comfortable, but it's nice and quiet in here."

Michael! She stood there, her gaze going over him frantically. He appeared completely all right, but a trace of that panic she had felt when she'd found he was missing was still with her. She hadn't been able to be absolutely sure she'd get him back until this moment.

Michael's smile faded, and he launched himself at her, his arms encircling her waist. "It's okay, Mom," he whispered soothingly. "Everything's going to be okay. We'll just have to make it that way."

Her arms tightened around him as she fought for control. After a moment, she was able to push him away and look down at him. "This is not okay," she said shakily. "This is all wrong, Michael. Do you know how worried I've been?"

He nodded gravely. "But I tried to make it as short as I could. I had to come with you, and this was the only way I knew you'd let me do it."

"I'm still not going to let you do it. This was crazy, Michael." She pushed his tousled hair back from his face. "I know you're worried about your dad, but you've got to let me handle bringing him back to us. I won't be alone. Jock and Cara are looking for him now. Jock is very smart about hunting, and he'll find him."

He nodded. "I know he's smart." He grabbed her hand and led her toward the last pew, where a dim glow emitted from the pocket flashlight he'd propped against the wooden back. He gently pushed her down before he plopped down beside her. "But I can help. I *have* to help. I have to be with him. He needs me."

"And I need you to be safe so that I can concentrate on getting him back. That's the way you can help him."

He shook his head. "There has to be more." He hesitated, then added simply, "Or he might die, Mom."

The certainty in his voice frightened her as much as the thought of losing Joe. "He won't die, Michael. We'll save him. You won't make the difference."

"I might. I believe I could." He looked into her eyes. "Because I think I can find him."

She stiffened. "What?"

"I know where he is. I can see what he sees. I've been able to do it ever since the minute that man, Svardak, hurt him. It scared me, and everything came clear. I have to concentrate, but I can see it."

She inhaled sharply. "That's not possible."

"You know better than that, Mom." His amber eyes were clear and shining into her own. His voice was very gentle. "I've always known I was able to do it with you, but you were afraid for me, so I stopped. But never with Dad, just wisps of what he was feeling and seeing now and then. Like I said, I had to get really scared before it kind of jarred me into being able to hear what he was telling me."

"*Telling* you?"

"Wrong word. Not exactly telling me. He doesn't know I'm even listening and watching yet." He frowned thoughtfully. "But if I concentrate hard, I might be able to talk to him a little later. The way I did with you. I'll have to see how it works out. But just knowing where he is and what he's thinking will help us, won't it?"

"Of course it would help us." She was staring at him, stunned. "And I'm supposed to believe this, Michael?"

He smiled at her lovingly. "You do believe it. You know I'd never lie to you. I can . . . do things. You always knew it was there. You've only been hiding your eyes because you want to keep me safe and happy. That's fine with me, but you can't hide them any longer. Not until after we get Dad back. Admit it, Mom. You know it's true."

She didn't want to admit it. Facing that truth would mean opening a new page in all their lives. One that might leave Michael vulnerable. Yet she did believe every word he had said. The knowledge of Michael's special uniqueness had been with her since before he was born. Only what he was saying about Joe came as a shock. So she wouldn't lie to him or pretend any longer. She smiled shakily back at him. "But I was much more comfortable hiding my eyes. It's a difficult world, and I want you to see all the good before you see the bad."

"You show the good to me every day." He took her

hand. "And we'll face the bad together when it comes." He paused. "Just like Dad's doing right now. But we can't let him face it alone. I told you, I can help. *Let* me."

She gazed at him in agony. He was only a little boy, dammit. There had to be some way she could keep him out of this. "What would you do if I said no?"

"I'd find a way to leave you and go by myself. I have to help him."

She tried another path. "And what if I paid attention to everything you said about Joe. The only difference is that you just stay away from where he—" He was shaking his head. She stared at him in helpless frustration. Her hands clenched into fists. "You're just a kid, act like one."

He grinned. "After we get Dad back. Anything you want, Mom."

"So unless I let you go with me, you'll be tearing around these mountains, and I'll have to chase after you when I should be helping your father?"

He nodded. "Though if you follow me, I might be able to lead you to him. But I really don't want to be alone."

And she didn't want him to be alone. After these last hours without him, the idea was unbearable.

She drew a deep breath. "I don't like this. The mere idea hurts me." She was silent again. "And the only way I can stand it is if we have rules you'll obey. I'm always in charge. You'll always stay with me. When I give you an order, you'll always obey with no questions. Understand?"

His eyes were suddenly twinkling. "I understand that there are a lot of 'always' thrown into what you're telling me."

"And should be. I'm serious. This is totally insane, and I'm having major problems with it."

"And I understand that, too," he said gently. "And

I never want to upset you. Now can we go and start looking for Dad?"

"Not yet." She leaned back in the pew and tried to regain her composure. "Give me a minute to get my mind clear. It's not every day that I'm idiot enough to let myself be blackmailed by you." She added grimly, "And it better be the last."

He nodded. "After we get Dad back."

"You keep saying that. And that's the only thing that's making me think that maybe I'm not a completely horrible mother and the ultimate fool." Her lips were trembling. "Because we have to get Joe back, and you might have the key to do it. But I guess I have to know more about that part of you that you said I've been hiding from. I have to decide how far I can trust it." She swallowed hard. "I'll need to ask you a few questions. Am I the only one you've ever been able to reach? I want to know how this works. It's kind of like mind reading?"

"Sort of, I guess. But it's different between us. It's warm and nice, like two rivers flowing together. I like it, don't you?"

"Yes. But you didn't answer me."

"Sometimes I feel as if I might be able to read someone else, but I don't do it. It would be an intrusion if they couldn't read back. Bonnie says it's important to be polite."

"Bonnie!" Her nails bit into her palm. "Bonnie knows about this?"

He nodded. "Bonnie knows about lots of stuff. But she says I've got plenty of time to learn how to handle it later, that it will all come to me."

Bonnie. Standing beside him, protecting him, smoothing the way. Beloved Bonnie.

"Very wise advice." She cleared her throat. "And was it Bonnie who told you that your dad was in trouble?"

He shook his head. "No, Bonnie wasn't there after I went to bed last night. It was Dad, and something dark was heading toward him." His eyes were suddenly haunted. "I didn't like that darkness. That was why I knew that I had to go to him when I woke up. Then, later in the day, when I *felt* his pain, it scared me. It hurt so bad, Mom."

Her eyes widened in alarm. "You actually felt it?"

"It only hurt for an instant, then it was dark. But I knew he was still alive," he added soberly, "And I was glad I was already on my way to him." His eyes were suddenly glittering fiercely. "And that Svardak man hurt him later, too. Dad knows he likes to hurt him. So he won't let him see it."

"And did you feel that pain, too?" she asked tensely.

"Only the start. I had to leave him. But we've got to stop it."

"Yes, we do." She swept him into her arms and held him close. Nightmare on top of nightmare. How could she have guessed that Joe's pain would also be Michael's pain? It was hard to believe that the bond he now felt for Joe was so strong it would bring this additional risk and horror. Would he continue to share Joe's pain? She had the terrible feeling that he would. "And we will, Michael." She kissed his forehead, then forced herself to release him. She couldn't let this new terror overcome her. He was right, she had to stop it before the pain came to either one of them again. Now there was no choice at all about her bringing Michael with her. If Michael might be in danger of suffering any pain, she had to be there for him. "Now tell me how we can find your father. You said you could see what he sees, if you concentrate? Tell me about it. What did you see?"

"Dad's wearing handcuffs and tied to a chair. I could see that man's face when he hurt Dad. I couldn't stay

with Dad when that happened. I tried, but I had to leave."
His lips tightened. "Next time, I'll be able to do it."

Because it was hurting him too much. Eve felt the
helpless rage tear through her at the thought. "You did
the right thing to leave him. Your dad would tell you
that, too. You couldn't help him. If it happens again, do
the very same thing."

He gravely shook his head. "I won't let him be alone
with it. It hurt so bad that it surprised me. I didn't know
what to do about it. But I think I learned a little bit. I'll
learn more, and I'll get better."

What could she do with him, she wondered helplessly. He wasn't going to listen to her. She could only
love him, be proud of him, and make any sacrifice necessary to keep him and Joe alive. She tried once more.
"Listen, I don't want this. Please, don't do it."

He looked troubled, but he shook his head.

She gave it up. "Then we'll just have to move fast
so that lessons won't be necessary." She hugged him
again. "And if they come, I'll be there with you." She got
to her feet. "Now let's get on the road. If we stay here
much longer, Cheknof, that guard Kaskov assigned us,
will be busting in here trying to rescue us. He insisted
on following me because you made him look bad to
Kaskov when you flew the coop."

"I didn't mean to do that. He was nice to me."

"Actions have consequences." She looked back at
him. "You're sure that's all you can tell me?"

"That's all I could see about where Dad is now."
He grabbed his flashlight and followed her toward the
front entrance. "But remember? I told you last night he
was excited when he was standing beside that lake and
looking at the woods and that funny house."

She looked over her shoulder. "And you believe that
was a part of all this?"

"I think it might have been the beginning," he said

quietly. "I wanted to be with him so much that maybe it happened. I thought it came later, but that minute was so real."

"Maybe?"

He was silent. Then he said firmly, "It did happen. I know he was standing there looking at the house. Let's go find that lake, Mom."

"By all means." She opened the door. "But there are a lot of lakes in these mountains. You didn't, by any chance, see a convenient sign or landmark that would help us?"

"No, but I might remember what Dad was seeing and thinking if I caught sight of it." He was frowning. "It was different than later, when everything was clear and I actually saw what was happening in that room where he was tied. This was kind of in his head . . ." He shook his head. "But will it help?"

"We'll make it help." Lord knows they didn't have any other clues that could lead them to Joe. "We know where your dad was during the last couple days. We'll just have to find your lake somewhere in that area. We'll head for the town where Cara and Jock are right now and start from there." She made a face. "Though we may have problems with convincing Jock that your dad's giving you directions."

"Cara will believe it."

"Yes, she will. We'll let her convince Jock." She was about to shut the door behind them when she suddenly stopped and looked back into the dark church. "I suppose we should lock this door. I can't believe they left the church open. It might be a house of worship, but it took a lot of trust."

"The front door was locked," Michael said. "I had to go around to the back to find an open door."

She looked down at him as she swung the door shut. "Why go to all that trouble?"

His gaze rose to the white neon cross over the door. "I've been thinking about crosses since Dad has been gone. I don't know why. I saw that cross, and I thought if I stayed here awhile it might come to me."

"And did it?"

He shook his head. "It's not a cross from a church . . . but it's still important, and it has something to do with Dad."

A cross.

Joe.

A chill went through her. Not a cross from a church. The only other cross she could think of right now were the ones that marked the graves in cemeteries.

"I don't think we'll worry about crosses right now." She started quickly down the steps of the church. "You've given us quite enough to work on for the time being. When we get on our way, you can start going through your computer and see how many lakes we can find that might resemble the one your dad might have been looking at last night . . ."

Jock gazed at Cara in disbelief as she pressed the disconnect after talking to Eve. "She's actually bringing the boy?" He cursed beneath his breath. "What is she thinking? She'll get him killed." His lips twisted. "Or she'll get us killed while we try to protect him."

"You heard her. She thinks he might be able to help find Joe." She was as much in shock as Jock, but she was trying to work her way through it. Eve had not given her the opportunity for more than a token protest before she had cut the connection. "And there's no way Eve would risk Michael if she could avoid it. It would kill her if anything happened to him." But it would also kill Eve if anything happened to Joe. The pain surrounding that decision must have been horrendous. "We just have to trust her to know what she's doing."

"He's a ten-year-old kid," Jock said. "He won't help. He'll get in the way."

"He's Michael," Cara said. "We both know he's . . . different. I've been with him from the moment he was born, and I've almost become used to expecting the unexpected from him." She smiled shakily. "Maybe not this unexpected. But I'll take any help I can get. We'll just have to make sure there's no cost to him or Eve."

"Or you," Jock said grimly. "I'm not going to let a wild card like Michael put you in even more danger than you are right now."

"We've got to find Joe," she said quietly. "And we've not had any luck so far. A wild card is better than no card at all." She paused. "Because if Svardak still has Joe by that deadline he set, I'll have to find a way to bargain with him."

"No!"

"You can say no all you please, but it won't change anything. You know that, Jock. I won't change my mind."

His eyes were glittering down at her. "And I won't give you up to him."

She smiled sadly. "Then try the wild card. No choice. Because that's what I'm going to do."

"Cara . . ." She could see the myriad of emotions conflicting in his face. Then he suddenly said through bared teeth, "I'll take your wild card. But you're wrong; I'm not without other choices. I won't put all my eggs in one basket." He was dialing quickly. "Let's talk to Kaskov."

"Why?"

"Ron Edding. Svardak is trying to gather all his old crew around him. I told Kaskov before that I wanted Ron Edding compliant and ready for me to use if I needed him as bait to draw Svardak. I don't doubt that

Nikolai managed to do it. If your Michael can't give us a lead on Joe, then we'll use Edding as Judas goat."

"You're hoping if Edding contacts Svardak, that Svardak will tell him where he's located?"

His lips twisted. "Not much hope involved there. He wouldn't trust him that far. Edding was the last man he hired for his team. All I can expect is that he might arrange to pick him up somewhere near his hideout and check him out. But that might be—"

"Where the hell are you, Gavin?" Kaskov said as he answered his phone. "I told you to report back to me."

"Aye, that's going to happen," he said sarcastically. "I'm going to need Edding. Is he ready?"

"How is Cara?"

"She's fine. Is Edding ready?"

"Of course. Nikolai says he'll be more than cooperative."

"We're near Ruell Falls. Have Edding make the call to Svardak to tell him he's made his way this far into the mountains and ask for further directions. Then put him on a helicopter. I want him here by dawn."

Silence. "I detect a hint of frustration. Is Cara on the line? I wish to speak to her."

"I'm here, Kaskov," Cara said. "What do you want?"

He was silent an instant. "I assume Eve has told you that I appear to have failed to protect her and the child as I promised. The child proved . . . difficult." His voice sounded oddly stilted. "But I do not break my word. Though it's not really my fault, I wished to express my regrets. They're under close observation once more, and it won't happen again." Then his tone changed to pure, arrogant Kaskov. "Though you know that because I understand they're heading in your direction. You will take care of yourself, *not* them. Do you understand?"

"We'll do what we have to do. We're family. Do *you*

understand? Probably not." She added wearily, "I'm not blaming you for letting a ten-year-old make your goons look bad. It would amuse me if it wasn't so terribly frightening." She drew a shaky breath. "And I'll take whatever help you can give us to get Joe away from that monster. But don't tell me that I'm more important than any other member of my family because I can entertain you. It's not true."

"I beg to disagree," Kaskov said. "My amusement is all-important in the scheme of things. Gavin, I'll deliver Edding. In exchange, I expect you to make certain Cara lives through this somewhat clumsy plan you've concocted. I'll be in touch if you don't." He cut the connection.

Cara shook her head. "That was a bit unusual. He sounded almost contrite. I guess his nose was out of joint because he's not accustomed to making mistakes."

"Perhaps." Jock's tone was noncommittal. "One can never tell what he's thinking. I prefer not to try unless it's necessary to ensure survival. At least he gave me what I needed in Edding this time. It will take Eve a few hours to get here. Kaskov will deliver Edding not long after. Now it's only a question of our waiting for it to all to come together and choosing which path is best." He was driving off the lay-by where they were parked deeper into the woods. "And for you to get a little rest before it does." He parked the car and turned it off. "I don't like all that bullshit you've been giving me. I'm hoping I'll be able to temper it if I can get rid of some of the stress that's tearing you apart."

"You mean that you don't like the idea of not getting your own way." But he was right, she was having trouble controlling the tension as the time passed. "I don't like to argue with you." She leaned back in her seat, her gaze on the almost total nighttime darkness out the windows. Here in the woods, the overhanging canopy of trees even shut out the stars. "I just have to be honest with you, Jock."

"Hush." He was unbuckling their seat belts and pulling her to him. "Just let it go."

She relaxed against him. "But you never let anything go. You just file it away and come at me from a different direction."

"I'll let it go tonight. Promise."

And Jock always kept his promises. She was silent as the tension gradually flowed out of her. He felt so good. The golden warmth, the smoky spice scent of him . . . But she couldn't quite let it go yet. "You said that we'd choose what path was best. But you've already made up your mind. That's why you called Kaskov."

He didn't speak, his hand was gently smoothing her hair.

"I don't want to use Michael either," she said. "But it's Eve's decision, and she must have a reason to risk him."

"But now we have Edding," he said softly. "And I have no problem at all about risking that bastard's neck. I'm only giving Eve a choice that won't involve putting her son in danger. I believe that will win the day."

"She said that Michael told her he'd go find Joe on his own."

"He's ten years old. I think I can make sure he doesn't interfere."

She raised her head to look at him. "How? You have no idea how stubborn he can be. You can't risk hurting him. And Eve would never permit you to take that chance." She paused. "Neither would I."

"I'll handle the problem," he said impatiently. "And he's a smart kid, he might listen to reason. I'll tackle him as soon as they get here. For God's sake, I'd never hurt him. I *like* him. I just want to keep Svardak from killing him." He added, "Or using him to kill you."

"I'll vote for that." She laid her head back down on

his shoulder. "I hope that everything works out for you. But I don't know if it will. I think we'll have to wait and see. Michael went to a lot of trouble to end up here in the mountains searching for Joe. Maybe there's a reason why we should pay attention to what drove him."

"Shh. I promised I wasn't going to talk about this." He kissed her. "Now try to nap."

"Okay." She closed her eyes. "But I liked what Eve was saying about Michael's being able to tell where Joe might be because of the bond between them. Wouldn't it be nice if we could all be joined like that? I wish we were able to be—"

"Very nice." He pulled her closer. "Maybe we'll discuss it with Michael when we see him. For now, I'm feeling very close to you right this moment."

"But you don't want to have sex with me?"

"I imagine that will be an ongoing factor throughout eternity. But you're new to all the nuances. This isn't the time. And holding you like this is more than enough at present. Just relax . . ."

"I was just curious." And she *was* relaxing. It was good being here like this with him, she thought drowsily. In this time of fear, worry, and tension, they were close and strong and together. So close . . . Maybe someday they'd be even closer, and the bond would be like the ones Michael seemed to be able to weave.

Maybe someday . . .

LAKE KEDROW RANGER STATION

"How are you, Quinn?"

Joe opened his eyes to see Svardak standing in the doorway across the room. His muscles tensed. The son of a bitch was smiling, and the feral malice was vicious and clear. "Better than you are," Joe said bluntly.

"You look a little pale. Are you sure that wound in your stomach hasn't turned septic?"

Svardak's smile vanished. "Nothing's wrong with me that can't be cured by watching that bitch being chopped into pieces. I've been taking my antibiotics, and I'll make it through until I finish with the lot of you."

Joe glanced at the darkness beyond the windows. "You must be getting overeager. Are you upping Cara's deadline? You gave her twenty-four hours."

"I didn't tell her that I wouldn't entertain myself with you until I called her." He glided forward. "In fact, I mentioned something of that nature, didn't I?"

"I don't recall."

"Let me remind you." He was next to him and pushing aside the bandage on his shoulder. He made a clucking noise with his tongue. "Oh, dear. So sore and bruised . . ." He rubbed the edges, watching Joe's face as he ran his nail beneath the puffy flesh. "That stings?" He savagely dug his nail deep into the raw flesh!

Joe bared his teeth, but he couldn't stop the groan that tore out of him.

"Ah, that's what I wanted." Svardak spent a full five minutes digging at the wound. But after that first break, Joe was able to keep from giving him the satisfaction he wanted. Svardak finally turned away in frustration and dropped down in the chair across from Joe. "You're a personal disappointment, but I still have to have an example to show Cara what to expect if she doesn't cooperate." He motioned to Abrams, who had entered the room behind him. "Make him hurt, Abrams. Not enough to fatally damage him. Just enough to bring me satisfaction and Cara extreme agony and guilt. Understand?"

Abrams grinned as he came to stand in front Joe.

"No problem. You'll be satisfied. I know just what you want." And then his fist buried itself brutally in Joe's abdomen with full force.

Michael screamed!

Eve glanced over in alarm at where Michael was curled up in the passenger seat next to her. He was jerking, flinching, his entire body writhing in pain. She had thought he was asleep, but his eyes were wide open, staring in blind agony straight ahead of him.

"Michael!" She yanked the wheel and pulled the Toyota to the side of the road. The next instant, she'd jumped out of the driver's seat and run around to jerk open the passenger's door. He was still having those horrible jerking spasms. "What's wrong? Tell me what's wrong." She gathered him in her arms and pulled him out onto the side of the road. She sat there on the rocks and grass, rocking him. Was she even doing the right thing? She didn't know what the hell was wrong with him. "Where does it hurt? Is it your stomach?"

"Yes." He whispered. "No. It's . . . all over." The jerking was going on and on. "Sorry . . ."

"What are you talking about?" She held him passionately close. "You're sick. Stop apologizing. You can't help this."

"Scared . . . you." His hands clutched at her as he gave another convulsive jerk. "But I think it's—done. He's not feeling it anymore . . . so they're stopping." He buried his face in her shoulder. "I stayed with him this time, but I don't—think that—he knew it. It was too—bad for him."

"Him?" She froze as she began to understand. "Your dad?"

He nodded. His hands still clutching at her. "Hurt. They *hurt* him, Mom."

Joe. Svardak had hurt Joe? The thought sent the agony spiraling through her. Her arms tightened around
Michael. "Are you sure? You were sleeping. A bad
dream?" But he had told her he didn't have nightmares.
She was just trying to avoid the horror of the truth Joe
might be facing. And not only Joe. She realized what
Michael had told her about being able to feel Joe's pain
had been too bizarre to be real to her. Dear God, it
was real to her now. "No, I know it wasn't." She added
shakily, "Was it the same as that time before when you
were with your dad?"

He nodded. "Sort of. I was sleeping, and I woke
up when Svardak started hurting him." His face was
pinched and strained. "It was really bad. But it was
worse after he told that man, Abrams, to beat him." He
was shaking. "Dad couldn't move, and he just kept hitting him and hitting him."

And Michael had felt every blow, she thought, sick.
He was still shuddering, though the violent convulsions
had stopped. She was aching for him as he had been
aching for Joe. She wanted to keep him close, hidden
in her arms, make him forget it all. But she couldn't do
it. Because there were questions she had to ask him.
"How badly . . . was your dad hurt? He's still alive?"

He nodded. "I heard Svardak tell Abrams that he
was only to damage him enough so that it would hurt
Cara to see it. I think Abrams stopped when Dad
passed out." She felt him shudder once more against
her. "I'm not feeling anything now. I'd know if he were
doing something to him."

She was torn between profound relief, anger, and
despair. "Michael, I told you not to stay with him if it
happened again."

"I thought I could help."

"And I know you desperately wanted to do it. But what
you were going through wasn't good for you either.

Your body was convulsing and shaking as if you had malaria. That's not good for even someone who is healthy. I was afraid for you. I'm still afraid."

"I know you are," he whispered. "But I'm learning all the time. I'll get better." He was trying to sit up, pushing her away. "I managed to stay with him. That was all that was important."

"You said he didn't even know you were there," she said desperately. "And it was terrible for you. Why was it so important?"

"Because I could feel how bad Svardak was, and I wasn't sure what would happen." He added simply, "I thought they might kill him. And I couldn't let him go through it alone."

She stared at him, stunned.

"You would have done the same, Mom."

She shook her head. "It's what I would have wanted to do." Oh, how she would have wanted to be with Joe during those last moments. To spend the end as they'd spent the years of joy . . . together. "But I would have stayed behind to take care of you and the family. That's what your father would have wanted me to do." She swallowed. "And it's what he'd want from you, too. But you said he was still alive, and that makes the question moot. We just have to keep him alive. I shouldn't even be talking to you about it. Because you're going to live a long life, and your dad is going to be there with both of us." She wiped the tears from her cheeks. "How do you feel? Can you get back in the car?"

"Sure."

"You didn't answer me. How do you feel?"

"Kinda stiff and sore. That's funny, isn't it?"

"Not the least funny." She was helping him into the passenger seat. "Listen to me. It sounds as if your dad isn't going to be dealt anymore punishment until they can do it in front of Cara. So stay away from him until we can get him away from Svardak. Okay?"

"I might not have to be with him to help." Michael was fastening his seat belt. "Before I dozed off, I found three lakes on my computer that could have been the ones Dad was looking at before he started hiking toward that house. I'll look at them again and maybe I'll—"

"No. Not now. Later." She kissed him, then hugged him tightly. "You sit back and close your eyes. I'm still wondering if I should take you to a doctor. If you don't feel well, you tell me immediately. Do you hear me?"

"What would you tell the doctor?" He smiled. "I'm okay, Mom. I'm getting better every minute. And next time I'll be—"

"I don't want to hear about next time." She slammed the door and ran back through the spear of headlights to the driver's seat. She stood there a moment before she opened the door, trying to get control.

Joe.

She'd had to hold inside all the agony and terror she'd felt about Joe while she tended to Michael, but now it was all right to take this tiny instant to think and pray.

We're coming for you, love. We'll never stop. You stay strong until we get there.

RUELL FALLS
5:40 A.M.

"They're coming." Cara moistened her lips as she watched Eve and Michael get out of Eve's Toyota and start walking up the bank toward them. "They made good time, didn't they?" She had to raise her voice to be heard above the roar of the falls cascading down the hill to splash on the rocks below. "But then Eve must have been in a hurry. Joe is everything to her and this had to be—"

"You're nervous." Jock's gaze was on her face. "It's a little ironic when you're the one who's been telling me that Eve should be here, even with Michael in tow."

"I'm not nervous." She drew a deep breath. "I'm terrified. Eve's given me everything, and now I'm responsible for taking away the one person she values the most." Her gaze went to Michael. "And risking her son. She'd have to be a saint not to resent—"

"Be quiet," he said roughly. "Svardak is the only one responsible. You've been trying to prevent this from the beginning. Eve realizes that, Cara. She's not going to blame you."

"But how can I not blame myself?"

"I don't like that kind of talk. It's dangerous. I should have known you'd have this kind of reaction when you saw her." His hands closed on her shoulders. "Joe considered Svardak as a job he had to do. He had a choice, and he made it. Now we have a choice, and I'm not going to let you mess everything up by getting all weepy at this stage."

She blinked, then laughed huskily. "Heaven forbid I get all weepy." She swallowed hard. "I just had a moment of sheer panic at the thought of what Eve's going through."

"I know. You've always had a fixation about helping her. *We* will help her. But you do nothing alone, understand?" He kissed her hard and fast, then whirled her to face Eve and Michael coming up the hill. "They're almost here. She has enough to worry about without you adding to the mix. She thinks she's just gotten you back. She doesn't need to see how you're teetering. She needs hope, dammit."

Wise Jock. In this moment, she could see the shining inside him he didn't even know he possessed. He was right, they all needed hope . . . and love.

"Eve!" She broke free of his hold and ran down the hill toward her. The next moment, she was enveloped in Eve's arms. Memories flooded back to her. Safety when there was no safety. Love when she had never known love without fear. Family when she had no idea what the concept meant.

Eve.

Eve pushed her back and searched her face. "How are you? You look a little . . . fragile."

Cara shook her head. *She* was fragile? When she had been so worried about Eve? "I'm not at all fragile. I'm just happy to see you." She tried to smile. "Though not in these circumstances." She turned to Michael and gave him a hug. "And you've caused your mom big-time headaches. Not good, young man."

"I know." He returned the hug and stepped back, his gaze on Jock at the top of the hill. "But I had to do it. He doesn't want me here, does he? I didn't think he would."

She wasn't going to lie to him. "None of us want you here. But Jock doubts that you'll be able to help and might get in the way. That's what you get for barging in without an invitation."

"I can help." His eyes were still on Jock. "But I'd better make sure that he knows that he's wrong." He looked at his mother. "Do you suppose you should show Cara those photos of the lakes in the computer? I guess we should start out pretty soon to see if one of them is the right one."

Eve's gaze followed Michael's to Jock. "That's a good idea." She turned to Cara as she took her computer out of her backpack and smiled. "He's given me the easy task. He told me that you'd have no trouble believing him." She made a face. "Well, maybe a little trouble." She sat down on the bank and opened the laptop. "Sit down. There are three lakes in the area that Joe might have seen the night he was taken."

Cara hesitated as she saw that Michael was no longer with them but climbing up the hill toward Jock. He looked so young and vulnerable in his jeans and navy sweatshirt with the dawn light shining on his red-brown hair. But his stride was eager and springy, and he waved cheerfully at Jock as he came toward him. Darn it, he was so endearing that she was reluctant to have anything disturb that wonderful picture of youthful faith and exuberance. He deserved anything that Jock said to him after what he'd done, and she'd certainly been rough on him. But he was Michael, and she wanted to run after him and protect him even from Jock.

"It will be fine," Eve said gently, her eyes on Cara's face. "When did you know a time when Michael couldn't take care of himself? We do all we can, but in the end, he seems to be able to survive on his own." She shook her head. "Though this time, it's been very hard for me to believe. He's pulled out a few special items from his bag of tricks that have me pretty dizzy. I guess he had to do it because of Joe. But it still scared me." She patted the ground next to her. "I'll tell you about it, but sit down and let me show you these lake photos first. It all ties in to Michael and Joe, and that's what we have to concentrate on." She gave another glance at Michael, who had reached Jock and was standing with legs slightly parted staring up at him. And then at Jock, whose face was totally without expression. "Because we might not have as much time as I hoped."

CHAPTER

14

"Hi, Jock." Michael smiled up at him. "It's pretty up here, isn't it? I like waterfalls. They always sparkle and seem to dance in the sunlight."

The words were as seemingly guileless as the sunny smile on Michael's face, Jock thought. And they accomplished his purpose, Jock could feel himself yield and soften slightly as he looked at him. "It's not the time or place for any of us to be admiring pretty scenery," he said dryly. "And, if that was your aim, you put your mom through hell to do it."

Michael's smile vanished. "I didn't want to hurt her. I think you know that, Jock. It was the only way I could think to help Dad. I had to be here."

"Because you're the only who could help him? That's very conceited. Your father has a few of us ready to step up to the plate who have a few years and experience on you."

"I know that, but it has to be me." He paused. "Mom told you and Cara that I could find him, but you don't want to believe her." He frowned, troubled. "You think it might be a waste of time, and that would be bad for Cara. It scares you."

"Does it? Maybe I just think you're a kid with an active imagination who doesn't realize it might hurt those around him. Yes, you're smart, but this is something else entirely."

He slowly shook his head. "You're scared." His bright, amber eyes were on Jock's, searching deep. "And you're never scared. You've seen bad things, you've even done bad things, and now nothing scares you any longer. You've been all over the world, and you've seen strange sights that not many people have seen. You know that maybe I can do this. But you're afraid to trust me."

Holy shit.

The eyes staring into Jock's were not those of a young boy. Or, if they were, they were seeing things about him that no one should be able to see. He took an instant to recover. Because Michael was right—he had seen things in India and Tibet that were fully as strange as a child's being able to find his father in these mountains. Seen and accepted them because they were no threat, but anything affecting Cara could be a threat. "As I said, you're very clever. I wasn't expecting this. It seems you're an entire other person from the boy everyone thinks you are. You have a real talent for pretense."

"No, I don't," Michael said. "That would be a lie. Mom's right about lies being bad. Pretty much what you see is what you get with me. I'm just a kid with a great family." He frowned. "But sometimes I see stuff or find out I can do something that would make people uncomfortable. So I just kind of ignore it."

"Until you're not getting your way and decide to spring it on someone like me to seal the deal," Jock said mockingly.

"Only because it's so important because of Dad," he said soberly. "And there's not anyone 'like' you. I could tell all those months I talked to you on the phone that something like this might happen. But I really needed Cara home because of Mom, and I thought it would be worth it."

"It wasn't," Jock said harshly. "And I won't have her go through anything more because you want to 'experiment.'"

"I love Cara. You know I do. I made a mistake." His eyes met Jock's pleadingly. "Help me make it right?"

"Is that supposed to sway me? I don't care about making you feel less guilty. I only care about finding Joe. You haven't shown me you can do it."

"Then just let me show you. Don't get in my way. Okay? Trust me."

Persuasive as a siren call, Jock thought. But there was sincerity and honesty beneath that persuasiveness. These last few minutes with Michael had stunned and challenged him, but throughout he had been aware of that element of honesty running through his words. He hesitated, then made a decision. "I don't have to trust you. I'm already setting up a backup plan that won't involve you."

"Great." Michael's brilliant smile lit his face. "That will make you feel better. And it won't interfere with what I have to do. You might even be able to help me a little? There are so many things I don't know. I've never had to do anything like this before. I promise it won't have anything to do with Cara."

"Everything about you and your family has to do with Cara," he said dryly. "That's why I'm scared." His gaze returned to Michael's face. "I always intended to help you, Michael. I like you, and Cara loves you. But you're an unknown quantity, and I've never liked operating in the dark."

"That's why I came up here to talk to you. But now you feel you know me better?"

"No, why should I? All I know is that you're way

deeper than anyone thinks you are. You're still an unknown quantity."

Michael sighed. "Yeah, I know. For me, too. But I'm
working on it, Jock."

Jock smiled faintly. "I have an idea it may take a
while for all of us to see what's below all those lay-
ers." He shrugged. "In the meantime, I'll accept what
you show me as long as it never hurts Cara. And I'll
always be there for you." He clapped him on the shoulder. "Now we'd better go down to Cara and your mom.
You think you can do this?" He started down the hill.
"Let's prove it. It's showtime."

Eve gazed warily at Jock and Michael as they ap-
proached where Cara and she were sitting on the bank.
Michael was smiling, and Jock's expression was as
noncommittal as it had been before. "Everything all
right?"

Jock shrugged. "Possibly. We'll have to see when we
go over those maps, won't we?"

"She's already shown them to me," Cara said. "Eve
tabbed the three lakes that Michael said might be the
ones that Joe was looking at. She said the one that's
on page one is Lake Cormack, and that's the closest.
It's about an hour from here. The other two are farther
north, and they're a good three hours. They're almost
right on top of each other, Lake Kedrow and Hunter's
Lake." She flipped the pages. "If Joe was here in Ruell
Falls, he would have had to have a good reason to go
that distance."

Jock's lips tightened as he looked at the photos.
"And if we go up there, and it's not the so-called right
lake, it will eat into the time that bastard gave Cara as
a deadline."

"But one of them could be the right one," Cara

said. She glanced at Michael. "Does one of them look more—" He was shaking his head. "Sorry to put you on the spot. I'm just not familiar with this kind of thing." She made a face. "And who knew that you would be?"

"Not me," Michael said. "It's kind of crazy. But if I see the lake, I'll know it, Cara."

"Then let's make sure you see it." She turned to Jock. "The closest one first? We might get lucky."

He nodded curtly. "That hasn't happened so far. But it has to be the closest one. I told Kaskov to deliver Edding here at Ruell Falls after dawn. I have to be back here to receive him." He turned to Michael. "Backup. Let's hope that we won't need him."

"He doesn't need that kind of pressure, Jock," Cara said quietly.

"He can handle it. He's tougher than he looks." Jock turned away. "But if you want to go with Eve and Michael to Lake Cormack to hold his hand, I think it would be a good idea. I'll follow her car and scout around, so there won't be any surprises." He smiled at Michael. "Be certain, but don't waste time. We have a tight schedule."

Michael nodded gravely. "I won't disappoint you, Jock." He turned and hurried down the hill after Eve.

Cara was staring after him. "What happened up there between you two?"

"Nothing much." He took her arm and urged her down the path. "Merely one of those rare moments of mutual enlightenment that comes along occasionally . . ."

LAKE CORMACK

"It's not the right one," Michael said flatly.

"You've only been looking around for fifteen minutes," Cara said. "Are you absolutely sure?"

He nodded. He was staring out over the lake to the green mountains beyond. "I wanted it to be the one Dad saw, but it isn't the right one." He looked at Eve. "I'm sorry, Mom. I thought it wasn't the one when we first drove up, but Jock told me to be sure."

Eve came to stand beside him. "And you did everything right. There's nothing to be sorry about. We just have to take the next step."

"If there is a next step." Jock appeared from the brush at the left of the path. "But I also saw no 'funny house' in the area that was on your list of descriptive real estate. So this lake has to be off the list for that reason, too."

"It just means that we have to go and take a look at Kedrow and Hunter." Eve stared Jock in the eye. "That's the next step. Michael has gone through too much to stop now. He believes what he's saying, so I have to believe it, too."

Jock held up his hand. "I never thought anything else. That's practically a mother's mantra. It's that tight schedule that's raising its head again. I can't afford to risk Cara if I put all my eggs in one basket. I'm going back to Ruell Falls and pick up Edding and see if I can find Svardak in some way that won't depend on a séance." He glanced at Michael, and said slyly, "No offense." He turned back to Eve. "But you can get on the road and take Michael up there yourself for a look around. If it's not another blind alley, I'll hijack Kaskov's helicopter along with whatever men he sends to bring Edding and be there in a heartbeat." He paused. "In those circumstances, I don't have to tell you that you'd be crazy not to hide out and wait until I can get to you, do I? I know that you're frantic about Joe."

Eve shook her head impatiently. "Of course I'm frantic. But this is purely an exploratory trip. I'd have to be truly insane to think I could barge in and rescue him without help. That's the kind of madness you and Joe would try to do. And I have to take Michael with me. Do you think I'd risk him?"

"No way." Cara took a step closer to Eve. "We'll just take a look around, then make a decision what we're going to do."

"We?" Eve whirled on her. "Forget it. You're not going with us, Cara."

"The hell I'm not."

"I don't need you. You'd be in the way. You think you'd be a help to us, but Svardak wants you. You're the beacon that draws him. He took Joe because it was his way to get to you. He'd use Michael the same way if he got the opportunity. I'm not going to take the chance of your being anywhere near him."

Cara felt stricken. She could see that Eve did not want to hurt her, but she was right. Because of her, Joe had been taken and the threat to Michael was very real. "I'm sorry, Eve."

"There's nothing to be sorry about." She took a step closer and gave her a warm hug. "But the best place for you is surrounded by Jock and Kaskov's guards, for your sake as well as ours. Understand?"

"I see where you're coming from, and I'll try not to be in your way."

Eve's brows rose. "That's no answer."

"As you said, Svardak is holding Joe because of me. I have to help him." She smiled shakily. "I'll find a way not to be a beacon."

Eve shook her head. "I may rue the day I used that word." She gave her a kiss on the cheek and glanced at Jock. "You're very quiet."

"I had nothing to say. You did all my work for me."

"But you had no intention of letting Cara go with us."

"I don't give Cara orders. It doesn't turn out well. She responds much better to your gentle influence."

"I wasn't so gentle today," she said ruefully.

"But you were honest," Cara said. She bent and gave Michael a hug. "You take care of your mom. Don't let her get into trouble."

"Okay." He whispered in her ear. "That's what Dad told me, and I haven't been able to do it. But I won't let that Svardak hurt her. I promise, Cara." Then he was gone and running to Eve. "Let's go. Didn't you hear Jock? We're on a tight schedule."

Eve shrugged. "Well, we wouldn't want to disturb Jock's schedule." She was whisking him away toward the Toyota. "But we do have an agenda of our own."

Cara shivered as she watched them drive away. "I wanted to go with them, Jock."

"I know you did. But she was right, you know. You're a beacon." He was pushing her gently toward his car. "And they're both safer without you. I wanted to go with them, too. I didn't like having to suggest that they go without me, but she wasn't going to let it go."

"No, she wouldn't."

"And Eve will be supercareful if she sees anything that appears off-kilter. She'll call us, and we'll be there for her in minutes instead of hours."

She smiled crookedly. "And you don't really believe that they'll find anything anyway."

"I didn't say that." He opened the passenger door for her. "I believe Michael might be able to pull it off. He's . . . unusual. I've seen stranger things happen. I just believe we have to hedge our bets with the semblance of reality." His lips twisted. "I won't let your and Joe's lives depend on anything mystical or psychic in nature. It's foreign to me. I know about reality, with all its complexities and ugliness. I can meld it to what I need it to be." He got into the driver's seat. "I leave it to Michael and Eve to deal with anything more *Star Wars* oriented." He added grimly. "And may the Force be with them."

RUELL FALLS

The large gray-and-cream helicopter descended slowly to the ground in the field across from Ruell Falls.

"It looks like the helicopter from *Blackhawk Down*," Cara murmured. "More military than commercial. Very impressive. But a little wasteful considering it's only a glorified delivery vehicle for Edding."

"Kaskov can afford it." Jock was moving toward the landing site. "He probably has quite a few uses for a military aircraft. Anything from drug trafficking to gunrunning." He was watching the door open. "And I don't give a damn as long as that copter is bringing Ron Edding. And I think it is . . ."

"Shit!" Edding screamed as he was thrown from the helicopter and landed in the dirt at Jock's feet. "Son of a bitch!" He rolled over, cursing as he struggled to his knees. He glared at Jock. "You didn't need to have him do that. Haven't I done everything I was told to do?"

"I don't know. Have you?" Jock looked down at him. "I admit it's very satisfactory having you in the dirt at my feet, but I didn't give the order." His gaze raked Edding from torn shirt to his stained boots. "But you look a little worse for wear, so I'd imagine you've been very good lately. I haven't been given a complete report so I—"

"Complaints, complaints, Gavin." Kaskov was jumping down from the helicopter. "You ordered, and I meekly brought him here to lie at your feet. Yet you can do nothing but whine."

Cara stiffened. "I didn't expect to see you, Kaskov."

"I thought about it and decided I couldn't trust Gavin to represent my interests where you were concerned. Particularly since Abrams told Edding when he called that he wasn't sure that he was needed since they'd been able to get several of Svardak's crew back in the last couple days. You clearly needed reinforcements." He turned back, and called into the helicopter, "Nikolai, it's almost time for that second call to Svardak. I'm sure Edding needs your encouragement to make it all it should be." He stepped aside as Nikolai and several other men in camouflage attire streamed out of the helicopter. He smiled down at Edding. "I'm going to tell Nikolai to ignore your extremely bad attitude when you renewed your acquaintance with Gavin. I realize Gavin can be very difficult."

Edding was suddenly wary. "He's a bastard."

"Without doubt. But I forgive him because we both have problems with the fact that you helped to keep my granddaughter prisoner at Lost Canyon. You told Nikolai you'd never seen her." He waved his hand at Cara. "You should meet her, and we'll see how truthful you were. Cara, do you know this man?"

"I never touched her," Edding said, panic-stricken. "I didn't have anything to do with her."

"Except make sure she could never get off that mountain," Jock said softly. "If that's all you did. I didn't have time to verify that you weren't lying to me at our last meeting."

"No!" Edding scrambled to his feet. "I tell you that I didn't do—"

"Stop it!" Cara took a step forward. Jock and Kaskov were standing there, looking as lethal as angels of death, and it was because of her. She hated for Jock to revert to that time and state that had almost destroyed him. Somehow, it was even worse to have Kaskov here like a mirror image of what he might have become. "Leave him alone. I don't know this man. The only one of Svardak's men I ever saw was that guard, Abrams. And I never really got a good look at him." She made an impatient gesture. "Besides, none of that matters now. Why are you wasting time when you brought Edding here for a purpose?"

"I believe we've been chastised, Gavin," Kaskov murmured. "She's been through a good deal, or I'd have to explain the consequences to her."

"Joe is being held by that monster and is probably suffering," she said coldly. "In the end, that's your fault. Don't tell me about consequences." She looked at Edding. "What can he do to help?"

"We shall see, now that we've determined what kind of treatment he deserves." Kaskov turned to Jock. "He made the first call to Abrams two hours ago and told him that he'd been wounded on the cliff but managed to get away. He said he'd been on the run in the mountains ever since, but he needed help for the wound in his leg. As expected, Abrams was not overly sympathetic. He said that Svardak didn't need anyone who couldn't function and to get lost."

"A philosophy you understood perfectly," Jock said.

"Which I understood enough to have a reply ready that Svardak would accept. Edding is going to tell Abrams that he literally knew where all the bodies were buried about the murder of that violinist in Bermuda, and he was afraid he might be forced to tell the police if he was caught. The British in Bermuda are very sensitive about threats to their citizens. Even I am careful when handling them. There was no evidence that linked Svardak to the other victims, but the Brits would stir up a hornet's nest. Abrams will realize that and go to Svardak." Kaskov smiled. "I think it will all go splendidly and that they'll soon be having a joyous reunion."

"He'll kill me," Edding said flatly. "Svardak doesn't fool around. He'll tell Abrams to get rid of me."

"Not if you handle it right," Jock said. "And you will handle it right. Or you won't have to worry about Svardak or Abrams. I'll get rid of you for them."

"I might as well let you do it," Edding said glumly. "You're as bad as Svardak. Either way, I'm dead."

"It depends on what you want to go through before you reach that point," Jock said. "I don't promise to keep you alive, but we'll have to take those manacles off you when you meet with Abrams. That will give you a chance to cut and run while you're on your way to Svardak's hideout. Who knows? We might be too busy to come after you."

"I won't get that far," Edding said. "I was safe until you had me threaten Svardak. Now he'll just send Abrams after me to shut me up."

Jock shook his head. "Not after you make the second call. Not if you tell him that you've written all the dirty details down and sent it to a friend in Nassau with instructions to FedEx it to the interested parties in case Svardak doesn't help you."

"Threats *and* blackmail? He'll still kill me. He'll just torture me first to find out where I sent the info."

Jock nodded. "Probably. But the chances are Svardak will tell Abrams to bring you to him so that he can share the enjoyment of tearing you apart. That will give me what I need and you an opportunity."

Edding hesitated, staring at him. Then he said belligerently, "I can tell you need this. Give me enough money to get me out of the country, and I'll do it."

"Wrong move," Jock said quietly. "You'll do it because I'll make certain the pain doesn't stop until you do. I'm very good with pain, Edding. I've been taught by experts."

Edding's face turned pale as he met Jock's eyes.

"No, Jock," Cara said.

"It's his call." She could see the icy stillness in his face. "He *will* do it, Cara. Don't interfere."

"Don't be selfish." Kaskov was motioning to Niko-lai, who was standing by the steps of the helicopter. "Of course he'll do it. But there's no use your being greedy about persuading him when he and Nikolai have formed such a close attachment in the last few days. We'll give Edding a little while to think about it. And then you can join them and listen to his chat with Abrams if you like."

"You're giving me permission?" Jock asked mock-ingly.

The ice was still there but now aimed at Kaskov, Cara thought, which was infinitely worse.

Edding obviously didn't agree, he was almost ea-gerly turning from Jock and letting Nikolai lead him away. Evidently, he was grateful to no longer have Jock's attention.

"You see?" Kaskov smiled. "Nikolai will do a much better job convincing him that he might have a chance to survive if you're not in charge. You're far too intimi-dating. Give him thirty minutes."

"And Nikolai is not intimidating?" Jock was relax-ing the slightest bit. "Perhaps not compared to you. But against anyone else, I think he'd pass."

"True. Because unfortunately he's had to smother his natural instincts. Life does that sometimes. Nikolai has a gentle soul." His gaze shifted to Cara. "Like our Cara. And not at all like either of us, Gavin. I don't believe she likes it when we show her glimpses of who we are. She finds it upsetting."

"I do find it upsetting," she said coolly. "I hate it. But speak for yourself. Jock is nothing like you. And I can smother my instincts if I have to do it." She repeated his words. "Life does that sometimes." She turned to

Jock. "And you will not tell me not to interfere. This is about Joe, and it's about you. I'll never stay out of anything concerning either of you."

Kaskov chuckled. "Besides the fact that she's obviously irritated that I indicated we belong to the same brotherhood. You should have caught that instead of being so single-minded about Edding." He turned away. "I'll leave you to make amends while I go to see that Nikolai doesn't get too enthusiastic to please me."

Cara watched him stroll away before she glanced at Jock. "He's right, it made me angry to see you together," she said curtly. "It reminded me that you consider yourself as much a killer as he is. You're not anything of the sort, and I won't let you believe it. That would mean I'd lose you, and that's not going to happen."

"No, I don't think it will," he said quietly. "I'm too far gone to let you go now. Though someday you may realize losing me could be the best thing for you." He smiled crookedly. "Actually, seeing Kaskov and me together might be a teaching moment."

"No, it won't. He might be my grandfather, but I barely know him, and I never had him to lose." She drew a deep breath. "But he's here and he's helping in his own fairly lethal way and I have to put up with him. So go and make certain that Edding survives both of you and that I can get Joe back. Because I could lose *him*." She took out her phone and turned away. "While I call Eve and see what's happening with her. She should be about halfway to those lakes by now." She looked back at Jock. "It sounded as if it might work. What do you think?"

"It depends if I'm right about Svardak's wanting to punish Edding himself. If he does, then we have a good chance. If he doesn't, then it will be more difficult." He shrugged. "But by all means call Eve and let her know that there's another option in the works besides

Michael. I could tell she was barely able to hold it together when she and Michael got in that car."

"She'll hold it together." She was dialing as she walked away from him. "I'm not the only one who has Joe to lose . . ."

"Okay, Mom?" Michael was staring gravely at Eve as she pressed the disconnect after talking to Cara. "It didn't sound as if anything bad was happening."

"No, kind of a holding pattern I think. Jock thinks that they might be able to track Svardak through one of his men."

"That would be good." He leaned his head back on his headrest, his eyes on the distant mountains. "And Jock would be careful so that Svardak wouldn't know he might lose Dad. That can't happen."

She stiffened. "Why do you say that?"

"Because he wants to kill him. He knows that it would hurt Cara. The only thing that's keeping him from doing it is that he thinks he can still get Cara by keeping him alive."

She drew a harsh breath. "You found all that out just by being in the same room with him?"

"He was hurting Dad. He was hurting me. It was all there in front of me. I told you that's why I had to stay with him."

"Yes, you did. Just not in detail." She had to ask him. "You said you'd know if Svardak was hurting your dad. You would have told me?"

He nodded. "He didn't do anything more to him." He paused. "But he didn't wake up."

She inhaled sharply. "What?"

"He's not dead," he said quickly. "That man, Abrams, might have done something, but I don't think . . . Dad's feeling hot, and his wound is hurting."

"Fever," Eve whispered. "Infection."

He nodded. "I guess it might be. Svardak had his nail digging in that wound."

She shuddered at the vision those words brought. "We have to get him out of there." But they weren't even sure where Svardak was keeping Joe. She could only pray that Jock and Cara could move fast enough to locate him if they failed to do it.

"How long will it be before we get to Lake Kedrow?" Michael asked.

She glanced at the GPS. "About an hour and a half. But Hunter's Lake is thirty minutes closer than Kedrow."

"I'm sorry that I couldn't help more," Michael said. "I should have been able to do this better. What if I'm wrong?"

"Don't *say* that," she said. "Do you believe you're wrong?"

"No."

"Then I trust you, and you'll have to trust me. There has to be a reason that you were able to reach out to your dad. That means that it has to be a way to save him." She swallowed to ease the tightness of her throat. Everything he'd said to her had frightened her. But in a world that had given her Bonnie, then Michael, she had to believe that Joe would not be taken from her. Not when they needed him so desperately. "This is alien territory for both of us. It will only work out if we do it together. Okay?"

"Sure." Michael's smile was gently luminous. "Okay." He leaned back and gazed out the window at the mountains again. "Together."

Darkness . . .

No, not complete darkness, Joe thought hazily.

There was a warm, golden cast that lightened it to the shade of deepest honey.

"Wake up, Dad. Mom got really scared when I told her that you weren't awake yet. I need to tell her you've come back."

Michael...

He stiffened.

Michael shouldn't be here. Svardak! He struggled to open his eyes, to tell him to get out of here. He couldn't do either, dammit. And he'd been talking about Eve. Did that mean Eve was here, too? God in heaven, she must not—

"Mom's not here," Michael said. "I guess I'm not really here either." He thought about it. "Yes, I am, but I'm in your head. Is that all right?"

"No, it probably means I'm going a little crazy. Or maybe it's okay if neither you nor Eve is here. You're sure she's not here?"

"I'm sure. Right now she's driving us to try to find the lake you were standing beside before you came to this place." He paused. "But I wish you'd show it to me again. We have to find it right away, Dad."

"Too tired."

"That's because you have a fever. But we really have to know. What's the name of the lake?"

"It doesn't matter... I shouldn't even be talking. They'll hear and come back and find you."

"You're not talking. No one can hear you, but me. Isn't that cool?"

"Very cool." He could feel himself smiling. Michael always thought that anything new and different was cool. It was one of the things he loved most about his son. Every day was a new discovery waiting to happen.

"But every day is like that for you, too, Dad," Michael said. "You taught me that I could learn to do

anything, be anything if I stayed open to everything around me. That was pretty cool, too."

"But I don't believe I taught you to do this." Joe was attempting to break through the haze that kept ebbing and flowing around him. *"Or maybe Eve did? This is a dream, isn't it?"*

"Sort of. But it's the kind that can help you. We have to get you out of here. They're . . . hurting you."

"Are you crying, Michael? You never cry."

"I never saw anybody hurt you before. It mustn't happen again, Dad."

"I'll try to oblige you. However, there are . . . a few roadblocks that might appear . . . on the horizon." He paused. Everything around him was strange and disjointed and he wasn't sure what was happening, but he could sense his son's worry and unhappiness. Why couldn't he help him? He'd always been able to help or guide Michael. But if he couldn't help him, he had to get him away from any threat. *"I think it might be . . . a good idea if you left here. I'll be fine. You know I'm always fine."*

"Yes, I know that." He cleared his throat. *"But let us help you this time. All we need to know is a couple things; and then I'll get out of here. Okay?"*

"No, it's not okay. I think I hear Abrams and Svardak outside. I want you out of here now."

"I tell you that it won't make any difference." He paused. *"But if you hear them, then you must be pretty close to waking up. Will you open your eyes and let me see everything that you're seeing, hear everything you do?"*

"Too hard . . ."

"Nothing is too hard for you. We need it, Dad."

Then, of course, he had to give it to them. He had to give them everything they needed. Concentrate. Get rid of that damn cloudy mist, banish the searing heat *that was scorching his body. He couldn't do it for long, but Michael needed it . . .*

He struggled to open his eyes. So damn hard . . .

Once . . .

Twice . . .

"You're going to owe me for this, Michael."

"I do owe you. For everything. Just a little more . . ."

And then his eyes were open, and the room was swimming before them. "Not worth it. Not much to see here." He could hear Svardak's and Abram's voices humming like bees in the background. "Enough?"

"Give me another minute."

"Too long."

"I might have enough. That door over there . . . And are those handcuffs like the ones you usually use?"

"Close enough. Go away, Michael." His lids were shutting again. "I don't know what you're up to, but keep your mother out of it. I told you to take care of her."

"I'm trying. Things happened."

"Don't try, do it."

"Yes, Dad. But it will be easier when you come home, so we have to find a way for you to do it. You work on it, and I will, too. You just rest, and I'll see you soon . . ."

The darkness was no longer dark honey but a deeper black now. Michael was gone. It was good that he was no longer here, he thought. There was danger, and Joe still couldn't be sure that it had only been a dream and not reality.

But now Michael was safe again because only the memory and the loneliness remained with Joe . . .

"Mom."

"We're almost there, Michael," Eve said without

looking at him. "Maybe another ten minutes until we get to Hunter's Lake. You were so quiet, I thought you'd nodded off to sleep." She glanced at him. "Is that what—" She broke off as she saw his expression. "Michael?" She reached out tentatively and touched his tear-wet cheek. Tears? She couldn't remember the last time Michael had cried. But now everything in the world had changed. She froze. "What's wrong? What happened? Is it your dad? Is he—"

"No," Michael said quickly. "He's still sick, but he woke up for a few minutes. And no one is hurting him."

Relief flooded her. "Thank God." She drew a deep breath. "You scared me."

He nodded. "I know you've been afraid. That's why I had to try to make it better for you. We had to know about him. I thought I could do it." He wiped his cheeks with the back of his hands. "And I did do it, but I'm not used to Dad's being sick. I wanted to let him rest, but we had to know stuff and he had to tell—"

"Michael, slow down." She pulled over to the side of the road. "First, I'm going to assume that my speech about doing everything together fell on deaf ears?"

"You were so scared, I could *feel* it. I thought if I'd reached him before, that I'd probably be even better at it now and I'd be able to—"

"But you didn't expect that seeing your dad sick would throw you for a loop," she interrupted. She had to know the worst about Joe. "Skip to the chase. How sick is he?"

"I don't know. It's the fever, like we thought. He was burning up, and he couldn't think straight. I tried to tell him what I was doing there, but he couldn't understand."

"What a surprise," she said unsteadily. "He's burning up with fever, and you expect him to comprehend that you've dropped in to pay him a visit that's purely psychic in nature. Not to mention that he has no idea you're even capable of it? It was hard for me to handle, and I had all my senses."

"I think he still knew what I was talking about part of the time. He's so smart, Mom." His eyes were glistening with tears again. "And all I had to do was tell him that we needed him, and he did what I asked."

"Yes, I can see how he would." Keep control. Michael was upset enough. "What did you ask him? Something about the lake?"

"I asked him the name, but he didn't answer me. He only wanted me to go away because he was afraid Svardak would know I was there. He didn't understand that it wouldn't— And he kept talking about taking care of you and how I had to leave." He stopped. "So I knew I had to find out another way. I asked him to wake up so that I could see what he saw." He swallowed. "It was so hard for him, Mom. I hated it."

"Then make it worth what he went through to give it to you." She paused. "Tell me it was worthwhile?"

"I think so. I thought there might be a photo of the lake somewhere in the room with a name, but there wasn't. But there was another photo that was on the desk of a man in a brown uniform with an older man and woman standing on either side of him. They looked happy and kind of proud. Like you do when I do something good in soccer." He was frowning with concentration. "And I found out about the cross. It was on the glass door leading out to the porch. It was a red cross with black letters, and below it said Officially Certified Facility."

"Red Cross," Eve said. "Facility." She could feel the excitement start to simmer. "And that's where they're keeping Joe?"

"A hospital?"

"Maybe. But in the wilderness it would more likely

be a mobile facility like the ones the Red Cross uses in disasters."

He shook his head. "On the news they look all small and cramped. The room where they're holding Dad didn't look like that. There was even a leather couch."

"What else?"

"Just the photo." He had another thought. "And a map on the wall with bears all over it."

"Bears," Eve murmured. "Not exactly the usual decorative accessory for a Red Cross facility. Anything else?"

"I asked about his handcuffs, and he said they were kind of like his, so you'll probably know how to get them open. But I didn't notice anything else in that room. Nothing that he saw. But he heard Svardak and Abrams talking out on the porch, that's why he wanted me to go. They were still talking when Dad woke for those couple minutes."

"And?"

"Svardak was cursing about someone named Edding. That's all, Mom." His eyes were big as he stared at her. "Is it enough? Maybe I could go back and ask Dad to help us again. But he was so sick, and I didn't—"

"No." She pulled him into her arms. "You did fine. We'll make it enough. We just have to pull it all together." But her mind was at a loss how to do that at the moment." She hugged him tightly, then let him go. The Red Cross. The photo of the man in uniform. A map with bears.

"But you have to do something else for me." She handed him his notebook. "You have a great memory. Can you draw me a picture of that man in uniform in that photo? Every detail?"

He nodded. "Piece of cake."

There was nothing resembling a piece of cake in this scenario, Eve thought. She was just glad she'd been able to give Michael something useful to do while she tried to put the rest of the pieces together. "With all due speed," she said as she drove back on the road. "In the meantime, I'll keep on the road toward those lakes. Maybe looking at Hunter's Lake will cause something to click into place for you, and we won't need to worry about soldiers or bears."

CHAPTER

15

They reached Hunter's Lake ten minutes later. Eve sat there for a few moments gazing out at the lake. Michael was still frantically drawing his picture, and she didn't want to disturb him.

It was a beautiful lake, with all the purple shadows and deep green shimmer of water that moved with the wind.

But was it the right lake?

She wasn't going to ask Michael at the moment. Give him a little more time. He'd already gone through enough during the last twenty-four hours. She unfastened her seat belt and got out of the car. She didn't know if Michael even knew she had left him. He was totally absorbed in his sketch.

She walked over to the edge of the cliff and looked down at the curving lake that ended in a stretch of forest. That sounded right from what Michael had told her. There was no house, but it might be hidden by a curve in the lake. She would just have to rely on—

"Here it is, Mom."

She turned around to see Michael coming toward her with his notebook in his hand.

"I think it's pretty good." He handed her the notebook. "He looks like a nice guy, doesn't he? And it's a neat uniform. Is he a soldier?"

She took the notebook. It was more than pretty good. Michael had given her all the detail she could have possibly wanted. The uniformed man did look like a nice guy and was probably not more than in his early twenties in the photo. Her gaze traveled from his face down to the uniform Michael thought was neat.

She inhaled sharply.

"Mom?" Michael's gaze was on her face. "Did I do okay?"

She couldn't take her eyes off that uniform. "More than okay." She turned on her heel and ran back to the car. "You couldn't have done better." She handed him back his notebook and reached hurriedly for her phone. "And that means we have a lot of work to do."

RUELL FALLS

"It's Eve," Cara said as she glanced at the cell ID. "They should have reached Hunter's Lake by now, Jock. Maybe we've got a break." She accessed the call. "You're at Hunter's Lake? Is it yes or no for us?"

"No, we're not at Hunter's Lake," Eve said quickly, and Cara could hear the excitement in her voice. "It was the wrong one. But we definitely have a yes, Cara. Right now, I'm standing on a bank of Lake Kedrow and staring at a three-story A-frame building that looks like the roof is part of a tree house. Is that weird enough for you?"

Cara went still. "You found it?"

"Michael and I found it. I would never have seen the house if I hadn't been looking for it. It's tucked in one of the coves and surrounded by trees. I would have wasted precious time on searching Hunter's Lake, first, if Michael hadn't steered me in another direction."

"Then Michael managed to identify this lake?"

"No, that didn't work out. He had to go another route." She hesitated. Then she drew a deep, shaky breath. "And I don't have time to go into all the details with you now. Joe is sick, and I don't know how bad he is. We have to get him out of that house before Svardak kills him."

"You're certain you've found him?" Jock asked gently. "You're not making much sense, Eve."

"Do you think I don't realize that, Jock? Yes, I'm sure that's where Svardak is holding Joe. I even made the calls to verify the uniform."

"What uniform?" Cara asked.

"Okay, I'll slow down. Michael drew me a sketch of a photo of a young man in a brown uniform that was on the desk in the room where Joe is being held. Michael thought he might have been a soldier, but when I saw it I knew he wasn't. I'd seen similar uniforms in the forests south of Atlanta. We have a rich forestry industry in Georgia, and the forests are patrolled by the U.S. National Forest Service. You must have seen some of the rangers, too, Cara."

"A few. Though I spent most of my time at the lake cottage or studying in New York."

"Well, that photo was of a forest ranger. Michael also said there was a map on the wall with bears all over it. Who would be more likely to have a map tracking bear migration? Or a Red Cross first-aid facility at the station to treat injured hikers and tourists?"

"My God," Cara whispered. "You actually found him."

"Michael found him. I only verified. That sketch Michael drew was incredibly accurate down to the ID badge the ranger wore in that photo. R. Billings. I called the U.S. National Forest Service in Charleston and asked if they had a ranger station in this area. They did, and I'm looking at it now. Lake Kedrow. The two rangers who run it are Bob Duggan and Randy Billings. They haven't reported in for a few days, but that's not too unusual at this time of year." She paused. "But I don't think they'll ever report in again, Cara. Svardak told me that he'd had some young fool take care of his wound because he couldn't go to a hospital. That man in the photo looked so young and happy. And Michael said there was another man and a woman in the photo with him and they looked proud of him. I think it might have been when he got his first job with the Forest Service." She cleared her throat. "I'm sending a copy of Michael's sketch to you. Along with a photo of the ranger station and Lake Kedrow. I'll leave it up to you to get what else you need and whip together a plan to use them. I didn't mention what I thought was happening at that station to those clerks in that Forestry Office in Charleston. All we need is for the police to come barreling down here in full force and get Joe killed." Her voice was suddenly hard and fierce. "Even though it's what I want to do. I'd like to blow the whole place into a million pieces. If Svardak doesn't kill Joe outright, then he'll just let the damn fever do it. I'm not going to let that happen."

"No one's asking you to," Cara said. "If we know where to find him, the battle's half-won. Get as far away from that lake as you can manage. I don't like the idea of your standing on the bank staring at that damn station. What if one of Svardak's men sees you? We'll take it from here."

"No, you won't. I have to know what's going on. I'm staying here until Joe can leave with me."

"Eve, that's not safe or—"

"Do you think I'm fool enough to do something

crazy? I'm not going to do anything that will endanger Michael. He's already risked too much. That's why I'm calling you. I'm taking him back to Hunter's Lake and calling Cheknof, Kaskov's man who's been shadowing us like the Grim Reaper, to meet me there. I'm going to turn Michael over to him and tell him to take care of him until I come for him."

"That didn't work out so well for you before."

"It will now. Cheknof is terrified of doing anything wrong that might displease Kaskov. Will you call Kaskov and have him reinforce it with Cheknof?"

"I won't have to call him. He's here with us at Ruell Falls. I'll go see him."

"Even better. I'll be through with my call to Cheknof in ten minutes. Ask Kaskov to follow up before I get to Hunter's Lake. That should give Cheknof time to be able to work himself into a very amenable frame of mind."

"And then what?"

"You mean after I try to convince Michael this is the best thing to do? He's never going to believe it. I gave him a great speech about working together that he totally ignored. Now it's my turn. Too bad. Time's running out." She paused. "I saw a boat-rental shop near Hunter's Lake. After I drop Michael off with Cheknof, I'll rent a boat and come back here. I'll look the place over and try to keep watch on Joe until you show up. I'll be okay. It's not as if I haven't lived in the woods all those years at the lake cottage. I'll try to give you as much information as I can about Svardak's sentries around the place." She paused. "Are you listening, Jock? Don't make any mistakes. Svardak can't know you're coming. Not one false step. I need Joe out of there."

"I hear you," Jock said grimly. "I'm going to be on the move for Lake Kedrow the minute we hang up.

Keep in touch, so I'll know where to find you. Don't *you* make any mistakes, Eve. Somehow, it's going to end up that I'm to blame if Cara loses either one of you."

"Good. I want to levy all the pressure possible on you right now." Eve hung up the phone.

Cara whirled to Jock in a panic. "It's too dangerous for her. She's an artist, not a cop. She has no business being out there alone. Svardak would love to get his hands on her."

"Not nearly as much as he'd like to get his hands on you," he said grimly. "I'll be with her as quickly as I can. If you think you can talk her into leaving, call her back. I knew I couldn't do it." The phone pinged, and Jock took it and pulled up the photos. "Good job," he murmured. "I think she might be right. It all makes sense. It's a perfect place for him to hideout. It's in the back of the beyond with the Red Cross First Aid Office where he could have his wound stitched. The rangers who failed to check in . . ."

"As long as you're ready to trust Michael as a source. Are you?"

"I have to trust him. I can't do anything else when Eve is so convinced. She'd never risk Joe's life if she wasn't certain." He was getting to his feet. "But everything is escalating now. I need to talk to Nikolai and Edding, then get moving to that ranger station."

"But we don't have to use Edding now that we have a definite location."

"Yes, we will. Svardak has to be as vulnerable as I can make him. I have to draw as many men as possible away from that ranger station if I don't want Joe executed the minute Svardak feels threatened."

She couldn't argue with him. She hadn't the slightest doubt that would happen, nor did Eve. And the moment he thought he wasn't going to get his hands on her, it would have the same result. There had been that instant of hope when Eve had called, but now reality was setting in again. "Okay, I can see that it would be dangerous for him. How can we get around it?"

"Keep the play basically as we planned. Except I go to the ranger station and leave Nikolai to handle using Edding as a target and distraction, but instead of forcing Abrams to take him to Svardak, Nikolai can stall to give me time. Then he can dispose of Abrams after I tell him I've taken care of Svardak at the ranger station. It will be much simpler now." His light eyes were shimmering, his face intent, and she could almost hear his mind clicking. "I'll have to coordinate the kill to get Joe out first, but that should be no problem."

"Easy." She shivered. Given his background, it indeed might seem easy for Jock, but the thought of his facing Svardak was terrifying for Cara. And she had been aware he had left out one important detail. "Now tell me what I can do."

"Not one damn thing." He met her eyes. "You don't go near him, do you understand? The quickest way to get me killed is to have me worrying about you while I go after Svardak. I promise Joe will be safe." His lips twisted. "And I promise Svardak will be dead. Just let me do it the way it needs to be done."

And then she'd have to worry about his doing the job that she knew belonged to her. She'd been fighting to keep that from happening since the moment she'd first faced Svardak at Lost Canyon. That monster had taken Joe; she couldn't lose Jock, too. "It shouldn't be that way, Jock. I'm going with you."

"It's the only way it can be," he said curtly. "Eve's already there, and I know I can't budge her. But I won't risk you. There's no reason. It's what I do. It's what I am." But he was gazing at her expression, and he muttered a curse. "*No*, Cara. My stomach is twisting at the thought of you even close to him. If you need to do something, be our contact with Eve. You said you were worried about her. Keep her safe until I can get to her."

As long as she could do it far away from Svardak, she thought with frustration. Did he think that would be enough for her? As she stared at him, she realized that there was no way she was going to be able to change his mind. His obsession with protecting her from Svardak was too strong after all they'd gone through. "You're an idiot, Jock. And you're doing the wrong thing." She turned on her heel and walked away from him.

"Where are you going?"

"I promised Eve I'd talk to Kaskov about speaking to this Cheknof. I'm going to keep my promise." She gave him a cool glance over her shoulder. "If that's all right with you. I wouldn't want to interfere with any of your plans. I think you said that I'm allowed to deal with Eve?"

"Cara."

"Not now, Jock." She strode toward the helicopter. "You're in a hurry, remember? Go talk to Nikolai." She was climbing the steps. "I guarantee he'll be much more receptive than I am."

She disappeared into the helicopter.

"Hello, Cara. You appear a trifle disturbed." Kaskov came out of the cockpit drinking his tea from a beautifully crafted Meissen cup. "Since I can't recall doing anything that might bring you to that condition, I assume that Gavin is to blame. Would you like a cup of tea?"

"No I would not." She handed Kaskov her phone. "Eve managed to locate the place where Joe is being held. It's a ranger station near Lake Kedrow. He's wounded and ill, and she's very worried about him."

"I'm sure she has a right to be. Eve's a very sensible

woman." He quickly flipped through the photos. "And why is that my concern? Gavin made it clear that he's in charge of any and all rescue attempts. I'm only allowed to contribute manpower and weapons." He handed her back her phone. "Which I've done so generously that Nikolai says Gavin will quite probably be able to pull off the capture of Abrams and company. And it seems that it might be relatively easy now to pick up Svardak since we know where he's gone to ground. Case closed."

"The hell it is."

Kaskov's brows rose. "There's that disturbance again. Would you care to explain? Just what do you want from me?"

Cara wanted to shake him. There was something mockingly tigerish about the way he was playing her. "I don't have to explain. I told you before what I wanted from you. I want to keep the people I care about away from Svardak. I should have been able to kill him in that cabin, but I screwed up. This is my battle, and I won't let him win by killing anyone else I love."

"Gavin is quite competent."

"Don't tell me that." Her hands clenched into fists at her sides. "I know what he can do. I have night-mares about it. I also know that he promised me that Joe would live because he knew it was important to me. Which means he'll risk anything to give me what I want. It will be twice as dangerous for him to go up against Svardak than it would anyone else."

"I can see that." He paused. "Unless perhaps it's you. And that's what you have in mind, isn't it? You've had this idea about using yourself as bait all along. No wonder Gavin has been keeping an eagle eye on you." He smiled faintly. "More than an eagle eye. Does he know that you might try to slip away from him?"

"It wouldn't surprise me. Jock knows me very well." She met his eyes. "And that's why you'll have to be very convincing when you lie to him. He won't trust either one of us."

"I'm to lie to him? Interesting."

"I might need a very fast way to get to Lake Kedrow. You have this helicopter. And Jock isn't going to let me go anywhere near that ranger station. That's okay, but I have to be able to find a way to divert Svardak while Jock and Eve are getting Joe out of there."

"How? What form is this diversion to take?"

"I haven't had time to think about it yet. For heaven's sake, Eve just called me. But since you're very intelligent and without conscience, we should be able to come up with something between us."

"I'm sure we would."

"It's not as if Svardak is invulnerable. Besides being insane, he's reminded how much he hates me every time he takes a deep breath and that wound stabs him. That will be on our side. Actually, now he hates me more than he does you. Though you'd still be very tempting to him. Can't you see? You're nearly perfect."

"I'm flattered." He added ironically, "And you wouldn't be troubled about having to consider your own feelings if Svardak managed to kill me?"

"You're wrong. I'd feel terrible. I hope neither one of us will be killed. But you're responsible for all this. You should try to make it right."

"Really?"

"And you *want* to do it. You've been hunting Svardak for years. You want to put an end to him. Why else did you point Jock toward Lost Canyon?"

"Why else?" He cocked his head, considering her words. "It's true that you're being completely logical. Heaven forbid I'd be influenced by all that same emotional nonsense you are. Of course, there is the matter of your music. Do you suppose that keeping you alive might have anything to do with it?"

"I don't know. Maybe. I've never known what you're thinking. You don't like me or anyone else to know, do you?" She made an impatient gesture. "That's not important. Are you going to help me? If you're not, I'll have to figure out something else."

He was silent. "I find I do want to do it." He took another sip of his tea. "Svardak is unfinished business that needs a period. But I'll have to consider the ramifications and get back to you."

"I can't give you much time."

He shrugged. "I don't like being pressured, Cara. I'll take as long as I wish."

"And Jock will ask you to keep an eye on me before he leaves to go to that ranger station."

"How humiliating for you. I'm sure you'll make him suffer. Don't worry, if I decide to do this, being an expert liar goes along with being intelligent and without conscience." He nodded at the door. "Run along, Cara. I have things to do. I'll get back to you later." The mockery was suddenly gone, and his demeanor was clipped and radiating pure power. "Is there anything else?"

For an instant she was caught off guard by that sudden coolness. Then she turned to the door. "Yes. You can call Cheknof and tell him that you'll draw and quarter him if he doesn't take good care of Michael. Eve is being forced to use him as a makeshift babysitter while she's keeping an eye on the ranger station."

"No problem," Kaskov said as he reached for his phone. "Cheknof has already made his one mistake, and he knows it. The boy will be safe."

HUNTER'S LAKE

"He will be safe," Cheknof said belligerently to Eve as he watched Eve and Michael walk toward his car.

"You did not have to call Kaskov again. The other was not my fault either." He glared at Michael. "He made me look like a fool."

"I'm sorry," Michael said gravely. "You're not a fool. You're very smart. I wouldn't have even tried to slip away if I hadn't had to get to my dad."

"You should not have done it."

Michael nodded. "I can see that now. I won't do it again. I'd never want to get you in trouble."

"It wouldn't do you any good to try." But a little of Cheknof's belligerence had faded. "Get in the car."

"Right after I say good-bye to my mom." He turned and went into Eve's arms. "You shouldn't be doing this," he whispered. "I should go with you. Let me go."

"Not this time." She swallowed to ease the tightness of her throat. "You've done your part. I have to know you're safe. Hey, you've been so good about accepting this. Don't spoil it."

"I would if I could," he said. "But I know you won't change your mind." He looked up at her, his eyes misting. "Don't you get hurt. Dad will blame me for not taking care of you."

"I promise I won't." She gave him another hug. "Now go back to Cheknof and don't give him a bad time. Okay?"

"Okay. You're right, Cheknof only wants to do what's best for me."

"Well, he's not *that* good-hearted. There might also be some self-interest involved."

He smiled back at her over his shoulder. "Then maybe we can convince him that to be good-hearted would be to his self-interest. What do you think, Mom?"

"Just do what he says. Take care, Michael."

He nodded as he got into the backseat. "You'll call and let me know when you get Dad away from him?"

"You know I will." She turned and headed for her

car. "The minute it happens." A few minutes later, she was heading down the hill toward the road that led to Lake Kedrow.

Michael watched her go.

He should be with her.

He should take care of her like Dad had told him to do.

Darkness had fallen, and he didn't like the idea of her being out there alone. Jock was supposed to be coming, but how long would that be? Not knowing all those things was worrying him.

He had to do something about it.

"You want a soda?" Cheknof asked. "I've got Coke in the cooler."

Michael shook his head.

"Your mom's going to be okay. I can tell she can take care of herself." He scowled. "She nearly got me killed when she thought I'd hurt you."

Michael turned to look at him.

Cheknof was not a good man, but he was not totally evil. And he had tried to comfort Michael. That meant Michael would probably be able to reach him if he made the effort.

And he would make the effort.

"Yeah, I just worry about her. I bet you worried about your mom, too." Michael smiled at him. "Could I please have that Coke now?"

RUELL FALLS

"I wasn't sure you'd even come to say good-bye." Jock threw his backpack into the helicopter and turned to face Cara. "You were very explicit regarding my stupidity."

"Not stupidity. Your idiocy. There's a difference.

And you're still wrong. I deserve to go with you. Joe and Eve belong to me." She glanced at his backpack on the floor of the copter. "What have you got in there?"

"C-4, rope, audio equipment, my Remington rifle, various other weapons that might prove useful." He paused. "Bandages and medical supplies in case I need them for Joe."

She flinched. "And possibly for yourself?"

He smiled faintly. "Not for me, Cara."

"How do you know?" she said jerkily. "Oh, yes, that's right, you're impregnable. How is this going to work?"

"Nikolai flies me to within an hour's hike of this ranger station and drops me off. He returns here to Ruell Falls. I make contact with Eve and look over my options." He shrugged. "And then I choose one. I'll call Kaskov and tell him if I need Nikolai and additional men to implement it."

"Why not take help now?"

"Because you want Joe alive," he said quietly. "Every man I take is an unknown quantity during an attack. I can't control the outcome."

"Like me?" she smiled bitterly. "I'm left by the wayside because I'm another unknown quantity?"

"No, I'm leaving you here because you're not unknown. I can predict what you'll do, and it terrifies me." He looked over her shoulder at Kaskov, who was strolling toward them. "I'm ready to go. You should have your copter and Nikolai back within forty minutes. I'll be in touch."

"If he's not too busy," Cara said. "There's always that possibility."

"I won't be too busy." He stared into Kaskov's eyes. "I've told you what I expect of you. Don't disappoint me."

"Why would you doubt me?" Kaskov asked. "When I told you that I only came because I didn't trust you to take proper care of an asset I value? Now you're doing exactly what I wish, plus working to give me Svardak's head on a platter. For once our aims coincide beautifully."

"That's why I'm doubting you. You seldom do the predictable." His voice was cold. "Do it this time. I want her safe."

Cara took a step forward, and said fiercely, "Then take me with you and see to it yourself."

"One final attempt?" Jock shook his head. "I thought that might be why you came."

"And that only proves what an idiot you are." Her eyes were glittering as she gazed up at him. "This is why I came." She launched herself into his arms. She held him with all her strength for an instant. "Did you think I'd let you go face that son of a bitch without seeing you one last time? Then *I'd* be the idiot, and he'd win." She whirled away from him. "Now get out of here with your C-4, fancy weapons, and all those other fabulous options."

She stalked away from him.

She didn't look back even when she heard the helicopter taking off.

"Do you suppose you could stop?" Kaskov asked mildly. He had caught up with her and was falling into step. "My men might believe that you're trying to escape, and I was chasing you. Not a good scenario for you." His gaze lifted to the sky. "And Gavin is out of sight and can't rescue you. Though I'm sure that he'd try after that touching farewell."

"Shut up." She was searching for her handkerchief and finally found it. "What else did he say to you?"

"Nothing. You upset him enough so that all he wanted to do was to get out of here and kill something. Preferably Svardak. It was excellent motivation." He

watched her dab at her eyes. "It's too bad it wasn't cal-
culated. I could not have done it better. Without all the
passion and emotion, of course. That's definitely not
my style."

"I wouldn't think so," she said dryly. "I'm not
ashamed of anything that happened, but I'd prefer not
to talk about it, if you don't mind."

"As you wish. It just surprised me. You constantly
surprise me, Cara."

The helicopter was almost out of sight, and her
glance shifted to his face. "What happens next?"

"We wait until Gavin has been dropped off and Nikolai is on his way back to us. I admit to being uneasy
unless Gavin is sufficiently far enough out of the picture to raise my comfort level."

She wasn't sure that she believed him. She'd never
seen Kaskov uneasy. "And then?"

"Then I let you phone Svardak and have a conversation that should prove interesting."

"You decided you're going to help me?"

"It depends on what you term help. I've decided that
I'm going to let you assist me in eliminating a problem." He paused. "Unless you've changed your mind?"

Svardak. Forty minutes, and everything would start.
Jock would be on his way to help Eve and search for his
damn option to save Joe. How could Cara risk less? "I
haven't changed my mind. I'll make the call."

LAKE KEDROW
8:32 P.M.

Three men on guard at the front of the station, Eve
noticed.

And she had noticed two other guards dressed in

ranger uniforms who had been going in and out of the interior of the station for the last hour. Abrams and Lacher?

That had to be where they were keeping Joe.

But she couldn't *see* him. Maybe if she could get just a little closer to that window at the side of the house . . .

Eve wriggled on her stomach through the damp grass so that she was closer to the tree line of the woods.

Careful.

No sound.

Don't startle any of them, or they'll hurt Joe.

If he was still alive.

Of course he was still alive. Don't even think anything else.

She stopped as she reached the tree line. Too much open area before she could reach that window, she realized desperately. She'd just have to rely on what Michael had described to her, along with what she'd found on the Internet about the general structure of the ranger stations. But who knew if this one was the same as the others? None of the others she'd seen on the net had a damn tree house as a third floor. Maybe go around the back and see if—

A hand clamped down hard over her mouth!

She instinctively bit down *hard*.

"Get your teeth out of me," Jock gritted. "And start backing back toward the lake. You're too close. If those guards were any good, they would have heard you moving through the brush." He wasn't waiting but was already on his way toward the lake without a whisper of sound.

She was following him as silently as she could. He was dressed in black and was wraithlike in the darkness. She almost lost him in the brush before he stopped beside the lake. She sat up on her knees and whispered, "You scared me to death. You're lucky you still have fingers. You were supposed to call when you got close."

"I wanted to do a little scouting on my own. Then I saw you moving through that brush and decided that I didn't want to startle you. You were making enough noise." He looked down at his hand. "And I'm not certain all those digits are still in place." His gaze was darting around the bank and the woods. "No guards here. We can talk if you keep it low."

"I wasn't planning on shouting," she said sarcastically. "And not everyone moves like a phantom, Jock." She drew a deep breath. Jock was in attack mode, and politeness was never at the forefront. But she was no longer alone, and no one would know better than Jock how to find a way to save Joe. "I thought I was doing pretty well, but I'm still glad you're here. Who's with you?"

"No one. But I can have a team here within twenty minutes after we decide it's safe for Joe." He paused. "You told me to be careful. Is he still okay? Have you seen him?"

"Not yet." She realized she was shivering. "I was trying to get close enough to that first-aid room to make certain. Michael said he was very sick."

"Michael's just a kid. I don't think we'll go along with his diagnosis on this." His smile was suddenly gentle. "Suppose I go take a look for myself."

"And how are you going to do that? I couldn't see how I was going to get near that porch without being spotted."

"I'll find a way." He was gazing thoughtfully at the station looming through the trees. "I was planning on planting audio and maybe a few other items in the house anyway. I'll just add it to the list."

Add seeing if Joe was still alive to his list? "Svardak has to be in there and probably Abrams and Lacher. I saw two men in uniform going in earlier. There might be more, Jock."

He nodded. "Plus two men standing guard in front. Three sentries are stationed in these woods near the south and west banks of the lake. And I saw one guard on the ridge leading to the main road when I was looking around. That should be all."

"That's enough," she said. "And you didn't tell me how we could manage to do it."

"We? I'll barely be able to get myself in there, much less you." He was turning and moving back through the woods. "Stay here. I'll come back for you."

"But I told you, there's no way you could get in through that porch."

"I'm not going through the porch. I'm going down through that tree house . . ."

He had disappeared.

Through the tree house? Eve gazed at the ranger station. The top of that house was composed of branches, and who knew how it was accessed from the lower rooms of the house. There would definitely be a noise factor to overcome. But no one would expect anyone to enter that way either. And when Jock entered the main house, he would only have to negotiate the corridors, avoid running into Svardak or his men, then set up his "items" where he chose.

And check to see if her Joe was still alive.

Only?

She could feel the muscles in her stomach tense as she strained to hear any sound issuing from the station.

God, she was afraid. If Jock was caught or killed, it could not only mean his death but Joe's. Who knew what Svardak's reaction would be to any intrusion?

Stop it. Joe had told her once that no one was more

capable than Jock at this kind of deadly game. Eve had
to believe he could do this.

Do as Jock had told her.

Wait for him.

Pray for him.

And pray that Joe was still alive.

She sat back on her heels. Her gaze on the tree house.
Waiting.

"Everything's okay, Eve."

Eve's gaze flew to the lake to see Jock emerging from
the tall grass in back of her. "Where have you been? It
must have been at least an hour, dammit."

"Fifty-four minutes. And you know where I'd been.
It took a little longer than I estimated because I had to
avoid Abrams and Lacher and set up a deterrent to get
them out of the house while I was working."

She stiffened. "What deterrent?"

"Nothing suspicious. I was prepared. I caught a
squirrel while I was in the tree house and let it loose in
the kitchen where they were having their supper."

"A squirrel?" It was too bizarre, and she didn't care
about Abrams or Lacher. "Joe?"

"I already told you that everything was okay, Eve,"
he said gently. "I knew you'd want to know that first."

"You didn't say Joe was okay. All you could talk
about was Abrams and squirrels and—" She broke off,
and said, "Joe's still alive? You actually saw him?"

"I saw him. I couldn't risk actually going into the
first-aid room, but I had a few minutes to study him
from a distance." He hesitated before adding soberly,
"And I hate to admit it, but Michael might be right.
Joe's pretty sick. He's unconscious, and he won't be
able to help us if we try to get him out of there."

Joe was *alive*. It was all that sank in for that first minute.

"If he's alive, that's all that matters. And Joe is always stronger than anyone thinks. We'll get him out."

Jock nodded. "No question. But it will make it more difficult." He was reaching into his pocket and pulling out two small devices. "And we have to know what's happening over there because of Joe. That's why I had to set up audio. It's extremely sensitive and will pick up any hint of sound in any of those rooms including phone transmissions. It would have been much easier just to blow the place."

"And no doubt explosives were on the list of items you left in that ranger station?" She tried to smile. "I'm certain Joe would appreciate your using the listening devices instead of the C-4."

"Until we get him out." He was tucking the electronic earpiece in his ear as he handed one to Eve. "Monitor Svardak as much as you can, particularly when he's near Joe. I don't want to make any precipitous moves, but Joe can't take much more punishment. It's not only the fever."

"I know. Svardak turned Abrams loose on them."

"Them?"

"Never mind." Eve was tucking the device into her ear. "I guarantee I'll know everything the bastard is doing. I take it you're going to be too busy to do any monitoring. Tell me you're not heading for that tree house again."

He shook his head. "I have to start getting rid of a few of Svardak's guards. I can't touch anyone near Joe yet, but I can eliminate the guard on the hill leading to the road. After that, I'll see if it's safe for Joe for me to go after the guards by the porch. Let me know if there's something important I should hear."

"Other than the fact that we aren't going to be able

to get to Joe unless we go through Svardak and his two stooges?" she asked bitterly. "You said he was in bad shape. We're going to need help, but that might get him killed, too."

"He's not going to die. Give me a chance. I'll work it out." Jock gave her the faintest smile. "I don't dare do anything else. I promised Cara."

"I admit that's formidable." She nodded jerkily. "Sorry, I lost it for a minute."

"I didn't notice."

"Liar." She looked back at the house. *We're so close, Joe. Can you feel me here? Just hold on.* "Just get out of here and do something to make a difference."

"Whatever you say . . ."

She didn't take her eyes away from the house, but she knew he was no longer beside her.

CHAPTER

16

He looks like death warmed over." Svardak gazed down at Joe Quinn with immense satisfaction. "At first I thought you might have gone too far, Abrams. I was afraid he might die on us. He might still die, but he'll linger long enough for me to tear our Cara to pieces."

"If he dies, it will be the fever." Abrams shrugged. "I've worked for you long enough to know you don't tolerate mistakes." He glanced at the clock. "And isn't it almost time for you to show her my handiwork? Is that why you're in here gloating?"

"I'm not gloating. That will come later. I'm just examining your work. Though I admit that I'm having trouble waiting for her. It's like a hunger—" He took out his phone. "But you're right, it's almost time and it won't matter if I start the clock a little early." He started to press the buttons. "Let's see what *she* says about your work. I'm eager to—"

His phone rang, and he smiled as he read the ID. "Ah, it seems our Cara is also eager to see if I've damaged Quinn." He accessed the call and pressed Face-Time. "Hello, Cara. Have you missed me that much?

You still have fifteen minutes before you have to bow down to—"

"Shut up. I need to know if Joe is still alive."

"You sound quite desperate," he said softly. "And there are circles under your eyes. Have you been tearing about the countryside trying to find me? What a pity. Because you didn't have Quinn or that Gavin who appeared so conveniently on the scene to help you. Stressful."

"Is Joe still alive?"

"Perhaps. But you had no right to expect it. I'm in control now, Cara."

"Is he alive?"

"See for yourself." He turned the phone toward Joe Quinn. "I'd say the answer is 'barely.' What do you think?"

"My God." Cara inhaled sharply. She closed her eyes for an instant. "Damn you." Her eyes were glittering with tears when she opened them. "What did you do to him?"

"I just amused myself while I was waiting for you to come back to me. Are you ready now?"

"After . . . you let him go," she said hoarsely. "You know my terms. Look what you've done to Joe already. Do you actually think I'd be stupid enough to believe that if I showed up on your doorstep, you'd release him? It would be an automatic death sentence for him." She swallowed. "And you'd win, Svardak. I swore I'd never let you win. You might be able to get your hands on me, but only if you give up Joe."

"You stupid bitch." Svardak could feel the rage sear through him. He knew how stubborn she could be, but he'd hoped against hope that she'd cave when she'd seen what he'd done to Quinn. He wanted this to be over. He wanted her to be back where he'd had her at the canyon. He needed to punish her, hurt her. He needed to *see* it. "Do you think that I won't tear him apart? I *have* won. You just don't know it yet. I'll show you that—"

"Stop ranting, Svardak. You're boring me. I've lost patience with both of you." Kaskov was roughly pushing Cara aside and taking her phone. "I've had enough of this. I've wasted entirely too much time on you."

"Kaskov?" Svardak stared at him, stunned. But he quickly recovered. "Cara ran to you when she was trying to save Quinn? Well, you couldn't find me either, could you? All these years, and you've never been able to hunt me down. You should have gotten used to it."

"Do you think you're that important to me? I barely know you're in my world," Kaskov said. "But lately, you've been getting in my way, and it has to end."

"Is that a threat?"

"It doesn't have to be." Kaskov was silent. "We can negotiate."

"Kaskov, what are you saying?" Cara asked incredulously.

"Be quiet, Cara. You no longer have any say in this. You're just in the way. Svardak's cost me time and manpower and money. I've been on the hunt for him for years; and then he pops up again when he started to kill those women. How long am I supposed to put up with it? Yes, I could continue indefinitely, but there comes a time to make the deal." He smiled. "You know a lot about me, don't you, Svardak? You know I'm primarily a businessman. That's why I'm successful. I leave passion and revenge to the fools who embrace it. Fortunately for you, you've caught me at a time when I need to concentrate on my new deal with Beijing."

"What does China have to do with anything?"

"They believe as I do that business has to be paramount. I've been getting rumblings from them that they think me weak for spending so much time on a family matter instead of devoting myself to completing our transaction." His smile vanished. "I cannot tolerate any rumors to that effect. The tigers are gathering. It would cause me problems on all fronts. I have to show them that I'm neither weak nor dominated by anything but the empire I've built for myself during these last decades."

"Which will vanish when I kill you. What are you saying?"

"If you'll listen instead of threaten, I'll tell you. You're not that important. I almost had you at Lost Canyon, but after that I decided to cut my losses. You were obviously going to be a constant headache to me."

"Until the day you die."

"Or not." He was silent. "I'm very fond of living. But I might give you something that might satisfy you."

"Money?"

"No, money wouldn't sway you." He smiled crookedly. "But what if I give you Cara? After all, she's my blood."

Svardak stiffened in shock. "What?"

"Why are you surprised? It would be payment for Anna, a way to settle this feud. Feuds are expensive."

"Kaskov!" Cara's voice was shaking. "Why are you doing this? You said that if I came to you, you'd help me."

"No, I said I'd let you help me. There's a difference. Unfortunately, you're expendable, Cara." He turned back to Svardak. "Now what about it? It's clear you have an obsession with her. Neither of us would have a total victory, but there are advantages. If I gave you Cara, you could still keep Quinn to play with until you choose to kill him in front of her. That's what you wanted, wasn't it?"

He was silent. "You'd actually do that?"

"Why are you surprised? You must have researched me enough to find I scarcely know her. It would be no real loss."

"And what would you get out of it?"

"I told you, it would give me exactly what I wanted. No one would ever question that I'd do anything I had to do to get what I wanted, even if it meant sacrificing family. Absolutely no weakness. And a chance to end this nonsense. I'm tired of it. I'm ahead of the game now. You're the last of the family on my list." He shrugged. "Of course, you might not be sated with Cara and still go after me later. But I'd still buy some time to finish the Chinese negotiations, which are crucial. And if the solution doesn't prove effective, I'll just go after you again, and this time I won't stop. It will just mean I'll have to make your end even more painful and bloody."

There had to be something wrong here, Svardak thought. Everything Kaskov had said made sense to him considering the bastard's deadly reputation, but it was definitely suspect. "I could keep Quinn?"

"Of course. Quinn is a cop, and he's only a hindrance to me. Enjoy yourself." His lips twisted. "By the look of him, you already have. Though I have a man who could have done it better. Do you need any tips about—"

"No!" Cara cried out as she launched herself and tried to grab the phone away from him. "Shut up! What kind of man are—"

Her head snapped back as Kaskov's fist struck her in the face. She staggered back and fell to her knees.

"You don't *touch* me." Kaskov stood over her, his lips tight, his eyes blazing. "You would have learned respect if I'd had the raising of you. But now it seems Svardak will have that pleasure." He lifted the phone again. "Yes or no, Svardak."

Svardak's gaze was still on Cara's shocked face. It had been a hard blow, and he could see the mark of Kaskov's hand on her cheek. He suddenly wanted it to be *his* mark on her, and he felt a rush of pleasure and anticipation that was almost erotic. "She looked the same the first time I hit her. I'd almost forgotten . . . but the blood reminded me."

"Yes or no."

He couldn't take his gaze off the blood on Cara's lower lip. "How would you handle it?"

"My men are very good at packaging. Tell me where, and I'll have her delivered."

"And scoop me up? I'm no fool."

"Kaskov, don't do this," Cara pleaded.

He slapped her again, hard. She fell to the floor.

"You would be a fool if you didn't take sufficient care, Svardak," Kaskov said. "It's wide-open country here in the mountains. You should be able to find a place that you could make certain you wouldn't be ambushed."

Svardak could see that Cara was having to struggle to sit up. So weak. So pliant to anything he wanted to do to her. He felt another flush of heat twist through him. "Tonight?"

"If you like, it's up to you."

Yes, it was up to him. The possibilities were making him heady with exhilaration. He was winning, and she could do nothing about it. "I'll send you the coordinates. Deliver her there in the next two hours. I want her bound and helpless. Do you hear me, Cara? Get ready for the chains again. I'll have them ready for you." He cut the connection.

Abrams was staring at him warily. "There's a good chance that it's a trap, you know."

"Of course, I know," he said curtly. "Only an idiot wouldn't suspect it." He paused. "On the other hand,

Kaskov is a ruthless son of a bitch who might want to rid himself of me in the most convenient method possible. He does think of business first, and I've been getting in his way. Cara even told me once that he cared nothing for her. He's quite capable of trading her for a truce." He thought about it. "Or risking her neck to make me think he was." He was staring at the blank screen of his phone. He could still see the image of Cara lying there, weak and in pain. "And Kaskov *liked* punishing her. I could tell." Because he felt as if he had been joined with Kaskov in those exquisite moments. "It won't hurt to play his game and see what happens. It will change nothing. It will only be a delay. I can afford to wait for Kaskov. I'll send him coordinates to Copper Flats, where I was going to have Cara meet us when she agreed to surrender herself. As long as you're very careful, there should be no problem."

"I don't like it."

"Too bad. You don't have to like it." He was still mentally seeing that delicious drop of blood on Cara's lower lip as he started to type in Kaskov's address. "All you have to do is make sure that if a trap is sprung, it won't be Kaskov's."

Oh, shit.

The muscles of Eve's stomach clenched as she pressed the device in her ear to turn it off. She should probably continue listening, but she couldn't do it right now.

Cara.

That Svardak call Eve had just monitored had been terrifying . . . and bewildering.

And she couldn't face it alone.

Her hand was shaking as she dialed Jock.

He answered on the second ring. "Problem?"

"Big-time. Can you come back right away? You need to hear this."

"Joe?"

Of course he'd think it was Joe who was threatened. He'd seen how vulnerable he was earlier tonight. "Cara."

"I'm on the ridge overlooking the road. It will take me four minutes." He hung up.

Four minutes sounded like a long time at this moment. She couldn't stop shaking.

Cara.

Kaskov?

Jock was there in three minutes. "What is it?" he said curtly.

She pulled out her earpiece and handed it to him. "I recorded the call as soon as I knew it was Cara." She drew a shaky breath. "It's crazy, Jock. What the hell can we do?"

He didn't answer. He was already listening. Even in the shadow-filtered moonlight, she could see the icy hardness begin to form in his expression. A few minutes later, he jerked the device out of his ear.

He wasn't moving. He was just sitting there with that terrible rage hardening his expression more every second.

"Jock?"

"Not now," he said hoarsely. "Give me a minute. I'm not thinking, I'm just feeling."

She had also needed time to absorb. She nodded jerkily. She repeated, "It's crazy."

He didn't reply for another couple minutes. "You're right, it doesn't make sense. That's what I'm hoping . . ."

"Kaskov. I shouldn't be surprised. I never trusted him. But I never thought he'd be that callous. He was ice-cold, Jock." She shuddered. "And he hurt Cara. They were talking about her bleeding."

"Don't talk about that right now. It's getting in my way." He was still once more, his brow furrowed. "But you were surprised, weren't you? Because, in spite of everything the entire world knows about Kaskov, you have a tendency to see deeper."

"You're wrong." Her lips tightened. "I don't have a clue about the man who hurt Cara tonight. I have no idea why he would do that."

He was silent again. "I do." Then he reached for his phone. "Cara. Let's see what she has to say about it."

She watched him in bewilderment as he punched in the numbers. "What are you doing? If she's being held by Kaskov, there's no way he'll let her answer you."

"The question is all in the word 'if.'" He hit the speaker button while he was listening to the ring. She could see the tension in every muscle of his body, desperation in each line of his face. "And Cara can be amazingly determined . . ."

"Hello, Jock," Cara said as she answered the phone. "I suppose you heard my call to Svardak? How angry are you?"

Eve saw an expression of unutterable relief cross Jock's face as his hand tightened on the phone. "I'm furious with you."

"I thought you would be. Will you please get over it?" she asked wearily. "That call almost drained me, and I still have a lot more I have to do before the night is over."

"I thought you might. Being a sacrificial lamb takes considerable energy, doesn't it? And you had me fooled until I realized that it was striking too many false notes in my experience with both of you. So it was all just a show that you and Kaskov put on to set you up for Svardak?"

"Yes. I was planning on calling you later if you hadn't had time to set up the audio so you could hear it for yourself."

"How kind. It would have been even kinder if you'd given me advance warning so that I wouldn't have to go through that hell. I want to strangle you, Cara."

"No, you don't. You're just hurting. I would have tried to warn you, but you'd have just argued with me. There was no question I'd change my mind." She drew a shaky breath. "And time was running out. I could tell Eve was in a panic about Joe. From what Svardak showed me, she had a right to be. Is she there?"

"I'm here," Eve said. "And I'm not sure I don't agree with Jock. I might be in a panic about Joe, but that doesn't mean either one of us would want you pulling something like this. What do you think you're doing?"

"As I said, trying to get Joe away from Svardak. Jock wouldn't listen to me. He just closed me out because he was scared. I had to go to Kaskov."

"And you both lied to me," Jock said through set lips.

"I didn't lie to you. I just didn't say what you wanted to hear. And you knew I'd do anything I could to help Joe if I got the chance. Because you were wrong, you *need* me. I can keep his attention away from Joe long enough for you to get him out of that ranger station and safe." She added quickly, before he could argue, "Yes, Edding might have proved to be a minor distraction, but I'm the main attraction as far as Svardak is concerned. But I had to have a good reason to be there because at some point he would have questioned why I gave in about Joe's release. Because he *knows* me, and it might have seemed too easy to him. But now all you'll have to do is concentrate on getting Joe out and leave the rest to me."

"Providing we're not concerned with what Svardak

will be doing to you while we 'leave the rest' to you," Jock said harshly. "That might be a major distraction in itself."

"I'll find a way. I know how to push his buttons. And Kaskov said that he might be able to have some of his men run interference for me. But, of course, it will have to be after you get Joe away from the station."

"Might? Of course? I can't say I'm liking Kaskov's extremely casual view on keeping you alive. In fact, I'm not liking his entire input into the matter."

"Don't blame Kaskov. It was entirely—"

"Enough, Cara." Kaskov came on the line. "I believe I can come to my own defense. You've already taken sufficient heat tonight. Go ahead, Gavin. It's not something I didn't expect."

"You're going to get her killed. Didn't you say that you couldn't trust me not to do that when you showed up at Ruell Falls? Well, here she is, directly in the line of fire."

"Come now. We both know she's a force of nature when she makes up her mind. I'm a reasonable man, I don't fight battles I can't win. Besides, she's my blood. It would offend me to see anyone but myself defeat her. You couldn't expect me to take your side against her."

"I could expect you to try to keep her alive. She's of value to you. That was my only hope. But you chose to use her to revenge your damn vendetta instead."

"It was certainly a consideration. Cara realized that when she came to recruit me. She's such a clever girl. But, then, she also had an idea how much I'd enjoy the actual hunt."

"I'm glad you were entertained," Jock said softly. "Because when this is over, I'm coming after you, Kaskov."

"You *are* angry," Kaskov said. "Interesting. I believe

most of the time you manage to overcome that blood-lust. What tipped the scales?"

"You enjoyed yourself a little too much. You *hit* her, you son of a bitch."

"Yes, I did," Kaskov said. "And I did it well. I imagine I made Svardak salivate. But I can't really claim credit for that action. It was Cara's idea."

"What?"

"For God's sake, Jock," Cara said impatiently. "Of course I told him to do it. Svardak *likes* to see me hurt. It's a power trip. If he had doubts, I knew it might have a good chance of blurring them."

"Then by all means it had to be done," he said sarcastically.

"Yes, it did." She was silent. "I have to go now. Kaskov has the coordinates, and it seems to be a flat about an hour's drive from the ranger station. He'll leave me there for Abrams to pick up and take to Svardak."

"Like a sack of potatoes?"

"Oh, I'm much more valuable than a sack of potatoes. And my packaging will be impeccable. Kaskov says that he has special chemically treated ropes that appear strong and foolproof, but will enable me to wriggle out of them if I try hard enough. When you see Abrams's car coming down the road toward the station, it will be your signal to get Joe out. I'll make a distraction to be sure that Svardak is out of that house for at least ten minutes. I might not be able to hold him any longer."

"And I'm just supposed to accept that? Just rely on you and Kaskov, who *might* be there for you?"

"I believe he'll try very hard. If you can think of something else, by all means do it. But not if it means not getting Joe out of there. That's not an option." She was silent, struggling to speak. "Don't rob me of this,

Jock," she whispered. "And don't you dare get yourself killed." She cut the connection.

Jock sat there, frozen, gazing down at the phone.

Eve knew how he felt. She was feeling that same panicky helplessness she was seeing in him.

Then Jock was swearing beneath his breath and jumping to his feet.

"Jock?" She sat up straight. "Where are you going?"

"Where do you think?" He was gliding silently toward the ranger station. "Didn't you hear her? I have my orders. I only have a few hours before I'm going to see her come down that road. I have to find a way to keep her alive. And that means timing the removal of those guards at just the right time." He glanced over his shoulder. "And you have to make sure that canoe you used to come over from that far bank is as close as possible to the station without anyone's seeing it. I'm going to need to move very fast to get Joe out of that first-aid room and both of you on your way across the lake to your car on the other side."

"And you won't be able to move that fast burdened by Joe and without help," she said curtly as she got to her feet. "Joe's no lightweight. I'll have to help you get him out of the station and down to the canoe." She held up her hand as he opened his lips to protest. "No," she said fiercely. "You probably don't want to risk either me or whatever plan you decide to go with. But I can do this. I'm no Wonder Woman, but I'm healthy and strong, and I'll be able to help. Cara was right. Not doing everything possible to get Joe out is not an option." She shivered. "She also said she could only give us ten minutes. The quicker we can get Joe down to that canoe, the quicker you can get back to help her." She turned toward the lake and started moving. "So shut up, Jock. Just figure me into being there to help Joe and not just rowing him across the damn lake. I'll call you when I get the canoe hidden closer to the station, and you can come and tell me what else I can do."

RUELL FALLS

"Gavin might still go after me, you know." Kaskov smiled ruefully at Cara. "Even if you manage to live through what that idiot, Svardak, is planning for you. Gavin was intensely annoyed about my abusing you."

"You didn't abuse me," Cara said jerkily. She was still shaken and disturbed after hanging up on Jock. If everything didn't go right, that could be the last time she would be able to speak to him, and the idea was terribly painful. "And I told him that everything you did was my idea. I'm the one with whom he was really angry."

"Wrong. He was really angry with himself for not being able to keep you from doing this madness. I came in second because I was on-site and had the ability to stop you and didn't choose to do it."

"You couldn't have stopped me."

He smiled. "Not true. I'm more ruthless than anyone you've ever known, Cara. I have no problem channeling that ruthlessness whenever it's necessary. Neither does Gavin, but he suffers from serious twinges of conscience on occasion. I've gone past that inconvenience." He sighed. "But Gavin always makes an exception where you're concerned. There might not be any twinges at all where I'm concerned." He leaned forward and gently touched her lower lip. "This hurt you."

"And it excited Svardak." She moved her head to escape his touch. "It might have pushed him over the edge. You did what I wanted you to do. Shouldn't we get going?"

"There's a little time. It's only a short helicopter ride from here. I've sent men to search the area to make certain there aren't going to be any surprises for me when I deliver you." He was still looking at her lip. "This displeased me. I'm a superb actor, but I found it difficult to give Svardak what he wanted. I believe I'll have to take something excruciatingly painful back from him to make up for it."

"Blood?" Cara shook her head. "I can't think about that anymore. I'm beyond wanting anything but to keep everyone I care about safe." She added wryly, "And maybe come out of this alive." She frowned. "You wouldn't have something I could use to help me ensure that I do, would you? I know you said that you'd use ropes that would let me free myself, and that should help. But Abrams is sure to search me for weapons. I thought you might be very clever about finding ways to get around obstacles like that."

"Oh, I am. But it's generally best to think in advance on devices of that nature." He shook his head. "You're such a novice, Cara. It's good that I was prepared for it. I might have something on hand that could be a little more efficient than that amateurish dagger you stuck the bastard with before."

"Might?" Amazingly, she found herself faintly smiling. "Jock didn't like that word."

"I remember. Perhaps I'll work on making it a little more positive." He shrugged. "Or perhaps not. I'll have to decide if you're worth it."

"You've already made that decision, or you wouldn't be planning on going to all this trouble," she said quietly.

"No, I've decided that Svardak's death is worth it. Your life is another matter. Perhaps I'm only interested in how you'll perform in this particular arena."

It was always performance with Kaskov where she was concerned. She was suddenly impatient. Her nerves were raw and on edge, and she wanted this over. "Whatever." She got to her feet. "May we go now? I want to spend some time working with those ropes that you said I'd be able to wriggle out of so easily. You're not the only one who doesn't want to be surprised. And I can't guarantee I won't disappoint you. You're right, I'm a complete novice. I'm afraid that I'll do the wrong thing and get someone hurt."

He was silent. "Yes, you *are* afraid." He was studying her expression. "Very well, we can leave. Keeping busy will be better for you." He got to his feet and headed for the helicopter. "But for your information, I don't expect to be at all disappointed in you, Cara. Are you not my granddaughter?"

LAKE KEDROW

Lord, the water was cold. With every step Eve was taking, the icy water washed against her lower body and waist, taking her breath.

Ignore it.

She was almost at the cove she'd chosen as the safest and closest place to hide the canoe. It had taken her longer than she had thought it would because she'd realized she couldn't use either the motor or oars because of the noise factor. She had to guide the canoe slowly along the bank, making it glide soundlessly, and the only way she could control that movement was to be in the water with it.

Eve tightened her hold on the rope she was using to guide the canoe along the bank of the lake.

Only seven or eight yards more to the cove . . .

Six.

Four.

Two.

Done!

Then she was boosting herself onto the bank. She sat there a moment trying to catch her breath and stop the shivering. The wind had risen in the last hour, and her lower body felt like an ice cube whenever it touched her. But that wasn't the only thing that was chilling her as she gazed at the ranger station. It looked so far away through the trees. It had been the very closest she could get without running the danger of being spotted. How long would it take them to get Joe, who might have to be almost entirely supported, through those woods?

She couldn't stay here and waste time worrying about it. She was already running late. Secure the canoe firmly, then go meet Jock.

She got to her feet and started to pull the canoe closer to the bank so that she could tie it to that pine tree a few yards from the bank. The rope was cutting into her hands as she fought with the sharp wind.

"I'll do it. Let me help, Mom."

She stiffened in horror. It couldn't be.

She looked down the bank.

Oh, my God. Michael was running toward her.

Here?

Then he was next to her, his hands on the rope with her own, pulling the canoe, helping her secure it to the tree.

"Is that okay? That's the knot Dad taught me." Michael was frowning worriedly. "You're all wet. You shouldn't be wet. You could get sick again."

That remark was so typical, it proved this wasn't a nightmare. He was really here. "It's *not* okay. Nothing is okay. You shouldn't be here. I left you miles away, where you'd be safe. How could you *do* this?" She ran her shaking hand through her hair. "And keep your voice down. They'll hear you."

He shook his head. "I don't think so." But his voice was lower. "Mr. Cheknof checked and said that there weren't any guards along this strip of the bank. He knows about things like that."

"Cheknof." This was still worse. She had thought perhaps Michael had gotten away from Cheknof and found a way to get to her. "Cheknof is here with you? Did something happen? Was there some reason why you had to leave Hunter—"

Michael was shaking his head. "Nothing bad happened. I just knew that I needed to help you, and Mr. Cheknof was the only one who could bring me. But it took a little while to persuade him, so I was only able to get here just now." He frowned. "But you're wet, and I should have—"

"Michael, be quiet." She drew a deep breath, trying to pull herself together and confront this new disaster. "I have to get you out of here. Cheknof is with you? Where is he?"

"He's coming." Michael nodded down the bank. "I could feel you up ahead and started running. Please don't yell at him. He only wants to help now, and like I said, he knows things. Some of it is bad, but it won't matter if he can help Dad."

"Jock and I are going to help your dad. All I need Cheknof to do is get you out of here."

He shook his head gravely. "I won't go this time. You need me." He reached out and touched her wrist. "I know you're afraid something will happen to me and that's why you wouldn't listen to me before." His gaze shifted to the distant ranger station. "You're going to have to get Dad out of there. But he's sicker now, and he's not going to understand or be able to help you. But if I get close to him, I can still reach to him and explain. I can make him wake up and stay awake until you have him safe. You know that would be a help."

"It doesn't matter. We'll do it without you. Do you think I'd let you go with us?"

"No, but what if I stay back here at the canoe and wait for you? I don't really have to actually be there. I could do what I did before." He smiled. "Besides, I'm not big enough or strong enough to help you get him this far, am I? You need someone like Jock." His gaze went to Cheknof, who was stalking down the bank with a scowl on his face. "Or Mr. Cheknof . . . Remember not to yell at him."

She started toward Cheknof. "No promises."

Cheknof slowed down warily as she approached. "I told the kid that you'd be angry. But I did take care of him. It's just . . . difficult."

"Tell that to Kaskov," she said grimly. "Never mind my being angry. I can't believe you'd disobey his orders. Do you have a death wish?"

He shook his head. "He won't be angry when I explain this is the best way to protect you and the child."

Her eyes widened in shock. "He won't?"

"Why would he? If I take out Svardak and keep him from hurting his granddaughter, I'll be a hero. Nothing else will matter to him."

He appeared absolutely convinced, Eve realized incredulously. A complete reversal of his cautious attitude before she had left him with Michael earlier that evening. "I wouldn't count on that."

He made an impatient gesture. "You don't understand. I had to think about it for a while myself before I realized the best way to handle everything to please Kaskov. But now I've got it right." He glanced at Michael and changed the subject. "And you shouldn't have run away from me. You promised you wouldn't do that."

"I forgot," Michael said solemnly. "It won't happen again, Mr. Cheknof. If you need to do something important for Mr. Kaskov, I'll stay here where I'm safe. That way you won't get in trouble."

Eve's mouth was open as she watched the interplay between them. Michael was being completely respectful but he was playing faultlessly to Cheknof's new attitude toward Kaskov. What was going on here?

It took me a little while to persuade him so I was only able to get here just now.

Persuade. Just what had Michael done to "persuade" Cheknof to do what he wanted him to do?

The answer was literally mind-blowing. She had an idea, but she was having problems accepting it. She didn't want to acknowledge even to herself how Michael had probably managed to shift Cheknof's thinking to suit himself so that he could get to his father.

"I'm sure it's comforting to you that my son is so concerned about keeping you out of trouble, Cheknof." She turned to Michael, and said grimly, "However, you're definitely in trouble in all kinds of ways, young man."

"No!" Cheknof's expression was suddenly menacing as his gaze swung back to Eve. "He's helping me. And you're getting in the way."

"No, she's not," Michael said quickly. "She's fine, and Mr. Kaskov likes her. She's just a little confused."

"That's certainly true," Eve said dryly.

"But you'll need time to talk to Jock, then tell us how we can help." He stared directly into her eyes. "Because we do *have* to help, Mom. Mr. Cheknof and I both really want to do it." He was suddenly smiling coaxingly. "I know you're probably in a hurry. Suppose we go back to the canoe and wait for you? That's a safe place, or you wouldn't have taken the canoe there." He turned and headed for the pines. "Come on," he said to Cheknof. "You can check out the canoe while we're waiting for them to come back . . ."

Eve stared dazedly after Michael and Cheknof, who looked like a giant wrestler lumbering beside him. She wanted to run after Michael and swoop him up and hide him away somewhere until this was all over. Get a grip. Where could she hide him that he wouldn't be in danger? He had made it clear that he wouldn't leave until his father did. In the short term, there was clearly no question that Michael would be as safe as he wanted to be until she could get back to him after her meeting with Jock. Cheknof had even been ready to attack her when he'd thought she was threatening him. It was only Michael's intervention that had saved her.

Which was as bizarre as the rest of what had happened since Michael had run down that bank toward her.

Accept it. He was here and determined to stay. And she doubted if she had time to change the course that Michael had put in motion if they were to save Joe.

She just hoped to God she could think of some way to keep them all safe. Don't try to do it alone. Talk to Jock about these new problems that had emerged from the shadows. Tell him she hadn't been able to get the canoe as close as she'd wanted. Tell him about Michael and Cheknof.

She suddenly stiffened as she glanced back at Michael and Cheknof.

Cheknof . . .

CHAPTER
17

"Good God," Jock said. "We don't need another complication, Eve."

"Don't tell me something I already know," Eve said curtly. "But it appears that Michael thinks that we do, so we have to deal with it. He's *here*, and somehow he's convinced Cheknof he'll be Kaskov's superhero if he helps us keep Svardak from killing Cara and Joe." She saw the skeptical look on his face and held up her hand. "I know. I felt the same way. But I think it might be true. As I listened to Cheknof, he sounded genuine enough. What if he is? You know we need all the help we can get. And Michael says Cheknof knows things. I assume he means that he's an expert at the violence and mayhem Kaskov appreciates so much."

"Aye. Kaskov always hires the best." His eyes were suddenly narrowed. "What do you want me to say? All right, if we were able to use Cheknof, it might be just what I need to solve a major problem." His lips tightened. "God knows, I've been looking for something, anything, that could work."

"You mean for you to get to Cara in time." Eve added quietly, "And to keep you from making a choice.

Do you think I didn't realize that might be an option?" She moistened her lips. "I told you that even the closest place where I could secure that canoe would still take at least four minutes to get there from the ranger station. And then you'd have to race back to get Cara. It would be a miracle if you made it in time to help her. That was why I was thinking long and hard about Cheknof on the way here to meet you. Michael mentioned something about how he wasn't big and strong enough to help with his dad. That it would take someone like Jock." She paused. "Or Cheknof. If Cheknof can help me get Joe through the woods and down to that canoe, it would free you to go after Cara."

"Yes, it would." Jock didn't look at her. "But it would be a risk for you. Cheknof is definitely an unknown quantity."

"Everything is a risk for us right now."

"You can't trust him."

"For some reason, Michael trusts him. I don't believe it was accidental that he mentioned you and Cheknof in the same breath." She said unevenly, "Look, I know you're trying to be fair and giving me all the sensible reasons to discard a possibility that's nowhere near as strong as we'd like. But I can see it's tearing you apart. Do you think this is easy for me? I'm scared Michael might be wrong, that the superhero might turn back into a cowardly lion. But this way we have a chance that Cara and Joe can both live. Joe wouldn't thank me if I didn't take that chance." She checked her watch. "Two hours to go, Jock. Stop arguing with me and tell me how we're going to do this. I have to get back to Michael and Cheknof."

He hesitated, then pulled out his small notebook. "I have a few things to do myself." He pointed to the rough sketch of the station he'd drawn. "There are three perimeter guards in the woods near the lake. I'll take them out as soon as the time is close enough so they won't be missed. Here are the two guards out front. Which is still the only way to get Joe out. Abrams and Lacher are on their way to pick Cara up now with three other of Svardak's finest. She said that she'd find a way to cause a distraction when the vehicle she was in left the main road and started toward the station." He pointed toward the exit. "There are heavy woods and brush that lead down toward the lower lake. But we don't know if she'll be able to use it or if she'll be able to do anything at all. If there's no distraction, I'll furnish one myself by shooting out the two front tires of the truck. That should bring the front guards and Svardak running toward it." He tapped the diagram of the front porch. "But you'll have to get Joe out of the station and in the woods in less than three minutes."

"Cara said that she could give us ten minutes."

"She may not have ten minutes," he said curtly. 'I'm going after her the minute I shoot out the tires." He paused. "And you won't have time either. I might need another distraction. I'll probably have to blow up the station."

She inhaled sharply. "That would definitely be a distraction."

"And if Svardak managed to survive, he wouldn't know if Joe was blown up with it." He put the notebook back in his pocket. "But I wouldn't worry, I'll see that he's doesn't have a chance in hell of surviving." He turned away. "I'll call you to come to the station after I take out the guards in the woods." He was striding back toward the station. "That will be your last warning." His voice crackled with tension. "After that, be ready to move!"

COPPER FLATS

The blue lights of the helicopter speared down, light-ing the stark, rocky landscape as the aircraft slowly descended.

Cara unconsciously tensed as it touched down. She had thought she'd braced herself for this on the way from Ruell Falls, but she'd been wrong. Kaskov had bound her himself before they'd left the Falls, and she felt claustrophobic and panic-stricken lying here on the seat.

"You still have time," Kaskov said quietly. "Would you like to stay in the copter until I get the report that Abrams is almost here?"

"No." She took a long breath. "You should leave me and get out of here. Abrams will be wary about you anyway. He might do something rash if the opportunity presents itself."

"As you wish." He pulled her to her feet and helped her to the door that Nikolai had just thrown open. "Then I'll just see that you're comfortable, as a good host should." He jumped from the copter and swung her to the ground. She looked around at the rocky plateau and multitude of boulders cascading all over the otherwise barren the landscape.

"It looks like a photo of a moonscape," she said.

"The moon is dead. There's nothing dead about this place." He gestured to a large, smooth, flat rock. "Lie down, please, I have to tie your ankles as well. I wanted to give you as much freedom as possible until the last minute." Then he was kneeling beside her and swiftly tying her ankles. "But we want to make certain that Abrams thinks that you're so securely bound that there's no reason for him to do anything else. I've always found that laziness always rules if you cater to it."

"And I now know the definition of hog-tied." The

claustrophobia was even greater now. "You're sure that this will work?"

"Don't insult me." He was taking rubber gloves and a bottle of liquid from Nikolai. He put on the gloves and began to rub a thick coat of the liquid on Cara's hands and arms. "Don't struggle with Abrams. And avoid having anyone touching you until the moment is right for you. This liquid is transparent, but the texture has to be a little thick. You don't want anyone to ask any questions. You'll spoil a perfectly good plan if you're stupid."

"I won't be stupid." Her arms and palms felt tingling and hot. "And all I'll have to do is touch the ropes and they'll dissolve and fall off me? It seems very high-tech and Disney."

"If Disney had hired scientists from labs in North Korea," Kaskov said dryly. "Disney wouldn't have appreciated that the North Koreans developed it to be used in their prisons when they tortured prisoners. Yes, they will perform just as I told you they will. But you'll have to be careful what you touch."

"You've already told me that."

"Well, I didn't tell you quite everything." He was stripping off his gloves. "You also wanted a weapon that would prove undetectable. I thought I'd give you two-in-one."

"What?"

"When you remove the ropes, they won't actually dissolve, the composition will just change so that the ropes will stretch and enable you to slip them off."

"Isn't that basically the same result?"

Kaskov nodded. "Except that when the composition changes, it becomes acid-based. You can use the ropes as a garrote that will burn through a man's throat in less than a minute."

"Acid." Her eyes flew to her hands, which were still tingling. "And it won't hurt me?"

"You now have a base protective coat. You can handle any of the ropes with no ill effects. But just touching the ropes will cause anyone else to be practically eaten alive." He smiled. "What a perfectly delicious idea. You may thank me now."

"You're enjoying the idea."

"How can I help it? I told you that I'd give you a toy that would put that dagger you conceived in the shade, and I did it. And I like the idea of your having that much power at your disposal. Though you probably won't appreciate it."

"You're wrong. I will appreciate it."

"Good." He reached out and gently touched her hair. "Because I've decided that your life is very much worth preserving. Which probably means I'll see you later, Cara." He got to his feet. "And, if you have second thoughts and start becoming softhearted, I believe I should tell you that Copper Flats is infamous because of the number of snakes that make it their home. Most of them are nonpoisonous, but there are also copperheads and rattlesnakes. Very unpleasant and terrifying when one is trussed and helpless as you are. Svardak was willing to risk the possibility of your getting a nasty bite to put you through that unpleasantness."

She shivered. "It doesn't surprise me. I suppose you took care of the problem?"

He nodded. "That's why I was in no hurry to bring you here." His phone pinged as he looked down at the screen. "But you have another reptile to deal with now. Abrams's truck is cruising the area to make sure he's not coming into a trap. I'll bet it will take him about twenty minutes to be reassured." He strode toward the helicopter. "Good luck, Cara."

"Thank you, Kaskov."

He looked back at her and smiled. "You thank me? You lie there bound and helpless, in this valley of serpents, waiting for the monsters to come and devour you. Some would say you're mad." He got on the helicopter. "But they'd be foolish because I've done everything superbly, and I deserve thanks. You're welcome, Cara." The door swung shut behind him.

The next minute, the helicopter was lifting and the lights were casting their blue beams over her body. It made her feel like a sacrifice on a stone altar as the helicopter disappeared into the darkness.

She was alone in the darkness.

Don't be afraid.

That rustling sound was her imagination, not the serpents with which Svardak had wanted to threaten her. Kaskov had said they were no longer there, and she trusted him. Yes, the monsters were coming, but she had an Excalibur sword to vanquish them.

It was twenty-five minutes before she heard the sound of a truck roaring up the road.

She went still, bracing herself. Don't think of what she was going to face yet.

Think of Jock.

Think of the passion and the love and all the memories that were special and golden that they'd woven through the years . . .

But the roaring was louder now, and the vehicle's lights appeared around the curve.

Then the truck screeched to a halt in front of her, and the headlights were blinding. She heard a laugh as the driver jumped out of the truck and came toward her. There were three other men tumbling out of the bed of the vehicle and surrounding her, but the driver must be Abrams.

"Well, what have we here?" He squatted beside her, his flashlight almost blinding her. "All gift-wrapped and ready for Svardak." He put his hand on her breast and rubbed it slowly, sensuously. "And I told him it was probably a trap. I'm tempted to open the package my-self." His voice lowered. "All he wants to do is hurt you, and that's such a waste. I wanted to have my turn when I was guarding you up in the thicket but he was selfish."

She stiffened. No! His hand was moving toward her bare arm. Kaskov had said no one must touch her exposed flesh. Stop him.

"Bastard!" She spat in his face. "He'll kill you!"

He swore, his fist lashing out and striking her cheek. His eyes were blazing down at her. "You'll think you're lucky if he kills you, bitch. He's going to be very happy to see you. He's been making plans. If you'd been smart, you wouldn't have left Lost Canyon." He got to his feet. "Check the ropes, then load her in the back-seat, Lacher." He strode back toward the truck. "I'll call Svardak and tell him that we have a present for him."

LAKE KEDROW

After Eve left Jock when she reached the pine tree where the canoe was tied, it was to see Michael sitting on the bank beside the boat.

But Cheknof was standing guard several yards away, with gun drawn.

"It's okay, Mom," Michael said quickly. "Mr. Chek-nof was restless and needed something to do. I told him Mr. Kaskov would want him to be on watch to make sure nothing had changed."

"Kaskov seems to be the magic word." She drew a deep breath and braced herself as she reached him. "All right. I'm not going to fight you any longer." She dropped down to sit beside him. "We don't have the time. And there are reasons why you could be right

about its being better for your dad that you and Cheknof are here."

"Cara," Michael said softly.

She was not even going to question how he had
immediately made the connection. "It's better if Jock
doesn't have to be the one to help me get your father
from the ranger station to the boat, then across the lake.
You said Cheknof would be willing and eager to help."
She stared him directly in the eyes. "Listen to me. I'm
going to trust you. But I have to be certain. Can I count
on him? Can your dad count on him?"

Michael nodded soberly. "I've been talking to him.
He knows what he has to do."

"That's more than I do." Eve shrugged. "Nothing
will be going by the book when I go after your dad.
It's clear Cheknof doesn't have any respect for me. I've
been worried that he won't do what I tell him to do."

"Use Mr. Kaskov," Michael said earnestly. "You
were right, he's the magic word. Mr. Cheknof respects
him, but he's mostly afraid of him. Once I found that
out, it was easy to reach him."

"Reach him?"

Michael didn't answer. He only repeated, "Use Mr.
Kaskov." He was looking at the station. "How much time
do we have?"

"*We* have?" She tensed. "I need Cheknof. You stay
here."

"I told you that I would." He paused. "But I haven't
been able to contact Dad yet. I think he's sicker than
he was before." He moistened his lower lip. "And he's
so hot with that fever. It's going to be hard for him to
understand me."

She tried to hide the panic his words brought. She
hadn't realized how much she wanted something, anything, to go right. "We'll manage if you can't do it."

He shook his head. "You need me. *He* needs me. I

can do it. I just haven't been able to concentrate because I had to make sure you'd be able to control Mr. Cheknof. How much time?"

"It will be over an hour before Jock calls me." She reached out and lovingly touched his cheek that still held the smooth softness of childhood. So young . . . This weird, bewildering talent that had been catapulted to the forefront must be a thousand times more difficult for him to accept than it was for her. Because he'd had to fight her as well as try to understand what was happening to him. "It will be fine, Michael." She pulled him into the curve of her arm and leaned back against the tree. "Just relax. I'll handle it. No one wants anything from you that you can't give. Not me. Not your dad."

"I know," he whispered as he laid his head against her shoulder. "I like this. I always feel safe and right as long as you're here. Dad feels like that when he's with you, too. There's much more, but he always wants—" He stopped. "Could you just stay here with me for a little while? He might *feel* you, and that would make it easier for me to reach him."

"Of course. I wasn't going to leave you until I had to. Whether it helps or not, it will be my pleasure." She brushed her lips on the top of his head. "Because I may not have your voodoo, but I feel as if there's not a minute of the day when I'm not with your dad. So being here with you will be like having the two of you home with me again . . ."

That dark honey darkness was back again, Joe realized. Wrong . . . It made him uneasy . . . Even through the heat and pain, he knew that it meant something wasn't right. It was taking him away from that other darkness that was now his constant companion. Then he remembered why it was wrong. It had signaled that crazy dream that was no dream. The dream of Michael who said he was only in his mind and yet was so sad . . .

"At last." Relief. "Stay with me, Dad."

Michael.

"You're here again?" Joe asked. "I told you that I didn't want you. It's dangerous. Go away, Michael."

"I can't do that, Dad. And you can't go away either. You have to stay with me."

"It's harder . . . now."

"I know. It took me a long time to get through to you. But now you're awake, and you have to stay awake."

"I'm not awake. Or maybe I am, but only for the next minute or two. Go away, Michael."

"No, you have to stay awake!" Joe could sense his son's panic. "If you don't, you'll hurt Mom. You don't want to do that."

Those words jarred Joe into opening his eyes. "Eve? Before you said she wasn't here. She can't be here, Michael. Get her out!"

"She's not here now, but she will be soon. And it won't be a dream, it will be real. I can't stop her. Only you'll be able to get her out. But only if you stay awake and help her. She won't leave here without you."

"Make her go."

"I'm only a kid. What can I do? You'd never leave her, would you?"

Leave Eve, his partner, his love, his center?

"She won't leave you either. You can either go back to sleep and leave her or help her get away from this place."

Go back to sleep? How could he do that? Eve . . .

He was trying desperately to fight the fire in his head, the searing that was beginning through his entire body. "Where? When is she . . ."

"Soon. But you'll have to stay awake and keep talking

to me until she gets here. Then it gets harder. You'll have to try to walk for a little while until you can get Mom to the lake, where she'll be safe. But I'll be with you all the time, Dad. Just listen to me, and we'll go step by step."

"That will be the day. Why should I listen to you, when you shouldn't even be here? Keep yourself safe. I'll handle everything."

Silence. "Mom just said something like that to me." He cleared his throat. "Sure, you handle everything, Dad. But since I'm here already, suppose I stick around and help Mom, too. Is that okay?"

"No." There was something basically wrong with Michael's still being here, but the fever was blurring Joe's reasoning processes. "I'm very annoyed with you, Michael. This is probably a dream, but I can't take a chance, can I? Not with Eve. I have to stay awake, dammit."

"No, you can't take a chance. But you can close your eyes until she gets here. I'll still be around, keeping you awake. But it's better that Svardak doesn't know how well you're doing."

"I'm not doing well. Let's face it. I might be dying."

Another silence. "You can't die. Mom needs you. I need you."

"Yeah, I keep forgetting about that. This fever . . ."

"You mustn't forget that, Dad. Not ever. Maybe the fever will go away for a little while. I'll concentrate and try to help . . ."

"We're almost there, Svardak," Abrams said into his phone. "No sign of anyone following." He glanced at Cara lying on the backseat. "She's been docile as a lamb the entire trip. Though I might have had something to do with it. I told her how eager you've been to see her again. Do you want to talk to her?"

"By all means. I want to tell her myself."

Abrams turned on the speaker and handed the phone to Lacher in the passenger seat. "Hold it and let Svardak welcome her."

Lacher grinned and turned around to extend the phone to within a couple feet of Cara in the backseat.

"Hello, Cara," Svardak said mockingly. "It appears that Kaskov doesn't have any family feeling for you at all. I wasn't sure that he'd actually go through with it."

"Neither was I," Cara said. "I actually thought he might help me. I didn't have anyone else."

"Kaskov has never cared for anyone but himself. Anna could have told you how he hunted her down. How he hunted my father and brother. He was never like us. He doesn't know the meaning of family."

"And you do? I guess you're right, you nearly crippled him because of your 'family' feeling. Maybe you taught him not to feel anything for anyone. So here I am."

"And I'm so happy you are." His voice lowered to soft malice. "I was looking forward to killing you where I could watch you join your friend Marian Napier, but Joe Quinn is much better. He's very sick, and just a few minutes ago, I kept hearing him mutter in his sleep. I can do so much with a helpless man that will wrench that soft heart of yours. I can hardly wait."

She felt sick. "I've already told you that you never really won anything from Marian. And Joe is so strong and good that he's way beyond what you'll ever be."

"We shall see. I've been thinking about crucifixion. You must tell me your view on it when I see you in the next several minutes. I can hardly wait. I believe I'll go out on the porch to wait so I'll be the first person you'll see when I welcome you home." He cut the connection.

Lacher was laughing as he handed the phone back to

Abrams. "You can't say he's not imaginative. Have you ever seen a crucifixion, Abrams?"

"No, but I hope he was talking about the bitch and not Quinn." He glanced over his shoulder at Cara. "I'd be glad to help."

"Several minutes," Cara said. "We're that close?"

"The turn off the main road is about five miles ahead," Abrams said. "Nervous?"

"Yes." She didn't care that the admission brought him pleasure. He could take that any way he wanted. She was nervous, and she was desperately trying to wrap her mind around the coming scenario. Abrams in the driver's seat. Lacher in the passenger seat. The other two guards in the truck bed. Any way she looked at it, there was probably going to be a collision with one of those tall trees that lined the road if she used that rope on Abrams or Lacher.

Hell yes, she was nervous.

Jock wiped the blood off his knife on a shrub beside the trail. Then he rolled the body of the guard he'd just taken out down the incline, where he wouldn't be readily seen.

Not that it would likely matter. He'd been the last of the men guarding the woods bordering the lake. Jock had taken out the others with no trouble, and it wasn't likely that anyone from the station would be checking on them in the next fifteen or twenty minutes.

And Cara would have arrived by that time.

Don't think about her now. It would disturb his concentration, and he couldn't allow that to happen.

And don't take anything for granted. Climb up to the ridge and see if he could see Abrams's headlights before he went to meet Eve and Cheknof. He turned and started trotting up the slope.

His phone vibrated before he reached the top of the ridge.

He went still as he saw the ID. He punched the access. "Why are you calling, Kaskov? I already know that you delivered her to Abrams." He had to ask it. "Was she . . . okay the last time you saw her?"

"As good as could be expected. No, better, she's extraordinary. It must be my blood. I'd like to expound on that theory, but I don't have time." His voice became brusque. "She should be arriving at that exit off the main road in about fifteen minutes according to the GPS I had Nikolai install in Abrams's truck while they were gathered around her congratulating themselves. I thought you'd appreciate advance notice. We'll be seeing Abrams's headlights before that."

He stiffened. "We? Did you decide to bring Nikolai and your band of goons to help her? It's a little late. You could get both her and Joe killed if anyone makes a false step."

"I'm not a fool, Gavin. Don't insult me. I'm well aware how delicately this has to be handled. Cara made it clear that Quinn must not be harmed. Which puts me in a difficult and awkward situation. If I brought in Nikolai or any other of my men, it would be too obvious." He paused. "But I found I couldn't bear that Svardak might get the better of me. So I decided that I'd come and finish up the matter myself and, at least, make certain that you don't get Cara killed."

"How?"

"I have no idea. Because of the circumstances, Cara is having to play this all by ear. I could only furnish her with an interesting and lethal weapon. However, with my invaluable help, that could make all the difference. We both know how brilliant I am. It shouldn't be that difficult."

"You're here at the station?"

"And moving around the property . . ." He added softly, "As you are. I've counted five of Svardak's men that you've taken out so far. There are probably more since you're so good at what you do. I just thought it time that I tell you that I'm here in case you get tired of the blood and gore and offer you my possible assistance."

"On your terms," Jock said curtly.

"Of course. Otherwise, we handle this on our own. Which I'd prefer anyway."

"I'll let you know if I need you." Jock cut the connection. He started back up the slope, then stopped. If Kaskov said fifteen minutes, then it would be an accurate time frame. He turned around and started back down the slope. No matter how arrogant Kaskov could be, he was every bit as brilliant and skilled as he claimed. Jock could rely on that about him, and in a life-or-death situation like this, he'd take whatever he could get.

He pulled out his phone and started to dial Eve to tell her to come and meet him.

It was time.

"I saw the truck headlights on my way here." Jock appeared from the brush beside the tree line where Eve and Cheknof were waiting near the ranger station. "Abrams should be hitting that exit road in a few minutes. Get ready."

"I don't need to be told that," Cheknof said. "You're Gavin? I've heard of you. You should be the one going with me instead of this woman. Kaskov would like it better."

"Tough. Wrong thing to say at the moment. I don't take orders from Kaskov." He gave him an icy glance. "And you'll hear a lot more about me if you don't do your job and get Eve and Joe out of there." He glanced at Eve. "Trouble?"

"Nothing I can't handle." She glanced at the two guards in front of the house, then at the Remington 700 rifle Jock was carrying. "You don't think Cara's going to be able to cause a distraction? You're going to shoot out the tires?"

"I'm going to be prepared to do it. I'll give Cara her chance. But I just monitored a call from Abrams to Svardak." His glance went back to the road. "They were very sure Cara was completely helpless."

And that call must have been hell for Jock to listen to, Eve thought. The thought of it was scaring her, too. *Joe. Concentrate on Joe.*

Her glance flew to the front porch of the station. In minutes, she'd be with Joe. In minutes, she'd be able to get him out of there.

Pray God, she'd be able to get him out of there alive.

She tensed as she saw Svardak strolling out on the deck of the front porch.

Her glance flew to Jock's face.

"Still okay," he whispered. "The arrogant bastard said he wanted to welcome her home. He's playing mind games with her." His hand tightened on the Remington. "One way or another, you'll be able to get Joe away from him, Eve. We'll just have to give Cara her chance to distract the son of a bitch first."

The headlights were spearing the road ahead, and Cara could see that there was a drainage ditch on both sides of the road. The woods seemed deeper, thicker along this stretch. In the distance, she could see the lights of a building glowing in the darkness.

Where Svardak was waiting for her.

It was time to try the ropes.

And she had to trust Kaskov that they would even work.

She shifted her bare palm coated with the liquid to touch the rope binding her wrists.

No hiss. No burning sensation. Just a stretching, loosening . . .

Maybe not loose enough . . .

Stop doubting.

She moved her hand to the ropes around her body. It took an instant longer, but they loosened. She couldn't touch the ones at her ankles yet. She wanted to wait until Abrams exited the main road, when the truck slowed down to a crawl to make the turn. How long had it taken her to loosen those ropes? Longer than she had thought. She was feeling the truck slow as Abrams put on the brakes to make the turn onto the exit.

Use the rope as a garrote, Kaskov had said.

What did she know about garrotes? But the ropes that had bound her wrists were the logical ones for the purpose.

She took the rope with both hands. The rope felt hotter than when she'd taken it off, as if it had been storing energy.

Imagination?

Then Abrams began to make his turn.

And Cara swung her legs to the floor and sat up! The next instant she'd looped the rope around Abrams's neck and pulled it tight!

He screamed! "What the hell are you—"

His throat smelled like burnt flesh, and he frantically lifted his hands from the wheel and tried to tear off the rope.

Lacher was gazing at him with mouth open.

"Get her!" Abrams shouted, his eyes bulging. "*Kill* her!"

The truck bounced down in the ditch and careened toward an oak tree.

Cara let loose of the rope and covered her face with her arms.

Crash!

CHAPTER

18

Holy shit!" Jock watched the truck hit the tree
and the smoke and fire ignite beneath the hood.
"What the hell did she do? That's not a distraction.
That could be suicide." He was already on the move.
"Go! Inside, Eve."

"Right." Eve knew they'd never get a better chance.
She had seen Svardak run down the steps and start toward the wreckage at the side of the road. The scene
was complete chaos. The brilliant headlights lit the
oak tree it had smashed against. Someone was lying on
the horn, and it was blaring raucously. The two guards
were leaving the station and running toward the wreckage. Svardak was shouting and cursing at the driver as
he saw someone crawling from the front seat. "Come
on, Cheknof." She was up the steps to the porch in seconds. Then she was pushing the glass door with its Red
Cross emblem.

Joe!

She inhaled sharply as she saw him. Dear God, he
looked ill.

Cheknof was pushing her aside. "Is he dead? No,

he's not dead. Kaskov won't be upset unless he's dead. We still have to get him out."

She was sick to death of hearing about Kaskov at this moment, which was all about Joe. She wished Michael hadn't seen fit to press that particular button. But now wasn't the time to do anything about it. "Yes, we do." She ran to the examining table. "You cut the ropes. I'll get the cuffs." She bent over Joe and pulled the wire she'd brought out of her pocket. She worked the wire back and forth in the cuffs. Her hands were shaking.

Hot. Oh, God, his skin is so hot.

She snapped off the cuffs.

"Eve . . ."

Her gaze flew to Joe's face.

His eyes were open. "You shouldn't . . . be here."

"Yes, I should."

He shook his head. "Have to . . . get you out." He was trying to sit up. "Told Michael . . . shouldn't be anywhere near here. Let's go . . ."

"Right." She put her arm around his waist. "Cheknof will help. Lean on him."

Cheknof was already half lifting him from the exam table. "You're worse than useless," he told Eve. "Gavin should have come. Now we have to move faster, or he might die. He'll probably die anyway. I'd leave him, but Kaskov wouldn't be pleased." He was dragging Joe across the room. "If I decide to do it, you'll tell Kaskov it's not my fault?"

"I won't have to tell him. Joe's not going to die." She took out her gun and pointed it at him. "And you're not going to leave him. If you try, I'll blow your head off, and Kaskov will give me a medal. But you're right, we do have to move fast." She slipped the gun back in her pocket. The warning might be enough. Cheknof was looking at her with distinct wariness. He was very familiar with violence, he just hadn't realized he could expect it from her. But she had to make certain she could do this alone if he caused problems. She looked up at Joe's face as she helped him toward the outer door. His eyes were open, and they were fixed on her. "Walk, Joe," she whispered. "Help us. This Cheknof is completely obnoxious, and he's driving me crazy. I'm not going to let him be right about this."

He nodded slowly, his gaze never leaving her face. For an instant the faintest smile indented his lips. "Ob . . . noxious . . . Eve?" He staggered forward.

Yes!

Then they were outside and moving down the steps. The truck horn was still blaring and she did not know how long they'd been inside. Not long. Svardak and the guards were still milling around the wreckage. She shot a quick glance to try to see where Cara had gone. Where was she, she wondered in agony. Not in the truck. Had she run into the woods? Svardak must think so since he was running in that direction.

She had to let it go. Not her job. Let Jock handle it. She had her hands full with getting Joe away from here. She didn't know how long she had before Jock would blow that C-4. She tore her eyes away from the wreck and tightened her hold around Joe's waist.

Another four yards, and they'd get to the tree line.

Two yards.

One.

The ranger station blew, sending glass and wood into the sky!

Eve staggered and had to struggle to keep herself from falling.

Then they were in the woods, the black smoke from the blast hiding them from view.

If they'd not already been seen.

Her head was bleeding, Cara realized dazedly. She pushed herself off the floor, where she'd been flung by the impact.

That horn blaring . . . It was driving her crazy.

The ropes around her ankles. She had to get them off . . .

Easy . . . Just like the others had been . . .

She was sore, but there didn't seem to be any broken bones.

A groan from the front seat!

She froze. Abrams?

Her gaze flew to the driver's seat.

She nearly threw up.

That groan hadn't been from Abrams.

His throat and neck were almost burned through, and the rope was still sizzling, eating the flesh and muscle.

Another groan.

It was Lacher. He was half out of the passenger seat and fell to the ground as she watched.

It jarred her into motion.

Svardak . . .

She had to get out of here, too.

The next moment she had thrown open the back door and was tumbling out onto the oil-wet ground. She lifted her head and saw that Abrams's three guards, who had been riding in the truck bed, had been thrown out during the collision. They looked dazed but were slowly sitting up, one man already on his knees. Down the road, she saw more men running toward the truck from the ranger station.

And behind them she saw someone else.

Svardak!

Run.

She rolled over and bent to jerk off the rope still wound around her ankle.

Heat.

She could still smell Abrams's seared flesh. Her hand instinctively started to open to drop the rope.

Svardak.

A weapon.

Her hand tightened on the rope.

She turned and ran into the woods.

"Dad!"

Michael jumped up and ran toward Eve, Joe, and Cheknof as they staggered out of the trees toward the bank of the lake.

"No, Michael. Get in the boat." Eve shook her head as they came closer. "He's really sick. It's a wonder he's still on his feet. But he's getting weaker all the time. We have to get him out of here and over to the other bank. We don't know what effect that explosion will trigger with those goons of Svardak's. They could be searching the forest for the people who did it right now."

But Michael was standing before Joe, his gaze on his face. "Not yet." There was such a look of glowing love as he looked up at him that Eve remembered that golden moment at the lake cottage when she'd watched them working on the Jeep together. Then he wrapped his arms around Joe for just an instant. "You did good." His voice was muffled against Joe's shirt. "You got her out and took care of her. But it's not over. Now we have to make sure she's safe, and she won't be safe unless you are. Just a little longer, Dad. You have to get across the lake and hold on until the doctors get to you." He took a step back, and Eve saw his eyes were glittering with moisture. "Do you hear me? You know I'm right. You have to do it."

Joe's lids slowly lifted. He looked down at Michael. "Of . . . course . . . I . . . do . . . I was just . . . resting . . . Nag . . . Nag . . . Nag . . ."

Michael nodded. "Yeah, but only until we get you to the hospital. Then we'll all be safe, and you can take over again." He watched Cheknof and Eve pick Joe up and place him carefully in the canoe, with his head on Eve's lap. Then he untied the boat and jumped in the canoe himself. "I like that much better, Dad. Mom will, too. I've been doing all kinds of things that she worries about."

"Bad . . ." Joe murmured. His eyes were closing again. "Have to . . . keep you . . . in line . . ."

Michael nodded. "You do that." He wiped his damp cheeks on the back of his hands. "Mom will tell you I'm getting out of hand. She needs you."

"Yes, he's right," Eve said huskily as she looked down at Joe's face. "How do you expect me to get along without you? Not fair, Joe."

He nodded. "Not . . . fair. Together."

"Right." Eve was reaching for her phone. "And we're almost on the other bank, so I have to call and get you some help. First, I'll call 911, then I'll call Kaskov as a backup."

"Kaskov first," Cheknof said. "He has to know what superior work I've done. If we can keep him alive . . ." He frowned. "Though we should really have gone after Kaskov's granddaughter before we—"

"Shut up, Cheknof," Eve said. "Or I'll drop you into this lake."

Michael was looking back over his shoulder at the burning ranger station and the black smoke rising into the sky. "Cara, Mom?"

"She's not in that fire." But she wasn't going to lie to him. "And Svardak didn't have her yet when we got your father out of that station." But the memory of that twisted metal smashed against the oak tree was still before her. "But other than that, I don't know, Michael. I guess we've just got to trust Jock."

"Where are you, bitch?" Svardak's shout was almost a screech of rage in the darkness behind Cara. "Do you think you can get away from me? Lacher told me that you killed Abrams, but I'm no Abrams. I don't know how you did it, but I'm going to hunt you down and slice you to pieces."

She ran faster, deeper into the forest.

She had to keep going.

Svardak might be alone now, but she was remembering Svardak's guards, who had been streaming from the ranger station toward the wreck. And Abrams's men picking themselves up after being thrown from the bed of the truck. Svardak would have help soon.

Jock would come.

Jock would help her.

But she didn't know what was happening to Joe or how much help he'd need. She had to try to help herself.

"Ah, there you are," Svardak called. "You look like a ghost in this darkness. Run, rabbit. Run."

A shot hit the boulder ahead of her! She darted left, down another path.

The dark trees loomed on either side of Cara like the drawings from a child's macabre Halloween coloring book as she tore through the woods. She had felt the explosion that had rocked the earth only minutes ago, and she could smell the acrid smoke of the fire that had demolished the ranger station. But Svardak wasn't even mentioning the explosion, it was as if he hadn't even heard it. He was so obsessed by the sheer rage that had consumed him when he'd realized that she had escaped him that he could think of nothing else.

"Was it Kaskov who gave you one of his toys to kill Abrams?" he asked mockingly. "He meant it for me, didn't he? He didn't really fool me. But nothing mattered as long as I got my hands on you. I was so tired of waiting. He sent you into the lion's mouth and abandoned you. Did he tell you he was going to follow you and save you? He lied to you. No one followed Abrams. I had him check from the minute he left Copper Flats. You're alone, Cara. As alone as you were at Lost Canyon."

A bullet suddenly tore into the pine tree next to her!

"Almost got you." Svardak was laughing. "I caught just a glimpse . . ." Then he snarled. "But you're gone again. I'm getting tired of this." He was panting now. "This damn wound is starting to bleed again. I'll make you pay when I catch up with you."

His wound . . .

He was sounding weaker. She probably had more strength than he did. But he had that gun, and that last bullet had been very close. If she kept on being his prey, then he might be able to get off a shot that would take her down.

She looked down at the rope in her hand. She also had a weapon, and it had worked before. But she had taken Abrams by surprise. She wasn't sure that she could do the same with Svardak.

She heard shouting coming from the direction of the road. It wouldn't be long before Svardak would be reinforced.

No choice. Go on the offense before he had any of his men to join the hunt. Lure him. Then strike him down.

Lure him where?

The thick stand of brush near the boulders bordering the lake. It should give enough cover . . .

She started running toward it, darting back and forth through the shrubs. Talk to him. Make him angrier. Bring him to her.

"That wound may kill you yet," she called back to him. "It's what I meant to do. I can still feel your blood on my hands. Did it hurt, Svardak?" She jumped over a log on the path. "I wanted it to hurt. I was remembering Marian and what you did to her. All the torment . . ."

"I only told you bits and pieces." His voice was a vicious growl. "I'll show you the rest when I have you. Like I'll show you what I do to Quinn." She could hear him pushing through the bushes on the trail behind her. "He's almost gone, but there's still time for pain. You'll see every minute of it."

Pray that wasn't true. Pray she'd given Eve and Jock enough time to free him.

"If you live that long," she taunted. "Are those stitches breaking open yet? I told you that I'd win. It just took a little longer than I thought." She was almost at the boulders. "If I keep you running long enough, I'll only have to stand and watch you bleed out."

She heard Svardak's growl of sheer fury as his pace increased. "Bitch!"

Two more yards until she got to that tall stand of grass.

"Do you think your Anna will be there waiting in hell for you? Since she was the ringleader of all that ugliness that brought down your family, I'd think it only fair."

She heard his cry of sheer rage as she ducked behind the grass.

Wait.

Hold her breath.

He was only yards behind her.

Then he was on the trail, right beside her.

She leaped forward, swinging the rope around his neck.

He screamed, his hands clawing wildly at the rope, as he dropped his gun to the ground. He screamed again, jerking his hands away in agony as he felt them burning. Then his hands were back on his throat, and he jerked the rope away from his neck and dropped it to the ground.

The sickening smell of burnt flesh. His eyes glaring fiercely at Cara as he looked down at his scorched hands. "You stinking whore."

Then he dived to the ground for the gun he'd dropped.

No! Cara dived after him.

But he'd already retrieved it and was swinging the butt at her head!

Pain.

Svardak was on his feet, looking down at her. His eyes were blazing crazily with agony and rage as he aimed the gun. "Win? You'll never win, you demon from hell. I won't let you—"

A dark figure hurtled toward Svardak before he could pull the trigger!

Kaskov, Cara realized dazedly.

Kaskov between her and that bullet.

A shot.

Kaskov was falling to the ground.

Dead?

Svardak was lifting his gun once more.

He was going make certain Kaskov was dead.

"No!" She was leaping toward the gun in Svardak's hand.

"For God's sake, Cara! Don't do it! Get away from him."

Jock?

Only a few yards behind Svardak, she saw Jock moving with that deadly speed and precision toward him.

But Svardak still had that gun in his hand and he was whirling to face the new threat behind him.

Not Jock. Never Jock.

She snatched up the rope Svardak had jerked from around his neck. She threw it over the hand gripping the gun.

That horrible cry. The acidic smell of burning flesh.

And the gun was no longer a threat, it was falling nervelessly from Svardak's hand.

Then Jock had reached him.

Jock's face, ice cold, filled with fury and a terrible lust for pain and vengeance. It was the expression she always hated to see on his face. She still hated it. But now she understood it. She only wished that she could be the one to mete out the final punishment to Svardak.

But it was too late. Jock's hands were on Svardak's throat, squeezing slowly, choking, causing maximum pain. His eyes were bulging as he gasped helplessly for air. She didn't look away. She stepped closer so that he could see her. He knew he was going to die. She wanted to be the last face he would see on earth.

His eyes were glazing over. Jock was letting him slip slowly from his hands to the ground. He was barely alive when she stepped still closer to look down at him. "Listen to me, you monster," she said fiercely. "This is the end for you. You failed in everything you've ever done, and your Anna knows it. She'll turn her back on you in hell because she'll hate you for being so weak." His eyes were wide as he stared up at her in horror. He was struggling desperately to speak as life was leaving him. "Can't you see? We've all beaten you. No matter what you did to us, it's all come down to this moment.

Marian. All those other poor women you tortured and killed. Joe. Kaskov." She paused. "Tribute. *And* retribution." She bent still closer, and whispered, "I win, Svardak."

"Cara." Jock was behind her, his hands on her shoulders. "For God's sake, are you okay?"

She whirled and went into his arms. "Jock." She buried her face in his chest. "I was afraid he was going to kill you."

His arms tightened around her. "You didn't answer me. I saw that damn truck crash into the tree. And by the time I got here, I had to track you through the forest. Are you hurt?"

"No. I don't know. Maybe a little sore." She couldn't let him go. She never wanted to let him go. "Joe?"

"I haven't heard from Eve yet. But I know she got him out of the ranger station."

She suddenly stiffened. "Kaskov!" She whirled and ran to where he was lying. "Is he dead? He can't be dead. He saved me, Jock. He just appeared out of nowhere and took Svardak's bullet for me."

"I know, I saw him do it." He knelt beside Kaskov and started to examine him. "He's not dead. But he's unconscious." He opened his leather jacket. "Blood. Wound in the rib cage or upper chest. But I don't know how serious it is—"

"Not . . . serious." Kaskov's eyes had opened. His voice was hoarse. "Do you think I'd allow that . . . scum to ruin my reputation? But you could have performed more efficiently, Gavin. I'm . . . disappointed in you."

"Why? It gave you the opportunity to be a hero. I had to eliminate those three sentries before they reached Svardak and gave him additional backup."

"Excuses. Excuses." He inhaled sharply as Jock cleared the blood to look more closely at the wound. "Or did you decide this would be a good way to finally get rid of me?"

"It's a thought." Jock was putting pressure on Kaskov's wound to stop the blood. "But you ruined any hope of its working by stepping in front of that bullet Svardak was aiming at Cara. Now I have to find a way to save you."

"True." His gaze shifted to Cara. "Look at her. She's in agony because . . . she thinks that I might have . . . given my life for her. When I feel a little better, I'll have to think of a way to . . . use that angst."

"Be quiet." Cara's voice was unsteady. "For all I know, you could be breathing your last breath. You're both so twisted that you think the fact that I'd care about it is funny. Well, it's not funny." She was reaching for her phone. "And I won't laugh even after the doctors tell me that you're not dying." She was dialing 911. "And, Jock, don't you let him die. I won't have Svardak sending me ghostly messages from the great beyond to tell me I didn't win, after all."

"Oh, you won," Kaskov said softly, his eyes closing. "For a novice you . . . did . . . very well . . . Indeed."

CHAPTER

19

He has not regained consciousness yet?"
Cara turned her head to see Nikolai standing in the doorway of Kaskov's hospital room. His gaze was on Kaskov in the bed across the room. "He should not have taken this long. He's very strong. Have there been any strangers in the room?"

He was in protective mode. Suspicious of everything and everyone. "You should know better than I," Cara said. "You've been hovering in that hall since the ER assigned Kaskov a room tonight. I'm sure you've checked everyone out."

"I am good. I am not perfect. Everyone makes mistakes. I could have missed someone." He inclined his head in her direction. "But you are no fool. You've been sitting there next to him all evening, and I don't believe you would have let someone slip past you."

"How kind of you to give me your seal of approval," Cara said solemnly. "You didn't even search me for weapons."

"Kaskov would not have approved. He makes exceptions for you." He was frowning as his gaze returned to Kaskov. "But he should not be here. It's too difficult to keep him safe. I could have arranged treatment be brought to him in a place where I could have controlled it."

"It was my decision. I didn't know how badly he was hurt. It might have taken too long to whisk him away and wrap him in the cotton wool that would have met with your approval." She paused. She could see he was troubled, and added gently, "I wouldn't let anything happen to him, Nikolai."

"Not if you could help it. But he is more of a target than you can imagine. He would be much safer if he did not constantly insist on your presence."

"I have a very good imagination. And you can discuss your opinion with him as soon as he recovers. Until then, he belongs to me."

"And on that remarkable statement, I feel forced to stop eavesdropping." Kaskov had opened his eyes and was gazing at Nikolai. "Interference, Nikolai?"

"It is true, sir." He inclined his head. "But I apologize for expressing it. It was not my place." He turned and headed for the door. "If you can forgive me, I will start planning to get you away from this hospital before your enemies find out how vulnerable you are."

"Oh, I believe I can forgive you." He smiled mockingly. "But you'll have to consult with Cara on the timing. She appears to have taken charge."

"Don't be ridiculous," Cara said crossly. "I only meant that I wasn't about to let you be taken away from me until I knew you were on your way to getting well. You saved my life. It was my fault Svardak almost killed you. I won't let Nikolai take you to some high-priced surgeon who could still be crooked as a dog's hind leg until I'm certain that you're on your way to recovery."

Kaskov's brows rose. "And at that point if I start

to fail, Nikolai will know the crooked physician is to blame and take action?"

"Exactly." She shrugged. "Because the ER doctors said that your wound wasn't serious. The only reason it took you so long to regain consciousness was that they gave you a shot to keep you out while they stitched you."

"And Nikolai permitted that to take place?" he said silkily.

"Gavin was with her at the time," Nikolai said quickly. "I judged him to be sufficient and that you would not want me to draw attention to myself."

"Yes, Gavin would be quite sufficient to handle anyone who might prove to be suspect. I'm just surprised he would bother." He glanced at Cara. "Your influence?"

She didn't answer. "Start making plans to get him out of here, Nikolai. And tell the head nurse at the nurses's station that he's awake."

Nikolai hesitated, gazing at Kaskov.

Kaskov was nodding. "It seems you have permission."

The next moment, Nikolai disappeared from the room.

"It was bewildering to have you here when I woke," Kaskov said. "I immediately thought of angels, and I knew that wasn't my destination. And, since you look amazingly healthy, I assume that Svardak did you no damage after I took that bullet. Were you hurt at all?"

She shook her head. "You gave me the chance I needed."

"You killed him?"

"No, it was Jock. But, yes, I certainly contributed." She did not want to dwell on that moment, and went on quickly, "So it's over, Kaskov. For you and for me." She drew a deep breath. "And Joe is doing well. Though not nearly as good as you. The infection will take time to heal. He's still having to fight that fever. But the doctors told Eve that he'd probably be able to go home in a few days if he kept improving. He's down the hall in the next wing."

"Then why aren't you with him?"

"I was there earlier. But he doesn't need me." She made a face. "And Eve certainly doesn't need me right now. She doesn't need anyone but Joe and Michael. She barely knew I was in the room."

"So you decided to come where you're appreciated? Sound decision."

"The only time you appreciate me is when I have a violin in my hands," she said dryly. "I just didn't want to be in their way. I'll see enough of them when we take Joe back to the lake cottage."

"The violin is always a definite plus, but I have found a few other qualities that I find tolerable in you." He tilted his head. "Think about it. How could we not form an attachment that's much more cerebrally based than an ordinary relationship? Our little jaunt tonight was intensely interesting and revealed that we had common goals."

"To kill a demon?"

"It worked for us," he said softly. "And you stayed with me to see that no other demons had their way with me."

"Of course I did," she said impatiently. "You took a bullet for me."

"And that's still another reason. The pact is constantly growing in substance, isn't it? You have such a giving heart, and you can't help but be grateful to me no matter what my motive was for doing it. I'm just pointing out that the bond between us appears to be strengthening, and you may feel yourself making choices that you ordinarily would not."

"You're wrong." Yet she felt a frisson of uneasiness. She had not realized how much he'd studied and learned about her during those visits when she'd thought he was only absorbed in the music. And he was not above using that knowledge to his advantage. He was lying there in a hospital bed, and yet she could still sense the sheer power Kaskov emitted. "My choices are always based on my family and the people I love. I can't see them changing." She shook her head. "And I'm certainly not going to worry about it. From now on, you can take care of your own demons." She got to her feet. "I am grateful, Kaskov. You not only saved me, but helped get Joe away from Svardak. But in the end, you were just putting a deposit down on the wrong you did all those years ago. Why should I believe I owe you anything?"

"Because it's your nature." He watched her walk toward the door. "And I'm too selfish to refuse reaping the benefit. Good night, Cara. Do give my best to Gavin. I imagine he wasn't pleased at having to run interference between the ER staff and Nikolai's men."

"Probably not, but he did it anyway."

"Because he knows about debts," he said softly. "Gavin's not like you. He wouldn't give a damn about any wrong I inflicted in the past as long as the end result was that I kept you alive." He smiled. "That's the only thing that would be important to him. I wonder if I'll have occasion to remind him of it someday?"

"No!" She whirled on him, her eyes glittering. "Leave Jock out of anything between you and me. I won't *have* it."

He chuckled. "I generally don't involve Gavin. Sometimes he seems to involve himself. Have you noticed?"

She had noticed, and this last interference had been

very painful for both of them. "Good night, Kaskov. I hope you get well soon."

"I'll make a point of it. I have a good deal to look forward to in the next several months. I'll see you in Arizona."

She closed the door behind her and stood there, her mind warily going over the conversation. Nothing that was threatening, but there were still shadings of the unknown present in every word.

Forget it.

Kaskov was a law unto himself, but he had never been a deliberate danger to her. He was just a dominant man who liked control. In the past, she had even allowed herself to occasionally be controlled by him.

There was really nothing different.

Except he had made that comment about Jock, and she hated the idea that Jock might feel he owed anything to her grandfather.

"What are you frowning about?" Jock was walking toward her from the elevator. He was grimacing. "Tell me that you've been released from bondage by Kaskov at least for the night and we can get the hell out of here."

"It was always my decision." She started walking toward him. "He could hardly call the shots with me when he already had a bullet in him."

"I'm not sure about that." He stopped, his gaze studying her face. "I'm not sure about anything about you any longer, Cara. It's as if you've turned a new page, and I have to learn how to read you."

"The only bad thing about that would be if you didn't want to learn," she said unsteadily. "For heaven's sake, Jock, we've known each other for so long, and we've never stood still. I don't promise not to change through the years. You'll change, too, and we'll argue, and we'll have to come to terms with each other, and it will all start again. And it will keep on changing until the day we die, because that's how long we'll be together. So don't tell me you're going to start complaining about it at this early date."

"I wouldn't dare." His lips indented in a faint smile. "And I wasn't complaining, I was just making a statement. Yes, it makes me uneasy that I can't predict what you're going to do next, and Kaskov always sends up red flags where I'm concerned. But then that's part of the challenge of loving you." He added softly, "And what a challenge it is, Cara, one that I'll look forward to meeting as long as you'll let me. Now will you stop being defensive and let me take you back to the hotel and prove it to you?"

Her frown disappeared as she looked at him. He was strong and golden, and the shining she had always seen in him was brighter now. It seemed to be shimmering just for her. Lord, she loved him. He was everything she'd ever wanted, and now she was going to have him. Why had she even been worrying about Kaskov or anything else when she had so much for which to be thankful? "My thought exactly." She was smiling brilliantly as she walked the rest of the way toward him. "And I've no intention of coming back in the morning. Kaskov's on his own. Let's get the hell out of here, Jock."

LAKE COTTAGE
THREE WEEKS LATER

"Jock's coming, Mom!" Michael shouted up to Eve from the driveway, his gaze on the road. "May I run down and meet him as he comes around the bend in the road? Cara said he rented a really cool Ferrari this time, and I want to see it."

"And you can't wait?" Eve asked teasingly. For three weeks, Jock had been going back and forth from here to London and New York to see Cara and check on Joe. Each time he had shown up in a vehicle that had intrigued and excited her son. "Go ahead. But don't get run over. Ferraris are powerful cars and not to play with."

"I'll be careful." Michael was laughing as he started running down the road. "But Jock doesn't agree with you. He says they're great toys, and I should learn to appreciate them."

"No use arguing with him," Cara said as she came out on the porch. "Jock has totally corrupted him. Michael and Joe have always been fascinated with cars, and Jock figured that if he periodically brings them a brand-new supertoy, he could keep Joe from spending hours taking his own cars apart. There's not much you can improve on a Ferrari." She made a face. "My fault. I told him you'd been having trouble keeping Joe on invalid status."

"Impossible," Eve said. "And I'm so grateful to have him back on his feet that I tend to let him tinker." She paused. "Though I think they both like working on the old Jeep better. I've been suspecting that Michael's enthusiasm might be a little feigned to keep Joe from doing too much."

"Only a little." Cara was smiling. "You forget, Jock is involved now. He and Jock are dancing around like two fencers and testing each other. They're enjoying it, and it's rather fun to watch."

"Not for me. I'm still having to balance being Michael's mother and keeping an eye on anything else that shows up on the radar."

"You're already farther along than you think you are. You've got the magic key."

"And what is that?"

"Love," Cara said simply.

"You're probably right." She tilted her head as she studied Cara. "And you seem to have it, too. You look as if you're ready to run after Michael to meet Jock."

"That's nothing new, is it?" Her smile was luminous. "I've been running to meet him since the day I was born. You said it yourself." She turned and started down the steps. "But I won't steal Michael's thunder. I'll wait for them in the driveway. Though I do have a few things that I need to tell Jock later."

"Anything that will impress him as much as that sleek monstrosity he's driving?"

Cara made a face. "No, he'll probably be relieved. He's got this guilt thing about my career. He doesn't realize yet that I can do both. You did."

Eve asked, puzzled. "What on earth are you talking about?"

"Never mind. On second thought, maybe it's one of those things that I shouldn't be talking about to anyone but Jock. I'm just so used to sharing with you." She ran down the rest of the steps and was waving at Jock and Michael as they came roaring down the road in the silver Ferrari.

"What a beauty," Joe murmured. He was standing in the doorway, gazing down at Jock now sweeping up the driveway. "An Aston Martin the last visit. Now this Ferrari . . . I wonder what Jock's going to come up with next? Maybe a Lamborghini?" His lips were quirking. "If he thinks that's too mundane, I'm sure that Michael might have a few ideas."

"You've got to admit that Jock's original. It's better than sending you a get well card with a bouquet of flowers." Eve got to her feet and crossed to where he was standing. His color was much better today, and his strength and vitality were growing in leaps and bounds. It was presenting problems, but she thanked God for it. "And I believe this is entirely Jock, and Michael has nothing to do with it."

Joe lifted a skeptical brow. "Really?"

She grimaced. "Well, I believe that *if* Michael did have something to do with it, Jock is fully aware of what he's doing. No more manipulation."

Joe was silent.

"Truly, Joe."

He smiled and drew her close. "Sorry. I just remembered how intense he was when he was trying so hard to get you not to overwork. Nothing was too much for him to do. It would be natural for him to follow the same course with me."

She shook her head. "He'd do something else that wouldn't break our rules."

He threw back his head and laughed. "Did you hear what you said? You accept that he'd do anything he has to do when he believes he's right or if he wants something very badly. But you still think that we have final control?"

"Don't you?"

His smile faded. "Yes. But I don't know how long it will last. I think we both knew the potential that was hovering in the background. I just didn't expect him to take the giant leap he did when he was in those mountains."

"It was because he was so frightened for you." She was silent. "And since he's been home, it's as if he never went away. He's acting just the same as he did before. Just a normal kid who's only worrying about his next soccer game. It's as if he took a time-out, and now he's back." She was thinking about it. "Crazy.

But a couple times when I was upset about what he was doing to find you and called him on it, he only said. 'When we get Dad back.'" She paused. "As if he couldn't be what I wanted him to be until he'd finished what he had to do."

"But now he has time to meet all your demands?" Joe asked teasingly. "And we all know how tough you are on him."

"I just wanted him to have everything a child could want from life." And Michael had chosen to go his own way to save his father. She still shuddered at the memory of holding him in her arms on the side of that road while he had gone through those painful convulsions. And all to stay with Joe because he might need him. She had not told Joe about that night because it would have hurt him as much as it had her. Perhaps after more time had passed . . . "I want him to forget about the last weeks."

"That might be difficult for him to do."

Her gaze flew to his face. There had been something in his tone . . . "How much do you remember?"

"Enough. Bits and pieces." He kissed her cheek. "But what I most remember is that everything was done with love and because of love."

She nodded. "He does love you so much, Joe. We all do."

"Of course. That's only because I'm surrounded by people with excellent taste," he said lightly. "What's not to love?"

"Let me think about it." She could hear the strong beat of his heart beneath her ear. To have him back and this close was everything she needed in this moment. She heard Michael laughing at something Jock had said and saw the sunlight gleaming on Cara's dark hair as she leaned forward and mockingly stroked the silver hood of the Ferrari as she gazed up at Jock mischievously.

Togetherness, humor, warmth, and family.

But what I most remember is that everything was done with love and because of love.

She smiled as she leaned back contentedly in Joe's arms. "You're right, what's not to love?"